The House on the Hill

Tony Bowman

CONTENTS

Foreword

Sometimes you have to take a step back. They talk about elements of a story - you might remember that from High School. The elements of a story: Plot, Setting, Theme, Character, Conflict, Point of View.

I've always had a grip on five of the six. I place Character at the top - for me, it's the most important. If my characters don't interest you, speak to you in some way, the 80,000 words I write are meaningless. Conflict comes next followed by Plot.

To tell you the truth, Character and Conflict dictate Plot.

Setting is important. I love my mountains. I rarely stray from them. Other times the setting is a Cadillac Eldorado with the top down, or a 200,000 pound rolling fortress called Valkyrie.

Point of View for me is generally third person. I like to tell you 'he said' and 'she said' with little glimpses into the character's minds, showing you what makes them beautiful and letting them hide what makes them ugly.

Theme, though? Theme is an elusive beast. I never set out with a theme in mind. Theme comes in the analysis at the end. I usually recognize the theme just before I go to press.

I believe the subconscious dictates theme. It wasn't until I finished Turning the Darkness that I realized the book was about predestination versus free will.

Nine Fingers was about responsibility and, in some ways, redemption.

Often, however, I find my central theme to be Family.

Every book I write has a group of people thrown together by adversity. They might be related, or they might not. But, in the end, they face the problems I inflict them with as a family.

The family becomes a character in and of itself.

Vales Hollow, Turning the Darkness, Valkyrie, Nine Fingers - all of them center on family. Sometimes they are dysfunctional, they have conflicts with one another. Some of the members have weaknesses and inner demons, enemies.

The House on the Hill is no different.

I have no idea why I write about so many dysfunctional or non-conventional families. I grew up in a hollow in the middle of the Appalachian Mountains surrounded by kin. My grandparents lived across the dirt road from us. My aunt and uncle and two cousins lived a few hundred feet away.

I have a multitude of aunts and uncles and a horde of cousins.

And, we were together almost every weekend to some extent.

I grew up in safety - nurtured, encouraged, and loved.

Looking back, it was idyllic. You just can't have a better childhood.

So, why on earth do I create these families in my books and subject them to such horror? I've collapsed the entire world around them and written about how they cope. They've faced vicious drug gangs, werewolves, demons, vampires, and nuclear holocaust.

Other than being a possible sadist and a definite sociopath, my only defense is that only a family can face such adversity and survive. It is the strength of the pack, the reliance on one another, that is the deciding factor in conflict.

I see this when I take a step back.

P.S. At present, I have forty books in me. Five have been written, thirty-five more are either outlined or in various stages of completion. These books span five different 'universes' - separate realities where the stories play out.

Twenty-nine of these stories occur in a reality I call the Appalachia Universe. The House on the Hill is one of those twenty-nine. Chronologically, it appears almost dead center in the timeline set in this reality. It happens a decade after the first Nine Fingers book, fifteen years after Vales Hollow, and right about the same time as Redbud Revue.

It's not important that you've read any of these books - some of the books are series that haven't even been written yet. However, The House on the Hill is its own story.

But, if at some point you honor me by reading any of my other books, you may hear names and remember events that tie these stories together. I hope those realizations make you smile or chill you.

Tony Bowman

29-May-2017

Dedication

For Laurie Ann Spivey
It's all in the name, you see.

Playlist

Act I
"Let It Burn," Red
"House on a Hill," The Pretty Reckless
"Freak of Nature," Broods

Act II
"I Love the Night," Blue Oyster Cult
"Big Girls Cry," Sia
"White Teeth Teens," Lorde
"The Vengeful One," Disturbed
"All the Tears that Shine," Toto

Act III
"We Belong with the Dead," Inkubus Sukkubus
"Better," Kodaline
"The Light," Disturbed
"Second Chance," Shinedown
"Only Love," Mumford and Sons

Denouement
"Children of the Sun," Poets of the Fall
"Long Black Cadillac," Shinedown
"Gabriel's Sword," Runrig
"And We Run (feat. Xzibit)", Within Temptation
"Ascent," Red

Creation is a game of chess that God plays against himself, warring with the two sides of His nature.
- Merlin Taliesin

...and we came upon them in the night, huddled together in unholy communion. They had no fear of the cross, and, when they were disturbed, they tore into us as harpies and gave no quarter.
- Bertrand du Guesclin, circa 1350 AD

It will have blood, they say; blood will have blood.
- Shakespeare, Macbeth, Act 3, Scene 4

In this house on a hill
The dead are living still,
their intention is to kill and they will, they will
Keep your children safe inside, out of pocket, out of mind
Until they drink the wine and they will, they will, they will
- Ben Phillips and Taylor Momsen, The Pretty
Reckless, House on a Hill

ACT I

The Burning

Gene Stinson watched the house burn from two streets away. His pickup was idling, heater blasting as the snow fell outside.

The flames climbed a hundred feet into the air, backlighting the heavy snow. It was almost beautiful: a snowstorm in hell.

And, at the heart of the inferno, it really was hell.

He heard their screams in his head as the fire found each one, trapped them, consumed them. Each one a victory - albeit a hollow one.

He had failed.

Gene had stood outside the house when it caught fire. Too close, but he no longer cared. He was happy to burn with it.

There were real, physical screams inside then as the occupants realized they were trapped. The fire burned on all four sides of the old Victorian, moving from the outside in, fueled by gasoline.

Gene fell on his knees and cried. It was finally over, after forty years, it was done.

Then he heard the roar of the engines.

Somehow they had gotten out, not all, but some.

The first car that appeared out of the smoke was the Lincoln, it swerved onto the street without noticing him.

The second was the old school bus, painted a pale blue with newspaper taped over the side windows.

Gene had grabbed his ears and almost buried his head in the snow as the bus passed. It was a useless gesture - the ear-splitting screams from the bus were *inside* his head, not outside.

The occupants of the bus were projecting their thoughts at him, at the entire neighborhood. Screaming in anguish and terror and hatred.

Gene scrambled for the pistol in his jacket pocket.

He got a glimpse of the driver as the bus turned onto the street.

Olc. He glared at Gene with his black eyes, and then put his foot to the floor.

The last vehicle was the pickup.

She was driving.

Miriam stopped in the driveway. Looked at him. Tears were streaming down her face. Her lips mouthed the word, "Why?"

Gene hadn't answered. He raised the pistol and fired. The bullet struck the metal door of the pickup two inches from her face.

She glared at him as she roared out of the driveway, dragging the small camper trailer behind her.

That had been barely fifteen minutes ago.

The fire engines roared by in a blur of red and silver. The police came next, blocking off the street.

But, there was little need. The streets around the house were empty. Their occupants had left long ago. Each would have had a reason for selling their home or simply abandoning it.

A 'seller's market' they would say, or, 'it's too cold in Minnesota.'

Few of them would have or even could have told you the real reasons. The feeling of cold even when the weather was warm. The nightmares that came like rats in the night gnawing into their brains and showing them terrible things.

The voices they heard when nobody was around.

The fact they could not will themselves to look at the old Victorian house that now filled the sky with flame and smoke and ash.

The neighbors had left, or they had gone insane and been removed.

There was no middle ground.

And, the firemen who dragged their hoses out as Gene watched? They would direct the jets of water at the wrong areas without even realizing it, some primitive part of their brains sensing the danger and whispering, "Let it burn."

The stereo in Gene's truck was expensive. The truck itself looked like junk, but the engine was new.

Social Security went a long way when your house was a pickup, your kitchen was any roadside diner, and your bathroom was in any truck stop you chose.

The radio was a splurge, with Bluetooth to connect his cell phone.

His truck was his entertainment room and his phone booth.

"This is Victoria Darke, and you are listening to 'Voices from the Darke' broadcasting live from Prescott, Arizona," the radio said. "It's open mike night. Do you have a story of UFOs, shadow governments, or things that go bump in the night? Then give us a call…"

Gene had listened to the show since Victoria Darke's father, Adam, had started it in the late 70s.

He turned off the radio and unmuted his phone.

"Our first caller tonight is an old friend, someone who has been calling in regularly since the show started. Our fearless vampire hunter, Gene Autry, is with us. How's it going tonight, Tex?" Victoria asked in her silky but insulting voice.

Gene listened to the show, but Adam Darke's kid was an asshole.

"They aren't technically vampires, kid," Gene said.

"Hmm, they drink blood, right? Makes them vampires in my book."

"Not important. I failed tonight. I got some, but not all."

She paused. "What... does that mean? You *got some?*"

"You'll see it on the news. It's too big to cover up. I got dozens of them, burned them alive. They'll find the remains of their victims in the basement, but there won't be much left."

"These are your vampires you're talking about, right, Gene? Where are you?"

"I told you. It'll be on the news. You'll know then."

"For those of you who are new to the show, Gene Autry here is a self-professed vampire hunter. He claims to be in his seventies and crisscrossing the country looking for a family of fun-loving blood suckers. Gene, didn't you see Twilight? Vampires are just misunderstood sparkly folk. Your time would be better spent looking for the Loch Ness Monster, Bigfoot, werewolves..."

"There's no such thing as a werewolf."

"Oh, no, that's right - just vampires with psychic powers who can walk around in the daylight and who can't stand heat..."

"Wow. You remembered..."

"Of course, I remembered. We've named you cuckoo bird of the year three years in a row - which reminds me, in your honor..."

The sound of a cuckoo clock came over the speakers.

"...you just got cuckoo bird of the night, and you are the first caller!"

"Cute."

"Okay, Gene, I'll play nice. So, you say you got some, but not all?"

"I burned their house down."

Victoria was silent again. "Adding arson to your list of accomplishments? Bravo. Hey, Gene? I got a crazy idea, why don't you take your old schizo ass to the nearest police station? 'Cause, normally, I think you're just full of crap, but I think there is a possibility you might have actually hurt someone tonight."

Gene sighed and looked at his hands. "If I'd gotten them all, I would have. Job's not done."

"So, you just called tonight to cry on my shoulder because you didn't kill enough people, cowboy?"

"They're not people. And, no. I called because there are people who listen to this show who believe me, and I need them to know: the family is on the move. They've left Minnesota. Look for unexplained deaths and disappearances, the smell of death and decay. And, nightmares. Bad nightmares that stay with you when you wake up…"

"Uh, oh… Minnesota? My producer is telling me there is a four-alarm fire going on in Minneapolis right now. Confirmed deaths. Did you set that fire, Gene?"

"Goodbye, kid."

"Why call me, Gene? You want me to be your biographer?"

"No. I call you because you get the word out."

Tears

Miriam Tillford cried. She had been crying for over 600 miles. Light rain was falling as they paralleled Interstate 64 at 2:30 in the morning.

They needed to stay off the main roads.

The caravan of cars from Minneapolis drove slow through the Indiana countryside, but not so slow as to attract attention. A Lincoln town car in the lead, an old school bus in the middle, and Miriam bringing up the rear in the Chevy Silverado pulling her white and green camper.

Everything had been perfect in Minneapolis. They had been strong there. Almost fifty young, a half dozen ancients, a dozen protectors like Miriam.

And Olc.

He drove the bus ahead of her on the rain slick highway. The red brake lights flashed heading into the turns. The bus meandered every so often into the left lane.

His sorrow was showing in his driving.

She could feel it rolling back to her like waves on the ocean. A fragment of Olc's thoughts, an image of one of those now dead and burned in Minneapolis, would pass by like a ghost left on the road.

Miriam made her thoughts calm. She had no psychic ability, but Olc was connected to her. Even though he was in the bus fifty feet ahead of her, his mind touched hers.

She felt him looking into her mind for solace, and she gave it.

The bus swerved.

Olc was calm, but his passengers were not.

A tidal wave of emotion spread out in a circle from the bus, a scream of anguished hate from the dozen young vampires who huddled together inside.

Olc was shaken, and Miriam cried out in terror as the emotions passed through her.

In a trailer a quarter mile from the road, a good and kind man woke from his sleep and strangled his wife to death.

Animals a mile away ran in a blind panic into trees and cliff walls, dashing their brains out.

Children five miles away awoke from nightmares that would leave them screaming for hours.

"Be silent…"
"Still…"
"Loss is fleeting…"
"An illusion…"
"We are forever…"

The words radiated from the town car ahead of Olc. The ancients sat in the back of the car. Their thoughts soothed, and, for a few minutes, the young were calmed.

But, only for a few minutes.

"Stop. Now," Olc's voice said in her head.

Miriam came to a stop on the rough gravel shoulder.

Across the field to her right, she could see the lights of an Interstate rest stop.

The graffiti written in Sharpie on the rest room's smooth subway tile read, "What are you looking up here for? The joke is in your hand."

Jerry Mitchell smiled as he pissed in the urinal. He had seen the same joke a thousand times in a thousand different restrooms over the years, but it was comforting to see it here in the predawn hours in rural Indiana.

He hated rest stops, but the urge had come on him before he could reach a Gas'N'Go. This late at night, the rest stop had been empty except for a couple of idling semis and a van load of sleeping Hoosiers on their way back from a football game.

He zipped up and flushed, ran his hands under the icy water from the lavatory.

Jerry heard glass breaking.

He looked at himself in the mirror, eyes darting left and right looking for any movement behind him. He turned off the tap.

The bathroom was silent other than the hum of the fluorescents.

Jerry breathed. The room smelled of old piss, disinfectant, and deodorizer.

Breaking glass again, farther away this time.

He walked to the door and listened.

Nothing.

He opened the door a crack.

Cold, late fall air poured in.

The open breezeway between the ladies' and men's restrooms was empty.

Jerry stepped out and walked into the parking lot.

He could see the sleepy faces of the college students moving in the van windows. The driver's side window rolled down, and a boy with dreadlocks and a knit cap leaned out. "Hey, man, did you hear that?"

Jerry nodded. "Sounded like glass breaking."

Jerry took a step toward the van and heard something crunch under his foot.

Shards of glass glittered under the street lamp.

He looked up. A shattered security camera hung by its wires from the light pole.

"The hell…"

A Chinese girl wearing a t-shirt that read 'Hoosier Hottie' was getting out of the van. "Did somebody break the security camera?"

"Looks like," Jerry said.

The girl was dancing in place and crossing her legs. "You think it's safe? I really got to go."

Dreadlocks opened his door. "Hold up, Mae. I'll stand guard for you."

"My hero. Just hurry. Please?"

Jerry nudged the broken glass with the toe of his boot.

He turned and walked toward his car.

He froze in place.

A smell permeated the air. Something dead mixed with strong body odor.

Jerry reached for his keys. His car was five spaces ahead.

He hit the remote unlock.

Something moved on top of his car.

It was a person crawling on all fours sliding down onto the hood of his car.

Its skin was gray, with almost a blue tint.

He thought it was a naked man at first, but then he could see the swell of breasts hanging down as she slid off his hood. She stood up straight and tall, skin shining almost as if she were covered in oil.

She walked toward him, and he backed away slowly.

The woman was bald and, as she drew closer, he saw she also had no eyebrows.

Her crotch was shaved bare.

She shimmered as he watched her. He felt a tingle in the back of his head.

And, then she was no longer a naked woman but a cloud of steam with two red eyes glowing in the darkness.

Jerry's bladder let go and dumped what little urine he had left into his boxers.

Someone screamed behind him.

From the direction of the semis, he heard gunshots and then screams.

Jerry turned and saw the doors of the van were open, and the college kids were running, scattering in every direction. Interspersed among them were monsters.

Some were vapor like the thing that approached him.

Others had leathery wings like demons.

Most were simply the gray-blue hairless things he first saw.

He turned back to the creature walking toward him.

She was a woman again, her skin no longer gray, but porcelain white. She had hair now, long blonde hair.

But, her eyes were black.

And, she was the most beautiful thing he had ever seen. Lust filled him, and he strained at his wet boxers. He reached out to touch her, unnerved by his overwhelming desire for her.

The smell was back. A dead animal and the stench of burning sulfur. The feeling of lust evaporated.

Jerry stumbled backward.

She opened her mouth, revealing long fangs behind her ruby lips.

Run.

She said nothing, but her words were in his head, and along with it came anger and hatred. The smell of burning flesh and something about Minneapolis and the words 'blood will have blood.'

Jerry turned and ran, ignoring the scene around him. The college students were screaming as the monsters tore into them.

He saw a girl stripped bare and then picked up and held in mid-air between two of the creatures. One was a gray blue man, the other looked like an enormous bear. The two creatures played tug of war with the girl's body.

A thin red line meandered down from the girl's left shoulder, cut across her left breast and down across her navel to her crotch.

The line widened, and she was ripped in two, her eyes still rolling in panic looking from one monster to the other.

The monsters each fell on their half of the girl and drove their faces into the blood.

Jerry ran. He reached the field beyond the rest stop and kept running.

He didn't look back.

He saw car lights ahead. A school bus sat idling, in front of it was a black town car.

Behind it was a pickup with a trailer hitched to the back.

A woman stood in front of the headlights of the truck and stared at him.

"Run!" Jerry yelled as he approached the woman.

"Why?"

"Behind me. Monsters. They're killing people."

She punched him in the throat.

Jerry was knocked backward off his feet, and he landed flat of his back on the gravel shoulder.

He couldn't breathe.

The woman stepped between his legs and drove the heel of her pump into his crotch.

He felt something give, and he screamed, but no sound came out. His throat was crushed.

She crawled over him, her heavy breasts pressing into his chest through her thin white blouse.

The woman leaned forward and kissed him gently on the lips.

She smiled and looked at someone standing behind him. "You should feed."

"No, Miriam," a man's voice said. "For the young."

The woman looked to her right and smiled. She motioned with her right hand. "Here. I stopped him for you."

The naked, blue-gray girl from his car crouched over him.

The woman in the white blouse kissed the monster girl's cheek, and then she tilted his head away from them. "Make him feel your pain."

Jerry felt something sharp tear into his throat.

The Badge

The morning after Minneapolis, Gene drove west to Milwaukee. At precisely 10:00 AM, he knew he had made a mistake. He was parked at a truck stop south of Milwaukee when his phone pinged.

He opened the text message, clicked the contents, and a map appeared with a single red dot.

Des Moines, Iowa.

"Shit," he cursed under his breath.

They had gone south. He had bet east.

Olc almost never traveled south. It was still warm to the south, and they couldn't take the heat. Their body temperature hovered around seventy-two degrees. Anything above seventy-two was as uncomfortable as one hundred degree heat to a normal person.

Ninety degrees and above would kill them outright.

Gene turned south toward Illinois. If they continued south, he would converge on them in eastern Missouri. Maybe.

The good news was the box he had bought off the kid on the Internet was working.

A tiny transmitter that woke up once a day, read the GPS location, and texted his cell phone. It would run for months on its battery.

The night before, Gene had hidden it under the front bumper of the school bus before setting fire to the house.

Just in case.

The next morning found him near Saint Louis.

The pinger said: Shelbyville, Kentucky.

East now.

But closer.

He drove east on Interstate 64 into the Indiana countryside.

Gene rarely stopped, only when he was hungry or when his seventy-year-old bladder couldn't take any more.

It was almost 2:00 PM when he saw the yellow police tape blocking access to the last rest stop before the Kentucky border. They would have passed by this location sometime in the middle of the night.

A lone sheriff's car sat on the exit to the rest area.

Gene pulled onto the shoulder just short of the tape.

He opened his glove compartment.

Over the years, he'd acquired a number of IDs. He pulled out a badge in a black leather cover and put it in his front pocket. Then he opened his door and got out of the truck.

The wind was cold, blowing in across an empty field beyond the rest stop.

A sheriff's deputy looked up from something he was studying in the parking lot. "You need to go back. Rest area is closed," the deputy yelled.

"Yeah," Gene yelled back over the roar of a passing eighteen-wheeler. "Thought you might need some help. Gene Kelly, U.S. Marshal's Service." He held up his badge as the deputy reached him.

The deputy was a tall man, thin and weathered. "U.S. Marshal? What brings you this way?"

"Passing through," Gene said. "Saw the tape. Thought I'd stop and see if I could lend a hand."

The deputy looked at him for a minute. "Don't take this the wrong way, but you're a little long in the tooth to be a marshal."

"Retired," Gene said.

"Well, I thank you for stopping, but..." he cut his words short. He was staring at the cap on Gene's head. "Air Cav? You in Vietnam?"

Gene looked down at the ground. "Yeah."

"When were you there?"

"I got there in January of '68."

The deputy's face turned pale. "You were there for the Tet offensive?"

Gene sighed and nodded. Another war, a lifetime ago. It seemed almost innocent to him after all these years.

The deputy held out his hand. "I'm Calvin Dawson. My dad was Air Cav, in country back in '72."

"An Loc?"

"Yes, sir," Calvin said as he raised the tape. "Come on through. Truth be told, I'd welcome another set of eyes on this. Whole damned county went nuts last night."

Gene fell into step beside the deputy as they walked toward the parking lot. "How's that?"

"Over the past fifteen years, we've had three murders in the county. Last night, we had four in the space of an hour," Calvin said as he stopped in front of a pool of liquid on the asphalt. "And, whatever in the hell happened here."

The puddles covered the parking lot, each tinged red from blood. The smell was acrid.

Calvin kept blinking, his eyes watering. He couldn't look at the pools for very long.

Gene stared at them without moving, his nose and eyes were used to the smell.

Calvin took a step back. "Last night, a friend of mine, a fellow I've known since we were in elementary school - he woke up in the middle of the night and strangled his wife. They've been married thirty-five years." He shook his head. "These puddles are everywhere, I don't know what..."

"Piss," Gene said.

"What?"

"It's piss. And blood. Mostly piss," Gene said. He motioned to the other puddles with his hand. "Every puddle, somebody died."

Calvin stared at him. "Piss? What could piss that much?"

Gene said nothing. He walked to the sidewalk that ran between the restrooms. He knelt down by the shattered security camera.

"All the cameras were taken out. I think they shot them with a .22..."

Gene shook his head. "They threw rocks."

"Come again?"

"From the field over there. Just outside the camera range. They threw rocks and broke the cameras."

Calvin shook his head. "Ain't possible. That's a hundred and fifty yards."

Gene stood up. "Look around. You'll find the rocks."

Calvin pointed toward the semis. "The truckers got off some rounds. Hit at least one of them. There's blood spatter."

"Show me."

The blood spatter was on a light pole beside the still idling semi. Another puddle of blood stained urine lay nearby.

Calvin leaned down beside the spatter. "Blood hasn't dried at all..."

"Be careful!" Gene said. "Don't touch it!" He swallowed hard.

"I wasn't going to."

"Bloodborne pathogens. That blood... could be dangerous. Tell your techs to be extra careful when they take samples."

Calvin stared at the spatter. "I can't understand. All this blood but not one body. I mean, at least ten people would have died here." Calvin sighed. "I just can't wrap my head around it."

He stood up and turned around.

Gene was walking away, already half way to his truck.

Calvin scratched his head under his hat. "What the hell?"

Gene climbed into his truck and drove away.

Outside Elkhorn City, Kentucky

Miriam could almost sense the ghosts herself. Olc talked about them often. Or, more accurately, he thought about them.

His thoughts poured into her mind more often now. Olc was losing his ability to speak.

He said the hills of eastern Kentucky and southwest Virginia were teeming with ghosts. Not that he was frightened by them, he said they were a curiosity. He liked to talk to them.

She sat at the small camper kitchen table and adjusted her lipstick. Bright red.

Olc liked the shade. His taste in clothing and accessories ran to the slutty. Miriam was okay with that - the two of them had been together for forty years, longer than most couples.

She stood up and looked at herself, admiring her legs in the mirror, accentuated by the high heels and leather miniskirt, the sheer white silk blouse.

Miriam smiled. Not bad for a sixty-seven-year-old.

Not that anyone would mistake her for a senior citizen. She looked twenty-seven, thanks to regular treatments with Olc's blood.

She stared into her own eyes.

Physically perfect. Mentally?

Her breath caught in her chest. She looked away. Changes had been made. Forty years ago, in a sweaty tangle of sheets. Olc had reached into her mind and made… changes.

He had wanted her, and he had chosen her.

Four decades later, part of her mind still rebelled.

But, that voice was distant and small, an echo from the late seventies when she had answered the door to find Olc. He hadn't said a word. Olc simply reached into her mind and twisted.

What followed was a lifetime of violence and tenderness, blood and love.

She opened the camper door and stepped out into the cold Kentucky night. The gravel parking lot was filled with pickup trucks and motorcycles.

Neon light glimmered in the dirty windows of the roadside bar welcoming them to The Dew Drop Inn. Loud country music caused the wood and cinder block building to vibrate along with the twang and bass.

"You take me to the classiest places," Miriam said.

She held out her hand, and Olc took it, guiding her down the small metal steps of the camper. His hand was icy, twenty-five degrees colder than her own.

He stood on the gravel in his long black trench coat with the boots and black hat.

An illusion, of course. The clothes were an hallucination, a mental picture projected from Olc's mind. In reality, he and the other vampires were naked.

Olc's eyes glimmered black in the bright neon light.

The young loitered near the door of the bar.

The three college students they had chosen to add to the family the night before at the rest stop wandered aimlessly around the gravel lot.

Miriam reached out and took the hand of the nearest student, an Asian girl with paper white skin dressed in jean shorts and a long t-shirt that read 'Hoosier Hottie.' As soon as Miriam's hand touched hers, the girl's illusion vanished, and she hissed at Miriam.

The girl was naked, her skin a slightly pink shade of gray.

"Shh," Miriam whispered. "I know you're hungry, but you have to concentrate."

Miriam ran her fingers through the girl's long black hair, and it fell away in clumps, revealing her gleaming scalp beneath.

The girl began to cry.

"No, no, it's all right. Just concentrate."

The girl's body shimmered like a heat mirage on hot pavement. The image of shorts and a t-shirt returned, along with a full head of lustrous black hair.

And, now, also, her makeup was perfect.

The girl smiled revealing long gleaming white fangs.

Miriam touched the girl's chin and closed her mouth. "Keep them hidden."

She held the girl's hand and led her to the door of The Dew Drop Inn.

Olc held the door open and motioned them in.

Miriam walked into the bar, followed by sixteen vampires.

The screaming started.

Gene stopped and ate dinner at a truck stop in Huntington, West Virginia. He stared at his map spread out on the Formica table. The pinger told him the family had been on Interstate 64 near Shelbyville, Kentucky at 10:00 AM. That was twelve hours ago, and it would be another twelve hours until the pinger woke up and sent him another location.

He couldn't be certain they had stayed on 64. They might have turned north and headed into Ohio.

Would they do that? Drive this far south just to double back north? If they thought they were being followed, maybe.

But, they had no reason to suspect that.

No, they were going east on 64. They wouldn't turn north again until they hit Interstate 81 or 95 in Virginia and finally go to ground somewhere in the Northeast.

North was always the destination, where the nights were long, and the winter was cold.

The farthest south he had seen them was Dallas, and that had been four decades ago when a hard winter had gripped the plains.

Gene closed his eyes.

He had been late getting home from his job repairing oil derricks. Two feet of snow on the ground, and he had stumbled into his house smelling of crude and grease.

He had expected to find Miriam waiting on him, a hopeful look on her face that he had found the thing she wanted.

Instead, he found the house empty, her clothes gone, and a hastily scrawled letter telling him she was leaving.

"Dessert?" the waitress asked.

Her voice startled him, returned him to the truck stop and the greasy food.

He looked up. She was pretty, maybe twenty years younger than him. Her smile was bright, but her eyes were tired. Just another lost soul washed ashore at this truck stop.

"No, thank you, ma'am."

She sat down in a chair across from him. "You sure? Our dessert is a lot better than our entrees."

Gene smiled. "No, thank you."

"It's quiet tonight. You're only my third customer since I came on at seven. My shift's over at midnight," she looked at him. There was a question in her eyes.

Gene folded his map. "Dessert would be good."

Miriam swayed with her hands on the jukebox. Crazy by Patsy Cline flowed out of the brightly lit glass box. "Now, that's country music."

A woman ran by her screaming.

Miriam reached out and grabbed a handful of the woman's long red hair and yanked her back, pulling out a handful of cheap weave as the woman tumbled backward onto the wood floor.

Two of the students dropped on her, and arterial blood sprayed up, ruining the silk blouse.

"Fuck," Miriam said as she wiped at the dripping blood. "Get your lips on the wound. Stop wasting it!"

The naked vampires did as instructed and the spurting stopped as they drank the woman's life away. Pools of urine formed on the floor beneath them as their modified kidneys began working overtime to process the quarts of fluid.

"Better," Miriam said.

Olc sat at a table cradling a brunette's head as she nursed from his left wrist. Her eyes had already gone black as she began the transformation. He absently caressed the woman's right breast through her red blouse.

Miriam felt a tremor of jealousy.

He smiled at her.

Olc enjoyed making her jealous.

The brunette's husband was sitting across from them transfixed on the scene. Olc was holding him paralyzed with the power of his mind.

Two could play at the jealousy game.

"Want to dance?" Miriam asked as she leaned over the paralyzed husband.

Around her, the room was a chaos of the dead and the dying. People screamed, and blood sprayed on the walls.

"What?" the brunette's husband asked.

She leaned over him and put her hands on his shoulders. He was staring into her cleavage. Miriam turned her head and smiled at Olc. "I should be able to have fun as well."

Olc shrugged.

He released his hold on the husband.

The man scrambled to his feet, but Miriam grasped his wrists. She felt the bones grind together.

He howled in pain as she pulled him to her. "Dance. Dance or I'll break your arms."

They began to slow dance as Patsy Cline lamented from the jukebox.

He looked over his shoulder. "What's he done to her?"

"Oh, something horrible. You really don't want to know."

He tried to pull away, and Miriam crushed his right wrist. He screamed in pain.

Miriam clamped her mouth over his and drove her tongue deep.

She pulled her mouth free when he stopped screaming. "You're a good kisser. Learned your lesson now? See how strong I am? Now, do exactly as I say, or I'll reach down and tear off your little nuts. Then, I'll make you eat them."

His right hand hung uselessly from his ruined wrist.

"Put your right hand on the small of my back."

He hesitated, and she ground the bones in his crushed wrist together.

He howled again, but he obeyed.

"Little lower. Cop a feel."

He looked out of the corner of his eye toward Olc.

"No, I…"

Olc wasn't smiling.

"Never mind him. Concentrate on who's hurting you now, not who might hurt you later."

Miriam laughed as he cupped her left buttock through her leather skirt in his right hand. She grinned at Olc.

He looked angry. It was delicious.

"Now, lift the skirt and really cop a feel," she whispered.

She felt her skirt lift.

Olc threw the brunette on the floor.

Miriam blinked, and Olc was beside them.

She heard a cracking sound and the husband's head flew across the room, a fountain of red blood sprayed upward and then drenched Miriam's face.

Olc pushed the man's body aside and grabbed Miriam by her upper thighs.

She squealed with laughter as he carried her backward and laid her upper body on a green felt pool table.

He tongued her face, licking the man's blood away from her eyes continuing down her neck, and lapping from the space between her breasts.

She wrapped her fingers around the back of his strong neck and pulled him harder against her chest.

Miriam opened her eyes.

Two women stood trembling on the pool table.

She looked at their high heels. "Nice boots," she said.

Olc began kissing his way down her body, and she laughed.

Gene lay behind the waitress in her bed. She was naked, and moonlight highlighted the curves of her body.

He ran a finger lightly down her side, and she moaned in her sleep. She leaned back against him.

Gene wanted to stay here in this bed with her. Tomorrow they would get breakfast and talk about her life. He would throw away his cell phone sometime before 10:00 AM. He wouldn't know where the family had gone. He wouldn't follow them.

And, if he was just a one night stand for her? Fine. He would go back to Texas, someplace hot like El Paso or Galveston. Somewhere it didn't snow.

Somewhere too hot for them.

He felt a twinge in his left arm. They were growing more frequent. He rolled away and picked up his pills from the nightstand. A doctor in Billings, Montana had told him he had the beginning stages of heart failure. If he took care of himself, cut out stress, and didn't over exert, he might have another ten or fifteen years.

At this rate, he might have six months.

She put a hand on his arm. "You don't have to go. I'm not expecting anything. It's just… it's nice not to be alone."

He felt the heart medication dissolve in his mouth. "I have to go tomorrow. But, I'll stay the night."

Olc pulled Miriam to her feet. She turned and leaned back in his cold arms.

The two women standing on the table were cocktail waitresses, wearing matching outfits of black short shorts and white halter tops. They both wore identical pairs of black patent leather go-go boots.

"I've been alive long enough to see the sixties make a comeback," Miriam whispered.

The women wore name tags: Tammy, a blonde, and Tina, a brunette with purple highlights.

"Why are they standing on the pool table?" Miriam asked.

"A present. For you," Olc whispered. He kissed her ear.

Miriam smiled. "That bar in Amarillo? The pool cues?"

Olc laughed.

Miriam shrugged free. She leaned on the pool table. "Hi, girls! How do you like the night so far?"

Tammy and Tina looked around the room.

The screaming had stopped. The vampires fed quietly on the floor or on table tops. A few were having sex, grunting and thrusting in the darkened bar.

Whether they were having sex with each other or with their still living victims or even their corpses was impossible to say.

Miriam sighed. "It's about this time of night that our parties start to wind down. I mean, we'd party all night, but you break so easily."

She leaned down and picked up two pool cues from the floor.

"Since you are literally the last two normal people standing, we like to make last call into a fun game."

She tossed the pool cues onto the pool table between them.

"Here's the game: you each get a pool cue and try to bash the other's brains out. Last one standing gets to become a member of the family. Loser gets to be lunch. Start on the count of three. One…"

Tina, the brunette stepped forward. "Fuck you, bitch! You want to kill us, just fucking do it. We're not going to fight each other. We'll die togeth…"

There was a sharp crack as the blonde swung her pool cue and broke it on the brunette's temple.

The bar erupted in laughter as Tina collapsed in a heap on the green felt.

Miriam shook her head. "Okay, you were supposed to wait till I got to three… but, I have to say I like the initiative, Tammy."

Olc paused outside The Dew Drop Inn.

He was soaked in blood, but the hallucination covered it. To anyone passing by on the deserted mountain road, he would appear to be a tall man in a trench coat and hat.

No one would stop by the bar. Even if they had been on their way to The Dew Drop Inn, something would make the driver go somewhere else. A voice in the back of their head telling them tonight wouldn't be a good night to sample cheap beer and honky tonk.

The young projected these thoughts from the school bus as they boarded, creating a psychic forcefield around The Dew Drop Inn.

Come, a voice sounded in his head, one of the ancients reaching out to him from the Lincoln Town Car.

Olc opened the back door and slid inside into the rear facing seat.

The three ancients sat side by side in the back seat.

The ancients were a blur of motion even as they sat still. Their thin skin was more translucent blue than gray. Their sex was indeterminate, their internal organs visible under their thin skin.

Olc's head was filled with a sound akin to the buzzing of bees as the ancients conversed among themselves at a speed too fast for him to understand.

The buzzing slowed. *Dangerous, coming here. Reckless violence*, the voice said in his mind. Whether it was from one of them or all three was impossible to say.

The young needed to slake their thirst. They needed revenge for the lost. Olc thought.

You indulge them, the voice said. *They must learn discipline.*

They are young. Their emotions are strong. If we don't indulge them sometimes, they will become uncontrollable.

Perhaps, the voice said. *You are taking us south, why?*

I fear we are being tracked. We must go in a direction they aren't expecting.

The woman's husband? Still following after all this time. But, his time is coming to an end. The heart slows, the flesh weakens…

Olc spoke out loud. "Still a threat."

Yes. A threat you should have taken care of long ago.

Olc let the insult go.

The voice continued, *This area. Dangerous. Steeped in old ways. Witches, ghosts… and to the east, far worse…*

Olc nodded. *We will only be here for a while. I know the dangers. Trust in me.*

Outside, The Dew Drop Inn erupted in flame.

They drove through the night. Olc took the lead in the school bus, and Miriam followed with the truck and camper.

The young were silent. They were preoccupied with the new vampires in their midst. Miriam could feel them cooing softly with their thoughts to the new arrivals as their bodies changed.

The young numbered eighteen now, including Tammy, the waitress who was so quick with the pool cue.

Olc followed twisting roads deep into southwest Virginia. He seemed to know where he was going, but Miriam knew better. Her lover was following some innate instinct through the dense forest.

She wondered if ghosts guided him or something darker still?

He slowed on a stretch of highway called Glade Mountain Road. The Appalachian foothills rose around them. This high up, the leaves were falling away from the trees in cascades of red and yellow.

Here, his voice whispered in her head.

He turned left.

Miriam panicked. There didn't seem to be a road where he had turned. But, as she followed him, her headlights picked out a deeply rutted dirt road, choked with dead grass. The trees formed a skeletal canopy as the vehicles climbed awkwardly into the forest.

The trailer groaned and complained behind her, the grass choking the axle.

The bus plowed forward, clearing a path.

The trees ahead opened up revealing an old farmhouse slowly being consumed by vegetation. Vines like ropes climbed up the white clapboard sides and seemed to be pulling the house down into the earth.

The barn was in better shape, and it stood like a dark sentry by its fallen comrade, the house.

The town car stopped, and the rear doors opened.

Moonlight illuminated the farm as the ancients moved almost faster than human eyes could see. Doors clattered open or simply fell off their hinges as the three shapes darted about the buildings.

Olc parked the bus and stepped down onto the wet grass.

One of the ancients stopped, quivering beside him.

Adequate, the ancient projected with a force so powerful it echoed in Miriam's head.

The three ancients darted into the house.

Olc turned toward the town car, and the car rolled into the dark barn.

Miriam climbed down from the truck cab and stood beside Olc.

"He'll be hungry," Miriam whispered as she took Olc's hand in hers.

"I can. You... rest," Olc said.

"Let me. He likes me."

"Join us. In the house. Tonight," Olc whispered.

Miriam watched the young vampires walk toward the falling down house. They supported the limp body of Tammy. Her only clothing was a single boot that clung tenaciously to her right foot. Long strands of blonde hair drifted off her head, leaving a trail as they carried her.

Tonight they would draw her into the tangle of their bodies as they slept on the rotting floor of the farmhouse, sharing their dreams.

Miriam shivered. "No. It's too cold tonight. I'll sleep in my camper." She kissed his cold fingers. "Sleep in the camper with me."

He shook his head. "The young. Nightmares tonight. Frightened." He smiled at her. "Tomorrow."

She watched him walk into the house.

It was easier before. Olc had emerged as a leader among them two decades before. The young followed him, depended on him as children needed a father.

The ancients trusted in him. He could still walk among the humans, something they were incapable of doing. They had become things too alien to camouflage with mind tricks.

The ancients were in the house, under the floorboards, conversing among themselves with their bee buzz of telepathy.

How many nights had she lain down with Olc in that tangle of vampire bodies? Feeling their dreams in her head as he made love to her in the cold and damp?

She walked into the barn.

"Are you hungry, Edgar?" she asked.

Low tittering laughter filled the barn, more in her head than from sound.

She walked back to the trunk. "Open please."

As the lid rose, she said, "Time to wake up, Tina."

Tina was awake.

The girl in the halter top rose up on her knees in the trunk and swung a tire iron at her head.

Miriam felt the blow in her left temple, felt her neck jerk to the side

The force of the blow made her tumble to her right.

The cold dirt floor smelled of neglect and decay as she lay on her side.

Tina leaped out of the trunk, landing beside her.

Miriam kicked out with her left foot.

Tina screamed as her ankle snapped, the heel of the boot twisting sideways as the bones failed. She went down hard.

Miriam rolled onto her butt. She saw double. "What... fucking idiot left a tire iron in your trunk?"

More tittering laughter followed by a telepathic question.

"Yes," Miriam said as she wobbled onto her feet. "I'm fine." She felt her skull shifting, felt the fracture knitting together.

Tina tried to get to her feet, put weight on her ruined ankle, and went down again with a scream.

"Here, let me fix that for you," Miriam said. She grabbed Tina by the left boot heel and yanked.

Tina screamed as her ankle was set.

Miriam sat down on the open trunk lip. "Serves you right. You better not have messed up those boots. I like them. I think Tammy's are too small."

Tina lay motionless on the hard packed ground.

"Wake up, bitch."

Miriam leaned down and grabbed her arm.

Tina rolled suddenly and threw a handful of dirt in Miriam's eyes.

Miriam staggered backward. She grabbed the edge of the car and wiped the dust from her eyes. "Too bad Olc isn't out here. He loves a good girl fight."

Tina was digging at the ground trying to crawl away while dragging her shattered ankle.

Miriam knelt down and rolled her onto her back.

Tina scratched and clawed. "No!"

"Lot of fight in you. I think we chose the wrong one," Miriam said as she wrapped her arms around Tina's waist and hoisted her to her feet.

Tina scratched Miriam's face.

Miriam head butted her.

The brunette's eyes crossed, and her head lolled backward.

"Yeah, we definitely chose the wrong one." Miriam sighed. "But, Edgar's hungry. Poor boy hasn't eaten in twenty-four hours. Enough chit chat."

Miriam clasped her hands together at the small of Tina's back and jerked.

Tina screamed as something snapped inside her. The sound echoed through the barn. "What... did you..."

"Broke your back. Just above your hips. See? Can't feel your legs, can you?"

Tina wailed.

"Tina, Tina. Now listen, I'll stop hurting you if you'll stop fighting me. I don't like to hurt people, Tina. But, Edgar has to eat." She hoisted Tina onto her shoulder and walked back to the trunk.

"I mean, you're going to die," Miriam said as she rummaged through the trunk.

Tina whimpered.

"There's no getting around it, Tina. You're like a gazelle on the African veld. It's sad when the lions tear them limb from limb, but the lions have to eat. You understand?"

Tina was sobbing, but she had stopped fighting. "Please don't eat me."

Miriam laughed. *"Please don't eat me,"* Miriam squeaked in a falsetto voice. "Really, getting close to your final words and that's the best you can do? That's pathetic."

Tina slapped at Miriam's legs with her hands.

"Stop that," Miriam said, and she jerked her shoulder forward and slammed Tina's head against the side of the car.

Tina went limp.

"There. That's better." Miriam walked toward a wooden ladder leading up to the old hayloft. "Actually, I'm not going to eat you. I'm not a Draugr - what you would call a vampire. I'm a protector. You know? Like Renfield from the old Dracula movies. The movies have it all wrong of course."

Miriam tested the ladder with her foot and free hand. She sighed. "Looks sturdy enough, but we might go tumbling. Don't worry if we do, I'll get you up in the loft some way."

Miriam began to climb the old gray ladder with Tina draped over her left shoulder.

At the top, she rolled Tina onto her back with her head hanging off the edge of the boards.

Below, the town car started up. It moved a few feet forward until the driver side door was directly beneath them. Then the engine turned off.

Tina's mascara rolled down her forehead along with her tears.

"Edgar, he's the driver. He's one of them, the Draugr, but, well, he has issues," Miriam whispered.

Miriam balanced on the ladder. She held up a coil of clear plastic tubing. One end was open.

The other end was a thick, gleaming hypodermic needle.

"Draugr kidneys are very efficient. They're huge. While they feed, the Draugr urinate - quarts at a time." Miriam put two fingers on the left side of Tina's throat. "There it is. Poor Edgar. His kidneys don't work right. Lots of fluid retention." She leaned close and whispered, "He can't get out of the car. He's sort of grown into the front seat. Honestly, we thought about putting him out of his misery. But, Edgar is just the sweetest guy. Everybody loves him. And, he's an excellent driver."

Miriam pressed the needle against Tina's throat.

Tina screamed and thrashed.

"Tina!" Miriam said as she slapped her. "Listen to me. I will break your arms. Do you hear me? I will break your arms, and you will be in excruciating pain. Is that how you want to die?"

Tina closed her eyes and sobbed. She shook her head.

Miriam stroked her hair. "No, it isn't. So, you have two choices: I break your arms and jam this needle into your carotid. You bleed out fast but in some major fucking pain. Not a good choice, right?"

Tina shook her head.

"Then we'll do option two: you lie here quietly, and I'll gently thread this into your jugular vein. No pain, and you'll just go to sleep. Then you wake up in heaven with all the angels and Elvis."

Tina opened her eyes. "You're a fucking lunatic."

Miriam leaned in close. "Bitch, you have no idea. Trust me. You're lucky. I have a head full of spiders. Sometimes, I'm scared shitless by the twisted crap in here." She pointed at her own forehead.

Then, Miriam kissed Tina's forehead and slid the needle into her neck.

Tina cried softly as red blood flowed into the tubing.

Miriam started to climb down, unraveling the slowly filling tube as she descended. "Oops, almost forgot." She climbed back up. She rummaged in her fanny pack and pulled out a small paper covered object.

She opened it and held it up for Tina to see.

A pink and lime green Carebear bandaid.

"Children just love these." Miriam peeled the backing off and placed it over the injection site, securing the IV in place.

"You know, fanny packs are a lifesaver." Miriam climbed down. She capped the end of the tube with her thumb as she reached the barn floor.

"Window down, Edgar," she said.

The driver's side window rolled down slightly.

Miriam put a fist on her hip. "Edgar. I've seen you. You don't have to be shy with me."

The window lowered.

Miriam smiled.

Above them, Tina screamed.

Miriam looked up at her. "Stop that. You'll hurt his feelings."

Miriam reached out and stroked the wall of gray mottled skin in the open window.

It had once been a face, but now there was only a single jaundiced eye was visible staring out above a swelling of slick skin.

She eased the tube into his crooked mouth.

Edgar began to suck.

"You like that?" Miriam asked.

There was a drop of blood clinging to Miriam's thumb where she had capped the tube. She licked it off. "Mmm, I could get used to this. Tina, you're delicious."

Her mind filled with laughter.

"What's that?" Miriam asked. She listened to the voice in her head and then burst out laughing. "Oh, Tina, this is why we love Edgar. Knock, knock."

"What?" Tina asked from the loft.

Miriam rolled her eyes. "I said, 'Knock, knock.'"

Tina cried. "Who... who's there?"

"Not Edgar he can't leave the car." Miriam giggled. "Oh, Edgar, that's great." Then she burst out laughing again. "Tina? Honk, honk."

Tina stared down at them with half lidded eyes. Tina whispered, "Who's there?"

"Probably Edgar." She leaned forward and kissed Edgar's massive cheek. "So funny."

Huntington, West Virginia

Gene slept with the waitress curled under his arm. It was the first full night's sleep he'd had in weeks.

His chest rose and fell with his deep breaths. Occasionally, his breathing would stop. He died, thirty seconds at a time as his brain stopped telling his lungs to work.

Sometimes he woke up gasping.

He needed a machine to keep him breathing - the doctor in Billings had told him this when he had prescribed the pills.

Gene had never gotten the machine.

One night, he knew he would simply stop breathing and not start again.

The waitress moved in her sleep. Perhaps she felt his breathing stop. She held on to him tighter, and he gasped. His breathing started again.

Gene dreamed. His eyes fluttered under his lids as they moved, matching their movements in his dream.

He was lying in the waitress's bed. She was curled naked against him, and it felt so good to be warm and wanted.

Two people stood at the foot of the bed.

A woman about his age wearing a plaid sundress. Beside her stood a girl, a brunette with purple highlights. She was wearing black short shorts and a halter top.

The brunette had a band-aid on her neck, and she rubbed it as she stared at him.

"You have to go," the older woman said. "You're going the wrong way." The woman's voice sounded southern or maybe hillbilly.

Gene stared at them. He couldn't move.

"Don't you fail them," the younger girl said in a thick Kentucky drawl.

Gene sat bolt upright. He turned to the bedside table and grabbed the notebook and pen he kept beside him when he slept.

TWO WOMEN SOUTHERN ACCENTS
'YOU HAVE TO GO, YOU'RE GOING THE WRONG WAY'
'DON'T YOU FAIL THEM'

He scrawled the words in the dark even as the dream faded.

Ghosts, he thought. It wasn't the first time ghosts had spoken to him in dreams. Never anyone he knew, always strangers.

Victims, he thought. He struggled to remember the dream. No. One was a victim, he thought of the girl with the band-aid on her neck. She was a victim.

The older woman wasn't.

The vampires gathered ghosts like moths to a flame.

And, some of those ghosts didn't like the vampires. The ghosts couldn't do anything to them, not directly.

But, sometimes they talked to Gene.

Sometimes they helped him.

The waitress was looking at him from the sheets. "Penny for your thoughts."

Gene smiled down at her and rubbed her hair out of her eyes. "Just ghosts, darlin'. Nothing but ghosts."

"You seem like someone who's haunted," she whispered. She rolled onto her back. "Stay. I don't mind ghosts."

He put his hands under her thighs, lifted her ankles onto his shoulders. "I'll stay for awhile."

She smiled up at him. "It's Ava."

"What?"

"My name. It's Ava."

Gene sat at the kitchen table while she washed her frying pan.

Ava was almost as good a cook as a lover.

He wanted to stay.

He stared at his phone.

ARSON SUSPECTED IN MINNEAPOLIS FIRE - DOZENS DEAD

The story said there were no leads.

It also said police were investigating the identity of numerous bodies found mostly intact in the basement.

Several had been identified as missing persons from the metro area.

Each drained of blood, Gene thought. The newspaper wouldn't print that, of course. But, he could imagine the discussions going on in the homicide room right now.

His phone beeped.

The map opened. The terrain in the image was wooded, high in the mountains. He zoomed out.

Glade Mountain in Virginia. Southwest Virginia.

They had gone south.

Two hundred miles south.

Ava set the pan on the small white stove. "I don't have to work tonight. We could spend the day together."

She turned and looked at him. Her smile faded. "You have to go?"

"I'm sorry. I don't want to go."

She looked away. "I understand. Just… are you married? It's okay if you are. Well, not okay, but I won't be angry…"

He stood up, wrapped his arms around her. "No. No, I'm not married. She died a very long time ago."

"Then why…"

"Something I have to do. When it's done, if I can, I'll come back."

Rural Retreat, Virginia

The pretty, redheaded reporter is illuminated by bright lights. Her breath forms clouds in the cold air. The background is bleak: fire scorched concrete walls and the charred remains of a wooden staircase.

The logo at the bottom of the screen said: Redbud Revue Video Blog.

"Minnesota is fucking cold," she says.

"We're filming, Luv," a voice off-camera says.

"Shit. You can edit that out, right?"

The off-camera voice laughs. "Of course, darling, anything for you. Let's just mind our potty mouth from here out, all right?"

She smiles. "Good evening, this is Diane Reston reporting from Minneapolis, Minnesota where it is fifteen degrees below zero. We are in the basement of the Minneapolis Murder House, the infamous site of the largest non-terrorist related mass murder in US history."

Diane points up, and the camera follows, revealing a star filled sky. "The house itself is gone, destroyed by fire over two weeks ago. An inferno which revealed a chamber of horrors in the basement."

The camera tilts back to Diane as she turns to her right. "Police still will not allow the press or the public on the grounds. We had to get over a twelve-foot tall fence topped with razor wire to access the site." She turns and smiles at the camera. "Nobody knows we're here, and we'll hopefully be long gone before this video goes online."

She points at the floor. "The floor has a thick covering of quicklime, which is why we're wearing heavy boots. And, over in the far corner, you can see the reason we came."

The camera pans right revealing a yellow, rusting piece of machinery. It is taller than the woman. There is a long rectangular pipe leading from the top of the machine, its end pointed at a break in the concrete wall. A large sewer pipe is visible through the hole.

"This is the way the occupants of the Minneapolis Murder House disposed of their victims: they were fed a piece at a time into this wood chipper, the gore was then ejected into this hatch the killers cut in a sewer pipe," Diane says. She looks at the camera. "Over forty-seven individuals were ground up in this machine. Forensics labs are still sifting through the evidence trying to identify the bodies. So far, only five have been positively identified."

Diane looks at the camera with a serious expression. "The actual number of victims may never be determined. And, thus far, the identities of the killers remains a mystery. The authorities have no leads, no trail to follow - all we can do is wait to see if they strike again."

Anne leaned over the back of the couch and stared at the iPad in her six-year-old daughter's hand. A video of a place called the Minnesota Murder House was playing on the small screen. "Why are you watching that?"

"It's educational," Tia said.

She kissed the top of her daughter's head. Her hair smelled of sunshine and blanket fuzz. "It's not something you need to be watching. Find a Barney video or something."

"Barney sucks," Tia said as she went back to the search screen.

Anne raised up. "Who taught her that word?"

Her teenage daughter dropped backward over the back of the couch, landing inverted beside her younger sister. "Life taught her that word, Mom," Kim said, a half eaten Poptart in her hand.

"Yeah, life," Tia said.

"And she's watching that crap because she's a borderline sociopath," Kim said.

Tia broke half the Poptart in her sister's hand and gobbled it down. "Am not."

"Enough iPad," Anne said. "You're going to be late for school."

"School sucks," Tia said as she closed the magnetic lid on her iPad.

"Stop saying that," Anne said. "It's not nice."

"Well, what am I supposed to say?" Tia asked.

"Say, 'School blows,'" Kim said. She smiled up at her mother.

"You are not helping," Anne sighed.

"Hey, Mom, your cell was ringing earlier," Kim said as she rolled onto her feet.

"It was?" Anne picked up her phone from the kitchen island and looked at the screen. "623 area code. What is that?"

"Phoenix, AZ," Kim said. "I looked it up. Long distance romance?" She smiled at her mother.

Anne frowned and shook her head. "I don't know anybody in Phoenix." She waved toward the hallway. "Tia, get your shoes on. You're both going to be late."

Anne stared down at the phone.

They dropped Tia at her school and pulled back onto the road to the high school.

"I'm going to ask Mr. Hamadi for some evening hours over the weekend," Kim said as she lounged back in the passenger seat. She had her feet on the Prius's dashboard.

"Oh, no, you're not," Anne said.

"Come on, Mom. I'm seventeen…"

"You are not working after dark at the Gas'N'Go. Convenience stores are dangerous after dark," Anne said.

Kim rolled her eyes. "Says the woman who drives out to meet strangers in the middle of nowhere and sell them houses."

"Yeah, well, I get paid a lot more than you, and I'm an adult."

"Hamadi's son is a year younger than me, and he works Saturday night."

Anne sighed. "I don't care how Hamadi treats his kids. That's his business, and you're mine. What are you trying to make more money for? Is there something you need?"

Kim looked out the window. "No."

"Hey," Anne said. She put her hand on her daughter's arm. "Talk to me."

Kim bit her lower lip. "I know he isn't paying support."

Anne teared up. "That's not for you to worry about."

"He's an asshole."

"Don't say that he's your father."

"Really? He hasn't called in three years, Mom. Do you even know where he is?"

"No."

"Shacking up someplace with the whore," Kim whispered.

"I suppose," Anne said as she pulled up to the curb at the high school. "Listen, you have every right to be mad at him."

"So do you," Kim said.

"Oh, I am. Trust me. If I ever see him again, there better not be any cutlery at hand," Anne said. She brushed her daughter's auburn hair out of her eyes. "But, one day, you and Tia will probably have some kind of relationship with him."

"The fuck I will," Kim said.

"Hey! Language," Anne said. The words were authoritarian, but the tone was tender. "You don't choose family. You're stuck with it, the good and the bad."

"I'll never forgive him."

"Never say never, kiddo," she smiled at Kim. "Now, I'd hug you, but one of those Barbie Doll wannabes you call friends would probably see and give you shit."

"Language!" Kim said and burst out laughing. She looked out the window. "Yeah, you're right, I do have a cold, bitchy reputation to maintain. I love you, Mom."

"I love you too, cold and bitchy."

Kim got out of the car and walked straight and tall along the sidewalk.

She didn't turn around, but that was okay. Anne was happy to help with the illusion that helped her daughter cope with high school.

Anne drove up the street.

She made it a block before she burst into tears, beat her hands on the steering wheel, and cursed her ex for the millionth time for what he had done them.

Phoenix, Arizona

Bad choices, Laura thought. They'd write those words on her tombstone. A series of bad decisions leading to an eventful though mediocre life of little consequence. She leaned back in the dusty leather chair, peeled the clear nicotine patch off her upper arm and flicked it away into the corner of the room.

It stuck to the filthy carpet.

She pulled out the last patch in the pack, removed the backing, and stuck it to her arm.

The patch didn't do shit.

She still wanted a cigarette. But, she was three months nicotine free, and she was determined.

Adam was draped over the bed with yellowing sheets, his arm trailing off the side, his fingers inches from the now cold crack pipe.

We all got our vices, she thought. Although, she couldn't really understand his: the pipe, the needle, the gang of misfits passed out in the living room outside.

The sex she could understand, not that he was worth shit after the pipe, and especially not after the needle. The sex lifted, the other junk tore you down.

She sighed, ran her hand along the olive drab canvas of her duffel bag.

Adam had been a port in a storm, but the storm was past.

"Adam, wake up."

He moved slowly, like a glacier receding.

"Adam, we need to talk."

"Time? What time is it?" He whispered as he smacked his lips together.

"Noon."

He rolled over and groaned. "Come back to bed."

"I'm leaving."

"'Kay. Pick up some marshmallows, will you?"

"No, Adam. I mean I'm leaving Phoenix."

He sat up, shook his head. "What? Why? I thought you needed to lay low."

"It's been six months. They aren't looking for me," Laura said.

Adam hissed. "So, that's it? Six months and then adios?"

"Thank you. Thank you for letting me crash here. But, it isn't my life."

"Hey, baby, listen, come on. Just stay till Monday."

She stood up and leaned over him, stroked his cheek. "That's the problem, babe. It is Monday." She turned and picked up her duffel. "It's Monday, and it's time for me to go."

"Fuck. You know what? Next time you need my help, you can just go to hell. I thought we had something…"

Laura looked down at him. "You need help, man. You're drowning here, and I'm not drowning with you. Get some help, Adam, before it's too late."

She hoisted the bag onto her narrow shoulder and left.

"Can I get a ticket to Rural Retreat, Virginia?" Laura asked at the Greyhound desk.

The old man punched in the destination on his computer. "We don't have that destination anymore. Closest I can get you is Wytheville. Same county, about twenty miles difference."

"That's fine." She pulled out her cell and tried her sister for the second time since early this morning.

"Round trip?" The man behind the desk asked.

"No. I'm going home." *I hope*, she thought.

Home is the only place where one truly exists. Living without a home is to live as a spirit without a soul.
> - Merlin Taliesin

Everywhere there was the smell of death in these cold lands. Parisian backstreets with open sewers flowing past abattoirs are pale facsimiles. The abodes were charnel houses where the dead decayed, forming sprawling necropolises. I asked my guide what manner of plague had befallen these lands. He replied, "Draugr."
> - Bertrand du Guesclin, Voyages dans le Nord, circa 1350 AD

She vied so fast, protesting oath after oath, that in a twink she won me to her love.
> - Shakespeare, The Taming of the Shrew, Act 2, Scene 1

There's so much I can show and give to you
If you will welcome me tonight
If only you had been there my dear
We could have shared this together
> - Donald Roeser (Buck Dharma), Blue Oyster Cult,
> I Love the Night

ACT II

Real Estate

Anne sat in her Prius and stared at the phone that buzzed in her hand. The number again. Someone in Phoenix who seemed determined to talk to her. Her finger hovered over the screen. Instead, she sent it to voice mail.

The clients would be here soon.

She looked out at the two-lane blacktop of Kinder Valley Lane. The road was empty in the early afternoon. Stubborn late fall snow clung in patches on the dead field beyond the edge of the road.

Above that was the old Victorian mansion, looking out of place on the barren hillside. This was a house more suited to old Hollywood movies, not the backwoods of rural Virginia.

The perspective of the behemoth always seemed out of kilter to Anne. The farther your eye traveled up the fading painted sides, the larger it seemed to loom. It was old when she was born, abandoned before the time of her mother.

The house on Kinder Valley Lane had been built before the turn of the last century when ornate corbels and ornamental dentil mattered just as much as strong walls and foundations. The copper roof glittered green in the waning sunlight.

They were late.

Anne shook her head. No, the clients were always on time. You could be early, heaven forbid you should ever be late - but the clients were always on time.

The black car eased along the lane toward her. A town car, something else out of place in this land of pickup trucks and economy cars. The windows were tinted dark black, the interior unfathomable.

The town car rolled to a stop in front of her Prius.

Anne stepped out into the chill air. She pulled her coat around her.

The rear door opened and a woman stepped out.

She was tall, made taller still by towering red heels. She wore a small black blazer over a red dress that showed off the curve of her legs.

Anne held out her hand. "I'm Anne Lawrence from Coldwell Banker. You must be Miss Tillford?"

The woman took her hand and smiled down at her behind pale blue eyes. "Miriam. Call me Miriam."

Anne felt small looking up at the woman. Miriam Tillford's hand was warm in hers.

"My associate, Mr. Olc," Miriam said.

A tall, emaciated man stood beside Miriam. Anne had never seen the man exit the car, he simply appeared beside them.

"Oh… I'm Anne Lawrence…"

"Enchanted," the man said. He towered over them both. He did not extend his thin hand to her. His face was pale, his head beneath the black hat he wore looked bald.

He wore a black trench coat that extended down to his ankles.

Miriam smiled. "Mr. Olc speaks very little English, I'm afraid. I do most of the talking. You'll be dealing with me for the closing."

"Closing?" Anne asked. "But, you haven't even seen the place yet."

"Perfect," Olc said. "Excellent."

"The house has been boarded up for years," Anne said. "It's going to take some work."

"Ghosts. So many ghosts," Olc said as he wandered toward the path leading up to the house.

"One would almost think you didn't want to make the sale, Anne," Miriam said. She was smiling down as she said it.

"No! No, it's not that… it's just… don't you want to see it first? The inside?"

Miriam released her hand and motioned toward the house. "Please. Lead the way."

Anne called out to Olc. "The house has been vacant since the early 1940s. The last family member died shortly after that. It's been in the bank's holdings ever since."

"Whore house," Olc said as he walked silently up the weeded path.

Anne laughed. "That is the rumor."

"Truth," Olc said. "Ghosts say."

Miriam took Anne's hand and whispered, "Mr. Olc is… eccentric. But, quite harmless, I assure you."

Olc turned in the path and stared toward the east. "Killings. The town. Bedford?"

Anne stared uncomprehendingly for a moment, and then she remembered. "Oh, the bear attacks out in Bedford? That was almost ten years ago. It's hours from here, and they destroyed the bear." She looked up at Miriam who merely smiled back.

The bear attacks in the small town of Bedford had made national news.

"Bears?" Olc said in his odd sing-song voice. "Yes. Bears. Fear bears. And wolves. Fear wolves. Far worse."

Anne smiled. "Bears we have - small ones, more of a danger to trash cans than anything else. But, there are no wolves in Wythe County."

Olc smiled with a mouth too wide and lips too thin. "Good."

Anne turned the old key and opened the big oak door. The smell of dust and age rushed out and collided with the cold air.

Olc followed her into the grand foyer and ran his hand on the smooth stair rail.

In its day, the house had been grand. A mansion paid for with profits from lumber or coal or any number of more nefarious endeavors. Her father had told her once: It's not hard to get rich in a place like Rural Retreat, but it's hard to keep your soul at the same time.

The floors were dusty and bowed in places, the finish worn from decades of feet making paths from living room to kitchen, bedroom to bathroom.

Red floral wallpaper adorned the walls. A kind of leprosy had taken hold throughout where the wallpaper had receded to expose the house's lath and plaster ribs.

"The bank pays annually to keep the house free of termites and rodents. The pipes are old, naturally, but the plumbing is sound. The water is shut off at the street," Anne said as she felt the floorboards give slightly.

"It's hooked to the city sewer, correct?" Miriam asked as she walked in behind Anne.

"Yes. They did it a few years ago."

Olc walked around the foyer looking up at the second floor. "Bedrooms?"

"Eight. Only one bathroom, unfortunately," Anne said.

Olc seemed mesmerized by the surroundings.

Anne studied him. He was old, although she could not have told whether he was sixty or ninety. His skin was thin and pale, but with no wrinkles to give a hint of his true age. It was as if his skin was pulled tight over his face and skull.

Olc's eyes were black and large, the whites not yellowed by age.

He was old, but he didn't *seem* old.

Anne took a step and felt the floor give.

Then it cracked, and she felt herself falling backward through a hole that had opened behind her.

Olc was there. A moment before he had been on the other side of the room, but now he was inches from her, his hands in her hands. She teetered on the edge of the broken floor.

His hands were strong but ice cold. "Old houses. Treacherous," he said and smiled at her, but all she could focus on was the coldness of his hands.

Another set of hands, Miriam's, closed around her waist, and Anne felt pushed forward toward the tall man made of ice and darkness.

He looked away over Anne's shoulder, locked eyes briefly with Miriam, and shook his head slightly, the smile never leaving his lips.

Olc stepped aside, put a hand on Anne's shoulder and guided her away from the hole.

Anne looked back at the two-foot diameter chasm. "I am so sorry. They assured me the floors were in good condition. The bank will have workmen out here at once…"

Miriam smiled at her and put her arm around Anne. "That won't be necessary. Mr. Olc has a large family, they will take care of the repairs."

Olc walked ahead of them again. "The town. Tell me."

Anne's heart was still pounding, and she rubbed her hands together trying to warm her fingers from the lingering cold of his touch. "Rural Retreat? We have almost 1600 people in town now. Most people work in Wytheville - that's the county seat. Some people commute to Abingdon. Not much in the way of amenities. There's a Gas'N'Go gas station, a pizza place, two Dollar General Stores…"

"A High School?" Olc asked as he leaned down to peer through the lath and plaster at the room beyond.

"Rural Retreat High School. My oldest is a senior this year."

"Adore the young. Potential. Great potential," Olc said. He opened a bedroom door and stepped inside.

Anne laughed. "Trust me, sometimes I'd like to give my teenager away."

Olc smiled at her as he left the bedroom. "Take them. Anytime. Welcome them. Family."

Anne's smile faltered. There was something in his tone above a joke.

Before she could think anything more about it, he looked away. "Tour complete. Acceptable."

"We haven't even talked about the price. The bank is motivated to sell…"

"The asking price is fine," Miriam said as she escorted Anne back through the foyer around the opening in the floor.

They stepped onto the porch, and Anne locked the door as Mr. Olc joined them.

Miriam continued as they walked back toward the cars. "We would like an expedited closing. Mr. Olc's family is in temporary housing and anxious to move into more spacious quarters."

"I'll get right on it." Anne laughed. "You know, I'm not doing much work for my commission on this. I wish all my clients were like you."

Miriam opened her car door for her. "Oh, trust me. We're absolute devils in other ways."

Anne sat in her car and stared at the two of them as they got back in their car.

Her hands were still cold from Olc's touch.

Miriam and Olc sat side by side in the back of the town car.

Olc looked toward the dark glass barrier separating them from the front seat. He did not say a word to Edgar, but the car began to move.

"You should have fed. You haven't eaten in days," Miriam said.

Olc closed his eyes. "Pain of hunger. Savored."

"It will weaken you," Miriam said.

"Strong enough," Olc whispered in his sing-song voice. "Miriam. Take good care of us."

Miriam smiled. "Is that a command or a comment?"

"Comment. No command for you. Never you," Olc said. He reached over and ran his hand up her inner thigh.

She closed her eyes and let her thighs part. She smiled as his cold fingers found the top of her stocking and slid higher.

She breathed in. "All those questions about Bedford? Why are you so interested in bear attacks?"

Olc laughed. The sound echoed in her head, amplified by the power of his thoughts. "Even in pleasure. Questions. Remarkable. Always so."

Miriam bit her lower lip as he manipulated her physically and mentally. "The.. attacks... Why do you care?"

He stopped his caresses, and she whimpered in protest.

"Monsters. Dangerous. Like us, but not. Danger there."

"Like us? But, there's nothing like us. Why haven't you ever said anything..."

His caresses began again in earnest. His thoughts blocked out her own.

Words came into her mind, unimpeded by his diminishing speech center: *There are more things in heaven and Earth, Horatio, than are dreamt of in your philosophy.' Demons, witches, different vampires... The monsters in Bedford are not for us, and we are not for them.*

"Bedford. Stay away," he whispered.

Then he put both hands on her thighs and pressed darkness and madness into her mind.

Miriam screamed out just as she had so many years ago.

Tucson, Arizona

Laura leaned her head against the bus window and watched the desert pass by. She looked at the phone screen and closed out the dialer once more.

Her sister wasn't answering. She didn't even know if this was still Anne's number.

She hadn't spoken to her sister in five years.

What was she thinking? Anne might turn her away at the door. Laura had missed their mother's funeral, and that had been the last straw.

She had a reason, of course. Laura always had a reason. Two weeks before her mother died, they had burned a logging executive's car in Seattle, and he was connected to the feds, and he called it domestic terrorism, and the FBI called it that too.

Laura had to lay low until the heat died down, just like she had to lay low with Adam for the last six months.

That first time it had only been a car.

This last time, a man had died.

Laura hadn't been the one who built the bomb. She hadn't been the one to place the bomb - if she had, she would have made damn sure it was set to go off in the middle of the night.

Instead, a logging company bulldozer blew up shortly after 1:30 PM, on April 7th, and Patrick Shaunessy was dead. Forty-two years old with three kids and a wife and a mortgage.

Laura squeezed her eyes shut. Patrick Shaunessy's face was burned into her mind.

She hadn't built the bomb. But, she had taught the other members of Gaia's Guardians to make bombs.

She hadn't set the bomb. But, she had an eight-year relationship with the man who did.

And, Oh, God, please believe she didn't know they were going to place the bomb and set it to go off when Patrick Shaunessy climbed on to that bulldozer just doing his damned job.

She wiped tears from her cheeks.

Get a grip, Laura. You didn't know.

Bobby Duncan got thirty years, those that were with him got five years each.

The minute she heard about the death of Patrick Shaunessy, Laura had packed her duffel, tossed her cell phone in a dumpster, and hitchhiked to Phoenix.

After six months, no one had asked about her. The feds weren't looking for her. If they had been, they would have found her.

This morning, she woke up from a dream about her mother.

"Time to go home," her mother said as she stood in Adam's bedroom in her plaid sundress. Laura could still smell the stench of Adam's crack pipe.

"Time to go home." Four words. Nothing more, and then the sun rose. Laura had packed her duffel.

And, now she was dreaming of her again. She fell asleep with her head against the window.

"You need to hurry," her mother said from the seat beside her.

In her dream, she opened her eyes. Her mom was still wearing the plaid sundress.

"Don't you fail her," her mother said.

"I always fail her," Laura whispered.

"Don't you fail her."

Laura jerked awake. "Mom?"

The young, pregnant Mexican girl beside her stared at Laura.

Laura was breathing hard. "Perdona, lo siento."

"Esta bien, Senora. Pesadilla?"

"Si, Pesadilla. Very bad dream."

The Gas'N'Go

"You know, Dude, I don't mind being your wingman, but you are on a suicide mission," Pauly said as they stood near the back of the Gas'N'Go convenience store.

David gritted his teeth. "Man, please shut up."

Kim Lawrence stood behind the convenience store counter thirty feet away. He watched her over the potato chip bags and Pop Tarts display. She was perfect. Green eyes glittering in her face framed by auburn hair.

"Hey, David, I'm just saying, she's way out of your league. I mean, she's like major league and you're like... peewee league."

"Thanks, Pauly. Really you're a great help," David said.

"I call em like I see em, hayseed." Pauly Delveccio was David's best friend. They were polar opposites. Pauly was tall and dark, David was medium height and blond.

Pauly's family had moved to the area from New York City when David was in middle school. Now both boys were juniors at Rural Retreat High.

"Okay, let's count all the ways in which you are never getting with that: one, she's a senior. Two, she's smoking hot. Three, you're a nerd. Four, sooner or later she's going to get one look at me and fall head over heels."

David glared at him.

Pauly laughed. "Relax, I'm joking, you freak. Bro code. I'd never make a move on a girl you are hopelessly stalking even though you have zero chance with," Pauly said. He sighed. "No matter how unbelievably hot she is."

David picked up a bag of chips. "Alright, I'm doing this."

Pauly slapped him on the back. "Go for it, champ. You got this. Crash and burn, man, crash and burn."

"I hate you," David said as he walked toward the counter.

"Of course you do," Pauly said as he turned around to the Slurpee machine.

Pauly hadn't seen the woman come in. She was standing directly behind him. She was blonde and at least three inches taller than him.

"Hi," Pauly said.

She looked down at him with an amused expression. "I admire your friend's courage."

Pauly glanced back over his shoulder. "Who? Hayseed? He's doomed."

"Aren't we all," the woman said as she turned and picked a bottle of water from the cooler by the Slurpees.

Pauly looked at her legs.

"Most people consider it impolite to stare," the woman said without turning around.

"Sorry," Pauly said.

She turned toward him and smiled. "Not me, of course. I like it when men stare at me."

She looked at Pauly, her eyes traveling up and down. "See? Did that feel impolite to you?"

Pauly shook his head.

She held out her hand. "I'm Miriam."

"Pauly," he said as he took her slender hand in his.

She rubbed the nail of her index finger along his palm.

Pauly's breath caught in his chest.

She walked past him toward the counter. "I'll be seeing you, Pauly."

"Wow," Pauly said.

David put his bag of chips on the counter.

Kim picked them up and ran them over the scanner. "$3.77."

"Hey, I think we go to school together," David said. "And, I think your mom works with my mom."

She looked down at him. The platform behind the counter was six inches higher than the floor.

She's a goddess, he thought. *And, I'm a moron.*

"Yeah," Kim said with a frown. "You're Pauly's friend."

David felt himself growing smaller still. "Oh, you know Pauly?"

"Everybody knows Pauly."

David looked down at the floor. "Yeah, he's a popular guy that Pauly." What was he thinking? Using Pauly for a wingman?

He dug in his pocket and handed her a five dollar bill.

"Actually, he's an asshole. We all laugh at him. You going to ask me or what?" Kim asked as she made change in the cash drawer.

His eyes grew wide. "Ask you?"

"You came up here to ask me out. Ask."

David looked up at her.

Her expression was as unreadable as the Mona Lisa.

He swallowed hard. "Um, would you like to go out with me?"

She frowned. "No. Thank you for shopping Gas'N'Go. Have a nice day." She dropped his change into his hand.

He grabbed the chips and turned away.

And, then she laughed.

David froze in place.

"Turn around," she said. "It was a joke, you moron."

David turned.

She was smiling now, leaning on the counter in her red and white Gas'N'Go shirt. "How old are you?"

"Sixteen. I'll be seventeen in April." He stood up straight, tried to look taller.

She stared at him. "Okay. Saturday. 6:15 PM. My house. Don't be late. Are you wearing that?"

He looked down at his vintage Ren and Stimpy t-shirt. "Uh, probably not?"

"Definitely not. Regular shirt, blue or white. Tucked in. You have a car?"

"Uh, my mom won't let me drive till I'm eighteen."

"Okay, fine, I'll drive. I like flowers. A corsage. Red roses, white baby's breath. Nothing gaudy."

He stared at her. "Are you joking?"

She turned her head sideways. "Do I look like I'm joking, David?"

"No?"

"No, I'm not. One more thing: your friend is a blabbermouth. No one hears a word of this. Don't act like you know me at school - seriously, David, if you see me in the hall, go the other way. We're going to Wytheville on our date, so nobody will know us. I'm a senior, and I can't be seen with a junior. Nothing personal."

"Yeah, no. I get it. I'll tell Pauly to keep his mouth shut."

"You do that. Bye-bye now."

David started backing away, and then he stopped. "Wait. I don't know where you live."

An older girl wearing a Gas'N'Go shirt walked out of the back room and leaned on the door jam. She rang up the bottled water of a tall blonde woman.

The blonde woman smiled politely and walked away.

Kim frowned down at David. "I like men who are resourceful, David. If you can't figure out where I live, I don't want to go out with you."

"No, no! I'll find it. I can do that." He stumbled backward.

He turned back to Pauly with a smile on his face.

When he was far enough away, the other counter girl, Fatima, burst out laughing. "God, you are horrible."

Kim turned quickly and smiled. "I know. It's a gift."

"He's cute."

"Yes, and thank God he's just awkward enough not to realize it."

"No fucking way," Pauly said.

"Saturday night. And, the best part is: she knows my name."

"Bullshit."

"Yep. She acted all cool about it, but she called me by my name."

They both turned and looked at her.

Pauly punched him in the shoulder. "My little Davey is growing up so fast."

"What are you doing?" Mr. Hamadi said as he stormed down the aisle toward Pauly and David. He was a small, bald man with thick hair coming out of his ears.

"Uh, shopping?" David said.

"No," Hamadi said. "You are ogling. There is no ogling in my store. In my country, staring at a girl that long is the same as a marriage proposal. And, you are both shiftless looking. Get out of my store!"

"Alright, take it easy," Pauly said. "We're going."

Pauly and David walked toward the front door.

David turned to Kim and smiled at her.

She turned away with a disinterested look.

He left the store smiling.

Hamadi walked up to the counter and pointed a thick finger at Kim. "Do you know what your problem is?"

"No, what?"

62

"You are too pretty," Hamadi lectured. "Pretty is a curse. Pretty draws teenage boys who stand around and buy nothing."

Kim pointed toward the parking lot. "He bought chips…"

"Don't interrupt," Hamadi said. "I have four daughters. All of them ugly. Ugly and now happy in arranged marriages."

Fatima threw her hands in the air. "Standing right here, Papa! Can't you see? You call me ugly, and I.Am.Standing.Right.Here."

Hamadi shook a finger toward her. "But happy! Tell me you are not." He walked past them into the back room.

Kim grimaced. "I'm sorry," she whispered.

"Don't be. Someday he will leave my siblings and me the store. And, when he is old, we will put him in a home. Where he will be so unhappy. And, we will laugh, Kim." She turned toward the back room and yelled, "We will laugh!"

From the back of the town car, Miriam Tillford watched the two teenage boys walk away from the store. She looked at the taller, darker one and smiled.

Edgar's thoughts touched hers.

She laughed. "Yes, I think so. He's very strong. So many protectors lost, he'll do nicely."

Real Estate, Part 2

"So, tell me all about our new clients," Jane Connors asked as Anne walked back into Coldwell Banker.

Anne's boss, Jane, had a penchant for too tight skirts, too tall heels, and too much makeup. Female clients despised her, male clients held her in higher regard. Her voice was full on southwest Virginia.

And, the boobs have to be fake, Anne thought.

Anne rubbed her hands together. They were still ice cold from Olc's touch. "They're odd."

"Honey, as long as they are rich. Their financials checking out?"

"They're paying cash."

"Sweet, Jesus, I am in heaven!"

Anne sat down at her desk and Jane perched on the edge.

"They want an expedited closing, full asking price," Anne said.

Jane put her hands up to her cheeks. "Oh, I think I just had a mini O. Am I flushed?"

Anne laughed and shook her head. "But, they are weird. Miriam Tillford looks like she just stepped out of Vogue magazine, and Mr. Olc looks like a refugee from a zombie movie." She wrung her fingers. "And, his hands were like ice."

Jane took her hands in her own. "Wow, your hands *are* freezing. Still, we can forgive cold hands as long as the money is warm. Good work."

"Wish I could say I did anything. Other than almost fall into the basement. The floor gave way during the tour." Anne said.

"And they didn't run away? Oh, I must have done something right in a past life."

"No, they didn't care at all. Said they would fix it themselves."

Jane hopped off her desk. "I'll call the bank and give them the good news. We're going out for shots tonight."

"Don't you have a teenage son at home?"

"What? The hermit who lives in that funky smelling back bedroom? He won't even know I'm gone," Jane said. "Matter of fact, he called about an hour ago. He asked this certain redheaded senior out this afternoon at the Gas'N'Go."

Anne stared at her. "Oh, God. Your poor son. Did she hurt him?"

"Noooo," Jane said. "She said yes. I didn't think your daughter even knew David's name."

Anne closed her mouth. "Are you sure she said yes?"

"Yeah, and you need to put a stop to it. My David is… not the sharpest tool in the shed. Takes after his father, my second husband, God rest his soul. He's going to be like the dog who chases cars, finally catches one, and then doesn't have the slightest idea what to do with it."

"Isn't he a junior?" Anne asked. "She never goes out with juniors."

"Hey, I'm serious. You're gonna see mama bear get her claws out if she tears his heart out and stomps on it," Jane said. She emphasized the words by making scratching motions with her red manicured nails.

Anne laughed. "She's not that bad. Not quite anyway. I'll talk to her."

"Tell you the truth, I'm thankful for anything that gets him away from that Yankee best friend of his. That boy is a bad influence," Jane sat down at her desk and stared off into space. "Cash… think about that. Having enough money to just buy a house outright. Must be how movie stars and drug dealers live."

Amarillo, Texas

The pregnant girl's name was Luciana, and she couldn't stand the smell of the chemical toilet on the bus. She tried to go in twice, but the stench was too bad for her pregnancy sensitive nose. By the time they stopped in Amarillo, Texas, the girl was in agony, and Laura helped her down the front steps of the bus.

"Hey, she ain't going to drop a kid on my bus, is she?" the driver asked. He stared at them over a scraggly gray handlebar mustache.

Laura turned and glared at him. She stared down at his pot belly and smirked. "No, are you?"

"Real funny. I don't want no water breaking on my bus."

Laura flipped him off and put her arm around Luciana's waist. She ushered her toward the bus terminal through thick diesel fumes.

"I don't think I'm going to make it to the bathroom," Luciana whispered.

"Yes, you are. Think dry thoughts. The desert. Crisp white sheets."

She was practically carrying Luciana when they reached the bathroom door.

"Can you do this?" Laura asked.

"Si, I'll be okay." She disappeared into the restroom.

Laura leaned against the wall. "Hey, you want something to eat?" She yelled through the door.

She heard Luciana's voice echo over the tile floor. "I am going to get a sandwich out of a vending machine."

"Ew, are you nuts? Three-month-old pimento cheese on wonder bread? You want your kid to come out with three heads or something?"

She heard Luciana laugh in the stall. "You are funny."

"Yeah, I'm hysterical," Laura said under her breath.

The terminal was lined with vinyl covered benches from the 1970s. Bums slept on a few of them.

The whole place smelled.

"Hey, good lookin'," a voice said.

She turned to see a skinny man in an old cowboy hat and a white wife beater come out of the men's room next door.

He was looking at her with an expression akin to starvation.

"Seriously? I am so not in the mood."

"Well, what would it take to get you in the mood?" He smiled showing missing teeth from too much meth and not enough toothpaste.

"Deodorant. Charm school. About two thousand dollars worth of dental work."

"You know, usually a girl who pours herself into a pair of tight jeans like that is a little more accomodatin'," meth boy said.

"Yeah, sorry Cletus, it's a fashion statement, not an invitation," Laura said as she walked away.

"I hate to see you go, but I love to watch you leave," meth boy called after her.

Don't turn around, Laura thought. This is how trouble starts. You turn around, and shit gets complicated.

She reached the snack counter and heard the ladies room door open behind her.

"Well, hi there, Mamacita," meth boy said.

Laura turned around.

Luciana was looking up at meth boy with a nervous smile. "Perdona."

He wouldn't let her out of the ladies room. "What's your hurry darlin'? I think pregnant girls are hot. You got that whole glow about ya."

See? she thought. Shit just got complicated.

She walked toward them. She felt her stomach muscles tightening, felt her fingers squeeze closed into a fist. She relaxed her hands, forced her fingers to open. Fights were won in the mind, not in the heart.

"Hey, cowboy," she said. Laura willed the sexy into her voice. She smiled.

He turned toward her and smiled his gap-toothed smile. "I thought you didn't want nothin' to do with me."

She put both hands on his shoulders. "A lady can change her mind, can't she?" Her fingers touched greasy black hair on his shoulders.

A mullet. She hated mullets.

He nodded. "Yeah, I suppose."

She pushed him backward, past Luciana who stared up at them with her mouth and eyes open wide.

She pushed him into the empty restroom.

"Oh, hell, yeah," meth boy said.

She smiled at him as she kneed him in the groin.

His face went beat red as he bent over at the waist.

Laura spun on her right foot and raised her left leg. Her sweeping left calf caught meth boy behind both knees.

His knobby kneecaps crunched as he went down into a kneeling position on the cold tile floor.

"What?" he breathed.

Laura planted her left foot and raised her right foot above her waist over his head.

His eyes drifted up to follow the motion of her boot.

She brought it down hard in an ax kick to the top of his head, and he went face down on the floor.

Laura looked toward the door.

Luciana stared at her. "Is he dead?"

Laura knelt and put two fingers on his throat. "Naah. World wouldn't be that lucky. Lock the door, will you?"

Luciana locked the door and Laura pulled meth boy's wallet out of his back pocket.

She pulled out his license. "Waldo Carruthers. No wonder he's such a jackass, name like that, he never stood a chance."

Laura opened the bill pouch of the wallet. She pulled out money. "Six hundred eighteen dollars." She peeled off three hundred dollar bills and held them out to her.

Luciana took a step back. "No! I don't want his money. Es muy malo."

"Hey, he got what he deserved. Spoils of war."

"It is not right to take money that doesn't belong to you. No robaras - it's in the Bible."

"Yeah, well, when God wrote the Ten Commandments he hadn't met this asshole." Laura rummaged in his right front pants pocket. She came out with car keys.

In his other front pocket, she found fifteen small plastic bags of meth.

She opened one and emptied it in his hair, tossed a few more around the bathroom, and shoved the rest of them down the back of his pants.

Then she walked into a stall. She dropped his wallet and keys in the toilet and flushed twice.

Laura walked to Luciana and offered her the money again. "Last chance."

"No robaras! Es muy malo. You should leave it here or give it to the Church."

Laura shrugged. "Not happening."

She unlocked the door and stepped out into the terminal.

Luciana looked down at the motionless man on the floor. Then she smiled and mock kicked toward him. She turned around and followed Laura.

Laura bought them food from the snack bar.

She used the money she had taken from meth boy, but Luciana said nothing in protest.

She took the roast beef sandwich Laura offered her with a smile.

They started walking back to the bus.

"Where did you learn to fight like that? You are like a... I don't know the word... Una Caballera."

Laura laughed. "A knight?"

"Si, a knight. Or, maybe a ninja."

"Yeah, well, misspent youth."

Laura touched the arm of the terminal's security guard. "Might want to call the cops - there's a meth dealer passed out in the ladies room."

The security guard grumbled and shook his head. "Great. Just great." He hurried toward the restrooms.

Laura and Luciana sat on the bus and looked out the windows.

"I am going to Oklahoma City. My Ricardo, he is waiting for me. We have an apartment, and he has a job working construction. Look, he made one of the bedrooms into a nursery," Luciana held up her phone and showed Laura pictures of a small room with a crib and a mobile of little plastic horses. "He wants a boy. But, I told him, Ricardo you will be just as happy if it is a girl."

Laura smiled down at her. "Looks perfect."

She shook her head. "Not perfect. Es familia. Family is never perfect, but it is the only thing that is real."

Luciana napped as they rolled toward Oklahoma.

When she was sure the girl was asleep, Laura slipped the six hundred dollars into Luciana's purse.

She heard her mother's voice in her head as she drifted off to sleep with her head against the glass. "You can't buy your way into heaven, Stringbean."

No, Laura thought. *But you can feel better about yourself on the way to hell.*

Rural Retreat, Virginia, Part 2

Anne walked into her kitchen with a sack of groceries to find her girls sitting at the kitchen table doing their homework.

"David Connors?" Anne asked.

Kim dropped her head on her open history book. "Hi, Mom, how was your day?"

"David Connors, spill."

Tia looked up from her spelling.

"God, I hate small towns. Everybody is up in your shit," Kim said.

"She swore," Tia said.

"Tia," Anne said. "Spelling."

Tia rolled her eyes. "I'm just sayin'."

"He's a junior, why are you going out with a junior?" Anne asked as she put a carton of eggs in the fridge.

"It's no big deal, dinner and a movie. Typical Saturday night."

"With my boss's kid. Not typical. You have to be careful with people younger and less mature than you."

"Jesus, Mom, he's sixteen," she said. And added, under her breath, "And muscled."

Anne froze with a can of tomatoes in her hand. "Oh, my God. You like this kid."

Kim scoffed. "Pfft. Don't be ridiculous. It's nothing."

Anne sat down beside her with a smile.

Kim glanced at her. "Get that look off your face. It's just a date."

"Oh, not to him: right after you said yes, he went straight home and called his mom to tell her."

Kim grimaced. "He went home and called his mommy? Crap. Maybe he is too young for me."

"Well, I think it's sweet," Anne said.

"Oh, I'm seriously going to throw up," Kim whispered. "David is going to have to cowboy up if we're going out."

Anne got up and continued with the groceries. "Just be careful. This is probably his first real date."

"Christ, Mom? What am I? The dragon lady of Rural Retreat?"

She walked over and kissed the top of Kim's head. "No. You're one of my two favorite people in the world."

"Are you going to see a Disney movie? Can I go?" Tia asked.

Kim leaned forward and grinned. "No. An R rated movie with lots of kissing and maybe butt cheeks and boobies."

Tia wrinkled her nose. "Gross."

"Give it a few more years. Cartoon bunnies and princesses will lose their appeal," Kim said.

"What do you mean you don't make corsages with roses?" David asked over the cell phone. "Out of season? But, I need one for Saturday night."

David paced back and forth in his room. Discarded magazines crunched under his feet as a video game soundtrack thrummed from his television.

"Roanoke? Ma'am, I can't drive to Roanoke. What about Wytheville?" David asked.

He sighed at the answer. "No. No, thank you for trying."

He hung up the phone.

Four years of building up his courage to talk to her, and he was undone by a corsage.

Why the hell did she want a corsage in the first place? Girls wore corsages to dances, proms, not to the movies. He was half convinced she was screwing with him.

Half convinced.

Maybe she was setting up a list of impossible tasks to see if he was worthy of going out with her?

He dropped into his desk chair and put his hands on his computer keyboard.

"David?" His mom called from downstairs. "I'm going out. There's fish sticks in the toaster oven. And, there's chocolate cake in the refrigerator - one piece though, it'll break you out something fierce. That Lawrence girl ain't going to go out with no pizza face."

"Thanks, Mom," David yelled.

He opened the tiny fridge under his desk. It was filled with prepackaged salads and protein shakes. David hadn't eaten one of his mother's toaster oven meals in a year. He pulled out one of the shakes. He would go downstairs later and put the fish sticks out for the cat.

It wasn't that Jane Connors was a horrible mother - she was kind, and he knew she cared for him. She just wasn't good at the whole mom thing.

She was good at going out and attracting rich husbands. She was between them now, which David preferred - switching stepfathers the way other people traded cars was tiring.

His own father died when David was in middle school.

His mother didn't talk about David's father the same way she talked about her other three husbands, and David liked to believe it was because she had truly been in love with his father.

Jane Connors kept his father's last name, no others.

David typed on the keyboard and smiled: Amazon.com had corsages with silk roses and baby's breath.

Another task complete.

Glade Mountain, Virginia

The woman's face fills the screen. She is videoing herself with her phone. Her black hair is cut short, and a single smudge of dirt extends down from the outside corner of her left eye to the midpoint of her tanned cheek.

She squints at the phone, and then she licks her finger and wipes the smudge away.

The woman smiles and begins to talk. "Hi, I'm Addie Watkins Joseph, and today is day one hundred fifty-two of my marriage to Chad Joseph, and the one hundred fifty-first day of our honeymoon walking the Appalachian Trail from Maine to Georgia. It is cold, it has been raining, I cannot feel my toes."

Snickering off camera.

She turns the phone away from her face revealing a man in a soaked rain slicker.

"That's Chad, putting up our tent for the evening."

Chad smiles and waves as he threads the tent poles through the bright red and blue fabric.

Addie turns the camera back to herself. "Now, for those of you who think this is just soooo romantic? Let me tell you: Chad smells. I mean really, really smells. I could track him through the woods with my nose. In the dark. With a head cold."

"Hey, you don't smell like roses either."

She smiles. "No, no I do not. And, I haven't shaved my legs since Maine. I look like a chimpanzee below the waist."

Chad makes monkey noises off camera.

"Don't be gross. And, my blisters have blisters. This is my fourth pair of hiking boots, and we still have at least a month to go." She looks distracted for a moment. "What are you looking at?"

She turns the camera toward Chad.

He has stopped putting the tent together and is staring across the meadow.

The camera shifts as Addie stands up. "What is it?"

"Two people."

The image jostles, and her face appears again as she switches to the main camera.

"Where?"

"Across the meadow. Right at the treeline," Chad says.

The image zooms.

Two gray shapes stand in front of the pines about a half mile away.

"Something's wrong with the camera," Addie says.

"What do you mean?"

"I see a girl in a t-shirt and shorts and a guy with dreads, but all I see on the screen are two gray shapes."

"Too far away I guess, phone cameras don't have great zoom."

Addie whispers, "What are they doing?"

"Staring at us."

"Why?"

"Gee, babe, I don't know. But, we're staring at them too, so…"

"Hi!" Addie yells.

The shapes on the camera stand for a moment longer, and then they walk back into the pines.

"Okay," Addie says. "That was creepy."

She switches the camera to front facing. Her face fills the screen. She looks around nervously. "Listen."

"What?"

"Do you hear banjos?"

Chad bursts out laughing.

She grins at the camera. "Oh sure, laugh it up. This is evidence in case I'm kidnapped and used for breeding stock by some clan of hillbillies."

The screen goes black.

Addie's face fills the screen. Her face is lit green by a night vision camera.

"I hate peeing in the woods," she says. There is the sound of urine splashing. "But, I've gotten good at it. When we first started walking, I made him stand a few feet away every time I had to get up to pee. Now I don't even wake him."

There is a rustling sound as she pulls up her pants.

"Except a few days back at Sharptop Mountain. That's Bedford County, Virginia where all those people got killed by the bear. Yeah, I did not pee alone."

"Okay, things I miss about Manhattan: toilets, showers, Cosmopolitans, makeup… did I say toilets? It'd be nice to take a piss without having to worry about poison oak."

A branch snaps.

Addie stops talking and looks to her right. She squints into the darkness. "Hello? Chad?"

She swallows. "Oh, hi. I waved to you earlier. Is your campsite nearby?"

Addie is walking backward. "I'm just going back to my tent."

She drops the phone.

There is the sound of running feet.

The screen shows nothing but pine trees and dark sky.

Chad Joseph dreamed. They were back in their Manhattan apartment. He looked at pictures on the wall. Their wedding followed by scenes from the trail. Addie smiling at him as she stood beside the red and blue tent.

Two women stood beside him in his dream. One was a young girl, brunette with purple highlights dressed in black short shorts and a white halter top. She had a Carebears band-aid on her neck.

The other woman was older and dressed in a plaid sundress.

They were screaming, pleading with him, but no sound came from their lips. Their mouths were wide open, their throats straining. They waved at him frantically.

Addie came out of the bedroom wearing shorts and a white t-shirt. The t-shirt read Hoosier Hottie.

He frowned. Neither of them went to Indiana. Why was she wearing a Hoosier shirt?

He heard whispers then. "Wake up!" "Run!"

Chad moaned in his sleep. He rolled onto his back.

He heard the sound of his sleeping bag zipper opening.

"Hey, babe. You cold?" he asked, his eyes still shut.

Addie's hand ran down his stomach, and he shivered.

Her hand was cold as ice.

She grasped him, and he grew hard.

She climbed on top of him.

Chad opened his eyes.

A Chinese girl sat astride him. Her hair was long and black.

"What? No," Chad said, but he was already sliding into her as she smiled down at him.

She was cold inside.

The woman rocked on top of him.

Her breasts rose and fell as she rode him. In the dim light, he could make out the words Hoosier Hottie on her t-shirt.

He shook his head and tried to focus. Something was wrong here, but he couldn't concentrate.

He blinked, and she was naked. She hadn't taken off the t-shirt, it simply wasn't there anymore.

Just a dream, he thought. A wet dream. He hadn't had one since before college, but this one was intense.

She smiled down at him as he put his hands on her waist. The woman seemed to be made of ice.

She held her wrist against her open mouth and bit down. Blood sprayed across the tent, spattering his face.

His face tingled where the blood touched it. His hands squeezed her hard, and he saw her grimace as his fingers dug into her. He grew harder inside her. The tent seemed to grow brighter inside.

She hissed, and for an instant, she changed. The face was the same, but the eyes were larger and black. She was bald, and her skin was gray.

Sharp fangs showed between her lips.

He blinked, and she was the same naked girl as before,

Blood poured from the wound on her wrist. She pushed her wrist toward his mouth.

He saw the ghost of the old woman outside the tent opening. She shook her head and turned away.

The blood touched his lips, and he was on fire. He orgasmed deep inside her.

He opened his mouth and drank the blood.

It was salty in his mouth. He felt his mouth fill, and he swallowed.

This is what it's like to die, he thought. And, in a way, he did.

Chad's mind cleared, went blank. His thoughts were a void. Nothing existed but the blood and the woman who still moved on top of him.

In the distance, he heard a roaring sound, like a waterfall or the sound of a jet engine. The sound grew closer until it was directly beside him.

Thoughts flooded into his mind. Not his own. He saw the girl's thoughts, pieces of memories. A dorm room, a football game, sleeping in a van, and then running from monsters.

Other thoughts followed. A girl named Tammy. She hit her friend in the head with a pool cue, but she was so sorry because it hurts so bad what they did to her it hurts, and it shouldn't hurt like this why does it hurt?

Chad screamed and the pain cleared.

He could not remember his name. He was no longer sure which thoughts were his own. Nothing mattered but the blood, which he drank by the mouthful.

Stop, a voice said in his head. It was a man's voice.

The girl pushed him away.

The illusion was gone. She stared down at him with her cold black eyes.

Tend to him, the voice said.

She lay down beside him and rubbed his hair.

It fell away from his scalp revealing gray skin beneath.

Marion, Virginia

Going for shots meant driving eighteen miles out of town to Marion, Virginia. Anne sat at the bar and stared at her Chardonnay. Jane was late, as usual.

"Sorry I'm late, had to cook dinner!" Jane yelled as she sat down beside her at the bar. "What the hell are you drinking?"

"Chardonnay," Anne said. People were staring. Jane attracted attention wherever she went with her volume level set a little higher than everyone else in the room, and tonight was no exception.

"What are you, eighty or something? I said 'shots,' not grape flavored water," she slapped the oak bar top. "Hey, bring us two shots of the good stuff!"

The bartender nodded.

"Not for me, thanks," Anne said.

"Oh, party pooper, why not?"

"Because it's a twenty-mile drive back home to my kids. I'd like to make it there in one piece. On top of that, we have to work tomorrow."

"Hey, I'll spring for the cab, and as for work, I'm the boss, honey. We're going to shut this place down!"

The bartender put both shots down in front of Jane.

"Well, as long as this place shuts down at ten o'clock. I don't want to be out late."

Jane knocked back a shot. She looked at Anne and shook her head. "You know, if my husband did to me what yours did to you, I'd be sewing me some oats, girl." She drank the other shot.

Jane looked around the bar. "Lot of prospects for oat sewing here tonight."

Anne followed her gaze to the men in the room. They outnumbered the women ten to one.

The bartender refilled her shot glasses.

"Bobby, what's with the crowd?" Jane asked.

Bobby, the bartender, looked up at her and wiped down the counter. "Doctors."

Jane turned and leaned back on the bar. "Ooo, do tell."

Bobby chuckled and turned to Anne. "Some kind of trouble up at the state hospital. Some of the inmates lost their shit."

Marion was home to Virginia's hospital for the criminally insane. It sat on a hill near the center of town surrounded by guard towers and barbed wire.

A man sitting a few stools down laughed and stared at his beer. "Yeah, lost their shit. That's a good term for it."

Anne looked at him. He was older, and he looked tired. His watch probably cost as much as Anne's Prius.

"What happened?" Anne asked.

He looked up at her through red-rimmed eyes. "Nightmares."

"Nightmares?"

"Yeah, the kind that makes you wake up and do things."

Jane leaned toward him. "What sort of things?"

"Oh, wake up in the morning and tear out your eyeballs, or reach over and rip the throat out of somebody you were playing cards with a minute before," he said and then took a sip of his beer. "We had to sedate everyone of them. They're all asleep, and they're going to stay asleep until they can figure out what the hell is going on."

Jane turned toward Anne. "Enough of that shit. Bobby, more alcohol."

The doctor leaned around and looked at Anne. "They brought me in from Richmond." He waved his hands. "Brought in psychiatrists from all over the state." He stood up and dropped money on the bar. "But, I'm going home now."

"Why?" Anne asked.

He glanced at her sideways as he walked away. "Because I'm starting to have nightmares too."

Anne started to say something.

"Am I interrupting anything?"

Anne looked up.

Miriam Tillford was looking down at her with an amused smile.

Jane turned and looked at her, and it seemed to Anne that Jane shrunk three inches. The expression on her face said it all: the queen bee had been outclassed.

Miriam seemed amused by Jane's expression.

"Oh, Jane, this is Miriam Tillford. She's Mr. Olc's assistant. You know? The house on Kinder Valley Road?" Anne said.

Jane's demeanor changed instantly. She grabbed Miriam's hand. "Oh, believe me, I know - you're the reason we are celebrating!"

Miriam smiled. "No doubt."

Jane stepped to the side. "Join us."

"Don't mind if I do."

Miriam sat down on the stool beside Anne.

Anne looked around the room. All eyes were on the tall blonde sitting beside her.

Bobby leaned toward her from behind the bar. "What can I get you?"

"A Chardonnay for me as well," Miriam said.

"Is Mr. Olc with you?" Jane asked.

Miriam laughed. "No. He's out with his family getting into some mischief or other. Their temporary housing is far too confining. They like to roam and explore."

"You mentioned he had a large family," Anne said as she rubbed a dot of moisture off the side of her Chardonnay glass.

Miriam nodded. "Mmm, yes. Growing every day it seems. Lots of nieces and nephews, and, of course, Mr. Olc's parents live with him as well."

"His *parents*?" Anne asked. "They must be…"

"Very old," Miriam said. "They don't leave the house often. Still, they are quite spry for their age."

Jane downed another shot. "That accent of yours, I can't quite place it."

"Oh, I've become a bit of a chameleon over the years. I was born in Texas, but I've lived all over the United States and Canada. Mr. Olc moves quite often - the family gets restless."

"Texas?" Jane asked. "I can't hear any Texas at all."

Miriam laughed, and her voice changed, took on a Texas twang, "Well, I can surely hear it in yours, darlin'."

Jane laughed. "Nope. Southwest Virginia all my life. We just sound like Texas."

"How long have you worked for Mr. Olc?" Anne asked.

Miriam looked confused. "Worked? Oh, no, dear, you misunderstand. I don't work for Mr. Olc, he's my lover."

Jane paused with her shot glass against her lips.

Anne didn't know what to say.

"Didn't you say Olc was old?" Jane asked. The whiskey was lubricating her vocal chords.

"Jane!" Anne whispered.

Miriam laughed. "No, no, it's alright. I know how it must seem, but I'm older than I look." She smiled at Jane and licked her lips. "And, Mr. Olc is extremely well preserved. The things he can do would… shock you."

Jane just stared at her.

Finally, Anne thought. Jane finally shut up.

Miriam turned back to Anne, and her expression became more reserved. "Americans have such odd notions about age differences in relationships - in Europe, we rarely even get a second glance."

Jane snorted. "I doubt you've ever been anywhere that you didn't get a second glance."

Miriam turned her head to the side and looked at Jane as if she were trying to decide if her words were a compliment. Evidently, she decided they were. "Thank you," she said.

Anne looked at her watch. "Sorry, but I have to go. I don't like leaving my kids this long."

"Aww, come on, Anne, things are just getting fun," Jane said. Her eyes looked a little unfocused.

Miriam Tillford touched Anne's hand. "Yes, please stay. I want to hear all about your children and the town."

Anne pulled her hand away. She stopped herself from pulling it away quickly. Miriam's touch wasn't cold like Olc's, but there was something… unnatural about it. She seemed fake, like a person wearing a mask.

Anne smiled. "Another night, perhaps." She stood up and dropped a twenty on the bar.

"Yes. Another night," Miriam said.

"Don't worry, Miriam, I'll hang out with you," Jane said. She sat down on the stool beside her.

Anne didn't look behind her as she walked out of the bar.

Laura's bus pulled into the Greyhound terminal in Wytheville, Virginia at eleven PM. She had watched out the window as the bus passed the exit to Rural Retreat twenty minutes before. Laura should have felt annoyed the bus was carrying her twenty miles too far.

She wasn't annoyed. Looking at the Rural Retreat turn filled her with dread.

Fluorescent lights buzzed and flickered overhead as she got down off the bus with her duffel bag and walked into the terminal.

Laura started to panic. What had she been thinking? She couldn't just show up on her sister's doorstep after five years.

The old man in the ticket booth looked up at her as she dropped her duffel bag on the floor in front of him. "I need a ticket."

"Where to?"

"West."

He looked up at her over the top of his glasses. "Whereabouts west were you thinking?"

"What's the next bus going west?"

He looked at his computer screen. "Got a four AM going to Nashville and Saint Louis."

Laura stared at him.

"Miss? Do you want a ticket?"

Laura squeezed her eyes shut. She swallowed. *Family is never perfect, but it is the only thing that is real.*

Luciana's words echoed in her mind.

"Miss?" the old man asked.

"No, thank you."

She walked out into the cold night air in front of the terminal. A single cab sat idling on the curb. Laura opened the door and got in the back. "Can you take me to Rural Retreat?"

Jane stumbled into the bar restroom, and Miriam steadied her on her feet.

"Whew!" Jane slurred. "That was too much booze." She teetered sideways into a stall and closed the door behind her.

Miriam leaned on the sink and stared at herself in the mirror.

"I'm going to pay for this in the mornin'," Jane said.

Miriam opened her purse and took out a small aluminum tube. It looked like a travel tube of toothpaste, but it was dull silver with no label.

Jane flushed and walked slowly out of the stall. She looked up when she reached the sink.

Miriam saw her staring at her in the mirror.

"I'd kill for your skin," Jane said as she turned on the tap on her sink.

"Oh, let's hope it doesn't come to that," Miriam said.

Jane looked at herself in the mirror. "Where did all these wrinkles come from?"

"Life," Miriam said. She opened the tube and squeezed a red drop of gel onto her index finger. She touched the drop to the corner of her eye and rubbed it into her skin.

Jane frowned. "What is that?"

"Wrinkle cream. A special blend," Miriam said.

Jane snorted. "What are you? Twenty-five? Your skin is perfect, you don't need wrinkle cream."

Miriam smiled and applied a dot of gel to the corner of her other eye. "I told you, I'm older than I look." She held out the tube. "Try this."

Jane took the tube from her. She turned it over and stared at it. "No label?"

"I told you. It's a special blend. You can't buy it."

Jane opened the tube and squeezed a drop on her finger tip.

Miriam smiled at the expression on her face. "Powerful, isn't it?"

"Stings a little."

Jane put the dot on the laugh lines at the corner of her eye. She drew in a breath. Her mouth dropped open.

Miriam leaned close. "Only on the skin. Don't get any in your mouth." She whispered in Jane's ear, "If you swallow it, bad things will happen."

Jane was staring at her face in the mirror.

Miriam saw that the laugh lines where Jane applied the mixture had completely disappeared. "Keep the tube," Miriam said. "I have plenty." She turned with a smile and left the restroom.

Laura sat in the taxi outside her mother's house. She had gone to Anne's house first. Strange vehicles and a basketball hoop sat in the drive. She didn't have to knock on the door to know her sister no longer lived there.

What if Anne had moved away? There was nothing to hold her in Rural Retreat now that their mother was gone. Her husband's family was from North Carolina.

Sitting outside her mother's house in the cab, she breathed a sigh of relief. A pale blue Prius sat in the drive - the same car her sister had when their mother had gotten ill more than five years ago.

Tom Lawrence's car was nowhere to be seen.

"That'll be thirty-five seventy-three, Ma'am," the cab driver said as he reached to turn off the meter.

"Keep it running," Laura said.

The driver shrugged.

Laura closed her eyes and bit her lower lip. Was she doing this? She couldn't picture herself knocking on her sister's door. Was this selfish? Showing up on Anne's porch after five years?

Yes. It was selfish.

But, she had nowhere else to go.

She unfolded a fifty dollar bill from her purse and passed it to the driver as she got out. "Never mind."

The duffel felt heavy on her shoulder as she walked up the driveway and onto the front porch.

What was she going to say? *"Hi, Sis, sorry I'm five years late for Mom's funeral?"* *"Hi, Sis, sorry it's been five years, but my friends and I were busy setting off bombs in Seattle. Really bummed I killed somebody?"*

She almost turned around and walked away.

She heard the cab pull away.

Laura reached out and pressed the doorbell.

A yellow light bulb came on overhead. She saw a shadow behind the frosted square of glass in the door.

The door opened.

A softer version of her own face stared at her. A few years older, the same green eyes, the same brown hair.

Anne's mouth was half open.

Laura started to say something. She wasn't sure what. Before she could, her tears began to flow. "Oh, Annie. I fucked up. I fucked up so bad."

Anne said nothing. She reached out and threw her arms around her sister, pulled her close. "It's okay," she said. "You're home now. That's all that matters."

Laura shook and cried on her sister's shoulder.

"Aunt Laura!" Kim yelled. She ran to them both and threw her arms around them.

Laura felt arms around her thighs and a face buried in her stomach.

Tia looked up at her. "Who are we hugging?"

Anne smiled down at her. "This is your Aunt Laura, Baby. She's come home."

Laura walked out the back door.

Anne was sitting on the picnic table in the backyard staring at the rhododendrons that formed the back fence of the property.

Laura hugged her sweater around herself. "Tia has excellent taste in bedtime reading. That 'Mr. Blueberry' is riveting reading. Personally, I think there really was a blue whale in Emily's pond. Ol' Mr. Blueberry was a shit for not believing her."

Anne turned and smiled at her over her shoulder. Smoke wafted up from her lips.

Laura stopped. "No fucking way! Marijuana? The Prius princess partakes of the devil weed?" She hopped up beside her on the picnic table.

"Not mine," Anne said as she took another draw. The tip glowed bright orange in the dark.

"What? Oh, I will kick Kim's ass..."

"Nope. Not hers either."

"Well, whoever it belongs to, stop bogarting it."

Her sister passed her the joint, and she took a hit. "Oh, wow. Smooth. That's Acapulco..."

"Wrong again. Pure Bland County... at least I think it is. Mom never said."

Laura choked. "Mom? This was Mom's stash?"

"The last of it. Doctor told her it would help - he was going to write her a prescription, but she just laughed and said, 'Don't bother. I know where I can find the best shit.' Drove off by herself, came back at dinner time with a shoebox full."

Laura laughed. "Our Mom who baked cookies for school bake sales?"

"Yep. You know? Come to think of it, everybody loved Mom's cookies."

"And, now Wendy Whitebread is smoking it."

"Hey!" Anne said as she poked her in the ribs. "I have a wild side. I just keep it hidden. And, this is a special occasion. Not every day my sister comes home."

Laura gave her back the joint. "I'm sorry. I should have been here."

Anne shook her head. "No. No, you shouldn't have. You didn't need to see it."

Laura burst into tears again.

Anne hugged her. "Hey, Stringbean, enough. If you'd been here, it would have just been one more person Mom would have had to have been strong for. She couldn't stand to see you cry, and neither can I, so stop it."

Laura wiped away her tears. "Was she okay at the end?"

Anne took her hand. "To everybody else, yeah." Anne shook her head. "But, no, she wasn't. She was scared and angry, and she didn't want to go."

Laura looked away.

"But, listen to me. She was always different with different people. You and Dad? She always put on a brave face no matter what was going on. The kids? Exactly the same. She didn't do that with me. I was the one that needed to be here."

Laura turned toward her. She saw so much of her mother in Anne's face now. "Do you hate me?"

Anne laughed and took a final hit before flicking the spent joint into the yard. "Oh, I was pissed at you. But, I got over it. And, like I said, you didn't need to be here. I did."

"What happened with you and Tom?" Laura asked.

"Oh, that."

"Yeah, that. I mean I thought you two were going to grow old together."

"Teeth."

Laura stared at her for a moment. "Teeth?"

"Teeth."

"Okay…"

Anne giggled. "Twenty years of marriage, asshole never gave a shit about his teeth. Then suddenly, he was going to the dentist. Frequent cleanings, checkups. Seemed like he was at the dentist every other week."

"He was having an affair with the dentist?"

"Worse. Nineteen-year-old dental hygienist."

"Ew. Tacky."

"Oh, fuck it. I don't blame him. She had boobs like basketballs. If I had a dick, I'd have done her too."

Laura burst out laughing, and Anne joined her.

Anne sighed. "Okay. I'm lit. It's a good thing that's the last joint."

"So, does he have visitation with the kids?"

"Haven't seen him or the whore in three years."

Laura squeezed her hand. "He skipped? Oh, I will track his ass down for you. I will make him pay."

"Don't you dare. I'm happier without him in our lives. Trust me. I sold the house, and we moved into Mom's - it's half yours by the way, and her bank account, half yours too."

Laura shook her head. "No. No way. You were here for her. This is yours."

"Hey, wait a minute…"

"No! I mean it, Annie. You and the kids, you're what matters."

Anne shook her head. "*We* are what matters. You don't want the money, fine, but please tell me you are here to stay?"

Laura smiled. "I got nowhere to go."

Anne nodded. "Gaia's Warriors. Yeah, I saw it on the news."

"Did the feds come looking for me?"

"Not since Mom died. They came here and questioned me after you burned that guy's car."

Laura groaned. "God, please tell me they didn't talk to Mom…"

"No. They came to me first. I told them we hadn't seen you."

"And, that's it? They just left."

Anne bit her lower lip. "Not precisely."

"What *precisely*?"

"They said, 'Your sister is a terrorist.' I said, 'Did she kill anybody?' They said, 'No.' I said, 'Good. Get the fuck out of my house.' And, then I called the ACLU."

Laura laughed. "Wow."

Anne sighed. "This last thing. The guy on the bulldozer…"

Laura shook her head. "I didn't know. I swear to you. We had destroyed equipment before in the middle of the night when nobody was around, but Bobby set that bomb to deliberately kill that man. I hate them for it."

"So, you're done? No more Gaia's Warriors?"

"Fuck the trees."

Anne laughed and hugged her. "Good. Damn things are overrated if you ask me. Now, let's talk about cursing. No more 'F' bombs. We have impressionable minors for roommates."

Laura nodded. "You got it. If Mr. Blueberry wouldn't say it, it's out of my vocabulary."

Glade Mountain, Virginia, Part 2

His name was once Chad. At least, he believed it was. Things were different now.

He had been sick in the tent, and it reeked of the day's breakfast, lunch, and dinner.

And, other things. He had thrown up things that weren't food.

Meaty things.

He felt thinner, and the tent seemed stifling hot.

All the while, the Chinese girl had lain beside him, sometimes naked, sometimes in the Hoosier Hottie t-shirt.

His hair was gone, and he felt self-conscious, but she didn't seem to mind.

So many thoughts crowded for attention in his head. Life stories played in fast forward in his mind. He could no longer pick out which memories were his own.

He opened his mouth to talk to the girl, but his words wouldn't come.

Think - the word came into his mind. *Think, it's easier.*

He thought about the beach on a summer day and sand castles. The smell of salt water and sun.

She smiled at him and then there was a kite in the air overhead in his imagining, puffy white clouds.

Were these his thoughts or hers? In the end, it didn't matter. They were sharing the experience.

He looked at her smile. Two long canines extended down far past the rest of her teeth.

There was a stab of pain in his gums.

She frowned and rubbed his face. *Not much longer.*

He screamed. Pain in the center of his stomach like someone was driving a knife into him.

She took his hand and pulled him with her out of the tent.

The meadow was illuminated by the moon and stars.

Shapes moved in the tall grass.

He felt their thoughts wash over him, welcoming him.

Olc stood beside the doused campfire.

He held one of the gray shapes in his arms: Tammy, the one in pain whose mind touched his earlier. She slept in Olc's arms.

Olc was soothing her in her sleep, his mind showing her visions.

He could see Olc's thoughts. The smell of fresh baked bread. Olc standing on a marble floor in a grand building full of columns. Strange words being spoken in Latin as someone laid a crown on Olc's head.

The past.

In the present, Olc looked up. "Feed," he said.

A woman lay on the ground at Olc's feet.

She was bruised and battered.

Images came to him from the others. A game. They had chased her through the woods, laughing when she fell in the dark or collided with briar bushes. They would let her get a few steps ahead, and then they would grab her, toss her in a different direction.

The sweet scent of her terror.

"Chad?" she asked. It was a whisper. Her eye was swollen shut.

That name. Was it his? He couldn't remember. The pain in his stomach grew.

And, then he could hear it. The steady pounding of her heart.

"Help me." She was crawling toward him.

He knelt down in front of her. Addie, her name was Addie. Chad was married to Addie.

Addie finally saw him clearly with her good eye, and she screamed. It was a pitiful sound. The sound of something tormented and near death.

He grabbed her by her hair and twisted her head to the side.

His teeth touched her neck, and he bit down.

"Chad! Don't! Please Don't," she cried. Her fists beat against him, but he could barely feel them.

He couldn't break the skin, and he growled in frustration.

"Be patient," Olc said. "Help him."

The Chinese girl knelt beside him. He was so glad she was there. She pressed her thumbs against his upper lip.

Something cracked.

He spit two teeth onto the ground.

He felt movement in the space the two teeth came from.

Long canines slid into place, gouging two holes in his lower gums.

He opened his mouth and smiled.

Then he lowered his head and ripped into Addie's neck.

His mouth filled, and he swallowed.

The phone camera records trees and stars. A dark shape comes into the frame, and the phone is lifted. It turns sideways, and a single black eye appears in the frame.

The image turns around, and trees pass by. The thing carrying the camera is walking.

They emerge into the clearing.

Gray shapes wander about the meadow.

Near the tent, Addie kneels on the ground as the gray creature that was once her husband drinks blood from her neck.

Olc stands over them, cradling one of the vampires in his arms.

Addie beats her fists against the vampire who was once called Chad, but the blows are inconsequential. Each successive blow is diminished from the one before it until finally, her only movements are convulsions as she is bled dry.

Atkins, Virginia

Tonight was a splurge. It was a cold night and sleeping in the truck on a cold night caused Gene's arthritis to flare up. So, he had paid cash for a cheap motel room in Atkins, Virginia, a town a few miles west of where the pinger said the bus was parked.

He had slept a grand total of two hours, which was par for the course. Two hours of restless dreams.

Gene lay on the bed and listened to the radio.

Victoria Darke was lousy company, but she was better than the ghosts that plagued his dreams.

"Tonight on Voices from the Darke, we have a bona fide academic. Professor Jennifer Larson of the folklore department of Southwest Virginia Community College. And, if you want to find it on a map, it's a little speck of fly shit between Mayberry and Bugtussle," Victoria said over the AM clock radio.

A woman's voice sighed. "Wow. You're a real charmer. And, sweetie, Mayberry is in North Carolina."

Her voice wasn't what Gene expected. There was Bronx in her dialect.

"Tell us professor, what is your field of expertise?" Victoria asked.

"I have degrees in history and parapsychology."

"Didn't know they taught parapsychology at DeVry or was it University of Phoenix? Something else online?"

Professor Larson laughed. "Appalachian State University."

"Let's cut to the chase, Doc. You're a ghost hunter, right?"

"Nobody needs to hunt ghosts, Victoria. They're all around us."

Gene laughed in the dark room. "You got that right, lady."

"Seen any ghosts lately?" Victoria asked.

"Everyday. Some people who die don't leave, whether through an inability to transition or by choice."

"So, they just hang around and haunt houses? Bummer of an afterlife."

"Not just houses. People. Sometimes they haunt people."

"And, you help people bust them ghosts?" The theme from Ghostbusters started playing in the background.

Professor Larson laughed. "No. I try to communicate with them, more often than not, it doesn't work."

"You try to get them to move on - go into the light, right?"

"Hey, if they wanted to go into the light, they would. I just try to help them communicate with those they haunt."

"Scary stuff."

"No, not really. We have nothing to fear from ghosts. Most of the time, they're just trying to help."

Gene sat up.

"So, what are they trying to do, professor? Warn us of impending doom? Tell us where we left the car keys?"

"Yes to both, but mostly it's small stuff. A warning about a bad relationship or a nudge in the right direction that keeps us from ending up in a head-on collision with a semi."

"Oh, so not only are they ghosts, they're clairvoyant?"

"It's not that simple. For the living, time is linear. We can remember things in the past, and we can speculate on what the future holds, but we are confined to the here and now. Ghosts aren't cemented in the present. They can move at will between the past, present, and possible futures."

"And, how do you know all this?"

"They told me, Victoria."

Gene turned the radio down. Was that how this all worked? Did the ghosts he saw in his dreams know what the future held? Were they guiding him to change the future?

He picked up his reading glasses and put them on. He unlocked his cell phone.

According to Google, Jennifer Larson was indeed a folklore professor at Southwest Virginia Community College. The college was less than ninety miles away.

She had written a book: "My Brother's Keeper, Living with a Ghost for Thirty Years." He skimmed the table of contents online. There was no mention of vampires.

Still, she could help.

And then what? She could be his translator to tell him what the damned ghosts wanted? He would put her in danger for no reason.

Over the years, he had drawn other people into his confidence. Those people were tombstones alongside the road of his life.

Or, they were now worse.

He didn't like to think about it.

You're on your own, old man, he thought.

Rural Retreat, Virginia, Part 3

Anne shook her head as she looked at the lump of blankets and pillows on her living room sofa. Somewhere beneath it, her sister snored softly, betrayed only by her left arm and leg that extended out from under the covers and brushed the hardwood floor.

"I'm going to work," Anne said.

"Mmph," the lump on the couch said.

"Teacher work day. The kids are home today."

Another Mmph.

"Don't sleep too sound. They're savages," Anne said as she walked out the front door and locked it behind her.

Things are getting better, Anne thought as she started the Prius. Laura was home, and the kids weren't moping. It was a form of normal. Normal hadn't been around in awhile.

For the better part of three years, they had normal's cousin, Abbie. Abbie Normal was better than awful, but not by much.

Anne drove through the small cluster of old buildings that made up Main Street. Old men in overalls waved as she passed the feed store. At the supermarket, women loading groceries into sensible cars while balancing babies on their hips waved as well.

She was Anne, Brenda Reynolds' daughter. She was married to that Tom Lawrence who ran off with that floozy from the dentist's office, and wasn't that an awful thing?

"*...small towns. Everybody is up in your shit,*" Kim had said the night before, and it was true. But, that wasn't such a bad thing. You didn't have to explain why you looked depressed on Valentine's Day - everybody knew. And, they were quick to offer up chocolate or a nephew who had never been married who would be perfect for her.

They never were. At her age, the unmarried nephews offered up for sacrifice were either gay, addicted to something, or on the rebound from someone who destroyed them emotionally.

She knew everyone in town took pity on her, but the sad truth was she didn't miss Tom Lawrence in the least. She was still pissed for what he did - and, for abandoning the kids? She was homicidal.

But, not having him in her bed wasn't even a minor inconvenience. Truthfully, she was better at pleasuring herself than he had ever been. She pitied ol' balloon boobs a little. When the man was cold, narcissistic, and emotionally distant, size truly mattered.

She smiled a little thinking of the poor, now twenty something dental hygienist who had taken him off her hands. She wondered if the girl had buyer's remorse?

Anne pulled into the gravel lot of Coldwell Banker and was shocked to see Jane's BMW parked in her usual spot.

As she walked into the office, a cold wind brought with it the smell of nearby wood stoves.

Jane sat at her desk squinting at her computer screen. She took off her reading glasses and rubbed her eyes. Then she dropped the reading glasses in her desk drawer.

"I'm shocked," Anne said. "I thought you were going to shut the bar down last night."

"We did," Jane said. "Guess I didn't drink as much as I thought I did."

Anne sat in a chair in front of her. "You change makeup brands?"

"What?"

"You look amazing."

Jane laughed. "Stop buttering me up. We don't get salary actions for another six months."

"Jane, I'm serious."

Jane opened her purse and took out her compact mirror. She stared at her reflection.

Anne leaned closer. Jane's soft wrinkles were gone. "How did you do that?"

Jane snapped the compact closed. "Nothing. It's nothing. I just changed makeup."

"What brand did you change to? Because I want some."

"I... ordered it. Online. I'll send you the link when I get home."

Jane looked nervous and maybe a little scared.

Anne stood up. "Okay. Thanks."

"You better call your clients. Take a look at what was just delivered." Jane pointed at a manila envelope on Anne's desk.

Anne picked up the envelope and opened it. She read the top sheet of paper. "Closing for 3800 Kinder Valley Road... what? That isn't possible. They just signed the contract yesterday."

"The bank called at 9:00 and said the funds were in order. Next thing I knew, there was a courier at the door with the paperwork. Closing is at 2:00. Joe Davis is the closing attorney."

Anne stared at the packet. "This should have taken thirty days."

"I ain't never seen the courthouse move so fast. That Mr. Olc must have some pull."

Laura felt eyes on her. She lifted the blanket away from her eyes.

Tia stood a few feet away staring at her with her brow knitted. "You snore."

Laura lowered the blanket back over her eyes. "Yeah. I have garlic farts and belch sulfur as well."

"That's disgusting."

"So's picking your nose."

"I don't pick my nose."

"You do in your sleep. I watched you last night. And, then you eat the buggers. That's why you wake up with that funny taste in your mouth every morning."

Laura peeked out.

Tia was running her tongue experimentally over her teeth.

She reached out and grabbed Tia and pulled her onto the couch.

Tia screeched.

Laura held her down. "You know what your Mom used to do to me?"

"What?"

"She used to hold me down and tickle me till I peed."

"No!"

"Yes!" Laura started tickling her ribs.

Tia screamed and laughed.

Kim walked in with her Pop Tarts. "So mature." She sat down on the couch beside them.

Laura shook her head. "What the f... hell... what the hell are you eating?"

Kim frowned at her. "Pop Tarts."

"No. No, no, no. That is the grim reaper in a foil pouch. They'll give you diabetes." She snatched the remaining Pop Tart.

"Hey! That's mine!" Kim said.

Laura got to her feet. "Trust me, one day you'll thank me. This shit causes acne, hemorrhoids…"

Tia jumped up. "Babies? Does it cause babies?"

"Does she mean rabies?" Laura asked Kim.

"No, she's saying 'babies' - she hasn't had the talk yet," Kim said as she grabbed for her Pop Tart. "Gimme."

Laura jerked the Pop Tart away. "Don't be ridiculous, Tia. Babies come from storks. Never ever go near a stork. Your Mom did twice and just look what happened."

Tia looked confused. "What do storks look like?"

"Strange looking bird with a really long beak... although sometimes their beaks are small, and they're really sensitive about it. So, never make fun of a stork with a short beak 'cause it makes them mean."

Kim burst out laughing.

"Pfft," Laura said. "What are you laughing at? Like you've ever seen a beak."

"Hey!"

Laura backed away. "Follow me into the kitchen."

Tia and Kim sat at the kitchen counter and watched Laura work at the stove. To Kim, it was like watching one of the chefs at the Japanese steakhouse in Roanoke. Laura's hands moved at breakneck speed, slicing vegetables and whisking eggs.

Kim's mouth was watering from the smell of omelets and French Toast.

Laura had tattoos on the inside of each wrist. On the right was an artistic rendering of the earth. A five pointed star was on the left.

"What do your tattoos mean?" Kim asked.

"Oh," Laura said without looking up from the stove. She held up her right hand. "The earth of course. I was an environmentalist."

"Aren't you anymore?"

"Well, sure. It's just... now I think people are part of the environment too. Before, they didn't seem so important."

"What about the other one?"

Laura laughed. "The pentagram? That one is misspent youth. Inverted pentagram on the left wrist - you know, the left-hand path?"

Kim shook her head.

"Witches. Witchcraft. Back in the day, I believed in all that shit." Laura sighed. "Hey, Monkey Face, come here."

Tia looked up at Kim. "Who's Monkey Face?"

Kim shrugged.

"You're Monkey Face, munchkin. And, your sister is Jugs."

Tia giggled.

Kim looked down at her chest. "Hey! Don't call me that."

"Look, I'm the kind of person who gives you nicknames, get used to it. And, let's face it, the boob fairy was kind. A little overly generous. I mean, one of yours makes two of mine," Laura said. "Monkey Face, get over here."

Tia hopped off her stool.

Kim shook her head. "Please do not call me… that name in front of anybody."

Laura looked thoughtful. "Hello, Reverend, have you met my niece, Jugs? Oh, hi cute boy Kim likes, did you know I call her Jugs? Bet you can guess why."

"Oh, God, you're more embarrassing than Mom," Kim said as she hung her head.

"I am exactly like your Mom, only without an ounce of shame and zero sense of responsibility." Laura leaned down to Tia. "Okay, Monkey Face, you may have noticed Aunt Laura has a bit of a potty mouth?"

Tia nodded. "Yeah, you talk like a sailor."

"I know, right? Well, I'm going to need your help. Every time I say a bad word, I want you to pinch me, hard, got it?"

Tia's eyes grew wide. She nodded.

"So, let's just say I said, 'shit.' What are you going to do?"

Tia reached out and pinched Laura's arm.

"Naah, you suck at pinching. Grab some skin and really twist."

Tia reached out and pinched again.

"Ow! Okay, yeah, you got it." Laura said as she backed up to the stove and rubbed her arm.

Tia reached out again.

Laura danced away. "Whoa! Only when I curse. You don't get to pinch me for kicks."

"Okay," Tia said as she climbed back onto her stool.

"Where did you learn to cook like that?" Kim asked.

"Necessity. Only a few ways to make money in the timber country of the great Northwest. Either on your feet or on your…" Laura snapped her fingers. "Monkey Face, pinch, please?"

"But, you didn't curse," Tia said.

"No, but I almost said something naughty. Close enough."

Tia shrugged, climbed down from the stool, and pinched Laura's arm.

"Ow!"

Kim laughed. "So, uh, I take it you made your money on your feet?"

"Short order cook. I cook a mean omelet." She turned around with the frying pan and flipped an omelet onto each of their plates.

Kim shook her head. "I'm going to get so fat with you here."

"Relax, Jugs, it'll all go to the boobs. All good," she leaned on the counter.

Tia reached out to pinch her and Laura slapped her hand.

"Boobs is not a curse word," Laura said.

Tia frowned. "Okay."

"Cheer up, the day's young. Plenty of time for negative reinforcement."

Kim smiled and took a bite of omelet. "It's delicious." She frowned. "Where's yours?"

"Me? Oh, I'm not eating that. I'm going to laugh at you two when you get fat." She picked up the discarded Pop Tart and took a bite.

Kim laughed.

Laura smiled, and Kim could see a hint of satisfaction in her aunt's face.

Olc and Miriam sat in the backseat of the town car.

"How many? Houses. Over the years?" Olc whispered.

She took his big hand in hers. "Forty years. Thirty-eight houses."

Olc sighed. "I remember. Spending centuries. One place."

"The world has moved on. You had to adapt."

Olc shook his head. "Our time. Maybe not much longer."

Miriam stared at him. "What makes you say that?"

He squeezed her hand. "Ghosts. So many. Cling to us. Death shroud."

She turned his pale gray face toward her with her fingers. She stared into his liquid black eyes. "After this town, we'll be strong again. We need new blood, and the family will be reborn. You'll see."

"Love of my life," he said.

She smiled and laid her head on his chest. She strained listening for his heartbeat. It was slow, an ancient mechanism.

Miriam looked up at him. "We need to talk about Tammy."

Olc looked away. "Later."

"Olc," she said. "The change isn't taking. She needs…"

"No. Don't say that."

She turned him toward her again.

Tears were running down his cheeks.

She smiled and wiped the tears away. "You can't save them all. Your heart is too big for your own good."

He nodded. "I know. Must be done. Wait a few days. To make sure?"

Miriam gave him a weak smile. "Okay. A few days."

Anne didn't like the closing attorney, Joe Davis. He always seemed to be undressing her with his eyes, even though he paraded a trophy wife around town. He had that look about him, black hair cut short, but not too short. His skin was tanned, but not too tanned. Expensive suit, expensive watch, but a good natured, good old boy grin and speaking voice that could bed either a waitress or an heiress with little effort.

He was the kind of man who went to the dentist often and slept with dental hygienists regularly.

She despised him.

Jane, on the other hand, couldn't get enough of him.

Anne watched them from the other end of the conference table.

Jane was perched on the edge of the table. Joe sat leaning back in his chair beside her. Jane laughed at the appropriate points and occasionally played with her long hair.

Just from watching their body language, she felt like she needed a cigarette.

The front doorbell chimed, and Anne saw Mr. Olc and Miriam through the glass wall.

She stood up and opened the conference room door. "Miriam, Mr. Olc, please come in," she said as she held the glass door open for them.

Olc smiled at her. "Miss Lawrence. Pleasure."

He held out his hand, but instead of taking it, Anne put her hand on his back and ushered him inside. "Good to see you as well."

Mr. Olc laughed. Had he noticed she wouldn't take his hand? Anne hoped he did not.

Joe Davis practically leaped to his feet as Miriam stepped into the room.

Jane smiled, but her flirtatiousness from earlier was gone. "Miriam, and you must be Mr. Olc? I'm Jane Connors, and this is Joseph Davis from Davis and Perkins, he'll be doing the closing."

Davis walked around the table and took Miriam's hand. "Miriam. That's a lovely name. I haven't heard it in some time."

Miriam smiled at him. "Why, thank you."

Davis pulled out a chair for her.

Miriam sat down, and he pushed the chair up to the table.

"Such a gentleman," Miriam said.

Davis was still holding her hand.

Anne looked at Olc. He seemed to have grown taller.

He glared at Davis who finally let go of Miriam's hand.

The smaller man took Olc's hand. "Joe Davis." The look on Davis's face went to one of shock.

Anne knew that look. Her own hands trembled from the memory of his icy grip.

But, there was something more in Davis's eyes: fear. He let go of Olc's hand and returned to his seat.

He looked at Miriam and smiled. "Let's get you folks in a house!"

The signing took twenty minutes, as Olc signed each sheet of paper beside the stick on arrows Davis's office had applied.

All the while, Joe Davis stared in rapt attention at Miriam Tillford.

Jane sat quietly beside Anne.

Everything about Davis's body language was an invitation to Miriam.

But, Anne saw that Miriam sat motionless and calm, like a statue. She laughed on cue, but her demeanor was one of mild amusement.

There were no hair flips or coy expressions.

Still, Davis poured on the charm.

Olc looked up occasionally from the papers he signed.

Anne could feel the cold radiating from him.

"Done," Olc announced.

"So soon?" Davis said as he took the papers. "Impressive penmanship, Mr. Olc. Cursive writing is a skill we young no longer excel at, unlike your generation."

Olc smiled.

Davis winced. He squeezed his eyes shut.

"Something wrong, Mr. Davis?" Miriam asked.

Davis laughed. "Sudden migraine. I'm sure it will pass."

"Perhaps," Olc said. "Sometimes migraines... indicate other weakness?"

Davis shook his head and looked away. He pushed the papers toward Anne. "Anne, darlin', could you make some copies for us?"

Anne rolled her eyes. "Sure."

She picked up the papers and left the conference room.

It was easy to see the female hierarchy in Davis's mind. Miriam was the prize, and Jane was the sure thing he could have whenever he wanted.

Anne was there to make copies.

She went into the back room and started the copier.

She looked at the top page of the legal papers.

Olc did have impressive penmanship. The letters of his signature were perfectly formed with flourishes.

Marcus Velerius Corvus Olc.

She had heard of people with two middle names, but she had never actually met one.

Miriam held Olc's hand as they stepped out into the overcast day. "I'm surprised you stopped with a headache. I half expected you to give him an aneurysm."

"Odd little man," Olc said.

Miriam laughed. "Boys will be boys. Always competing with one another to see whose is bigger - even when one of the boys is over twenty-four hundred years old."

He squeezed her hand, and Miriam gasped. She felt her bones grinding together.

"Does it hurt?" Olc whispered.

"Yes."

"Should I stop?"

Miriam gritted her teeth. "No."

He smiled at her, let go of her hand, and caressed her face. "You are mine?"

"Yes."

"Good," he said as they walked toward the car.

Up the street, Davis was unlocking the door of his Mercedes convertible.

A tall brunette in a purple running outfit jogged around the corner and waved to him.

Olc and Miriam stopped to watch.

Even from this distance, Miriam could see the diamond on the woman's finger.

The brunette stopped in front of him on the street and threw her arms around his neck.

"Oh, he has a toy," Miriam whispered.

Olc smiled.

Miriam stared up at him. "Such a predictable boy. You always want things that don't belong to you." She leaned up and whispered, "Were you this incorrigible when you were Caesar?"

"Never Caesar. Such titles came later. Consul, six times. Dictator, twice." He smiled down at her and pushed his thoughts into her mind, *And, yes, I took many senator's wives, just as I took you from your husband.*

David Connors sat on his bedroom floor and played his XBox. His mind was elsewhere, and he navigated the on-screen carnage in a daze. His thoughts were on Kim Lawrence.

As far back as he could remember, she had been his obsession. Until last night, he didn't even know she knew his name. He remembered her from when he was in the second grade, and she was in third. He had fallen for her then when she had scabby knees, and he had trouble tying his shoes.

For the past year, he had taken an interest in his appearance, eating healthy and exercising. He wanted her to notice him.

But, until last night, she'd never even acknowledged his existence.

What had changed? Could it possibly be nothing more than the fact he had finally built up the courage to ask her out?

It couldn't possibly be that simple, could it?

David heard a board creak in the hallway.

He pressed pause on the game controller, and his room was silent.

There were two boards that squeaked just outside the door to his bedroom.

It was way too early for his Mom to be home.

David crept over to his door.

No more squeaks.

He closed his eyes and listened.

He held his hand just above the doorknob. He couldn't hear anyone breathing.

David jerked the door open.

A werewolf snarled at him a few inches from his face.

"You're pathetic," David said as he turned away from the figure in the rubber mask. He sat back down on the floor and picked up the game controller.

"Aw, man! Come on. You had to be scared just a little," Pauly said as he dragged the mask off his face. His black hair was mussed, and he stopped to fix it in the mirror on the back of the door.

"Nope."

"How the fuck you do that? I'd be pissing myself."

"Why would I be scared of a dope in a werewolf mask?"

"Yeah, but, how did you know it was me?"

David sighed as he played his game. "Teacher work day, I knew you'd come over sooner or later. In the past five years, the only two people who have been on the second floor of my house are you and my Mom. Therefore, a noise in the hall at this time is in all likelihood you. "

Pauly dropped onto David's bed and dangled the mask in front of his face. David pushed it away. "Yeah, but this mask is killer. Why weren't you scared?"

David laughed. "Well, there's no such thing as werewolves, dipshit."

"Fine," Pauly said. "Still going to be killer for Halloween."

"Yep, you're going to scare the shit out of five-year-olds and old ladies."

Pauly sighed. "At least my trip to your house hasn't been completely without some reward."

David glanced up.

Pauly had a lacy pair of black panties over his face.

"Where the hell…" And, then David realized. "You sick mother… Put them back!"

Pauly laughed and breathed in loud. "Damn, your Mom smells fine."

"She's my Mom, you freak!"

"Hey, I can't help it if she's hot."

David stood up. "Put them back."

"Relax. I steal your Mom's undies all the time," Pauly said with a smile from the leg hole of the panties. "Besides, I already sort of used them…"

David sighed and shook his head. "You are a twisted son of a bitch, Pauly." He sat down and picked up the controller. "FYI, I think this is how the Boston Strangler and Ted Bundy started out: stealing women's underwear."

Pauly took the panties off his head and stuffed them in the front pocket of his jeans. "No shit?"

"Pretty sure," David said. "What's your fixation on older women anyway?"

"I don't know. 'Cause they know shit, I guess. Like that walking Barbie doll in the Gas'N'Go - I'll bet she knows all kinds of shit."

David laughed and shook his head. "I think you're full of crap. How come I didn't see this goddess you keep talking about?"

"Man, you couldn't see anything except Kim Lawrence. But, damn, she was fine, David. I think she's the one."

David grunted. "Yeah, sure, Pauly."

"No, I'm serious, man. I keep dreaming about her. Weird, freaky shit."

David held up his hand. "I don't want to know."

"No, no, not like that. I mean like violent, horror movie shit."

"What do you mean?"

Pauly shook his head. "Blood, man. There's all this blood in the dreams I have about her."

How do you take a village? Olc thought. He stood on the hill beside his new house and stared toward the small town of Rural Retreat a half mile away.

He had stood on many hills in the twenty-four centuries he had walked the earth and wondered this same thing. In the early days, he had commanded legions of soldiers.

Now, he commanded a very different army. As a general, he had a reputation for caring about his soldiers in those days of the Roman Republic - a characteristic that had made him wildly popular.

But, those he commanded now were not soldiers. They belonged to him as children belonged to a parent. He loved them.

One of them ran to his side. A girl he had found at the rest stop in Indiana. He thought her name was Mae. It didn't really matter now. It would be several centuries before her memories returned and she developed an individual personality.

Around her was an illusion of how she looked when she died: a pair of shorts and a white t-shirt that said Hoosier Hottie.

She was staring in the same direction as he.

Olc smiled and caressed her face.

She cooed and rubbed her cheek against his hand.

"Hungry?" Olc whispered.

She licked the palm of his hand.

"Soon. The town."

She smiled showing her long fangs.

He hugged her to him.

Olc could remember the first centuries after he turned. The confusion was constant. Luckily, there had been mature vampires to watch over him during that time.

Still, the life expectancy for the young was astoundingly low. They couldn't recognize danger, and they were completely driven by their compulsion.

He was now the only mature vampire in the clan, and they were all his responsibility.

The ancients took no notice of the young. They had evolved beyond.

Olc knew he would be like them soon, leaving behind the concerns of the flesh. He resented it in a way.

He enjoyed being the father figure.

He turned back toward the house. The young were settled in the parlor, the ancients in the basement.

Miriam waited for him in the upstairs bedroom.

They had left the falling down house on Glade Mountain with a half dozen drained bodies moldering in the dirt filled crawlspace. Sooner or later, those bodies would be found. But, they would never be traced to the family living in the house on the hill in Rural Retreat.

He stared over his shoulder at the town.

Tomorrow, he would begin the siege.

Gene didn't need the pinger to show him where the family had gone. He had followed them from a half mile back as they left the dirt road on Glade Mountain. He watched them pull up the drive to the house on the hill.

Another Victorian. They were nothing if not predictable.

He would watch and wait.

And, when the time was right, he would burn the house to the ground with them in it.

Any army can lay siege. The cost is high on both sides. Only a gifted general can take a stronghold without firing a single arrow.
- Merlin Taliesin

The Norse had little fear of the black death that raged all around us. These men feared nothing save the devils they called Draugr. The Draugr dined on the blood of the living and could take on any form: a trusted ally, a lover, or a giant who could crush you underfoot.
- Bertrand du Guesclin, Voyages dans le Nord, circa 1350 AD

...the devil hath power to assume a pleasing shape.
- Shakespeare, Hamlet, Act 2, Scene 2

And you saw me low,
Alone again.
Didn't they say that only love will win in the end?
Didn't they say that only love will win in the end?
- Lovett, Dwayne, Mumford, Aubrey, and Marshall,
Mumford & Sons, Only Love

ACT III

Friday

An American town is not an island. It cannot be blockaded by a navy, and, if one decided to lay siege using an army, a larger army would come to liberate it - an army paid for by taxes and manned by the most frightening creatures in the history of humanity: eighteen-year-old Americans with automatic weapons who have no concept of their own mortality.

To lay siege in this time of laws and smart bombs requires camouflage and subterfuge. The scale cannot be large, and the siege engines must be invisible or appear benign.

The best way to lay siege is to subvert.

Anne drove to work through the slush-filled streets. Overnight snow met the dawn and turned to melting glaciers perched on the curb.

She had slept poorly.

Anne had dreamed of her mother, and for Anne, dreams of the dead were silent movies. Her mother tried to speak to her, but no sound came from her lips. Anne could see the frustrated desperation in her mother's expression as they stood in the wet grass of the back yard.

In the end, her mother had simply held her hand and then turned away.

Anne awoke to the sound of crying. Half awake, it took her a moment to realize the crying was coming from Tia's room.

She had jumped to her feet and run to her daughter, only to find Laura had beaten her to Tia's bedside.

"Shh, Monkey Face. Just bad dreams. It's okay," Laura whispered in the dark.

Anne stopped just inside the door. She smiled. It was nice to have a team again. It was so much easier raising kids when there was a team.

Anne shivered in the car. She reached out and turned up the heater.

Warm air washed over her as she passed the feed store. She smiled at a single old man who was trudging to his car.

Her smile faltered as the old man turned away.

The supermarket lot next door was empty.

The cold and snow brought with it a malaise that seemed to grip the town.

Anne walked into the real estate office to find Jane staring at herself in her desk mirror. This was her normal routine now. She spent at least half the day staring at her reflection.

"Morning," Anne said.

Jane was silent for a beat. Then she looked up. "Morning."

Jane Connors looked a decade younger than her age - a noticeable change even from yesterday.

Anne had stopped asking her about this miraculous facelift in a bottle. Whatever the secret, Jane was keeping it to herself.

Debbie Kincaid loved her cats. Other than her job at the high school and the small single wide trailer her father left her, they were the only joy in her life.

Pictures of her cats adorned her desk at work. She smiled at the pictures as she played her solitaire game on the school computer. She looked up at the clock. Just five hours to go and she would be back at home with them.

She looked up from her game at the two figures who stood in front of the wide counter. She made it her job to know all the parents with children at Rural Retreat High School.

These two were new: an older man dressed in a black coat and hat and a young blonde woman dressed to the nines.

Debbie smiled up at them. "Welcome to Rural Retreat High School. How can I help you?"

"Debbie," the man said. His voice was smooth as silk. She found herself staring into his black eyes.

The blonde woman took her hand over the counter. "Debbie. We need you to get us some information. Can you do that?"

Debbie blinked. She shook her head. "What information?"

His eyes seemed to drill into her. Memories came flooding into her conscious. In her mind, she was at home with her cats.

"Lovely creatures. Cats," the man whispered.

Debbie smiled up at him.

"If you press too hard, you'll turn her brain to mush. She's of no use to me as a vegetable," the blonde woman whispered, but Debbie was oblivious to the words.

The man laughed. The sound was magical to Debbie. "Little difference."

The woman sighed. "Debbie, we need you to print us a list of all the juniors and seniors along with their home addresses and phone numbers, but only those who are healthy. No one with a chronic illness or deformity, no epilepsy or mental abnormalities,"

The words echoed in her head as if the man was repeating the woman's words to her.

"Okay…" Debbie said. "Wait. No. No, I can't give out that information."

More of her memories played in her mind. A boy, years ago when she was in high school. He was lying on top of her in the backseat of his car. Pressing down on her, and she was uncomfortable, but she was doing it, and everybody said she should be doing it by her age. She felt him again inside her, and she groaned because it hurt just the way it did that night, and she hadn't spoken to him again.

"Yes, you can, Debbie. I want you to draw little smiley faces by the ones who are pretty or handsome, and a big star beside the most popular senior girl. Can you do that, Debbie?"

She was becoming frightened. More memories came into her mind, along with them came a realization: she wasn't bringing up these memories, *he* was. He was digging in her head, searching.

His eyes looked into her, through her. He found deeper memories and brought them forward. Private things, things she wanted to forget. Uncomfortable things she did when she was alone.

"Stop. Don't. It hurts," she whispered.

"First time. Always hurts," he said.

There was a screaming wail inside her head. Something… moved. Inside her skull, something moved. It twisted.

She was calm. She turned to her keyboard and began typing.

He laughed. The sound was inside her head, and it seemed to echo, like laughter in an empty hall.

The printer buzzed to life beside her.

"List is printing," Debbie said. "It'll take me a few minutes to mark the smiley faces. Regina Kerns is the most popular girl in the senior class. Fucking slut. Probably didn't hurt her the first time, or the hundredth."

Regina Kerns walked along the faux marble hallway floor. She held her books against her sweatered bosom. It was always quiet in the hall between classes.

She opened the door to the main office.

Cat Lady Debbie was tearing paper into strips at her desk.

The door to the principal's office was closed.

"You called me in?" Regina asked.

Cat Lady shook her head and continued tearing the paper into strips. She pointed at a tall blonde woman.

Regina frowned. The strips Cat Lady was tearing were pictures of her cats.

The blonde woman held out her hand. "Oh, Debbie, I can see exactly what you mean."

"Slut," Cat Lady whispered.

Regina glanced at Debbie. "What did you say?"

A tall man stepped in front of her. "Regina. Pretty name."

The man stared at her, and she felt herself falling.

Inside her head, something snapped.

David ate his corn dog in silence. Kim Lawrence was sitting three tables over.

Pauly sat down beside him in the school cafeteria and poked him in the ribs. "Why ain't you sittin' with her?"

David looked down. "She doesn't want anybody to know we're going out. She's a senior, you know?"

"Yeah, man, I feel you. Still, that's pretty cold. I mean, shit, she's worth it, but... that's stone cold."

Regina Kerns walked to their table. It came as no surprise to David that she was staring at Pauly.

Pauly immediately leaned back in his chair and stretched his legs. "Hi ya, cheerleader."

Pauly always lapsed into his Brooklyn accent when there was a girl to impress.

"I'm having a party Saturday at 6:00. My parents are out of town."

Pauly stared at her. "Wait. You invitin' me to your party?" Pauly asked.

"Yes. You're cute." She looked stoned.

David looked at Pauly in shock.

Pauly looked Regina up and down. "There going to be booze?"

Booze? Was Pauly crazy? David thought. The most popular girl in school just asked him to come to a senior party, and he was asking questions.

She looked confused for a moment. "Sure. Lots."

Pauly smiled. "What about my boy here?" He pointed at David.

She turned her glassy eyes toward David. "No. He's a nerd. I don't want nerds at my party."

David rolled his eyes.

Pauly shook his head. "If my boy ain't invited, then…"

David shoved him. "Don't be an asshole. I have plans Saturday, remember?"

Pauly smiled. "Hey, that's right! Yeah, okay, cheerleader. I'll be there."

She walked away.

"Holy shit," Pauly whispered.

"What the hell, Pauly? You almost screwed it up," David said.

"I'm in shock, man." Pauly shook his head. "Correct me if I'm wrong, but did the head cheerleader just invite me to a party?"

"You've arrived, Mr. Delveccio. In the parlance of your people, you are a made man," David said with a laugh. He stopped smiling when he saw Regina stop by Kim's table.

No, he thought. If she invites Kim to the party…

Kim looked up and smiled at Regina.

Shit, David thought.

Then, Kim shook her head.

Regina looked confused and walked away.

Kim turned, looked David in the eye, and smiled.

"Drop you. At home," Olc said. He and Miriam sat in the backseat of the town car as Edgar pulled away from the high school.

"Are you going somewhere?" Miriam asked.

Tittering laughter in her head coming from Edgar.

"Errands."

Miriam stared out the window. "Let me guess. The lawyer's wife?"

"The man. Challenged me."

"You want her?" Miriam asked.

"Of course."

Was it jealousy? she thought. Perhaps. The thought of him wanting someone else infuriated her, even though both of them regularly indulged in other lovers.

"I could go with you," Miriam said. She took his hand.

"No."

"Why not? We can have fun together."

"Not today."

She let go of his hand. "So, what will she be? Protector, Draugr, or lunch?"

"Undecided. Jealousy? Unbecoming."

"I'm not jealous. I would gladly go with you and do anything you wanted. Not including me hurts me. It makes me feel like you don't want me."

"Ridiculous," he grabbed her wrist and twisted it.

She cried out.

He leaned close and pressed his words into her mind, *I created you.*

Brittney Davis's treadmill could incline up or down. The left and right sides rotated independently and could act as a stair master if called upon. A flat screen TV hung from the ceiling in front of the machine. A computer brain controlled the movements of the treadmill and projected first person scenes of running on the TV.

If she wanted, she could run up Kilimanjaro, through an Egyptian spice market, along the beach on the French Riviera, all without leaving her bedroom.

Today, she was running through Parisian streets. The people on camera spoke French.

"Bon soir, Madame," Brittney said as she passed the smiling old French woman on the video. It was a ritual, part of the illusion of the treadmill. Each time she ran the Paris workout, she made sure to speak to the woman on the video. If she didn't, it didn't feel real, and she would suddenly see herself back in the oversized bedroom running alone on a treadmill.

The machine had been her second anniversary present.

The first year had been breasts. *Their silicone anniversary,* she had joked.

Lucifer, her Rottweiler, had been her first birthday present after they married. He looked up from the floor at the sound of her voice and cocked his head to the side.

She smiled down at him. His name had been Joe's idea. Given his sweet and loyal disposition, it was a misnomer. She would have named him Lucky, and, truth be told, when Joe wasn't around, she called the dog Lucky.

The display announced she was now on mile number five. Only two more to go.

Normally, she liked to run outside, but the overnight snow made for good indoor running weather.

The house was huge and airy - an interpretation of a Frank Lloyd Wright original, flat roof and all. It blended into the twenty-seven acres of woodland at the edge of Rural Retreat.

Brittney was the middle wife. That's how she thought of herself. Connie, Joe's ex was the first wife. She had the kids, the estate, and the vacation home on Hatteras.

Brittney was the middle wife. The trade up, fifteen years younger. In a few years, she would have *the baby.* A single child that she would love with all her might. The baby would go to the best schools and be spoiled, but not to the point of rottenness.

Then, of course, Joe would find the last wife. An eighteen-year-old who would become wife number three. Something to brag about at the country club and to be gossiped about at the bridge club.

Last wife would come when Brittney was no longer a size four and Botox became a weekly regimen.

And, Brittney was okay with this.

When she had gone to work as a cocktail waitress at the bar in Roanoke, this setup was the endgame; although, she had been hoping more for a young intern from the hospital a block away.

She wanted to be first wife. First wife got to have the big family.

Second wife got one child, two at the outside.

Better than third wife, who was forced to have sex with a senior citizen or the gardener when time and opportunity arose. No children for third wife.

Instead of a young intern, she drew a middle-aged lawyer looking to unload first wife and upgrade.

Not that she didn't love Joe, she did. She just didn't have any illusions.

Romance in this world of outward appearances was more of a profession than an act of love.

So, she put in her time on the treadmill and bid good afternoon to the recorded French woman whenever she saw her.

Lucifer stood up and walked to the sliding glass windows that led to the second-floor deck.

Stairs led down from the deck to the expansive backyard and woods beyond.

A man stood in the backyard looking up at the house.

Brittney felt a moment of panic. There was a man on the property staring up at her.

The panic faded. There was a man in the backyard. It was okay.

She looked back at the screen. The old woman on the monitor. Bon soir, Madame.

There was a man in the backyard, a tall man in a dark coat and hat. He was staring at her, but it was okay.

One mile to go.

Lucifer looked through the glass door and growled. He paced back and forth.

There was a man in the backyard, a tall man in black with pale gray skin, and he climbed the outside stairs to stand on the deck just beyond the glass door.

But, it was okay. Even though she was running wearing only purple yoga pants and a jog bra.

A half mile to go.

Lucifer barked once.

And, then it wasn't okay. She stopped running and turned off the treadmill. The bark. She looked from the dog to the man on the deck and screamed.

He was smiling with a mouth too wide and too many teeth. There was no dark coat, no black hat. He stood naked on the deck.

The man was tall and gaunt, his skin was the color of smoke and it hung in sagging pouches down his body.

He reached out with his hand and took hold of the door handle.

Brittney dived onto the bed and grabbed her cell phone.

The door gave a snapping noise and shards of metal clattered onto the sill. The door opened.

Lucifer barked and lunged through the opening door.

The man smiled as the dog ran past him, claws tapping across the deck and down the steps.

Lucifer dashed across the backyard and into the woods beyond.

Brittney punched in numbers on the phone.

The phone dialed as the gray man walked across the carpet.

"The number you have dialed is not a valid number," the phone said in a woman's voice.

She stared at the numbers on the screen: 1-1-9.

She whined and typed again.

"The number you have dialed is not a valid number."

The screen said: 1-9-1.

He took the phone out of her hand as she sobbed. He laid it beside her on the bed and sat down. "Shh. No fear."

She could smell him, and she gagged. He carried with him the smell of death and decay, body odor, and milk that had curdled - the smell of the grave and worse things, far worse.

"What are you?" she whispered.

He smiled showing long sharp teeth. "Something old."

He reached out and caressed her cheek with a long ragged nail.

She retched and tried to roll away, but he caught her face in his hand and pulled her closer.

The smell was overpowering, and her breakfast was coming up.

He squeezed her mouth shut. "Swallow."

She tried to shake her head. The taste in her mouth was eclipsing his stench.

"Swallow."

She forced it back down,

He laughed.

She felt something moving in her head behind her eyes, like insects scurrying along her optic nerves. A blood vessel gave way in her left eye and clouded her vision with red.

Brittney had always heard your life passed before your eyes as you died. It was true. Her entire life was playing in fast forward as the gray man's black eyes bored into her. Every mistake she had ever made haunted her, the greatest being Joseph William Davis, father of three who could only get it up when she cheered him on with self-deprecating vulgarities. He had been the biggest mistake of her life, and she wished she had never left Bristol, Tennessee.

Cold. Time had slipped. She was in the big shower still wearing her yoga pants and jog bra. Ice cold water jetted on her from all directions. She looked at the digital display on the shower controls: seventy degrees. She reached for the hot water control, but he was there, standing behind her. He pulled her hand away from the control.

Brittney tried to run, but he pulled her back against him.

He was hard, and she could feel it pressing into the small of her back.

And, the smell, even with the water blasting them, the smell remained.

She was shivering. His arms were just as cold as the water.

She cried out as he ripped the yoga pants and broke the straps on the bra.

His lips touched her ear. "Mine. Mine now."

She shivered and sobbed.

Thoughts rushed into her mind, and she went rigid.

A field of tall grass. A brute of a man wearing fur. A boy walks out into the field. The boy has the gray man's face, but he is younger. He is handsome. He carries a short sword in his right hand.

The brute is laughing at him. The boy is tall, but the brute is taller still.

A bird lands on the boy's shoulder.

A raven. It hisses at the boy, but then it takes flight and scratches at the eyes of the brute.

The brute panics swinging wildly.

The boy runs him through with the sword.

An army cheers.

The boy's name is Marcus Velerius, but they will call him Corvus after this - the Raven.

Later years now. He is old and gray, his face still handsome but closer to the gray man than the boy. A woman stands above him, her skin gray and infirm.

The woman's voice in the head of Marcus Velerius Corvus. *Drink. Drink and be damned.*

He bites into the sagging ruin of her left breast, and his mouth fills with her blood.

Brittney retched at the taste in his memory, but then she realized she was nursing at a gash in his left wrist pressed tight against her lips.

"Drink. Drink and be damned."

She tried to pull away.

But, the blood tasted... sweet.

She swallowed just a little.

Her body caught fire.

The cold water now felt warm.

He pulled his wrist away, and she cried out.

"Patience," he turned her around to face him and picked her up.

She began to laugh.

He smiled down at her as she wrapped her legs around him.

He leaned her back against the tile of the shower and pressed his bloody wrist against her lips.

Brittney drank as fast as she could.

He was sliding into her, and she arched her back drawing him deeper.

Debbie Kincaid, known unaffectionately as the Cat Lady at Rural Retreat High sat in the drive thru and stared at the speaker. "I want two cheeseburgers, two orders of chili fries, and two chocolate milkshakes."

"Does that complete your order, Ma'am?" the disembodied voice asked over the PA.

She scanned the menu board. "Yes."

"That'll be $28.73."

Weight Watchers was not going to be happy, she thought. She burst into laughter, and then stopped as she looked up into the rearview mirror. Was she the one laughing? She wasn't sure. Someone had been in her mind before, and he had made himself at home.

She stared into her own reflected brown eyes. *Shit brown*, her Dad had called them. He was a charmer, her Dad. He died flat of his back pissing in a bag.

She laughed at the thought of this and, again, stopped suddenly, as if some switch had been thrown in her head turning off her laughter.

There's someone in my head, and it's not me, she sang to herself. She didn't even like Pink Floyd.

She pulled up to the window.

A chubby blonde girl looked at her and smiled. Then she looked down at the order.

She recognized the girl from Weight Watchers. Wendy or some shit name like that who wanted to fit in her size eight wedding dress come June, but she was still cruising size sixteen in October.

The girl leaned out. "Oh, Debbie, you don't want this," she whispered.

Debbie shoved money into her hand. "Yes, I do. Give me my food."

"Debbie. You've been doing so well. Everybody at the meetings is so proud of you. Don't do this." There was actual concern in the girl's eyes.

A few hours earlier, that concern would have moved Debbie to tears.

"Give me my fucking food."

The girl recoiled as if she had been slapped. "Debbie, what's wrong? What happened?"

Debbie leaned out her car window and grabbed the girl's hands. She pulled her part way through the window. "Someone's in my head! Now, give me my food!"

The girl pulled away. She grabbed Debbie's bags and change and held them out to her with shaking hands.

Debbie snatched the bags away and tossed them on the passenger seat. "Keep the change. You're going to need it to let out that dress. On your wedding night, just tell him to roll you in flour and look for the wet spot."

The girl began to cry, and a large black girl joined her in the window. "You get out of here! You ain't got no cause to say shit like that to her!"

Debbie held up her middle finger and drove away.

She reached the stop light. The smell of the cheese fries was enticing. She ripped the bag open and scooped out a handful of potatoes, chili, and cheese. She mashed the fries against her open mouth, feeling the excess slide down her chin.

She wiped the excess chili fries on her blouse.

Debbie stumbled into her trailer and dropped the grease-stained bags on the counter. She took out one of the milkshakes, tore off the top, and poured the contents down her throat.

She leaned against the sink and stared out the window.

"Mama's home," she said.

Normally, the cats were all over her as soon as she came through the front door.

She walked into the living room.

The cats: two Siamese, two Orange Tabbies, and a Calico sat in a line on the back of the couch and stared at her.

"I'm home," she repeated.

One of the Siamese hissed at her.

She reached out to the Calico, her oldest cat.

The cat pinned its ears back and hissed.

"What's wrong with you?" she asked.

The cat lashed out, and bright red blood ran down Debbie's hand.

Debbie staggered backward as all the cats began to hiss.

"What's wrong with you? It's me."

The Siamese cats began to howl.

Debbie started to cry. "It's me. I'm the one in my head. Nobody else."

The cats began to move, coming toward her, pushing her back to the kitchen.

Debbie bumped against the stove.

She reached behind her and picked up her heavy iron skillet by the handle.

"It's me," Debbie whispered. "I'm me."

She walked toward the cats.

Snow was falling outside as Laura helped Anne cook dinner.

"So, Friday night is still spaghetti night?" Laura asked as she checked the sauce on the stove.

Anne leaned against the kitchen counter. "Mom's tradition. I wanted to keep it going."

Laura smiled. "I like that."

Tia was watching the small TV on the kitchen counter.

The talking head on-screen spoke. "Park Rangers along with law enforcement authorities in Wythe County are searching for two hikers last seen near Glade Mountain on the Appalachian Trail."

The image changed to show two still photos: a pretty woman with short black hair and a blond young man.

Tia gasped.

Laura leaned down beside her.

The news anchor continued. "Chad and Addie Joseph of Manhattan have been missing for over seventy-two hours. Their last known campsite was on Glade Mountain…"

"What's wrong, Monkey Face?" Laura asked.

Tia pointed at the screen. "I saw her."

"Really? Where?" Laura asked.

"In my bad dream last night."

Anne wiped her hands on a dish towel. "Oh, honey, I don't think."

"She said her name was Addie. She's dead now."

Anne knelt down beside her. "Sweetheart, sometimes our brains play tricks on us. You probably saw this story last night, and your head made up a dream about it."

"No," Tia said. Her eyes were wide.

Laura hugged her. "Listen, Monkey Face. Your Mom is right. Those hikers just got lost. You watch, they'll find them any time now."

"She's dead. The bad people ate her."

"Tia," Anne said. "Come on. You know that couldn't be real."

"It is real, Mama. The bad people in the big house ate her."

Anne shook her head. "What big house, sweetie?"

The cordless phone rang, and Laura picked it up. "Reynolds residence. Oops, sorry, Lawrence residence."

Anne kissed Tia on top of her head and turned back to the stove.

The voice on the phone hesitated. "Kim?" It was a boy's voice.

"Nope, sorry, this is her aunt."

"Oh. Um, can I speak to Kim?"

Laura grinned. "May I ask who's calling?"

"Tell her it's David."

Laura pressed mute. "Hey, Jugs! Phone!"

Kim ran out of her room and into the kitchen. "Don't call me that!" she whispered.

"What? Jugs?"

Kim growled and snatched the phone out of her hand. She slapped her hand over the mouthpiece. "Who is it?"

"A booooy. He said his name was David, and he likes long strolls in the park with bubbly redheads…"

"Jesus!" Kim hissed. "Please tell me you muted this."

Laura pursed her lips. "Hmm… did I mute it before I called you Jugs? I just can't remember, Jugs."

"Aiggh!" Kim said. She held the receiver to her ear. "Hello?"

The line was silent.

She pressed the mute button.

"Hello?"

"Hi, Kim?"

She muted the phone again. "Mom! Do something about her!" She ran to her room and slammed the door.

Anne started laughing.

"Hey, she's getting what I got from you. My puberty was a gauntlet of hell."

Anne shrugged. "No complaints. Keeps her on her toes."

Kim lay down on her bed and unmuted. "Hi, David."

"Hi."

"How did you get my number?"

"White pages. I had to find your address, so…"

"You know, we're not really at the stage where you can just call me out of the blue like this."

He paused on the phone. "I'm sorry. It's just… I know Regina invited you to her party, and I want you to know if you'd rather go to it than go out with me, it's okay."

Kim rolled onto her back. "Oh, it wouldn't bother you?"

"No, of course, it would bother me, but if that's what you want…"

"Don't you want to go out with me, David?"

"No! I want to. I was just being nice…"

"Stop being nice, David. It's not a turn on."

"Fine."

"What time are you going to be at my house?"

"6:15."

"How are you getting here?"

He was silent. "Uh, I don't know. My mom will be out, so… I'll ride my bike?"

"Oh, and show up at my house sweaty?"

"No. No, I'll get a ride, somehow."

"Better. Now, I'll be driving on our date, but you are paying for everything. Gas, dinner, the movie, understand?"

"Sure."

"Where are we eating?"

"What?"

"Where are we eating? I like steak, David."

"I can't afford steak."

"Lovely."

He was silent. "You can have a hamburger."

She rolled onto her stomach. "I want steak."

"You'll have a hamburger and like it."

"Oh, my God! Did you just get snippy with me?"

"Yeah," he said. He paused for a second. "Yeah, princess, I got snippy. You know, you can be a real bully sometimes."

She started giggling. She tried to clamp her hand over her mouth, but it was too late.

"Are you giggling?"

"A little."

"You know, maybe I should go…"

"No! Don't go," she said. "I am a bully sometimes."

"It's okay. But, why are you being one with me?"

Kim twisted her hair with two fingers. "I don't know. I just don't want you to get a swollen head."

He laughed. "And, you think you do that by treating me bad?"

She sighed. "I guess not."

"You know, you and I should have a long talk."

"I know, but I have to go eat spaghetti. See you tomorrow?" Kim asked.

"Yeah. I'll be there."

The smell no longer bothered Brittney. She could barely detect it as she lay in Marcus Velerius Corvus Olc's arms in the dark bedroom.

She was drowsy. Images flooded her mind as she let go of consciousness.

Ireland in the Middle Ages. Marcus's thoughts were becoming more lucid after centuries as something mindless. She had images of sleeping in a pile of other... vampires? They were communal, sharing everything, even each other in the cold depths of a cave.

She saw through Marcus's eyes as he ventured out alone, raiding villages at night. Taking anyone he wanted.

They called him Olc - the Irish word for evil and unclean.

Brittney rolled onto the edge of the bed and threw up on the floor. Long strands of her hair fell onto the floor from her head as she retched.

His hands were on her, comforting her.

She wiped her mouth and rolled back against him.

It was getting hard to think.

"He will be home soon," she whispered.

"Prepare for him."

Debbie sat on the living room floor and ate her cheeseburgers. The blood stained iron pan lay beside her.

Tears ran down her cheeks as she chewed.

Her cell phone rang on the coffee table beside her. It vibrated and crawled across the faux wood. It nudged against a dead Siamese causing one of the clawed hind feet to move.

Debbie began to sob.

The phone fell on the floor beside her. She picked it up and answered.

"Debbie?" a voice asked on the other end.

Debbie stared at the phone, convinced it might bite her. "Who is this?"

"I'm the woman from earlier. Remember? We came to the school. My name is Miriam."

"Now's not a good time," Debbie whined.

"What's wrong, sweetheart?"

Debbie broke into sobs. "My friends are gone."

"What friends, dear?"

"Miffy, Chloe, Cindy, Raylene, and Jessica."

"Where did they go?"

Debbie broke down. "They're dead. I came home, and they started hissing at me like they didn't know me. I only wanted to scare them, but they kept scratching me…"

"Are we talking about cats, dear?" Miriam asked.

Debbie wiped her nose with the back of her hand. "Yes."

"Well, these things happen."

"Do you think I can get more cats?"

"Um, I don't think it would be a good idea, Debbie."

She cried harder.

"Debbie?"

"What?"

"Could you stop crying for a moment?"

"But, I'm sad," Debbie whined.

"I know. We're always sad when we kill our friends."

"I don't have any friends left," Debbie whispered. "Even Wendy or whatever her name is from Weight Watchers hates me now."

"I'm going to be your friend, Debbie."

She sniffled. "You are?"

"Yes. We're going to be great friends, you and I. As a matter of fact, you're coming to a party tomorrow. 1500 Larkspur Lane at 5:00 PM. Can you remember that?"

"A party?"

"Yes. Repeat it to me."

"5:00 PM, 1500 Larkspur Lane," Debbie whispered. "Should I bring anything?"

Miriam laughed. "Just yourself. Now, you go take a nice long shower and go to bed."

Debbie looked around the room at the dead cats. "I have to bury them."

"Nonsense. Just put them in the freezer, and I'll help you bury them later."

"You will?"

"Of course, I will. We'll have a little service for them and everything."

Debbie laughed and blew her nose. "I'd like that."

Brittney sat in the dining room. She was wearing a white dress with her hair pulled back. She smiled down at a string of pearls around her throat.

Olc stood beside her.

"I'm home," Joe Davis said as he came in from the garage. He put his briefcase by the refrigerator and stared at Olc.

Joe squinted. He rubbed his eyes and shook his head. "Damn, for a second, I could have sworn…"

"What?" Brittney said.

"I thought I saw that old fossil from earlier today. Eyes are playing tricks on me," he leaned down beside her and kissed her forehead.

He shrank back. "Brittney, honey, you are cold and clammy. You coming down with something?"

Brittney giggled out loud. Then she closed her mouth and bit her lower lip. "No."

"How was your day?" he asked as he washed his hands at the kitchen sink.

"I ran almost seven miles after lunch. I took a lover to my bed and the shower. He did nasty things to me."

Joe turned around as he dried his hands. "What?"

"I said I ran almost seven miles after lunch."

"That's my girl," he said. "What's for dinner?"

She pointed to a plate at the far end of the table. "Liver."

Joe sat down and frowned at the plate. It was piled high with glistening pinkish gray meat. He poked it with a fork. "Jesus, is it cooked?"

"Better for you raw. They said so online." She started giggling again.

Olc laughed as well.

Joe's eyes darted up from the plate. "Did you hear that?"

Brittney clamped her hand over her mouth and shook her head.

Olc was standing right beside him, but he couldn't see.

Brittney laughed louder.

Joe speared some liver with his fork and held it under his nose. "What is that? Some kind of curry?"

"Bile."

He took a bite and shrugged. "Aren't you having any?" he asked as he swallowed.

She smiled and shook her head. "I tasted it when it came up the first time."

Joe stared at her. "You ain't making sense tonight. You sure you feel okay?"

She stood up and walked to his side of the table. She sat down on the table beside his plate. "I feel fine. Now. Before, I felt ill. But I threw up a lot of things I don't need anymore, like my liver." She pointed to the plate.

He shook his head and took another bite. "I can't understand a word you're saying."

"I drank his blood," she said. She reached out and tilted Joe's face up toward hers. "It changed me inside. I don't need a stomach anymore or a large intestine or a liver or a pancreas. I'm almost hollow inside."

Joe stared at her, his eyes unfocused.

She tilted his head to the side and lowered her mouth to his neck.

"Your tongue," Olc whispered. "Touch his neck. The carotid. Pulses."

She ran the tip of her tongue over Joe's neck. He never stopped eating.

Brittney felt the pulsing in his neck. She bared her fangs and bit into it.

Joe spasmed as she drank his blood.

She gulped it down. As the blood filled her, her mind drifted away. She couldn't remember her name.

She felt a pressure in her bladder. She tried to stop drinking, but Olc put a hand on the back of her head and held her lips to the wound.

He reached down with his other hand and massaged her abdomen just below her navel.

Her bladder emptied on the floor, and she drank faster, not wanting to miss a drop.

Saturday

Jane Connors looked at herself in her bathroom mirror. This was her face from twenty years before. Years before David's birth.

The face that got her free drinks and any man she wanted.

But, the hands were a different matter altogether.

Her hands shook like she had Parkinson's.

She squeezed her fingers together, balled her hands into fists, and they still shook.

She had done her makeup three times in the last hour, and now her forehead was once again beaded with sweat.

She pounded her fists on the bathroom sink. "Stop. Stop. Stop."

Her stomach lurched.

She held up the empty aluminum tube and stared into the opening.

There was no trace of the red gel. She had used it all, taking the last smear from the crushed tube last night with a toothpick.

Jane picked up her phone and dialed it.

Miriam's number went straight to voicemail.

She waited for the beep. "Hi, Miriam, this is Jane Connors calling again. You haven't returned my calls." She sat down on the toilet in her short black skirt. "I really need more of the wrinkle gel. I'm totally out, and I don't..." what could she say? Her hands were trembling, she was broken out in a cold sweat? "I don't feel well. I think I need more. So, I'm just going to come over to your house. Okay? Maybe your phone is broken, so I'm just going to come over."

She hung up.

She hurried out of the bathroom.

Jane stopped by her son's room and peeked in. "I have to go out."

David nodded from the floor as he played his video game. "'Kay."

She forced herself to linger. "Big date tonight, huh?"

David looked up at her and smiled. He saw her face and his expression changed. "Mom? What's going on with, you know, your face?"

She rolled her eyes. "Nice thing to say to your mother."

"No, I mean, you look great. Younger even. Do you feel okay?"

She nodded quickly. "I'm... I'm great. I... I just have to go. Good luck tonight."

He smiled at her. "Thanks."

"I love you, David."

David stared at her open mouthed. "I... love you too, Mom."

"I know I don't say that enough," she said. "You're a great kid. Better than I deserved."

He shook his head. "Don't say that."

"It's true," she said as she nodded. "We both know that. But, I'm going to be better. I promise, David."

He smiled as she walked away.

Debbie's stereo blasted 'Big Girls Cry' by Sia as she carefully wrapped the last of her five cats in plastic wrap.

She rubbed the Calico's head, being careful not to touch the bloody dent on the left side of its face. "Big girls really do cry when their hearts are breaking, Miffy." She choked back a sob. "Because my heart is broken."

She danced across the old linoleum with the dead, plastic wrapped cat. She placed it lovingly in the freezer with the other four. Debbie had to make more room in the overhead by disposing of a freezer burned trout from at least a year before her father died.

She closed the freezer door.

Debbie smiled as she picked up her keys.

She heard laughter outside.

Debbie moved the curtain on her living room window slightly.

Her neighbor, Gwen, was standing on her small wooden porch.

A redneck was kissing her goodbye, his big hand caressing her booty shorts.

She despised Gwen. Her bleached blonde hair never covered her dark roots. Men came and went at all hours.

Rumor was she was a prostitute.

First time. Always hurts, the man's voice said in her head.

She shivered.

The redneck walked to his pickup, and Gwen dropped into the cheap plastic lawn chair on her porch.

He said something and Gwen raised her long skinny legs and set her heels on the porch railing.

The man laughed.

He pulled away in a spray of gravel.

Debbie waited, hoping Gwen would go back in her trailer.

But, despite the cold, the woman seemed intent on sitting outside. A puff of smoke came up from her vape machine.

Debbie opened her door and stepped outside.

"Well, hi there, Cat Lady," Gwen said through a cloud of fake cigarette smoke.

Debbie didn't look up. "Hi."

"Hope me and Earl didn't keep you up last night. Once he gets going, I gotta make a lot of noise. You know what I mean, don't ya?"

Debbie nodded. "Sure. I know."

Gwen gave a hoarse laugh. "Yeah, I bet. Where you headed? Going to buy some cat food?"

"No. I… I got rid of the cats. I took them to a farm. Lots of mice and rats and things for them to chase. They're going to be happy there."

"Nasty goddamn things. Can't stand having them around, sure as shit not in the house. Where you going?"

Debbie hesitated with her hand on the car door handle. "I'm going to a party this evening. I want to get a new dress."

"You? A party? No shit. Well, I'm proud of you," Gwen said as she blew another mushroom cloud of smoke heavenward. "What kind of dress you going for?"

Debbie hesitated. "I… I don't know." She hadn't really thought about it.

"I know a place over next to Roanoke in the mall where you can get a leather minidress. They got them plus sizes and all. That's what I'd do if I was you. You got a lot up top."

"You… think that would work?"

"Shit, yeah. Cat Lady, if I had boobs like you, I'd be out of this trailer park and makin' some serious cash."

Regina Kerns, the most popular girl at Rural Retreat High School, captain of the cheerleading squad, and member of the National Honor Society, dragged her father's corpse by the ankles through the hallway.

In the past four hours, she had committed patricide, matricide, and two counts of fratricide. She was now a mass murderer.

Her brothers had been easy to drag down to the basement. Neither of them was close to her weight. Her mother wasn't much trouble either - she had always prided herself on her svelte figure, and as she had maneuvered her mother's body down the basement stairs, Regina had been thankful for that.

Her father, on the other hand…

He was a massive hulk of a man, and even using the carpet runner to sled him across the polished wood floor was proving to be a Herculean task.

She paused and sat down on the floor. Regina looked at her watch. Plenty of time to get ready for the party.

The Regina of yesterday, before the tall gray man came and made her see things in such a novel and exciting way? That Regina would have been horrified by her actions. She had murdered her family - well, not technically. They were still alive.

At least, she thought they were.

Not that they were going to get better, of course. The gray man had been very specific: take an ice pick while each slept and drive it into the back of the head. Swizzle. Repeat. They were still breathing, hearts still pumping, urine and feces still flowing (which was disgusting), but their brains had shuffled off the mortal coil.

She had asked the gray man why he wanted to keep them in that vegetative state instead of just killing them outright.

"Waste not. Want not," he had said.

Regina sighed. She stood up and grabbed her father's ankles, sliding him on the runner toward the open basement door.

Such was the price of promised immortality.

She tugged harder. She had a party to plan.

Jane stood on Miriam's porch and stared at the ancient doorknob. She was sweating, even though the temperature was only in the forties.

Tremors wracked her hand as she reached out and knocked.

She heard footsteps on the stairs.

The doorknob turned, and the door creaked open.

Miriam Tillford smiled at her. "Jane, what a surprise!" She leaned against the door frame in an expensive silk dress.

It wasn't even 10:00 AM on a Saturday and Miriam Tillford was ravishing.

"I… I left messages for you."

Miriam nodded. "I know."

Jane frowned. "You... know?"

"Yes. I heard them."

"But, you never called me back..."

Miriam took her hand, and then she reached up and stroked her forehead. "I wanted to see if you had the balls to come here. You poor dear, withdrawal is hideous isn't it?"

"Withdrawal?" Jane asked. She teetered on her feet.

"Yes, darling, your body is literally ripping itself to pieces because it doesn't have any more... wrinkle cream."

Gene watched the woman arrive at the house on the hill. He didn't recognize her, but he caught a brief glimpse of Miriam as she opened the door. He had the crosshairs of the sniper rifle on Miriam's face, his finger on the trigger. If she had lingered a moment more, Gene could have taken the shot.

But, Miriam led the woman inside and shut the door.

He hummed "Billy Don't be a Hero" as he lay on the cold ground of the hill on the opposite side of the road from the house. He focused on the tune and nothing else. The earbuds helped - he had started out with a Walkman back in the day. His smartphone had the capability to play the same song over and over again, which was a hell of a lot easier than swapping cassettes and changing out batteries constantly.

The vampires could pick up on human thought within a half mile, read your mind outright closer than a hundred yards. But, music seemed to blind them. Especially repetitive music. The trick was to focus on the words while still doing what you needed to do.

Like lying in wait with a sniper rifle a quarter mile away.

"Did you... give me heroin or something?" Jane asked as Miriam led her into the house.

"Something. Mind the hole in the floor."

Jane felt dizzy as she looked down into the chasm in the foyer floor. "I thought... you were fixing that?"

Miriam shrugged. "Oh, just as easy to walk around it." She led Jane to the staircase.

"Where are you taking me?" Jane asked.

"To get you what you need... maybe. Come."

Jane stumbled on the stairs, and Miriam caught her. "Now, Jane, don't make me have to carry you. I can, but it's undignified."

She tried to pull away. "I need to go to the hospital."

Miriam snorted. "Hospital? Oh, this is far beyond those witch doctors."

She put her arm around Jane's shoulders and ushered her upstairs.

Miriam opened the door to a bedroom and led her inside.

The room was sparse. A four poster bed, a low dresser with a mirror, and a small chair were the only furniture.

The bed looked freshly made with a thick comforter.

Miriam left Jane standing in the middle of the room and sat down on the bed. "Olc's family keep the house ice cold. They can't stand the heat. If I didn't have a thick comforter and blankets, I would freeze."

The room was spinning, and Jane wobbled on her feet.

"Stay on your feet, Jane," Miriam said. Her tone was commanding.

Miriam went to her dresser. "Now, let's see... wrinkle cream." She opened the top drawer. "I could have sworn..."

She rummaged through the drawer. "Nope. Sorry. No cream."

Jane stumbled backward. "Take me to the hospital. Please."

Miriam turned around and leaned against the dresser. "They really can't help you. I mean, they can help with the withdrawal of course. You feel like you're going to die, but you really won't. Couple of days in a hospital bed and you'll be good as new."

Jane turned around and stumbled toward the door.

"But," Miriam said.

Jane paused, turned, and fell back against the door.

Miriam sat down at the dresser and turned away. "Once you're over the withdrawal, you'll just be plain middle-aged Jane again. Wrinkles and sags and fading dreams." Miriam picked up a lipstick tube.

Jane closed her eyes.

"I know. Not what you wanted, right? I mean, who wants to grow old and fade. What you really need is a mega dosage of that special red gel."

Jane jolted awake. "You could do that?" Jane asked.

Miriam didn't look toward her. Instead, she applied the lipstick. "Of course. If you get a major dose of the... gel, it works for years.

Decades sometimes. Just one big dose and you can be a twenty-something for years and years. Would you like that, Jane?"

Jane nodded. "Yes. Yes, I would."

"Hmm. I suppose we could work something out."

"I can pay..."

Miriam laughed. "Don't be silly. If I sold this, it would cost more than you could possibly afford. But, there are other ways."

"Other ways?"

"I have needs, Jane. Very specific needs." She brushed mascara on her lashes.

Jane rubbed her eyes.

So, that was it? She'd never done that before. She wasn't sure she could.

The thought of not having any more of the gel made her want to scream.

Could she do this? She took a deep breath and unbuttoned her blouse. Then she unzipped her skirt. She let it slide down. She carried both items of clothing in her arms as she walked to Miriam.

She laid her clothes on the bed.

She reached out and touched Miriam's shoulder.

Miriam turned. She burst out laughing.

Jane stumbled back and grabbed her clothes off the bed.

"Oh, no!" Miriam giggled. "You thought I meant..." She laughed out loud. "Oh, my poor Jane. You *are* desperate."

Jane burst into to tears.

Miriam stood up and put her arm around her shoulders. She guided her to the bed and sat down beside her.

"Now, now, let's not cry. I didn't mean to be cruel to you. You just surprised me with your offer. However, I'm not gay, I'm just perverted." She rubbed Jane's hair out of her eyes. "I will tell you, if I ever decide to try the other side, you're the first woman I will call."

Jane burst out sobbing. "You said you had needs..."

"Umm, not precisely carnal needs. I need help. I need an assistant. Several actually. Taking care of this family is a huge responsibility, and it is growing so fast. That's the deal. You help me protect the family, and I will make sure you get all the red *gel* you ever need."

"Protect?"

Miriam nodded. "Yes. The family has enemies - narrow-minded people who can't accept them for what they are. We protect the family."

Jane shook her head. "I don't understand."

Miriam squeezed her hand. "Easier just to show you."

Miriam helped Jane down the steps after helping her get dressed.

Miriam talked as they navigated the stairs. "The family has had many names over the centuries, most of them inaccurate. They are the *Draugr* - an old Scandinavian name. They were persecuted and hunted almost to extinction."

They reached the bottom of the steps and turned toward the parlor. "Humans kill what they don't understand. They fear the unknown. It's really perverse when you think about it. In the wild, the prey certainly fear the predator, but they rarely band together and kill them. It just isn't natural. Predators only take what they need - numbers wise, there's no real danger to the prey population as a whole."

Jane stared at her uncomprehending.

Miriam put her hand on the parlor doorknob. "Now, Jane. I'm going to show you something. It's going to be confusing and more than a little upsetting. It's okay to be frightened. You can scream, and I won't be in the least bit cross with you if you lose control of your bladder. But, you mustn't run. If you run, I'll have to stop you. I don't want to hurt you."

She opened the door.

The human mind loves patterns. The familiar. It's good at categorizing and classifying.

When it sees something utterly alien, it revolts. It focuses on the pieces it can identify. The rest is chaos.

A gray shape moved on the parlor floor. The furniture had been piled haphazardly in the corners, leaving a wide open space of bare wood floor.

The gray shape writhed in the middle of the open space.

Jane could identify pieces. Eyes stared out at her. *Here* was a slim gray arm and hand, *there* was a woman's leg.

Jane struggled to understand what she saw as a *whole*.

Hairless, gray-skinned people, dozens of them, lay in a pile, entwined in each other's embrace. The pile was in constant motion, bodies rotating up or sinking down in the chaos of arms and legs and torsos. A woman rose to the top, her head thrown back in ecstasy, only to sink into the crowd and be replaced on top by another.

"What... are they?" Jane whispered.

A face appeared in the side of the mass. A man's face, his liquid black eyes opened, and he smiled at her.

His teeth were long and sharp.

Jane shrank back.

Miriam squeezed her hand. "It's all right, Jane. They won't hurt you. They love you. Unconditionally and without limit. Pure love."

"I don't..."

Miriam smiled and touched the corner of Jane's left eye. "You're marked. Marked with their blood. They would know you in a pitch black room."

An overwhelming stench reached Jane. "Oh, God, that smell."

Miriam laughed. "You get used to it. They can't help it. It's what they are. When they're hunting, they can mask their scent and appearance with their psychic gifts."

"It smells like death."

"Yes."

"What are they?"

"The only known predator of man. They are the Draugr, created by feeding Draugr blood to human beings. We are the Vakt, the protectors, created by absorbing Draugr blood through the skin or eyes," Miriam caressed her face. "They are immortal and so are we - or at least you will be soon."

"You called them 'predator of man'?"

Miriam smiled. "Vampires, dear. They're vampires."

Jane sat down on a rickety chair by the parlor door and watched the ever changing swarm of bodies. "I can't tell where one ends and another begins."

Miriam knelt beside her. "Neither can they. Can you hear them singing?"

Jane shook her head. "No. I can't hear anything but their bodies moving."

Miriam smiled. "Not with your ears. Inside your head."

Jane closed her eyes. It began as a murmur inside her mind. If she concentrated, the sound went away, but if she let her mind drift, she could make out voices. And, then laughter.

She opened her eyes. "Oh, my God."

"Amazing isn't it?"

"I'm going insane, aren't I?" Jane asked.

Miriam took her hand. "No."

Jane took a deep breath. "They kill people... that's wrong."

Miriam nodded. "I know. But, they have no choice, Jane. They have to survive." She stood up. "There are only a tiny number of Draugr, but there are billions of human beings. The family only takes what it needs."

She turned to Jane and smiled. "And, they offer so much. Eternal life. You won't grow old, you won't ever get sick. Think about it. Whole religions are built on that promise, but here it is - not a fairy tale. Real. Tangible."

"I can't hurt people," Jane whispered.

"Olc will help with that. He will explain it to you in a way I can't." She turned away. "He'll make *changes*. Afterward, you'll feel wonderful." She knelt beside Jane. "Isn't that what you want, Jane? Don't you want to feel wonderful? To be happy?"

Jane looked at the floor. "How do we start?"

Miriam smiled and clasped Jane's hands in hers. "You won't regret this." She turned to the cluster of bodies. "Unfortunately, we start with violence."

Miriam stood up and walked to the mass of Draugr. "You have to give her to me now," she whispered.

Jane felt voices scream in her head. She winced.

"I know," Miriam soothed. "I know. I don't want to. I know you love her. But, she's incomplete. She's not getting better."

The screams in Jane's head became sobs.

The mass moved, and a shape came to the top.

It was a body, small and curled in a fetal position. It lay still.

Jane stood up to get a better look.

It was a woman with gray skin. She rested in a transparent bubble, almost like an amniotic sack.

Miriam turned and looked at Jane. "This is Tammy. Sometimes, when they drink the blood, it doesn't take. Usually, there's a defect or deformity. But, sometimes, there's no reason, it just doesn't work. She's in pain. They put her in this cocoon - I don't know how they do it. They produce it with their bodies somehow. The cocoon keeps her still and quiet, it relieves the pain. She's asleep."

Jane leaned close. The emaciated woman within the sack looked like an embryo.

Miriam reached out and dragged her red lacquered nails across the cocoon. It gave under her touch. Ripples spread through the liquid within.

A gray hand emerged from the mass below and grabbed Miriam's wrist.

Jane took a step back.

But, Miriam merely knelt down and kissed the hand that held her. "Don't. You know I have to."

The hand relaxed its grip and slid away back into the tangle.

Miriam placed the nails of both her hands on the top of the bag and tore it open.

Clear liquid flooded across the floor and Jane danced away.

Along with the flood came a doubling of the smell: too many people packed too close together for too long, something dead. She felt faint and leaned her hand on the wall to steady herself.

She turned to see Miriam stand upright with the gray, dripping thing in her arms. Its mouth opened revealing long white teeth. It moaned.

Miriam carried the woman in her arms as if she weighed nothing, but Jane knew she weighed at least a hundred pounds.

Jane followed her through the parlor door.

Miriam whispered to the gray woman in her arms as she walked, soothing it as one would soothe a sick child.

The door to the basement stood open in the hallway.

Jane followed them down as Miriam's heels echoed on the old wooden stairs.

The basement smelled of mold and decay.

"Turn on the light, please?" Miriam asked.

Jane flipped a switch on the wall above the first step.

The basement was huge, red steel posts extended up from the concrete supporting the floors above. The great hole in the foyer opened overhead like an oculus.

Bags of quicklime lay stacked on pallets around the basement. An old white claw- foot bathtub sat in one corner. It wasn't hooked to any plumbing. A chain attached to a pulley hung over the tub.

A wood chipper sat in the opposite corner. It was yellow and had blemishes of rust.

The teeth of the chipper were tinged red.

A jackhammer had been used to create a massive hole in the concrete wall behind the chipper. The chipper's ejector was pointed toward this hole. The jackhammer lay forgotten on the floor.

In the dim light, Jane could see a steel pipe in the hole.

"What is all this for?" Jane asked.

"Waste," Miriam said as she lay the vampire down on the dusty floor.

Jane stared at her uncomprehending.

Miriam laughed. "Oh, come now. Use your imagination."

Jane leaned against the cold wall and shivered. "I don't believe any of this."

Miriam walked to one of the pallets and picked up a roll of duct tape. "Let's review: the wrinkle cream? Do you believe that?"

Jane nodded. "Yes. It did something to me."

"It made you younger."

"It made me ill."

"Undoubtedly, but younger. Agree?"

Jane sighed and nodded. "Yes."

Miriam knelt beside the gray woman on the floor. "And, this is a vampire, isn't it?"

Jane shook her head. "I don't know. I can't explain what it is."

Miriam smiled. "Should we invite someone into the house so you can watch them feed?"

"No," Jane whispered. She looked at the roll of duct tape in Miriam's hand. "Why are you going to use duct tape on her?"

"It's not for her," Miriam said as she stood up. "Strip."

"What?"

"Take off your clothes, unless you want them soiled."

Jane shook her head.

"Oh, come now. A few minutes ago you were ready to hop into bed with me to get more wrinkle cream. Now you turn into a prude?"

She walked up to Jane and caressed her face. "I want to give you a gift. I will make you young and beautiful forever. All that is required is for you to trust me."

"I don't."

Miriam shrugged. "Then leave. Stay plain, middle-aged Jane."

Jane looked at the floor. She started unbuttoning her blouse.

Miriam turned away. "I like it better when people choose. I didn't have a choice. Olc wanted me, so he took me and made me who I am. Forty years later, I still don't know if this is my will or his. You will never have that worry. You chose this. Take comfort in it."

Jane stood naked on the basement floor. She shivered as Miriam tore off a piece of duct tape.

"Please don't. I'll do what you ask."

Miriam shook her head. "The tape isn't to bind you, it's to protect you." She placed the tape over Jane's mouth. "You must not get any in your mouth. If some goes in your nose, just blow it out. Do not swallow."

Jane shook her head. She couldn't understand what Miriam was talking about.

Miriam led her to the tub.

Jane stepped over the edge, and Miriam helped her sit down.

"He'll be angry with me. He wanted more time to see if Tammy improved, but it's hopeless. Shouldn't let her go to waste." Miriam opened a bag on top of one of the pallets. She withdrew a syringe and a bottle of white fluid.

Jane whined and tried to get out of the tub.

Miriam shook her head as she filled the syringe. "Propofol. It's an anesthetic. Not for you." She leaned down beside Tammy and slid the needle into her arm. She kissed Tammy's cheek as the Propofol went into her vein. "Sleep now, darling. No more pain."

Tammy went limp on the floor.

Jane dropped the syringe and picked Tammy up off the floor.

She took one end of the chain attached to the pulley and wrapped it around Tammy's ankles. She locked the chain with a clip.

Then, she took the other end of the chain and pulled.

Tammy rose feet first into the air, her lifeless arms hanging down at her sides.

She fastened the chain to a hook in the floor.

Jane looked up. The vampire hung directly over her head, her black eyes staring down at her unblinking. Jane looked at Miriam and shook her head violently.

Miriam just smiled. She took a straight razor out of her pocket and slashed Tammy's throat from ear to ear.

Blood rained down on Jane's bare skin as Miriam stepped away.

Jane screamed behind the duct tape gag. The red blood coated her. It was cold like ice.

She tried to climb out of the tub just as a seizure gripped her. Every muscle in her body went tense.

The tub was filling. There was so much of the blood, too much. There shouldn't have been that much blood in the dying creature who hung over her, but it kept pouring from her like a waterfall of crimson.

It was seeping into her skin, coating her face. It went in her eyes, and she raked at them with her fingers, trying to clear them of the red blood.

The seizure stopped, and Jane went limp.

She floated in the red stained tub, feeling the blood climbing into her body.

A feeling of calm passed through her as the flow of blood from Tammy ebbed until it was only single crimson drops that fell from the jagged slash in her throat.

Jane stared up. A single drop fell, and she watched it until it spattered red across her left eye. Her breathing slowed. The red liquid around her felt warm. She moved her hands slowly in the blood.

Gene swung the sniper rifle left as the town car pulled in.

It stopped beside the house on the way to the detached garage. The rear door opened.

A tall brunette woman stepped out. She seemed a little unstable on her feet. She wore a white blouse and pearls.

As he watched the clothing changed. She was wearing a black overcoat.

Olc stepped out.

Gene put the cross hairs on his bald head. *One shot would end this*, he thought. But, would it? The ancients were still inside along with what now numbered at least two dozen Draugr.

And, the protectors. How many now?

He followed Olc with the rifle.

They would swarm him if he took the shot.

His mission would be incomplete.

He let Olc walk into the house with the new vampire on his arm.

Miriam was sitting on the steps waiting as Olc and the woman stepped inside. She looked at the Draugr that had once been Brittney Davis. "Twenty-four hours," Miriam said. "You don't often spend that much time with an acquisition. She must be special."

Brittney stared up at Olc with reverence.

"Exceptional," Olc said as he caressed Brittney's neck.

Miriam turned away. "Already able to project camouflage. Not many can do that."

Olc nodded. "Personality. Already asserting itself."

Miriam stood up and turned away. "I took Tammy to the basement."

Olc looked at Brittney.

Brittney nodded and walked into the parlor.

Olc glared up at Miriam. "I said…"

"She was in agony. I ended it. I had my own exceptional acquisition. She's in the basement waiting on you," Miriam glided up the steps. "Not that you deserve a gift."

Miriam hesitated at the top of the steps. She heard Olc open the door to the basement, listened to him descend the steps.

She heard Jane's voice and Olc's laughter.

Miriam continued on to her room as she heard Jane begin to scream.

David sat in Pauly's Dad's delivery truck a block away from Kim's house.

Pauly didn't have a car, but his Dad let him borrow the delivery truck now and then.

It was ten minutes till six.

"You got this, my man," Pauly encouraged from the driver's seat.

"You think?"

"You ain't dressed like a slob, you got that lame-assed corsage. You're ready," Pauly said with a grin. "You use deodorant?"

"Twice."

"Good man. You brush your teeth?"

"Yes. And, mouthwash."

"You got mints?"

"In my pocket."

Pauly snapped his fingers. "Oh, I know one thing you didn't remember." He fished in his pocket and held out a foil wrapped packet.

"A condom?" David said. "Seriously? It's the first date, Doofus."

"Seniors, man. Rules don't apply. She might have expectations."

"Jesus," David whispered. He took the packet and read it. "Extra large?"

"Yeah, I got the box of them when I was 13." He added with a grin, "Too snug now."

"Asshole." David stuffed the condom in his wallet.

"Go make us proud, young Connors."

David stood in front of the door, the plastic-boxed corsage in his hand. He reached out and touched the doorbell.

The door opened. The woman inside was tall and thin, a brunette version of Kim, only three inches taller. "Yeah?"

"I'm David."

She studied him. "David who?"

"David Connors. I'm here for Kim."

The woman nodded.

"Uh, is she here?"

"Yeah."

David looked at his feet. "Could you tell her I'm here?"

She never took her eyes off David's eyes. "Monkey Face, go tell your sister there's another boy here. This one's taller than the last one."

"Last one?" David asked.

"Popular girl, my niece."

"Oh, you're her aunt?"

"That's the way it works."

Kim's little sister ran up the hall. "Kim! David's here!"

A woman leaned her head out of the kitchen. "Hi, David. I'm Anne, Kim's Mom." She was smiling.

David smiled back. "Hi, Mrs. Lawrence."

Anne wiped her hands on a towel. "I'll be out in just a minute. This is my sister, Laura. Laura? Invite him in."

David smiled at Laura.

She didn't smile back. "Won't you come in?"

David followed her into the house.

"It's a lovely house."

"You like houses, David?" Laura asked.

"Uh, yeah."

"Really? Because your comment sounds like nervous chatter to me. You nervous, David?"

His voice cracked. "Yes." He cleared his throat. "Yes, Ma'am."

"Got a reason to be nervous, David?"

David was now beginning to understand where Kim's personality came from. It was inherited.

"No, Ma'am," David said. He looked down the hall. "You think Kim will be out soon?"

"You like baseball, David?"

David stared at her. "Yes, Ma'am?"

"I don't. All those bases. I don't like bases, David."

They were standing just inside the door and Laura was only a few inches from him.

"You planning on playing baseball with Kim?" Laura asked.

"No, I don't think…"

"Sure, you are. Boys like you are always about baseball." She took a step back and looked at him. "You're not hideous, so you're probably going to get to first base."

"I don't know what that means."

"Kissing, David. That's first base," Laura said. "I got no problem with you hitting a single, David."

"Okay…"

"But, you'll try to stretch that to a double, because you're a guy, and that's what you do."

"Again, I don't know."

"Touching, groping."

"Oh…"

"Keep it above the waist. I mean it."

"Oh, I will. I don't…"

"Because, David, I swear to God if you even think about sliding into third or stealing home, I will end you."

He looked into Laura's eyes and believed every word she said. "I…"

Kim appeared behind her aunt. "Hi, David."

David smiled. Kim Lawrence was wearing a green dress that reached just above her knees. It glittered the same color as her eyes.

Laura stepped away and gave Kim a mischievous grin.

Kim looked at David's hand. She pointed at the box. "What is that?"

"Corsage. Red roses and baby's breath." He held it out to her.

She took it and stared at the corsage inside its plastic case.

"It's silk. I couldn't get real ones at this time of year." He reached out for the box. "Want me to put it on you?"

She looked up at him. "No," she said. "Don't be silly. It's just a date. I only wanted to make sure you were resourceful. It's an important trait. I'll just put this in my room." She turned back to the hall.

David glanced at Laura. "Can I come with you?" he called after Kim.

"Nooooo," Laura said. "You cannot."

Kim opened the door to her room. She opened the box and caressed the silk flowers. She smiled.

Laura shut the door as the two teenagers left.

Anne came out of the kitchen. "Oh, no! Did they leave already?"

"Yeah," Laura said. "Don't worry. I had a talk with him."

Anne burst out laughing. "Oh, not Dad's baseball talk?"

Laura grinned. "Generations of Reynolds girls have gone out with that warning. I was carrying on a family tradition."

Anne shook her head. "And, did that ever stop our boyfriends or us?"

Laura pondered for a moment. "No. But, it's a ritual. Sort of like when the Aztecs cut the heart out of human sacrifice victims."

Tia sat down on the couch. "Why did you talk to him about baseball? I hate baseball."

Laura sat down beside her and hugged her. "Me too. It's boring, and boys are gross."

"Yeah."

"Do you feel emasculated because I'm driving?" Kim asked as she drove onto Main Street. "I mean, it must be kind of embarrassing."

David rolled his eyes. "Well, it wasn't before, but it sort of is now."

Kim laughed. "I'm pretty rough, aren't I?"

David shook his head. "A little. But, it's okay. I like the abuse."

"No, you don't."

"No, I don't. But, being in the car with you and taking the abuse is better than not being in the car with you at all." He smiled at her.

Kim glanced at him. "You're weird, David Connors."

"Likewise, Kim Lawrence."

"How'd you get to the house? We don't have Uber."

"Pauly. He drove me in his Dad's delivery van."

"Does he have his license?"

"Hell, I'm not even sure he ever got a learner's permit. It's Pauly."

She laughed. "You two don't seem like the best friends type."

"How so?"

"I don't know. You're quiet, he's not. You're smart. He's…"

David laughed. "Not quite as dumb as he acts." David looked at her for a long second. "Please, tell me you didn't go out with me just to get closer to Pauly."

"Whoa!" Kim said. "Paranoid much? No, he's not my type."

"And, I am?"

"Maybe. Or, maybe I just feel sorry for you."

He stared at her.

"Geez, it was a joke, Connors. Grow a sense of humor."

"Why are you going out with me?"

She shrugged. "I don't know. Seemed like a good idea at the time."

"And, now?"

"The night's young. You haven't screwed up bad so far."

He smiled at her.

They reached the end of Main Street. Police cars had both lanes blocked just before the interstate.

There was an old pickup truck in front of them with Texas plates. The driver whipped the wheel to the left and did a U-turn in the middle of the road.

Kim looked up as the old man passed by, a look of determination on his face.

"Sobriety checkpoint?" David asked.

"If so, I think Grandpa there was fairly sure he wouldn't pass the test."

"I thought they only did these during the summer?" David asked.

A cold rain pelted the windshield as they pulled forward a car at a time.

There was a red minivan parked on the shoulder with its hazard lights blinking.

"Oh, looks like an accident," Kim said.

When they pulled forward again, Kim saw paramedics wheeling a woman away on a stretcher. She was strapped down.

The woman was straining against the belts and screaming. Two policemen carried her small children toward the ambulance in front of her.

Kim was startled by the sound of a flashlight tapping on her window.

A Rural Retreat town cop stood outside wearing rain gear.

She rolled down the window. "Trouble, officer?"

"Naah. Drivers license and registration, please?" the cop said.

Kim leaned over and opened the glove compartment. She pulled out the registration and then pulled her license out of her purse.

The woman on the stretcher was arching her back and screaming at the top of her lungs. "Help me! There's nothing wrong with me!"

Kim hesitated.

"Ma'am?" the officer asked.

She handed him the paper and card. "Sorry. Is that woman all right?"

He took the documents. "Out of town crackhead. High as a kite and with kids in the car, no less." He shined his flashlight on the license. "Kim Lawrence. Where you headed tonight, Miss Lawrence?"

Kim stared at him. "Wytheville. The movies."

He smiled. "I thought all you seniors were going to Regina Kerns's house for the big party?"

"You know about the party?" Kim asked.

The woman was still screaming, and she didn't act high to Kim. She seemed terrified.

"Small town. Word gets around. Nasty night like this, you two might want to go to the party instead. Be better to stick closer to home."

"We weren't invited," Kim said.

The cop smiled and nodded. "And, who are you, son?"

"David Connors."

The paramedics loaded the woman and her kids into the ambulance. She was still screaming as they closed the doors.

The cop seemed to be turning something over in his mind. "Well, you two have a nice night - no drinking now."

Kim shook her head. "No, sir."

He waved them on, and Kim rolled up her window as she followed the ambulance. It made a U-turn and headed back toward town.

Kim shook her head and looked in the rear view. "That was…"

"…fucking weird," David said, completing her sentence.

Two more ambulances passed them heading toward the roadblock.

Gene cursed under his breath as he drove back toward town. They had almost caught him at the roadblock, but he had made a U-turn before he reached it.

He needed to ditch the Texas plates.

He shook his head. They were getting bold.

This wasn't the usual behavior. The family liked to get established and grow slowly. They had only been in the house a few days, and they were locking down the town?

It was Gene's fault. It had to be. He had hurt them badly in Minnesota. Olc was trying to grow back to full strength in a hurry.

This town was doomed, and Gene was trapped inside it unless he could find a safe passage and get away.

Pauly parked on the long driveway leading to Regina Kerns's house. Cars lined both sides of the narrow asphalt as well as the street in front.

Regina's father was a doctor in Wytheville, and the house was a mansion by Rural Retreat standards: an eight bedroom Tudor with a carefully manicured lawn.

He walked along the wet driveway.

Pauly could hear loud Techno music coming from the house. A crowd was gathered outside the door, and he pushed his way through.

Most of the junior and senior classes of Rural Retreat High School were there.

The dining room table had been moved into the living room, and Pauly determined Monday morning would bring two things: Regina would be the most popular girl in the history of the high school, and she would be grounded until she reached menopause.

The table was lined with hundreds of bottles of booze, from craft beer to Absinthe, and everything in between.

The windows rattled from the loud Techno that throbbed from ceiling height speakers.

Two senior linebackers stood on either side of the winding staircase in the middle of the foyer. No one was going upstairs, but, as he watched Regina appeared at the top of the stairs in a sapphire blue dress. She smiled down at him and flowed down the steps.

"You came!" she yelled over the music as she took his hand. The stoned look in her eyes from yesterday was gone.

"I wouldn't miss it," Pauly yelled.

She turned toward a pimply kid who was running the stereo. She made a slashing motion across her throat, and the music stopped.

Pimple face ran up to her and handed her a wireless microphone.

She smiled and held the microphone to her lips. "Hi, everybody!"

The whole house cheered.

"I hope everybody is enjoying the free booze my Dad left us!"

More cheering.

She lowered her eyes and whispered into the microphone. "Monday, I'm going to be sooooo fucked!"

They cheered again.

"But! A few ground rules for this party!"

They booed.

She stamped her foot, and they stopped. "On this floor, anything goes."

She ran part way up the steps. "But, there is a separate party going on upstairs, by invitation only! Don't try to go upstairs without being invited, or Leon and Bruce will rip off your arms and beat you to death with them!"

Leon and Bruce, the linebackers smiled and nodded.

"Also," she said as she ran back down the stairs. "There's a party in my Dad's study." She pointed to a door off the living room. "Invitation only! Other than that, no rules!"

Regina walked around the crowd. "Now, the first invitation to the upstairs party goes to... Betty!"

Betty was Regina's best friend, and Pauly held his ears as the girl shrieked and ran to the steps. Her boyfriend followed, but one of the linebackers stepped in front of him.

"Not you, Todd," Regina said. "Maybe later."

Betty put her hands on her hips. "Regina!"

"My party, my rules, bitch. Don't worry, you'll see him in a while."

Betty shook her head, blew her boyfriend a kiss, and went up the stairs.

Regina held the microphone toward pimple faced boy, then she snatched it back. "Oh! One other thing. Stay out of the basement. That's where I put the bodies!"

Everyone laughed.

She handed the microphone off and took Pauly's hand. "What do you think?"

The Techno started again.

"You know how to throw a party, cheerleader.," Pauly said.

She led him into the living room. "You are a special guest."

"Oh, am I?"

"Yes," Regina said. "You were singled out for special treatment." She led him toward the study door.

"Huh?"

"You get to go to the extra special party."

Pauly stopped in mid-step, and Regina jerked to a halt.

"Yeah, cheerleader, I've seen Carrie. This is the part where I get pig blood poured on my head, right?"

She stared at him. "Pig blood?"

"At the end of Carrie, you know, the bucket of pig blood?"

She shook her head and dragged him toward the study. "Why the fuck would I do that?"

She opened the door and pulled him through before closing the door behind them.

There was a fire in the fireplace.

The tall blonde from the Gas'N'Go was sitting on an overstuffed leather sofa. "Hello, Pauly."

The burger place was right beside the movie theater in Wytheville. The rain had stopped by the time Kim and David finished eating. They walked on the sidewalk to the theater.

David took a deep breath, and then he reached out and took Kim's hand.

She didn't pull away, didn't give him a snide comment, instead she laced her fingers in his.

He felt ten feet tall.

"Why did you go out with me?" David asked.

"Jesus. Do you ever stop?"

"No. I want to know."

She squeezed his hand. "Fourth grade."

"Fourth grade?"

She laughed. "I was in fourth grade. I was out on the playground at recess. I was on the swings. This little boy, a kindergartner, was playing with a Hot Wheels car on the sliding board. He was just setting it on the slide and letting it roll down. He was laughing."

Kim stopped by the movie posters. "These two fifth grade boys came up. And, they took his car. He started crying. Just stupid shit that kids do. They wouldn't give it back."

He stared into her eyes.

"And, I got off the swing and went over. I don't know what I was going to do. They were bigger than me," she said. "And, then out of nowhere comes this third grader. And, he tackles the biggest one, knocks him down, knocks the wind out of him. Then he turns and kicks the other one in the shin, brings him to his knees."

David looked away.

"He was smaller than both those bullies. But, he grabbed the Hot Wheels car and handed it to the little boy. And, he says, 'Run, kid. I got this.'"

"Only, he didn't have *this* at all," David said.

Kim shook her head. "I've never seen anybody get beat so bad. But, you just kept getting up. You just wouldn't quit."

"If the teachers hadn't come running," David laughed. "They might have killed me."

"I know. That's why I ran and got them."

David turned and looked at her. "That was you?"

She nodded and took his other hand. "And, I thought, as the teachers carried you away, that's the kind of guy I wanted: a good guy who just didn't know when to quit." She laughed and shook her head. "In my defense, I was hooked on Disney's Sleeping Beauty at the time, and when the prince is fighting the thorns, I kind of got a tingle."

David laughed. "I remember that movie."

"You have a thing for Sleeping Beauty?"

He laughed. "No, actually I had a thing for the evil sorceress."

She linked her arm in his as they walked into the theater. "Ooo, well played, David. Well played."

Regina left his side as soon as they went into the study. The blonde smiled at him. "You remember me, don't you? Miriam?"

"Of course. I just wasn't expecting to see you here," Pauly said.

"The party was her idea," Regina said. She walked up beside a thick woman standing beside the fireplace. She was wearing a leather minidress. "Got any?"

The woman in the minidress handed her a bottle of red liquid.

Pauly did a double take. The woman was the school secretary, Debbie something or other, but everybody called her Cat Lady Debbie.

Regina unscrewed a dropper from the top of the bottle and dripped a single red drop into each of her eyes.

Miriam patted the spot beside her on the couch. "Come on, I won't bite."

Pauly sat down and then gasped.

He hadn't seen the woman sitting across from them until he turned to sit down.

David's mother, Jane Connors was smiling at him. "Hello, Pauly."

"Miss Connors? Uh…"

"Jane's my date," Miriam said with a smile.

Jane groaned. "Are you ever going to let that go?"

"Couple of hundred years, maybe."

Miriam rubbed a lock of black hair out of Pauly's eyes. "Poor Pauly, you must be so confused."

Pauly laughed. "You think?"

"Maybe this will help," Miriam said. She kissed him, her tongue slipping between his lips.

She broke the kiss, and Pauly glanced over at Jane, his face red with embarrassment.

"Don't feel uncomfortable. Jane doesn't mind me kissing you, do you?"

Jane shook her head. "No. But, you could have lined one up for me."

Miriam smiled and rubbed Pauly's cheek. She looked at Jane. "Go pick one. Any one you like. Just remember, he needs to be practical, not just spur of the moment. We can afford to be choosy."

Jane stood up. "Regina, give me your list. I don't want to accidentally choose somebody for the second floor."

Regina looked at her with bloodshot eyes and handed her the paper list Debbie had printed the day before.

"What about you, Debbie. Want to go pick a friend?" Jane asked.

Debbie turned back to the fireplace. "I just want my cats back."

Jane rolled her eyes. "She's an excellent choice, Miriam."

Miriam was still staring into Pauly's eyes. "She just needs time. You'll see."

Jane walked out of the study.

Pauly watched her. She was David's mother, but she was different. Younger, somehow. It was like someone had taken twenty or twenty-five years off her age.

"Hey!" Miriam said. "Keep your eyes on me. I'm a very jealous woman, Pauly."

"No. No, it's just…"

"She's younger?" Miriam asked. She put her hand on the inside of Pauly's thigh and caressed her way up.

He jerked as if shocked. "Yeah."

"I like you, Pauly," Miriam whispered. "I think you like me too."

"Yes. I do like you."

Miriam raised her hand and snapped her fingers.

Regina handed her the bottle of red liquid.

Miriam removed the dropper. "Tilt your head back."

Pauly shook his head. "I don't do drugs."

"It's not a drug."

"It sure looks like a drug."

"It's vampire blood," Miriam said with a smile.

Pauly laughed. "Yeah, right."

"No, it is, Pauly. Real vampire blood. I'm going to put some in your eyes, and you're going to be mine forever," Miriam said as she massaged his upper thigh.

It was hard to focus on her words when her hand was working magic on him.

"Now, tilt your head back."

He leaned his head back against the warm leather. Fire shadows danced on the ceiling. He saw the dropper above his eye, felt her hand close on him. The drop clung to the end of the glass dropper for an instant, growing into a fat, translucent red orb. It fell in his eye.

His body went stiff as if an electric current passed through it. And, just as he recovered a second drop colored his other eye blood red.

Kim and David sat in the far back row at Kim's suggestion. They balanced a bucket of popcorn between them. Their hands kept touching as they dug in the bucket, and David was happy.

"They always have it so cold in here," Kim whispered.

"Yeah," David said.

She was looking at him.

"You want me to go get your jacket out of the car?" David asked.

Kim looked away. "No."

She sat quietly for a minute or so. She sighed out loud.

"What's wrong?" David asked.

"I'm cold."

"Well, what…"

"Jesus! Put your arm around me - are you slow or something?"

"No," David whispered. "It's just… that counts as fondling, and that's second base. I wasn't sure…"

She stared at him like he had a third eye. "Aiggh!" she grumbled. "The baseball talk. Which one gave you the baseball talk?"

"Your aunt…"

"Oh, I'm going to kill her." She poked him in the ribs. "Arm. Now."

He put his arm around her, and she leaned against him.

There was that feeling of being ten feet tall again. "Did I just go straight to second base?" he whispered.

She shook her head. "In about a minute. You have to tag first before that," she whispered.

She kissed him, and they both forgot about the movie, the popcorn, and metaphorical bases.

Pauly was lying on top of Miriam on the leather couch. She smiled up at him.

Whatever she had given him, the effects had subsided. He could remember nothing other than kissing Miriam after the drugs hit his eyes.

He looked to the side.

Regina was watching them with a bored expression from the seat across from them.

He leaned down and whispered in Miriam's ear. "Could we go someplace?"

"Where?" Miriam whispered.

"Away from cheerleaders and cat ladies?"

Miriam smiled. "You are shy, aren't you?"

"They're creeping me out."

Miriam looked at Regina.

The girl was looking at her nails.

"I see your point. To tell you the truth, I thought this would be appealing to a sixteen-year-old. Maybe I should ask Jane to come back in?" Miriam asked with a smile.

"Please don't. I'm going to need therapy as it is."

Miriam laughed. "You are full of surprises."

Pauly sat up, and Miriam turned to Regina. "Keep the party going. Jane is in charge. When it's time, bring the upstairs party downstairs."

Regina nodded. "I got it."

Miriam stood up, and Pauly took her hand.

She led him out into the living room.

Jane was sending people upstairs one at a time.

Miriam waved to her as they walked out into the cold.

A black town car roared to life as they exited the house. Pauly opened a rear door for her when she pointed to it. He sat down beside her and closed the door.

One teenager every five minutes came up the stairs. The hallway was dark, but the teens found their way to the party by following the sound of the music. The sound upstairs was louder, the bass fuller.

One by one, they entered the family room on the second floor. The room was dark, lit only by a single candle. Gray shapes writhed on the floor.

Each teen was grabbed from behind and lifted into the air. A cold wrist was pressed against their lips. Blood seeped into their mouths, and they each drank their fill.

David and Kim walked out of the theater with their arms around each other.

"What movie did we see?" Kim whispered.

"I'm not sure," David said. He kissed the top of her head.

"We should probably know in case somebody asks."

"On Monday, am I supposed to act like I don't know you?" David asked.

She leaned her head on his chest. "You better not. You better act like I'm the best thing since sliced bread."

"Definitely. So, this means we're dating?"

She nodded. "Until somebody better comes along."

"Oh, you're right. I guess I should kiss some other girls to keep my options open."

She punched him. "You keep those lips away from other girls. I like those lips. If we do break up, I want custody of the lips."

"And the tongue?"

She shook her head. "You had to make it weird, didn't you? I was being all sweet, and you had to make it weird." She ran a few steps ahead toward the car. "But, yeah, I want custody of the tongue, too."

He chased her to the car.

Miriam Tillford's room was cold. The wind howled outside, and Pauly could swear the candle flickered with each gust.

He lay naked in her bed, as she sat naked at her dresser.

Pauly traced the gentle curves of her hips and back with his eyes. "Come back to bed."

She turned in the small chair, her breasts jutting out. His breath caught in his chest.

"Was I your first?" she asked.

"Yes."

"Don't lie."

"No. I met a girl over the summer back in Brooklyn."

"Was she like me?"

"No. There's no one like you."

She stood up and walked to him.

"I think I love you," he said.

She smiled. "She didn't do the things I did for you, did she?"

He shook his head.

"She didn't tell you all the things to do to her, like I did, did she?"

"No."

She lay down beside him on her stomach.

He put his hand on her warm skin. He wanted her. He was ready for her again.

"I love you, Miriam."

She put a finger against his lips. "Pauly, I didn't know you would be like this. I looked at you, and I thought you were like a male version of me. I was wrong."

"I don't know what that means."

"Listen to me. Pauly Delveccio, go downstairs. Get in the town car. Edgar will take you back to the party. Don't go in."

"I'm not going anywhere."

"Listen to me. Get in your car and drive. Drive away from this place. Put it in your rear view mirror. Don't ever look back."

He rolled her onto her back and kissed her. He pressed her legs apart with his knee.

She shook her head. "You are damned. I'm trying to save you, can't you see that?"

He entered her, and she groaned. She wrapped her legs around him.

Some time later, she reached under the bed, found the bottle of blood, and drenched them both in it.

A little after midnight, Regina and Debbie left the study. Debbie went to the kitchen where she stood at the back door, while Regina joined Jane to guard the front.

Regina waved to pimply boy. He cut the music and ran to her with the microphone.

"It's time to really get this party started!" Regina said. "Let's bring the upstairs party downstairs!"

Everyone turned to the staircase. The two linebackers even turned to look. Something moved in the darkness at the top of the stairs.

Most people on the first floor were drunk. They stared incoherently at the people who descended the stairs. Some were their friends, but most were just gray shadows that took the stairs two at a time.

A girl screamed, and then the entire floor was screaming as a swarm of gray bodies poured down the steps. They leaped on the nearest screaming teenagers and ripped into them. Blood sprayed the floor.

One of the linebackers turned to run. Something grabbed him from behind, lifted him into the air and brought him down in a crash on the marble floor.

A girl ran toward Jane, and she slapped her - so hard that the girl's jaw dislocated and twisted sideways. The girl went down and was instantly pounced on by two of the gray shapes.

Regina was laughing, shoving the crowd backward as they tried to reach the doors.

Pimply boy started the music again as the vampires danced and people died.

The first floor was silent as Olc descended the stairs. Mae walked beside him in her Hoosier Hottie t-shirt.

Olc smiled at the bloody scene on the floor. Slurping noises came from the newly turned vampires as they drank from their victims.

Debbie stumbled out of the kitchen on her high heels. She looked at the dead and dying on the floor with indifference.

Jane smiled at Olc.

"Where is Miriam?" Olc asked.

Jane shook her head. "The boy. She took him to the house."

Olc frowned. "The bus. Get it. Time to go home."

Regina looked around in horror. "Who's going to clean up this mess?"

"Leave it. Lock the doors," Olc said. "You come. With us."

The roadblock was gone from Main Street as Kim and David drove home.

Something gray darted past them on the empty street, and Kim slammed on the brakes. "Did you see that?"

"All I saw was mist."

"No. It was a person. I think. They ran in front of the car."

David rubbed her red hair. "Maybe someone jogging?"

"Well, they're going to get themselves killed."

She drove on.

The ancients ran through the streets from house to house. They placed their hands on doors, felt with their minds, finding the parents who were up late worrying about their children out late at some senior party.

One by one, the parents went to bed, their worries whispered away by the soothing voices in their heads.

No, he isn't late. He can take care of himself.

Or, worse, *you have no child.*

In the space of an hour, one hundred fifty sixteen and seventeen-year-olds were erased from their parents' memory, soon to be forgotten by an entire town.

Miriam slept, warm in the boy's embrace. The sheets were stained with blood. He curled against her back. Any movement on her part brought him to life. He took her over and over through the night.

She opened her eyes to see Olc watching them.

He stared at her with his cold, black eyes.

She swallowed. "Be gentle with him. Make him cruel, but leave his love for me. Twist him, but leave some piece of his innocence. I beg you. If you've ever loved me, do this for me."

Olc shifted his gaze to the boy.

Pauly whined in his sleep.

He clung to her as Olc looked into his mind and made changes.

Sunday

Debbie knocked on her neighbor, Gwen's trailer door at 9:00 AM.

Gwen came to the door wearing a white t-shirt that had long ago faded to yellow. The woman was half asleep, but the vape machine was already attached to her hand.

Debbie waved the smoke away from her face. "I brought cocktails!"

Gwen was trying hard to focus on the plastic tray with two tumblers on it. Her eyes seemed to cross and uncross. "Bitch, what time is it?"

"I don't know, bitch. It's like nine or something," Debbie said. She was aware of the silly grin plastered on her face, but she just didn't care.

Gwen turned and looked over her shoulder. "I got a guy in here. I think he's a truck driver."

Debbie nodded. "That would explain the semi parked on the lawn."

"You're different," Gwen said as she sat down in the plastic lawn chair.

"My life has taken some odd turns of late." Debbie looked from the tumblers on the tray to Gwen and back again. "Aren't you thirsty?"

"Darlin', I know I may look like ten miles of bad road, but I don't get sloshed before noon."

"Oh, I made them special."

Gwen eyed her curiously. She shrugged and reached for a tumbler.

Debbie pulled the tray away. "Not that one! The other one."

Gwen stared at her. Then, she took the other tumbler and took a drink.

Debbie grabbed the first tumbler and set the tray on the porch railing.

"Well, what do you think?"

Gwen shrugged. "Not bad. A little fruity. Tastes like a Bloody Mary."

Debbie giggled. "Could be Mary. I don't know their names."

"What?"

"Drink up!"

Gwen drank the tumbler down and handed it to Debbie.

Debbie set both cups on the tray and clapped. "Yay!"

"I'm... going back to bed now," Gwen said.

"You should. It's better if you can lie down."

Gwen tried to get out of the chair. She fell back into it. "Whoa! That was strong."

"You're kind of a waste," Debbie said.

Gwen looked up slowly. "What did you say?"

"Your life. I mean, you're a whore living in a single wide in a trailer park."

Gwen shook her head and rubbed her eyes. "Bitch, you don't know me. You don't know anything about me."

Debbie laughed. "Oh, please. I know everything about you. You're very loud in bed, and I've never seen the same guy come out of your trailer twice. Other than the grocery store, the liquor store, and the truck stop up on I-77 where you pick up your men, you don't leave your trailer."

Gwen stood up, and Debbie shoved her back into her seat.

Gwen's expression changed from anger to fear.

Debbie frowned. "I can't have cats anymore. They're afraid of me. I figure dogs will hate me too. But, I've always had pets."

Gwen winced in pain and held her stomach. "The fuck did you give me?"

"My Dad, oh he was awful. Mama left, and he hated me. I mean really, really hated me. Never had a kind word to say."

"Debbie, did you poison me?"

"A child has to have love in their life. I had cats. They always loved me unconditionally - see, I understand all the psychology behind it. The cats were a substitute for my parents not loving me. I learned that at community college."

Gwen reached around with her hand and pounded on the trailer wall. "Help me! Wake up! She's poisoned me."

Something thudded on the floor.

"I have to have something that loves me unconditionally. I have to have a pet. I don't exist without something to love me," Debbie said as she waited in front of the trailer door.

"What the hell is going on out there?" a man's voice called from inside.

The door burst open.

The man was at least six and a half feet tall.

Debbie reached out and grabbed him by the throat.

She lifted him into the air as the man fought to hit her.

Debbie slammed his head into the door frame and tossed him back inside.

"Hope I didn't kill him. You can't drink from somebody who's dead. They have to be alive."

Gwen fell out of the lawn chair and tried to crawl away. Clumps of her hair fell on the deck. "Oh, God. What did you do to me?"

"Don't cry," Debbie said as she reached down and scooped Gwen up in her arms. "It's going to be okay. Your life is going to be better because I'm going to take care of you."

She carried Gwen into the apartment and put her to bed.

Then, she went to the shed behind her trailer and got her Dad's tools.

David lay in his bed on Sunday morning. Last night had been a good night.

He smiled as he opened his smartphone. He went to the text app and messaged Pauly.

Dude, you up?

He heard movement from his mother's room. He climbed out of bed and walked across the hall.

Jane Connors was packing a suitcase.

"Going somewhere?"

She didn't look up. "You're going to have to fend for yourself."

"Sure," David said. "Where are you going?"

"I'm moving in with some people. Out on Kinder Valley Road."

"You're what?"

She turned and faced him.

David took a step backward. His mother now looked like a twenty-year-old. "Mom? What happened?" He reached out to touch her face.

She slapped his hand.

"I'm moving out. You'll be fine here in the house by yourself."

"What are you talking about? I'm sixteen, Mom. I can't live by myself."

"Please, you've been taking care of yourself since your father died."

He shook his head. "You can't just… abandon me."

"It's always about you, isn't it? What about what I need? Sixteen years of my life, just gone. All to raise the son of a man who couldn't do anything right."

David gritted his teeth. "Don't say that."

She laughed. "It's true. He was a failure at everything he ever did. Christ, he couldn't even satisfy me. Do you know where I was the night he decided to end it all?"

"Don't you say that!" David screamed.

"What? That he killed himself. Oh, he killed himself alright. You know he did. Fucking coward. Left me alone to look after you."

She turned around and put more of her clothes in the suitcase. "I was in bed with his business partner when the state police called me."

He took a step forward, and his mother straightened up, her back to him.

"Are you going to slap me, David?" She asked. "Now, what would little Miss Redhead say to that?" She turned around and faced him. "Go ahead. Take your best shot."

David started to cry. "Mom, please…"

She struck him.

It took a moment for it to register in his mind. She pushed forward with both hands and hit him under the chest.

His feet left the floor, and he flew backward. He saw the door frame pass overhead. He saw the popcorn ceiling flash by, like video from something landing on the moon.

His shoulders hit the hardwood floor, and he slid all the way into his room.

She stood over him with the suitcase. Her eyes were cold, her lips emotionless. "Pathetic. If you decide to try suicide for attention, don't do it like your father. Don't take so many pills that they can't revive you. Better yet, do. That Lawrence girl deserves better than you."

She walked away.

He lay motionless on the floor looking up at the ceiling.

He heard her descend the steps, heard the garage door open.

David heard her car as she drove away.

He just lay there and looked up at the ceiling.

Debbie finished bolting steel grating over the windows in Gwen's trailer. Finally, she put a padlock on the outside of her trailer door.

She didn't want Gwen wandering off - worse yet, she couldn't have Gwen's food getting away.

Debbie stepped inside.

The man on Gwen's floor had given her problems when she came in the last time, so she had broken his knees and elbows and bent them backward, and then tied him with clothesline.

He moaned behind the duct tape gag and writhed on the floor.

Gwen was lying on her bed. Her hair was gone, and her skin was turning gray. Her eyes were liquid pools of black.

Debbie sat down beside her and stroked her forehead.

Gwen whined.

"It's okay. You're almost done. A couple more hours, and you'll be ready to take on the world - or, at least that twisted man pretzel on your floor." Debbie giggled.

Gwen nuzzled her hand and licked it.

Debbie laughed with delight.

Kim stared at her phone. It was after noon, and David had not called or texted. He had not messaged her on Facebook. He had gone radio silent.

She felt like a fool, lying on her bed upset that he hadn't called.

It was silly, and it made her feel weak.

And, she didn't like that feeling.

She tossed the phone on the comforter beside her.

Had she misread him? Was he not the nice guy she had set him up in her mind to be?

She grabbed the phone and dialed.

It rang three times, and she was convinced it would go to voicemail. She had a speech in mind for the recording, full of words like "immature" and "hurtful."

He answered in a hollow-sounding voice. "Hello?"

"David?"

"Hi."

"Hi? That's what you have to say? You don't call me all day…"

"I'm sorry."

Something in his tone made her stop. There was pain in his voice. "Are you okay?"

"Yeah, yeah, I'm okay. I had a fight with my mom."

"What kind of fight?"

"A bad one. She left."

"Left?" Kim said. "Moms don't leave..." *Dad's do*, she thought.

"Yeah, well, mine did."

She rolled onto her back. "It'll be okay. She'll come back."

"Maybe."

"David, don't be silly. She'll come back. She's your mom, she can't just leave you."

"I'm okay," David said. "Really."

"Want to come over? My aunt is frying chicken. She's a really good cook."

He paused. "No. No, she might come back. I need to be here. I'll call you later, okay?"

"You promise?"

"Yeah, I promise."

"Okay."

David hung up the phone and stared at his reflection in the bathroom mirror. Two bruises the size and shape of his mom's hands covered his lower ribs.

Gene sat in somebody's house and thanked whatever gods were watching over him that the electricity and water were working. The house was at the end of a long driveway with a 'For Sale' sign on the road. He had pulled his truck into the woods behind the abandoned house and broken in through the back door.

He had then set about repairing the minor damage he had inflicted to the door. Gene was not a criminal. He left two-hundred dollars on the kitchen counter. This was payment for squatting in the house.

The house had been set up to show, but there was a thick layer of dust on the furniture. It had been on the market for a long time, and, with any luck, no one would notice him.

He cleaned his guns in silence with the curtains drawn.

When he came to Rural Retreat, he counted only Olc and his family as his enemy. Now, he could add the local police, fire department - all the first responders. Most likely the local government as well.

Olc was an infection, and the infection was rampant.

He had no doubt the police had his description. They would be looking for him.

Monday

Kim Lawrence walked into first period English to find the room empty.

Her teacher, Mr. Gatlin stared at her with a bemused smile.

"What's wrong, Miss Lawrence? Didn't you get the memo on 'Senior Skip Day'?" he asked.

"There was a memo?" Kim asked.

He shook his head. "No. But, as you can see, you're the only one here."

"I thought 'Senior Skip Day' was in the spring?" Kim asked.

"Evidently, your class is starting a new tradition - and, they neglected to tell you. You on somebody's hate list?"

Kim shrugged. "Guess so." Kim bit her lower lip. "Guess it's too late to call in sick?"

He smiled. "Open your book to Hamlet Act I Scene I - you'll be reading aloud to a class of one today, Miss Lawrence."

Kim walked into the hall when the bell rang. She had a new respect for Shakespeare and actors in general.

David was waiting for her in the hall.

She took his hand. "I am officially the most popular senior at Rural Retreat High School. Because I am the only senior at Rural Retreat High School. Which, oddly enough, makes me the least popular senior in Rural Retreat itself. I can't believe nobody told me."

"Don't feel bad. Half the junior class is AWOL as well." David looked at his phone. "Weird part is: Pauly isn't answering texts, and he isn't posting on Facebook which is impossible because he is addicted to Facebook."

Kim looked around. "You know... the people that aren't here? They're the people who were invited to the party."

"Holy shit, do you think they're all that hung over?"

Kim shrugged. "Well, if they are, we missed a hell of a party."

David stared at her. "You complaining?"

She put her arms around his neck and smiled up at him. "No way."

Mr. Gatlin walked by. "Not at school. I better see air between the two of you.

Kim rolled her eyes and stepped away from David.

"Sorry, Mr. Gatlin," David said.

"Suck up," Kim whispered.

"It's called being polite. You should try it sometime," David whispered.

"I'm going to be a bad influence on you."

"Promises, promises," David said. He looked both ways and pulled her into his arms. He kissed her.

She hugged him tight, and he winced.

"What's wrong?" she asked as she let go of him.

He gritted his teeth and shook his head. "Just a little sore."

She touched his ribs, and he drew in a breath. "What happened to you?"

"Nothing, I fell," he said. He took her hand and opened his phone with the other. It dialed. Kim could hear the voicemail beep. "Pauly, you piece of shit. You don't call me by noon, I swear to God I'm going to call your mom. You can't go around scaring people like this, Shithead."

Just before lunch, David dialed Pauly's mother. He knew if Pauly was off doing something stupid, this would get him in trouble, but in all the years he had known Pauly, he had never known him to drop off the face of the earth like this.

"Delveccio residence," Mrs. Delveccio said.

"Hi, Mrs. Delveccio. It's David Connors."

"Oh, hi, David."

"Is Pauly there?"

"No."

"Do you know where he is? I've been trying to reach him since yesterday morning."

"No. But, he's fine, David."

"You don't know where he is?"

"No. But, he's fine."

"Do you know when he's coming back."

"No. But, he's fine."

Always the same words each time. David thought for a second. "Did he come back after the party Saturday night?"

"No. But, he's fine."

David felt ice cold. "You haven't seen him since Saturday. You don't know where he is."

"No. But, he's fine."

David paced back and forth between the high school main building and the gym. "Mrs. Delveccio knows where he is all the time. If we're gone for an hour longer than we said we would be, she's calling."

Kim sat on the high school steps. "Maybe she's trying some new parenting thing. Giving him space. Christ, I wish my mom would do that."

David shook his head. "No. Believe me. You do not."

"She'll come back."

David sighed. "She's not the problem now. My best friend has disappeared off the face of the earth."

"Along with the entire senior class and most of the juniors," Kim added.

He sat down beside her on the steps. "Babe, I am really starting to get freaked out."

"One: don't ever call me babe. Two: there's an explanation for all this."

He laughed. "No babe?"

"Definitely not," Kim said. "We'll come up with terms of endearment at some point…"

"Like snuggle bug or sugar dumpling?" he asked with a smile.

"Do you want to die a virgin?" she asked.

He looked at her wide-eyed. "Did you just go there? Home run?"

"No baseball talk or you will never have sex." There was a dare in her eyes.

"Are we at that point? I didn't even know it was on the table."

"God, no. But, if you ever want to get to that point, no cutesy-pie names."

He smiled and nodded. "Fair enough, Miss Lawrence."

She stood up and took his hand. "Now, let's see if maybe the principal's office knows anything."

Debbie Kincaid looked up from her filing as the two teenagers walked into the office.

The boy waved to her. "Hi, Miss Kincaid. Is Principal Perkins in?"

She looked at the closed door to the principal's office. "He's in conference. What do you kids need?"

The girl, Debbie thought her name was Kim, said, "There are a lot of juniors and seniors missing today…"

Debbie shook her head. "Oh, that. Some kind of unofficial ditch day. They'll probably be back tomorrow." She turned her head and smiled at them. "What are you two doing here today? Didn't you get the memo?"

The boy - she remembered him, he was Jane's son. He was always polite and well mannered. David, that was his name.

David spoke up. "Miss Kincaid, Pauly Delveccio has been missing since Saturday night. He went to a party and never came back…"

Debbie nodded. "That Kerns girl's party. I heard about that. Got wild or so I'm told."

"Wild?" Kim asked.

Debbie looked conspiratorial. "Booze and drugs. And, I hear there was a lot of S-E-X going on."

"What should we do?" David asked.

"About what, sweetie?"

"About Pauly. Should we call the cops?"

"Did you try his parents?"

"Yeah."

Debbie looked from Kim to David. "And… what did they say?"

"His mom said… she said he was fine."

"Well, there you go," Debbie said.

"But, Miss Kincaid," David said. "She doesn't know where he is, and it's like she doesn't care."

Debbie shook her head. "Honey, I'm sorry, but there's just nothing I can do."

"For every action, there is an equal and opposite reaction - that's Newton's Third Law," David's Physics teacher said.

David wasn't listening. He was staring out the window, trying to come to terms with the events of the last three days. He now had a girlfriend, and she had been his heart's desire from elementary school on.

But, his mother had walked out. He didn't know if she was coming back. Worse, he wasn't sure he wanted her to come back after she had tossed him twelve feet through the air - he had measured it with a tape measure.

He had been knocked off his feet and thrown twelve feet across the house by a woman five inches shorter than him who weighed maybe a buck thirty.

He didn't know what to make of it. He also didn't know what would happen next. What if she didn't pay the mortgage? Would he be put out of the house? Without money, how would he eat? Would social services come and move him into foster care?

He wanted to ask someone all these questions, but he couldn't because it would force the issue.

What's that, David? Your mom moved out? Well, we have to get you into foster care. You'll be finishing out high school fifty miles away. Say goodbye to Kim. Oh, and forget about college, 'cause you are flat busted broke.

Maybe she would still pay the bills. He could just pretend she was there if anyone asked. Once he was eighteen, it wouldn't matter.

But, it was a long way to eighteen.

And, now, Pauly. Where the hell was he? Where the hell was everybody?

"David Connors to the principal's office," Miss Kincaid's voice called over the intercom.

David walked through the empty hall. This could be news about Pauly, or it could be news about his mother. He paused outside Kim's classroom.

She was sitting in the front row, the only student in Calculus. He tried to get her attention, but she was head down in the book.

He kept walking.

Debbie Kincaid was waiting on him outside the office. "David, I haven't been quite honest with you."

"What do you mean?"

She took his hand. "Well, I know where Pauly Delveccio is, and I'll take you to him, but you got to promise not to tell."

David stared at her. "Yeah, fine. I won't tell anybody."

"Pinky swear," she said. She held out her little finger.

The woman had always seemed weird, but now she seemed like a nut case. "Yeah. Okay." He hooked his little finger into hers.

"There!" she said with a smile. She took his hand and pulled him through the hallway.

He held back. "Wait, where are you taking me?"

"To Pauly, of course."

Debbie drove through misty rain as David stared out the window. They were driving into the poor side of town with its trailer parks and rundown houses.

"After the party Saturday night," Debbie said. "David went home with this tall blonde woman - I think her name is Miriam."

"How do you know this?" David asked.

"Oh, I hear things. People talk to me all the time. They confide in me. I think it's because I got a kind face," Debbie said with a smile. "Anyway, when he was at the house on Kinder Valley Road…"

"Did you say Kinder Valley Road?" That was where David's mother said she was going Sunday morning.

"Yes, do you know the house? It's really grand."

"But, we're not going toward Kinder Valley Road," David said.

"No. No, that's because he didn't stay there. He met this other girl - her name is Gwen. She lives in the house beside me. He's with her now."

"Oh. Okay. So you live out here?"

Debbie brightened. "Oh, yes. I have a cute little trailer. I used to have cats…" She looked down at the steering wheel. "Only, now I don't."

David gave her a weak smile. "I like cats."

She grinned from ear to ear.

"So, he's with this Gwen?"

"Yeah, he's fucking her. God knows it's all the woman does."

David just stared at her.

She glanced over at him. "Oh, I cursed didn't I? I don't know what has gotten into me over the last few days. There was somebody in my head, but it's all me now, so I don't know why I'm still talking like a sailor."

David didn't say anything.

"I don't... I don't talk like that, David. Not normally. I don't even do *that*, you know that *word*? I tried it once, and it hurt, and yeah I know first time always hurts, but... you don't hurt girls, do you, David?"

He shook his head. "I don't think it's supposed to hurt."

"Really?" She looked at him as if he had just explained particle physics.

"Are we almost there?"

She cut the wheel and pulled onto a white gravel drive leading to a small trailer park. "Better than that, we are here."

She pulled up in front of two trailers sitting side by side. One had flowers planted all around.

The other had steel grates on the windows and a padlock on the front door.

She hopped out of the car, and David followed her toward the one with metal grates. They stepped onto a rickety, wooden trailer porch with an algae stained plastic lawn chair.

Debbie smiled. "She's not much of a housekeeper." She unlocked the padlock.

"Wait, you have a key to the padlock?"

"Oh, yeah, Gwen and I are good friends. We have keys to each other's houses."

"But," David said as he took a step back. "Miss Kincaid, if the padlock is on the outside and it was locked, how could your friend Gwen get out? I mean, you said she's in there with Pauly, right?"

Debbie stared at the padlock in her hand. "Oh... you're right. Um, there's another door on the other side."

David pulled his cell phone out of his jacket pocket. "Miss Kincaid. Do you have Pauly and this Gwen woman locked inside the trailer?" He dialed the phone.

Debbie sighed. "Stupid. Stupid. Stupid... of course. The padlock. That would never... I'm such an idiot. I used to be smarter than this."

She moved fast, faster than David was prepared for. She snatched the cell phone out of his hand and clamped her other hand around his neck.

He swung at her, but she lifted him into the air with the one hand, and he only hit thin air.

"I'm really very sorry, David. I never wanted to hurt you. You were always kind to me. You never said mean things to me." She walked toward the door. She laid his cell phone on the porch railing while still holding him a foot in the air.

An overpowering stench came out of the trailer as she opened the door with her free hand, but it barely registered with him.

Debbie Kincaid was squeezing with her right hand, cutting off his breath and the blood flow to his brain.

She dropped him on the floor of the trailer and slammed the door shut.

David gasped for breath on the dirty trailer floor. He had landed with his back against the bathroom door. Mute sunlight drizzled through the small window in the front door.

He took a breath and gagged.

The smell in the trailer was overpowering. Body odor and old sweat, and, underneath it all the smell of something dead. Meat gone bad.

The door clicked as Debbie put the padlock in place outside.

David jumped to his feet and pounded on the door. "Let me out!"

Debbie's voice came from the other side of the door. "Don't fight. It's better if you don't fight. Just lie down and close your eyes."

David stepped back from the door. He looked around the trailer. He was standing in a narrow hallway. The bathroom was behind him. On his right, there were two doors - one on the same side as the bathroom door, one at the end of the hall.

To his left, he saw an empty, filthy kitchen and, beyond that, a bare living room.

Something moved behind the door to the room at the end of the hall.

"What's in here with me?" David asked. He started backing toward the kitchen.

"I told you," Debbie said from outside. "My neighbor, Gwen."

There was a loud thump as something fell on the floor in the room at the end of the hall.

"I lied about Pauly. I'm sorry. He's still in the house on Kinder Valley Road."

"Why are you doing this?"

"You were asking so many questions, and, well, Gwen has to eat. She's my responsibility. You have to take care of your pets."

The doorknob on the door at the end of the hall began to turn.

David was hyperventilating in the stench laden air. "Miss Kincaid, Debbie, please. You have to let me out. I won't tell anybody what you did. Just let me out."

"Are you going to cry? Don't cry, David. It won't hurt that bad. Just don't fight. Keep your eyes closed."

David turned away from the door, away from the turning doorknob. He didn't know why he was so frightened of the door at the end of the hall, but he was. He was terrified.

He jerked the kitchen drawers open. They were empty. All the knives, cutlery, even the pots and pans had been removed from the drawers and cabinets.

He dropped to his knees and opened the cabinet under the sink.

If there had ever been cleaning supplies in the cabinet, they were gone now, leaving only roach and rodent droppings.

The door to the room at the end of the hall creaked open.

He couldn't see it from the kitchen, but he could hear the door.

Something was breathing heavy in the hallway.

He started to stand when he saw a piece of wood sticking out under the bottom of the cabinet.

A wooden spoon, about a foot long.

You've got to be kidding me, David thought.

He snatched up the wooden spoon and backed toward the living room.

The hallway was dark.

The carpet squished under his feet.

The floor was wet, and it reeked of what could only be urine.

He looked down to his right.

The man's dead eyes stared up at him. He was lying on his back, his arms and legs bent and tied with cord. White bone gleamed where someone or something had broken his knees and elbows.

His throat was a mangled mess, and most of it was missing. He could see the opening of the windpipe, the white bones of the man's neck.

David swallowed hard.

He had his back against the living room wall.

He looked around. There was nothing in the room he could imagine would help him.

David took hold of the end of the spoon handle and broke it. It broke jagged leaving him a sharp, narrow shiv at the end of the old spoon.

He held the spoon part in his right hand, the point toward the dark hallway.

He heard footsteps on the porch and watched through the grate as Debbie Kincaid walked away.

"Screw you, bitch!" he yelled. He felt like an idiot. The words came out thin and reedy, his voice cracking. He wanted to sound defiant. He wanted to sound brave.

Instead, he sounded pathetic: a sixteen-year-old kid with a broken wooden spoon facing... what? What was in the hallway?

Something capable of snapping a grown man's joints and ripping out his throat.

There was a light switch on the wall beside him. He flipped it but wasn't surprised when nothing happened.

Something was standing in the hall.

It looked like a person. It was a gray shape, thin, and not very tall. It was motionless. Just staring at him.

Its outline was vague as if it were wrapped in fog.

He gripped the spoon tighter as it stepped forward.

"Stay back!" David said.

The shape paused. It flickered like someone was projecting an image on a screen.

David felt a pain behind his eyes. He blinked.

His mother was standing in front of him. She was the shape in the hall. Jane Connors was wearing the same clothes she had been wearing on Sunday when she knocked him across the house.

"Mom?" David asked.

She smiled. She took a step toward him, and, in that instant, the image of his mother flickered, like someone passing their hand in front of a projector.

The flicker lasted only an instant.

But, David saw the thing clearly in that brief snapshot.

The woman's gray skin looked loose on her body, and it had an oily sheen. The lips were thin, but the teeth behind them were long and sharp. She was nude and hairless. Her tiny breasts sagged on her anemic chest.

Her eyes were ink-black pits.

"Stay back!" David yelled again. He held the spoon tight.

Pain behind his eyes again.

The woman's image flickered again.

Pauly was standing in front of him. The smile on his face the same as his mother's.

"You're not Pauly. You're not my Mom. Get out of my head," David growled.

Pain once more.

And, now the thing was Kim, long red hair cascading down her bare shoulders, framing her full breasts.

The smile was the same.

David shook his head. "You're not her!"

The illusion evaporated.

The gray skinned hag stood in front of him. She snarled.

She leaped from across the room, and David brought his right hand up and under.

He drove the jagged wooden spoon into her abdomen, felt it rip open like a blister.

Cold liquid flooded over his hand.

She slammed him against the cheap paneling, and he slid sideways and down, landing on top of the dead man.

She drove her face down toward his neck, but he blocked her with his left arm.

Her teeth broke the skin of his forearm, but he didn't feel it.

He was stabbing her in the stomach with the broken spoon, plunging it at random, trying to hit something vital if there was anything vital to hit.

His right arm felt strong, powerful. He felt rage build inside him, and he drove the spoon deep.

He pulled it free, stuck his hand into the air, and brought the sharp end of the spoon down on her back.

She threw her head back, releasing his arm from her bite. She hissed and grabbed behind her trying to reach the spoon that was skewering her lungs, her heart.

David yanked it out.

He threw her on her back on the urine soaked carpet.

David straddled her waist and brought the spoon down over and over, destroying her chest with a hundred punctures.

Kim looked at her cell phone at the kitchen table.

"No texting at the table," Anne said as she put mashed potatoes down beside her.

"I'm not."

Anne stroked her hair. "Put it away, honey."

"Mom. He left school early. He hasn't called." Kim said.

Laura stirred the stew on the stove. "Maybe he finally caught up with that boy Pauly?"

"But, he would have told me. He wouldn't just leave me alone at school like that. It was so creepy there today."

Anne nodded. "His mom didn't show up for work today either. Left a sticky note on my computer that said she was running errands."

"She moved out," Kim said as she stared at the mashed potatoes.

"What?" Anne asked.

"They had a fight. His mom left. He hasn't seen her since yesterday morning."

Laura and Anne looked at each other.

Anne shook her head. "That's not like her."

"Yeah, well, he's freaking out. I'm starting to freak out a little myself."

Tia walked to her Mom. She had her head down. She handed Anne a piece of paper.

Anne took it. "What's this, sweetie."

"Permission slip. Miss Henson said I had to give it to you to sign."

Anne read it. "A field trip on Wednesday?"

Tia nodded. Her eyes were dark as if she had been crying.

"It doesn't say where you're going," Anne said. She knelt down beside her.

Tia shook her head. "It's a history thing, Miss Henson said."

Anne smiled. "You like history, don't you?"

Tia nodded.

"Don't you want to go?"

Tia shook her head.

"Why not?"

Tia looked up. "Grandma said not to go."

Anne smiled at her. "Grandma Lawrence called you? When?"

Tia shook her head. "Not Grandma Lawrence."

Anne's smile faded. "Honey, that's not..."

"It was your mommy, Mommy. She said not to go."

Laura looked down at them wide eyed.

"When, honey?" Anne asked.

"Last night. While I was sleeping. She was there, and she told me not to go. And, that girl Addie, the one the monsters ate, she was there too. And, she told me..." She broke into tears and threw her arms around her mother.

Anne held her tight. "What, baby, what did she tell you?"

"Hide," Tia whispered.

David sat in the kitchen and stared into the living room. The trailer was dark. There was a street light outside, and the light from it shown through the grate on the living room window.

The dead man's eyes no longer stared straight up. His neck was now canted more severely by the struggle that took place on top of him.

The gray woman lay motionless on the wet carpet. David left the spoon buried in her heart, and it stuck up out of her. It was almost comical.

He was shaking.

He had washed the blood from his body, especially his hand. His body tingled where it touched him. He felt strong.

David had tried all the windows and the door.

Debbie had done an expert job of turning the trailer into a cage.

He was trapped.

He desperately wanted his weapon back, but he didn't dare remove the wooden stake from the gray woman's heart.

In the movies, vampires sometimes came back if you pulled out the stake.

He put the thought out of his mind. It was insane.

There was no such thing as vampires.

And, yet.

The gray woman was empirical evidence to the contrary.

He looked at the puncture wounds on his forearm.

David had cleaned them with water from the tap as best he could. There was no soap.

The furniture was gone.

The bathroom toilet was missing.

The two beds had no frames, just bare, filthy mattresses on the stained floor.

Anything that could have been used as a weapon had been painstakingly removed.

Everything except his spoon.

Debbie had even removed the dead man's belt.

He still had his own belt, but what good was that? Debbie had picked him up with one hand and tossed him around like a rag doll. He doubted a firm slap with a leather belt was going to impress her.

He stared at the wounds on his arm again. Was he going to turn into one of them? Was that how it worked?

He could see lights from Debbie's trailer through the grates.

She was there.

Was she waiting for Gwen to finish eating? What would she do then?

What would Debbie do when she found her beloved pet with a wooden spoon stabbed through her heart?

Debbie would kill him. She would grab him in that vice-like grip and squeeze his neck until his head popped off.

He needed a plan.

"I don't want any more talk about missing people around Tia," Anne said. It had taken her an hour to get Tia to bed. "She's terrified."

"I'm terrified," Kim said as she stared at her cell phone.

Anne, Kim, and Laura were sitting in the living room. They were waiting on the eleven o'clock news to come on TV, just in case there was any word about missing people in Rural Retreat.

"Should we call the police?" Kim asked.

Laura shook her head. "What are we going to tell them, Kimmy? That your boyfriend hasn't called you? They won't take it seriously until he's been gone twenty-four hours."

Kim wasn't listening. She was looking at the television. "Turn that up."

"...authorities are searching for Monica Deskins of Emory, Virginia, who disappeared on I-81 sometime on Saturday. She was traveling with her two small children en route to Baltimore, Maryland. They were last seen driving a red Chrysler minivan..." The image on the screen was of a smiling woman with brown hair.

"Shit," Kim whispered.

"What's wrong?" Anne asked.

Kim pointed at the screen. "Sunday night. They took her away in an ambulance. Out at the end of Main Street just before I-81."

"Oh, Kimmy, are you sure?" Anne asked.

"There was a police roadblock, and they took her away on a stretcher. She was strapped down and screaming."

Anne stared at her. She bit her lower lip. "Okay, that's it. I'm calling the police."

She picked up the phone and dialed 911. "Can you connect me with the Rural Retreat Police Department?" She put the call on speakerphone.

There was a pause.

"Rural Retreat Police," a woman's voice said.

"Hi, my name is Anne Lawrence. The woman and children that are missing? My daughter Kim saw them in Rural Retreat Saturday evening."

"Where was this?"

"A roadblock at the end of Main Street just before the interstate. It was about 6:30. She says the woman was taken away by an ambulance..."

"Yes, Ma'am, we're aware."

Kim and Anne looked at each other.

"You are? But, they didn't say anything about that on the news," Anne said.

"They don't have all the information."

"Oh... Ok. Are Miss Deskins and her family alright?"

"It's an ongoing investigation, Ma'am. I really can't comment."

"I see. Should my daughter come in and give a statement?"

There was a pause on the line.

"No, that won't be necessary. But, thank you for calling."

The line went dead.

Anne stared at the phone in her hand.

"Okay, that was fucking weird," Laura said. Then she sighed and pinched her own arm.

Tuesday

David fell asleep twice during the night. Both times he jerked awake, convinced that either the dead man or the woman with the spoon in her chest was crawling toward him.

He awoke gasping for air.

The bodies had not moved.

Dawn came, and the street light went out, which made the trailer darker for a few minutes.

He stared at the bodies in the dark. Shadows played with his mind.

He could have sworn her eye moved, but it was only reflected light from the rising sun.

Would she burst into flame when sunlight finally reached full force through the grate?

A few minutes later, he had his answer. The sun illuminated her gray face. There were no flames, no smoke of charring flesh like he had seen in hundreds of horror movies.

There was only an anemic gray woman's face lit by the sun.

Lights came on in Debbie Kincaid's trailer.

David ran to the front door. He opened the door to the bathroom and backed inside.

He took a stance like a football player, crouched on the yellow stained linoleum, facing the back door.

He had one shot, one possibility of escape.

"Gwen? It's Mommy. Wakey, wakey, eggs and bakey," Debbie said from the other side of the door.

David was filled with an overwhelming rage at the sound of her voice. For the first time in his life, he wanted to kill someone. *I got your eggs and bakey right here, bitch*, David thought.

The padlock clinked as Debbie removed it.

The doorknob turned.

The door opened a half inch.

And, David launched himself forward.

He threw his shoulder against the opening door.

David felt a weight behind the door and then it was gone.

The door flew open wide as Cat Lady Debbie flew backward.

She struck the porch railing, and it broke outward.

She screamed as she landed on her back in the gravel driveway.

David was out the door.

He wanted to jump on top of her, beat her to death.

He didn't.

David ran down the gravel driveway.

Debbie continued to scream.

Looking behind him, he could see why: she was lying on top of the ruined railing.

Long rusted nails protruded from her legs.

He slowed down.

She was grabbing at the redwood stained boards. "You! You cocksucker!" She yanked a board free from her bleeding leg and threw it at him.

The missile sailed past his face and traveled another fifty yards before sticking in the dirt.

David ran.

"What did you do?" he heard her scream behind him. Her voice was growing more distant. "What did you do?"

He reached the end of the driveway when he heard her scream. "Gwen!"

"Why don't you just stay home today?" Anne asked.

Kim shook her head as she gathered her books from her bed. "I can't. He might come to school. I need to be there."

"I'm letting Tia stay home."

Kim looked up at her mother. "I think that's a good idea."

She put her hands on Kim's shoulders and looked up into her eyes. "My giant baby."

Kim laughed. "I can't help you're short."

"I'm not short. You're tall." She smiled a weak smile. "You keep your phone on you all day. You call, and I'll come running."

"My mom the cavalry," Kim said, returning the smile.

"Damn right. I mean it. Anything... weird happens, you call."

"What are you looking for in Mommy's closet?" Tia asked a few minutes after her Mom and Kim left.

Laura looked over her shoulder. "Thought you were watching cartoons."

"Cable's out."

"Well, that sucks," Laura said as she moved pillows and boxes on the top shelf of the walk-in closet. "Did you ever see an old shoe box up here?"

"A green one?"

"That's the one."

"I wasn't supposed to touch it because Grandpa's gun was in it."

Laura looked at her. "That's right. Never, ever touch a gun. Where is the box now?"

"Mommy took it to the police and gave it to them."

"Shit," Laura said as she put her hands on her hips.

Tia walked over and pinched the skin at the top of her left hip.

"Ow. Well done, Monkey Face."

"You sure all this pinching is worth it? You're gonna be black and blue."

"Change only comes through pain, babe." Laura pulled her against her hip and hugged her as they left the room.

"You want the gun to protect us from the bad people, don't you?"

Laura sighed. She leaned over and kissed her brown hair. "I just like to be prepared."

"Grandma said you're a protector. Like a knight."

"You talk to Grandma a lot?"

Tia nodded.

"Yeah, that's me. Una Caballera."

"What?"

Laura smiled as they walked down the hall toward the kitchen. "That's a word somebody called me recently. It's Spanish. It means 'knight.' Now, where do you suppose Mommy keeps all her cleaning supplies?"

The little girl frowned. "Under the kitchen sink and in the laundry room, of course."

"Let's go find out."

"Why?"

"Because Aunt Laura is not only 'una caballera' - she's one dangerous bitch when she wants to be."

Tia pinched her.

David didn't stop running until he made it to his house. He had no idea how far it had been, but he felt like he had run at least five miles.

A million thoughts were going through his head.

He needed to go to the police.

But, what would he say? Debbie Kincaid had locked him in a trailer with a vampire, and he had killed it?

He had to think.

He went to his room and peeled off the blood stained clothes. He grabbed fresh clothes out of his drawer.

He needed a shower, but it would have to wait.

David put on his clothes and reached for the phone.

A car pulled into the drive.

David put the phone down and stepped to the window. He moved the shade just a little.

There was a Rural Retreat Police cruiser in his driveway.

Thank God, he thought.

A town cop got out of the driver's side.

Debbie Kincaid got out of the back.

He shrank back from the window. *What the hell?*

The doorbell rang.

Why was Debbie with him?

He looked around the room.

Someone knocked on the outside door. "Hello? Anybody home?"

David grabbed the blood stained clothes and dragged them with him as he crawled under his bed.

"There's nobody here," a man's voice said.

"He has to be somewhere," Debbie said. "Kick it open."

David heard a thud and the sound of wood splintering.

"David?" Debbie called from downstairs. "Are you here? I'm not mad anymore. I just want to talk to you."

He fought to control his breathing.

"David, this was all a big mistake."

"He's not down here," the cop whispered.

David heard the steps creaking.

"I know you're confused," Debbie said. She sounded closer. "I want to explain everything to you."

He heard the door to his mother's room swing open, heard the sound of coat hangers moving in her closet.

Footsteps in the hall.

From his vantage point he saw his bedroom door open.

He could see the cop's black shoes and Debbie's flats in the door.

The cop walked in.

"David, are you here?" Debbie asked.

He heard his closet door open.

"He's not here."

Debbie sighed.

David almost cried out when he heard a heavy thud on the door frame.

Debbie must have punched it.

"You need to find that little shit. He killed my Gwen," Debbie hissed through gritted teeth.

"You need to call Miriam," the cop said.

"We need to find him first."

"The others can track him easier…"

"Just do what you're told. Or, do you want me to have Mr. Olc talk to you?" Debbie asked.

"No! No. I'll find him."

He watched their feet as they walked away. He heard them on the steps.

The police cruiser started and pulled away.

Still, David didn't move for ten minutes.

When Kim arrived in first period English, the room was empty. Not only were the students gone, but Mr. Gatlin was also a no-show. She sat in the room and stared at the clock. She was gathering her books to leave when the door opened.

Pauly Delveccio was smiling at her. "Hi, Red."

"Pauly!? What the hell? Where have you been? David has been worried sick."

He leaned against the door frame and stared at her.

His eyes seemed wrong.

She crossed her arms over her chest. Something in his stare made her feel uncomfortable.

"Party got wild. Took me a few days to get over it."

"David called your mom, she didn't know where you were either."

Pauly laughed and shook his head. "Yeah. I'm going to get back at him for that. Calling a guy's mom on him is a definite violation of Bro Code."

"He was just worried about you." She gathered her books in her backpack.

"Where is our boy David, anyway?"

"You haven't seen him either?" Kim asked.

"I just started looking for him."

Kim walked up to him, holding the backpack in her arms. "Aren't you supposed to be in class."

He was staring into her eyes, smiling. "It's history. History sucks."

She tried to push past him.

He slid his foot against the opposite side of the door frame, blocking her exit. "You know, I see it."

Kim looked him in the eye. "See what?"

"Why he likes you. The hair, the eyes. The body. I get it."

"Would you please move?"

He drew in air through his nose. "The smell too. Like flowers. What is that?"

She swallowed, but still looked him in the eyes. "Honeysuckle."

He closed his eyes and breathed in again. "Mmm, yeah. That's it. Something else too. I love the smell under that." He opened his eyes. "I really like the other smell. Something ripe."

"Move your foot, please."

He grinned at her and stepped aside.

Kim walked away down the empty hall. She wasn't sure where she was going. For now, anywhere away from Pauly Delveccio was preferable.

"Hey, Red? You see David, you tell him I'm looking for him."

She could feel his eyes on her with every step.

David peddled fast as the light mist seeped into his hoodie. He had it pulled up to cover his face as he guided the bike around rain puddles.

The cops were part of this. How many? He didn't know. Was it the whole department? How could it be?

What was *this* anyway? Vampires? It just didn't make sense. Last night, in the trailer with the bodies around him, it had seemed the only logical explanation.

But now, as his legs pumped the pedals, and he sped away down back streets and empty country lanes? Now it sounded insane.

He wanted to talk to Kim. He needed to talk to her.

His second stop would be the school.

His first stop was insane. He couldn't believe he was actually going to do this.

Saint Mary's Catholic Church stood in stone, Gothic splendor on the east side of town.

He wasn't Catholic. Jane Connors didn't believe in much of anything, certainly not an all powerful God in heaven. He had been Christened. Not in a Catholic ceremony, but in his father's Methodist heritage.

He stopped on the brick sidewalk in front of the church.

Thinking of his father distracted him.

She had been right, of course. All the horrible things she had said to him on Sunday. His father had left them to fend for themselves. Things might have been different if he had been here.

But, he had left - taken a coward's way out. He couldn't understand his father's reasoning in downing a handful of downers along with a fifth of vodka.

Regardless of what his mother was. Even if his father had found out what she was, he had left David alone with her.

He had quit, and no matter if David had found a way to forgive him for that, which he had, he could not understand it.

Because no matter his other faults, David Connors would not quit.

He set the kickstand and walked into the church with his backpack on his back.

The priest was younger than he expected, with only a touch of gray on the man's temples.

He turned and smiled as David walked in.

There was huge crucifix with a pained looking Jesus staring down at him from behind the altar. There was a smaller gold plated crucifix on the altar with a Bible beside it.

David bowed.

The priest shook his head. "He doesn't expect you to bow. A simple genuflect will do. Regardless of what you may have heard, He's not a stickler for protocol."

David smiled.

The priest walked up to him. "And, a handshake for the local priest? I'm Father Tobias."

David shook his hand. "David... Cochran. David Cochran."

"You're not one of my meager flock, are you?" the Father Tobias asked.

"No, sir. I'm from the high school. We're collecting food for the Wythe County Food Bank." David looked at the font filled with holy water beside him.

"It's not a bird bath. Looks like one, but the water's consecrated."

David nodded. "I know."

"Food bank, huh? Noble cause. I believe we might be able to help." The priest looked at him. "You're soaked. You want a towel or something?"

David shook his head. "I'm fine."

Father Tobias nodded. "Okay. Well, if you'll wait here, I'll go see what we can spare."

Tobias turned and walked to a door beside the altar. "You can talk to the guy behind the altar. He can be pretty good company."

Tobias put his hand on the doorknob.

"Father?"

Tobias turned to him.

"Do you believe in evil?"

Tobias looked at him and nodded. "Yes. I believe in the evil people do to one another, the evil they do to themselves…"

"No. I mean like pure evil. Supernatural evil?"

"You mean the devil?"

David nodded.

Tobias shrugged. "If you want an objective opinion, you're asking the wrong guy. I'm a company man."

David looked away.

"Yes, David. I believe in the devil. I think he whispers in our ear and asks us to do evil things."

"Why would anybody listen?" David asked.

Tobias shook his head. "Weakness. Greed. Lust. Envy. Wrath. Take your pick. The devil isn't an ugly monster - if he were, nobody would listen. Does that answer your question?"

David nodded. "I think so."

Tobias nodded. "So, yeah, I believe in the devil. But, I believe in Christ more. His sacrifice, his innate goodness and love." He pointed at the cross. "His light. Drives away the shadows. Against that, devil's nothing but a con man." He smiled and pointed at the door. "Let me get the canned goods, and we can talk more?"

David nodded.

"Been quite awhile since I had somebody come in before Mass and ask me about the nature of evil," Tobias called through the door.

He searched through the church pantry.

"Reminds me of college." He looked at the cans in his hand. "Sure hope the food bank is okay with Beanie Weenie. I can't stand the stuff myself."

He placed a dozen cans in a double plastic bag.

He walked back into the chapel. "I doubled the bag so I don't think it will break. Now, where were we?"

The boy was gone.

"David?"

He looked toward the altar. Tobias sighed. "Son of a bitch." The gold plated crucifix was gone along with the Bible. "Tobias, you've been robbed." He paused then and looked up at Jesus. "Actually, you've been robbed. My bad."

He ran to the front. The door was open, but the boy was nowhere in sight.

Tobias looked at the font. It was half empty. He stared at it and trailed a finger through the water. He shook his head.

Tobias walked into his office and picked up the phone. He started dialing.

And, then he stopped.

There was something about the boy's face, the way he had been so serious when he asked about the nature of evil.

This was a kid who needed a cross, needed a Bible, and, for some reason, needed some holy water.

He hung up the phone and took the crucifix and Bible off his bookshelf to replace the ones on the altar.

David said a prayer in his head as he pedaled down side streets toward the school. He had robbed a church, but he believed Jesus would understand. Desperate times called for desperate measures.

He slammed on the brakes and skidded sideways at the high school driveway.

There was a police cruiser sitting outside the front entrance.

Of course, he thought. *They're looking anywhere they think I might go.*

He knew Kim was in there, probably hoping he would show up. But, he couldn't do her any good if they got him. "Please, be safe," he whispered.

He rode down the street and turned onto Kinder Valley Road.

He needed to find Pauly.

Anne looked out the window of Coldwell Banker.

Main Street was empty.

She had seen only a handful of people all day.

What's happening to my town? she thought.

A police cruiser pulled up in front of the office.

What now? she thought.

She had seen this man before. Taggert or something.

He opened the door, and the bell jingled. "Hello?"

Anne smiled. "Can I help you, officer?"

"Maybe," he said. "I'm looking for David Connors." His name tag read Taggert, just as she remembered.

"Somebody finally realized he was missing?" Anne asked.

"Ma'am?"

"He's been missing since yesterday."

Taggert shook his head. "Don't know anything about that. We're looking for him on a different matter."

"What matter?"

"I'm afraid I'm not at liberty to say. But, you say you haven't seen him?"

"No."

Taggert turned his head sideways. "You sure about that?"

"Yeah, I'm sure."

Taggert looked stern. "Ma'am, aiding and abetting is a serious offense…"

Anne's eyes narrowed. "No. Aiding and abetting a *criminal* is a serious offense. Not a sixteen-year-old boy."

Taggert shook his head. "I know he's screwing your daughter, but…"

"What did you just say?"

Taggert looked confused. He squeezed his eyes shut. "No... wait... that wasn't what I meant to say." He looked like he was about to faint.

"I think you need to leave," Anne said. Her fists were clenched at her sides.

He staggered backward. "I... yes. I'll leave. But, listen, if you see him..."

"If I see him I'll get him a lawyer before I call you. Get out."

He turned and went out the door.

When he drove away, Anne pulled out her cell phone and dialed. "Kim. Go to the front entrance. I'm coming to get you."

Gene sat on the hillside in his rain poncho and watched the house on the hill though binoculars.

The vampires were coming and going now. They would leave the house one at a time and run into the forest toward town.

They were hunting. Sometimes they came back carrying a limp body in their arms.

New recruits.

Occasionally, Olc, Miriam, or one of the other protectors would leave the house in the town car.

He had gotten a glimpse of a boy earlier. Nothing more than a flash of black hair as he got in the town car and it drove away.

He had a sketchbook and pencils at his side, protected in a ziplock bag. When a new protector, or a vampire able to camouflage, came out, he drew it. He needed to memorize the faces.

It would make them easier to spot when *he* started hunting.

The Asian girl came out in her Hoosier Hottie t-shirt. She wasn't running toward town the way the others did. She and the tall brunette vampire who wore illusionary pearls always stayed close to the house.

They were the smart ones, the ones who matured quicker.

The dangerous ones.

In order of danger, the ancients were first. They were almost invisible when they moved.

Olc was second most dangerous.

Hoosier Hottie and Pearls were next.

Then the protectors - Miriam, the blonde teen, the chubby girl, the tall brunette who had shown up human Saturday morning and left looking like a stone cold bitch Saturday evening.

And, the boy with black hair, whoever he was.

Lost in thought, he almost missed seeing the boy on the bicycle as he rode off the road and into the trees just short of the house.

"The hell?" Gene whispered. He grabbed his rifle and raised the scope to his eye.

A young boy with blond hair wearing a backpack was lying prone under a bush, his bicycle laying beside him.

He was staring at the house.

"Dumb ass." He swung the rifle to the left.

Hoosier Hottie was smiling. She walked into the woods above the boy.

"Nice knowin' ya, kid," Gene whispered. He turned back to the house.

David opened his backpack and pulled out his camera. It was a nice one his mom had bought him for Christmas a few years before.

It had a telephoto lens. He brought it to his eye and peered through.

The house looked like it was abandoned.

The weathered siding had peeling paint. The window glass was wavy from age.

He zoomed in on a window.

Nothing moved behind the glass.

He knew he would have to go inside.

He needed to find Pauly, and he needed to get pictures of the things he suspected were inside. People would believe pictures.

And, his mother?

He shook his head. She wasn't his mother. She was whatever Debbie Kincaid was: a monster.

David knew in his heart this was a bad idea. He had no idea how many of the things like Gwen were in the house.

He had no idea how many of the things like his mother and Debbie were inside either.

But, he had to try.

Something moved in the bushes farther up the hill.

He dropped the camera and reached into the backpack for the golden crucifix.

She appeared out of nowhere: an Asian girl wearing a t-shirt that read Hoosier Hottie. She wasn't wearing a bra, and her breasts pushed the fabric out.

Her shorts were small and black.

She had to be freezing in the cold rain.

David looked into her black eyes. They drew him in like magnets.

She smiled at him.

He shook his head. Blinked. He held up the crucifix. "Stay back."

She giggled. "Pretty."

He couldn't tell if she was talking about the golden crucifix or him.

He rolled onto his feet and grabbed his backpack.

David held the crucifix at arm's length.

She walked down the hill toward him.

"I said stay back!"

She shook her head. "I meant you. Pretty."

"You have to be afraid of this."

"This? Why this?" She turned her head to the side with a pout.

"It's a symbol of God."

"What God? I am a god." Her words were simple and terse as if spoken with great effort.

David closed his eyes. "Work. Please work." He dug in the pack and pulled out a stake he had made from the leg of one of the kitchen chairs. He slung the bag on his shoulder.

David held the cross in his left hand and the stake in his right. "I've already killed one of you. Stay back." He was backing toward the road.

She frowned. "Lie. We would know. Who did you kill?"

"Gwen. I killed Gwen. And, I'll kill you."

She shook her head. "No. No Gwen. We do not know Gwen."

David felt the asphalt under his heels. He doubted he could outrun her.

"No. You can't. Why run? David? Your name. Pretty David. Kim? Kim made you hard. I can make you harder," she said as she walked closer to him.

David's heart pounded in his chest, and suddenly he felt lust. He wanted her. He knew what she was, and he still wanted her. He dropped the stake.

"Pretty David. I won't hurt you. I'll make you like me. Perfect. Immortal. Drink from me. Drink and be damned." The last words came out in a different voice, something lower from a more guttural dialect.

David was crying as he backed away. "Please... don't... stay back."

She smiled at him in pity. "Shh. Billy, don't be a hero. Don't be a fool with your life?"

David hesitated. "What?"

She looked confused. The image of her flickered. "Billy, don't be a hero, Come back and make me your wife."

She stood before him in her true form, the glamour gone. She was a gray thing like Gwen, hairless with sagging, wet-looking skin.

Her black eyes opened wide. She started to turn and look behind her.

The pistol crack was silenced, little more than the sound of a twig breaking.

But, the right side of the girl's face disintegrated in a spray of gray and blood red.

An old man in a baseball cap that read Air Cav was running down the hill toward him. He had earbuds in his ears. He waved the pistol toward David. The old man jumped over the fallen vampire and past David. "Run, you stupid mother."

David ran after him as they crossed the road and ran into the field beyond.

The old man put the pistol in a shoulder holster as he ran. "Idiot. What the hell was that shit?"

"Who are you?"

"The dumbest asshole in the damned world. That's who," the old man said. He paused and cradled his left arm. "Not now," he whispered, wincing as David caught up to him. He started running again.

David followed the old man over a small hill.

A beat up pickup truck was on the other side.

"Get in," the man yelled as he jumped in the driver side.

David ran to the other side, opened the door, and climbed in. "Who are you?"

"Shut up!" The truck started with a rumble, and they tore across the field.

"Where are you going?"

"What part of shut up do you not get?"

The truck plowed through tall, dead grass before pulling onto a dirt road.

They kicked up mud behind them.

The old man looked in the rear view. "By all rights, we should both be dead right now." He shook his head. "Blind, dumb luck."

The dirt road merged onto Kinder Valley Road heading back toward town.

The man glanced at him. "Crucifix. How'd that work for you?"

"It didn't."

"Yeah, no shit, Sherlock. What made you think it would?"

"I… I don't know…"

"Movies. Yeah, I know. Movies and books got it all wrong. Draugr don't care about God or Jesus or Buddha or Mohamed."

"Draugr?"

"What else you got in there?" he grabbed the backpack off the seat.

"Hey, that's mine," David said.

"Shut up," he said as he dug through it with one hand. "Bible. You can read it while they're draining you dry." He tossed it on David's lap.

He drove one-handed and kept one eye on the rough road. The old man dug in the bag and pulled out a plastic bottle. "Holy water?"

"Yeah."

He shrugged. "Okay. You hold them down, you might be able to drown them with it." He tossed the bottle on David's lap. "What else?"

He pulled out one of the wooden stakes. "Yeah, this will work. Got to get close though. You get close enough to use this, it'll probably tear your head off."

"I killed one with a stake last night," David whispered.

The old man stared at him. "No shit? Well, you're one lucky little peckerwood, I'll give you that. Now, where can I drop you?"

"What?"

"Where can I drop you? And, I'll warn you, I ain't going much closer to town."

"I… I got nowhere to go."

"Yeah? Good luck with that."

"Please. I don't know what to do next."

The old man sighed.

"I'm David…"

"I don't give a damn who you are, kid."

"Thank you for saving my life."

The old man looked at him and burst out laughing. "Saved your life? Kid, I didn't do anything except give you a stay of execution."

David stared at him. "I don't understand."

The old man shook his head. "You don't get it, do you? The last thing old Hoosier Hottie saw back there before I deconstructed her skull was your face."

"So?"

"Jesus. They're all connected together, like a hive mind. They all know she's dead, and your face is the last thing she saw."

David looked at him wide eyed.

"Yeah, now you're catching on. They're going to find you and bleed you slow. Every one of them is looking for your narrow ass now."

"What do I do?"

"Run. To the south. Don't stop till you hit the gulf coast." He said as he pulled onto the shoulder. "Vaya con Dios, Chico."

David looked out into the dark woods off the shoulder. "You'd do that? Just put me out and tell me to run?"

The old man smiled and nodded. "Scoot."

"Mister, I know you don't owe me anything. But, you just risked your life to save me, so I know you aren't heartless enough to put me out on the side of the road like this."

"Watch me."

"Please, mister. My mom is with them. They took my best friend, and I haven't seen my girlfriend since yesterday. I need your help."

The old man closed his eyes. "I've been doing this forty years. The only thing that's kept me alive is not taking in strays. Run. Trust me, you have a greater chance of survival if you just run."

"Please. I don't even know what they are." David held out his hand. "I'm David Connors."

The old man shook his head. "Gene Stinson."

"If you could have seen him, Mom. Pauly was always a lech, but he was, I don't know, respectful. Like it was all a big joke on him. But, today? He was like a sleazeball from some biker movie," Kim said as they all sat at the kitchen table.

"What's a lech?" Tia asked.

"Stranger danger," Laura said.

"Oh."

Anne tapped her nails on the kitchen table. "I'm thinking about calling the state police and telling them about the Deskins woman. And, about David going missing."

"Let's just get the hell out of Dodge," Laura said. She looked around the table. "Seriously, Annie, let's just leave for a few days. Go to the beach. Go down to Disney."

Kim shook her head. "Mom! I can't leave until I find David. I won't."

Laura rolled her eyes. "Aw, come on, Kim. Dial down the hormones. You went out with him once…"

"It's easy for you to just leave," Kim said. "Isn't it? Whenever things get bad, you just run."

"Kim. That's enough," Anne said.

"Well, the last time you ran away? You left Mom to clean up the puke. You left her to hold Grandma's hand while they pumped poison into her veins trying to save her life. You left Mom to bury her. Alone." Kim stood up from the table and glared at her aunt. "Mom forgives you for that because that's who she is. I'm not that good a person. And, I hate you for it." She ran away from the table.

The door to her room slammed.

Laura was paralyzed. She just stared straight ahead.

"Hey," Anne said. She took her sister's hand. "She didn't mean that. She's scared, that's all."

Laura shook her head. "Yes. She did mean it. And, she's right."

David shoveled road stew into his mouth as fast as he could swallow.

Road stew was one of Gene's staples: a can of baked beans mixed with chunks of beef jerky and Velveeta cheese. No refrigeration required, and you could cook it on a campfire in ten minutes.

They sat in the kitchen of the abandoned house.

"How long did you go without eating?" Gene asked.

"Lunch yesterday," David said between mouthfuls. He took a drink from his soda can. He looked around the room, his eyes settling on the counter. "Does that phone work?"

"No."

David looked at his hands. "I need to call Kim, my girlfriend. I have to tell her what's going on. Do you have a cell?"

"I do. It won't do you any good. They got somebody in the local cell office. Cell phones calling out on the local system with anything other than the local area code won't work. They're smart. Damned smart."

David sighed. "Does your phone's internet still work?"

Gene shook his head.

"Damn it."

"Yeah, it's seriously eating into my Netflix watching."

"You called them Draugr?"

Gene nodded. "Lots of names for them. Most of the stories are inaccurate. Draugr is closest to correct. It was a Norwegian folk tale about monsters that drank human blood and could make themselves look like anything they wanted - shapeshifters. The Hindus knew about them too, called them Rakshasa."

"Are they undead, like vampires?"

Gene shook his head. "No. They're alive. There's a virus in Draugr blood. It can be absorbed through the intestines - if you swallow it, the virus rewrites your DNA, makes you one of them."

David stopped eating. "I got some on me. On my hands when I killed Gwen…"

"Gave you a rush?"

"Yeah," David said. "Like I was on drugs or something."

"Absorbed through the skin or eyes, it makes you strong, younger… hell, taller even. Get enough on you at regular intervals, it makes you immortal."

David looks at his hands. "That's what they did to my Mom?"

Gene nodded. "She was the pretty brunette lady from Saturday morning?"

David nodded.

"Yeah."

"So, it makes you into a monster? That's why she hates me now?"

"No. No, it makes them high. It makes them feel invincible. Influences them I suppose. But, that's not what makes them into monsters."

David looked at him.

"Olc. Olc does that."

"I don't understand."

"The Draugr have mental abilities. They can get in your head - you've seen that?"

David nodded. "Gwen. She… looked in my mind."

"Took on a shape she thought wouldn't frighten you?"

"Yeah."

"Sometimes they do that. Other times, they just want to terrify you. All of them can look inside your mind, read your thoughts, sift through your memories like it was a file cabinet."

Gene stood up. "But, Olc? He can do more than just look. He can drill into your head. Change what you think. Change your entire personality." He turned away. "He can take your wife, someone you love and who has loved you for years and turn them into a stranger. Make them into something you don't recognize. Something they wouldn't recognize themselves."

"That's worse than killing someone," David said.

"Yes. Yes, it is. If he wants he can reach inside your brain and pop a blood vessel, kill you on the spot."

"What happened to Hoosier Hottie out there? She started saying strange shit just before you killed her."

Gene laughed and faced him. "Billy don't be a hero?"

"Yeah."

Gene took his phone out of his pocket and slid it over to the boy. "'Billy Don't be a Hero' Bo Donaldson and the Heywoods. God, I hate that damned song. Gets in your head. Gets in their heads too, 'cause they're constantly listening in on people's thoughts that come near them. You listen to a repetitive song like this, it jams Draugr radar. Disorients them. I keep it playing through the earbuds all the time when they're near."

"I don't understand. If Olc is as powerful as you say he is, how are you still alive."

Gene nodded. "Knowing. If you know what they can do in your head, it's like your subconscious is immunized against their mind tricks to an extent. He can't burst a blood vessel in my head. And, now he can't do that to you either."

"Because I know?"

"Yes."

David laughed. "It's like quantum physics."

"Huh?" Gene asked.

David smiled and shook his head. "Never mind."

"Anyway, none of that shit you were packing would have worked. Heat is the best thing to use against them. Over ninety degrees kills them outright, so a nice house fire is best." He took the silenced pistol out of his shoulder holster. "This works pretty well too." He slid it toward David but kept his hand on it. "You know how to shoot?"

David nodded.

"Really?"

David shrugged. "XBox."

Gene chuckled. "Ain't quite the same thing, son. Here." He took his hand off the gun.

David picked it up.

"Keep your finger away from the trigger. Keep it on the trigger guard."

David nodded and put his index finger straight along the frame around the trigger.

The barrel with the silencer attached wavered toward Gene.

"Shit, kid! Don't point it at me."

David swung the barrel to the side. "Sorry."

"That'd be just my luck. Hunt Draugr for forty years and get my nuts shot off by a sixteen-year-old eating beans and jerky." He glared at David.

"I'm sorry, I've never held a gun before."

"Yeah, that's obvious."

David rolled his eyes.

Gene sighed and walked around the table. "See if you can hit that vase on the coffee table in the living room."

"You want me to fire this in the house?"

"Not my house nor yours," Gene said. "Besides, would you rather wander around outside in the dark?"

The vase was baby blue. It looked cheap.

"Why the vase?" David asked.

"About the size of a skull."

"It's barely twenty feet away."

"Yeah, most times they'll be about that close." He reached out and worked the slide, cocking the gun. "Feel that lever under your thumb?"

"Yes."

"Press it down. Line up the vase in the sights and squeeze the trigger."

David breathed out and squeezed.

There was a loud snapping sound, and the vase exploded.

David smiled as Gene eased the gun out of his hand and made it safe.

"Don't get cocky. Shooting a vase is a far cry from a Draugr that's running at you."

He handed it back to the boy. Then, he took off the shoulder holster and handed it to him as well.

David stared at the holster. "You're giving me this?"

Gene nodded. "I got plenty more."

"Is there any hope for Pauly?" David asked.

"Been in the house since Saturday night?" Gene asked.

David nodded.

Gene shook his head. "He's either Draugr, Protector, or he was dinner. Sorry, kid."

David picked up the shoulder holster and studied it. "I have to get to Kim."

Gene shook his head. He went to his green backpack and took out a map. He spread it out on the table.

The map was of southwest Virginia. "This is where she lives?"

David looked where Gene was pointing. "Yeah."

"That's five miles as the crow flies. They'll be scouring the countryside looking for you."

"If we took your truck…"

"We wouldn't even make it to Main Street. They'll have the roads blocked. Remember, they're probably expecting you to go to her house."

David pounded his fist on the table. "Damn it. There has to be a way. She doesn't know they're out there, and I can't even warn her."

Gene folded the map and handed it to him. "I'm going to give you some free advice. Take it, don't take it. Your option."

David took the map.

"First light, you hike straight north until you reach the interstate. Walk through the fields beside it about seven miles to the northeast. You'll run into a Gas'N'Go truck stop. Hitch a ride on a semi going toward Charlotte. Keep going south till you can't take the heat. Live a life." Gene said. He opened his wallet and took out five one-hundred dollar bills. He handed the money to David.

The boy stared at the money and map in his hands. "If I could get to the state police…"

Gene nodded. "If they don't just cart you off to the loony bin, the first thing they're going to do is call your mother. Maybe they get her, maybe they don't, maybe they'll drive you kicking and screaming back home, or maybe they won't - but, one way or another, the Draugr will find out where you are. And, they'll come for you."

Laura stood at the kitchen window and stared out into the darkness.

Anne walked up beside her and hugged her. "It's going to be okay, Stringbean."

Laura gave her a weak smile.

Anne pointed to the back door. "What is that?"

One of the kitchen chairs was propped under the doorknob. There was a sticky note above the knob that read: Do Not Open!

"Always the weakest point in the house."

Anne leaned up and whispered. "I think you're overreacting, Sis."

"No. The over reaction is on the other side of the door. Don't open it, okay?"

Anne looked at her sideways. "What did you do?"

Laura shrugged. "Just don't open it."

"Hey, I got kids in this house! You can't be setting traps…"

"Monkey Face helped me - trust me, she won't go near it. And, I'm going to let Jugs know right now…"

"I'll tell her…"

"No. No, I need to talk to her."

"It might be better to wait."

Laura shook her head and walked away. "It never is."

Miriam sat in her bedroom and listened to the Draugr wail in the parlor. They had been screaming for three hours. Jane, Regina, and Pauly stood in the center of the bedroom and stared at Debbie.

Debbie was leaning against the bedroom wall and staring at her feet.

"How could you be so stupid?" Jane whispered.

"I said I was sorry," Debbie blubbered.

"That's enough recrimination," Miriam said. "There's no more point. Debbie now realizes the Draugr aren't our pets, don't you, Debbie?"

"When Olc finds out what she did..." Pauly said.

Debbie looked up with a look of terror.

"He won't find out. Because we're not going to tell him. We're going to put it out of our minds. And, we're not going to speak of it ever again," Miriam said.

Regina glared at Debbie. "Why? I don't see a reason to lie for her..."

Miriam stood up. "She is one of us." She walked to Debbie and tilted her face up. Miriam wiped away the woman's tears. "Now, no more crying. What's done is done."

"Doesn't change the fact Mae is dead," Jane said. "She was one of his favorites."

Miriam laughed as she leaned forward and kissed away Debbie's tears. "Oh, he has many favorites. He will recover. They all will. Now, tell me about the boy."

Laura knocked on Kim's door. There was no answer. She opened it.

"I didn't say you could open my door," Kim said. She was lying on her stomach on the bed, facing away from the door.

Her room was a pale blue color, the walls covered with posters of rock bands and boys. Laura recognized some of the posters.

"Used to be my room," Laura said. "I never had that innate decorating sense your mom has - all the pinks and lace."

"You want it back? I'll move," she said, her voice cold.

"I'm sorry."

"Not the one you should be apologizing to," Kim whispered.

"Your mom? I have apologized, for what that's worth. I'm going to keep on apologizing and making up for it till it sticks."

"Good luck with that."

She sat down on the bed and Kim scooted away.

Laura sighed. "I'd like to apologize to *my* mom, but that ship has sailed. I got that one on me forever." Her voice cracked. "So, that leaves you and Tia."

"Don't bother. I don't need anything from you."

"Whew. Man, you're tough. Reminds me of somebody…"

Kim rolled onto her back. "Don't you dare say I remind you of yourself! I am nothing like you!"

Laura shook her head. "I'm sorry."

"Stop saying that. I don't want…"

"It's not for you."

Kim stared at her.

Laura shrugged. "It's for me. One hundred percent selfish motivation. Because I screwed up so bad. I have nothing but you and Tia and your mom. People make mistakes. *I* made mistakes. So, I'm begging you not to stop loving me. Please."

Kim sat up. "Are you crying?"

"Of course, I'm crying. What? Do you think I'm some kind of robot or something?" She lowered her face, and her tears fell on her thighs.

"Don't. I'm…"

Laura looked up with red-rimmed eyes. "No. No, you have nothing to be sorry about. Everything you said was true. And, I am going to spend the rest of my life making up for that. If you'll let me."

Kim sighed. She nodded. Then she looked at her. "I'm not leaving without David."

Laura nodded. "Okay. We'll find him. Tomorrow. Me and you."

Kim hugged her and laid her head on her shoulder. After a moment, she said, "This is kind of a letdown."

"What do you mean?"

"I thought maybe you were a robot. Like fembot Amazon Barbie or something."

Laura laughed. "Sorry to disappoint. I'm all organic." She looked down at Kim. "Which begs the question, are those real?"

"What?"

"The fun bags?"

"You are obsessed with my breasts."

"Nobody in the family had those."

"They're real. I'm not even eighteen - you really think Mom would buy these for me? The genes come from a maiden great aunt on my Dad's side."

"Seriously doubt she was a maiden. Not with jugs like that."

"Can we please stop this conversation?"

"Yes. One other thing?" Laura asked.

"Yeah?"

"Don't go on the back porch. I set a trap."

"What kind of trap?"

It was as if the town of Rural Retreat held its breath.

There was no moon that night, and heavy clouds blocked out the stars. It was cold with no wind.

No cars moved on the street.

The road leading to the interstate was blocked, as was the road leading to the south.

The patrolmen manning those roadblocks were mute - sitting in their cars staring straight ahead. Their minds were blank, doing nothing but processing their surroundings.

They were like machines in some kind of sleep mode, waiting for an interruption to bring them to life.

Most of the houses were dark. The front doors hung open on some, and these were the quietest of all.

Sometimes, a front door would be opened, and a shape would step inside.

It might be a woman or a man, a towering giant, or a minuscule imp. Occasionally, lights would come on. Sometimes there were screams or gunshots.

But, mostly there was silence.

This is how a town dies.

The houses were visited by monsters, many disguised as relatives, friends, or lovers. Or, shapes meant to instill fear.

Because fear seasoned the blood - the rush of adrenalin and a flood of glucose. Salty and sweet.

A taste savored by the monsters who visited, picking and choosing the residents as either nourishment or to welcome into the fold.

Ishmar Hamadi stood behind the counter of his Gas'N'Go and fretted. Since dusk, no customers had entered the store, and it was almost eleven PM.

Something was wrong.

He stared out the windows into the empty parking lot. The overcast sky was low, the clouds lit by the street lights.

It felt like the town was encased in some cocoon.

Fatima took his head. "Papa? Let's close up."

He squeezed her hand. "No, no. We mustn't do that. People need gas, they might need groceries."

"Papa, no one answers at home. I am frightened," Fatima whispered.

He drew her close and kissed her cheek. "Okay, okay. Start shutting off the lights."

The front door hissed open and the overhead heater cut on with a roar.

The woman entering looked up at the ceiling and cringed. She hurried past the forced, heated air.

Hamadi smiled. "Mrs. Davis! Such a night to be out." He leaned over to Fatima and whispered. "See, Habibty? Everything will be okay."

Brittney Davis stared at him. She was dressed in a white blouse, black skirt, and pearls. She seemed puzzled by his words. A moment later she broke into a wide grin. "Mr. Hamadi... Yes, the night is chilly."

Hamadi felt his smile fade. Such a cold night for her to be out in nothing but a thin blouse. "Yes." He touched Fatima's arm. "I'll start closing up in the office. We'll go home as soon as you help Mrs. Davis."

Fatima smiled and nodded.

Hamadi turned and walked into his office.

Gene watched the boy sleeping on the couch.

He wasn't much older when he stepped off the plane in Viet Nam.

But, in Viet Nam, Gene had his training and the Air Cavalry behind him. There were air strikes when things got bad and Medevac when things got worse.

The boy had nothing - just an old 1911 Colt and advice from an old man who couldn't run a hundred yards without his heart threatening to blow a gasket.

The advice was something the boy wouldn't take, and Gene knew it.

Brittney Davis walked up to the counter empty handed.

"Is there something I can help you find?" Fatima asked with a smile.

Brittney stared into her eyes. "Stand very still. Be very quiet."

Fatima felt drowsy.

Yes, she should stand very still. She should be quiet.

She should stand very still and quiet even as the tall woman walked around the counter and into the office.

"Did you need something, Mrs. Davis?" she heard her Papa say.

Fatima wanted to turn. She wanted to warn her Papa that something was wrong. But, she had to stand very still. She had to remain very quiet.

She heard the sound of something breaking.

A single tear slid down her cheek as she heard the sound of something like a kiss coming from behind her. It turned into the sound of someone drinking.

There was feminine laughter and then gnawing and slurping.

Fatima wanted to run, but she had to stand very still.

She wanted to scream, but she had to remain very quiet.

She heard the sound of something heavy hitting the floor.

Fatima heard the gentle click of high heels on the floor.

Brittney Davis leaned around in front of her.

Blood ran down from the woman's mouth. She smiled showing gore-stained sharp teeth.

She leaned forward and kissed Fatima on the lips.

The metallic taste of blood filled her mouth.

Brittney leaned back and smiled.

And, Fatima wanted to die, because she knew where the blood came from.

But, she had to stand very still. She had to remain very quiet.

Brittney held up her hand to reveal long, ragged talons.

Brittney ran the talon on her index finger gently down the side of her own throat.

She put her hand on the back of Fatima's neck.

She guided Fatima's lips gently to the bleeding wound.

"Drink," Brittney whispered. "Drink and be damned."

Tia Lawrence slept in a bed decorated with Hello Kitty. She dreamed. A reprieve from the nightmares of the past week.

In her dream, she slept, her head on her grandmother's lap - a woman she could remember only as feelings and emotions, and soft hands that stroked her hair as she slept. Addie, the woman who had died in the woods, stood nearby.

They held vigil over the child.

It's what ghosts do.

The thing that had once been Chad Joseph, hiker, and husband of Addie, ran through the wet, cold grass. Blood dripped from his face.

He had found a house a few minutes before. A woman alone with two small children. A simple twist of the doorknob and the mechanism within shattered.

The door opened, and he entered as a clown. Blue paint around his eyes and red around his lips and sharp teeth, all on a pasty white face.

The little boy on the floor above was afraid of clowns. His blood was sweet with fear, much better than the blood from his sister's half awakened body.

He had taken the mother, forcing his blood into her mouth at the same time he penetrated her.

Chad left her convulsing on her bedroom floor.

Now, he stood outside a small two story house with a Prius in the driveway.

Four people slept inside.

A mother, her sleep troubled.

Her sister, who dreamed of a woman who said, "*Not perfect. Es familia. Family is never perfect, but it is the only thing that is real.*"

A girl, who did not dream.

A child, who dreamed of her grandmother's soft hands.

He smiled as he stepped onto the front porch. His hand touched the knob.

Addie.

The name? Did he know that name? It was there on the tip of his tongue.

He saw an image of a smiling woman with short black hair.

Addie.

His hand hesitated above the knob.

He was confused. The smell of the blood inside the house was intoxicating. The child was afraid of monsters. He would appear as himself, gray and horrifying, when he woke her from her dream. The blood would be sweet.

He reached for the knob again.

Addie.

He stepped back as if the doorknob had an electric charge.

He snarled and ran around to the back of the house.

Laura snapped awake when the screaming began. She rolled onto her feet wearing a Grateful Dead t-shirt and black panties. She was disoriented. She was on her mother's couch in her mother's house.

The screaming continued.

"What the hell?" Anne yelled as she came down the steps two at a time.

Kim ran behind her.

Tia was in the rear. "We got one!" she yelled.

Laura jumped to her feet, everything came to her at once. She tossed the blanket on the floor. "Stay behind me!" She ran into the kitchen.

Laura grabbed a butcher knife out of the butcher block knife holder.

She held it overhand in her right hand. She canted her wrist, so the flat part of the blade ran down her outer forearm, the edge pointing outward.

The chair was still propped under the kitchen doorknob.

The screaming was grown faint. The screamer was running away.

"Oh, God, I hope that wasn't David," Kim whispered.

Laura glanced over her shoulder. Her sister and the kids were gathered behind her.

"Your boyfriend going to try to break in the back door at three AM?" Laura asked.

"I… No. I don't think so."

"Annie, can you pull the chair out from under the door?"

Anne nodded. She reached out and touched the chair.

"Don't open the door, Mommy. There's a monster," Tia whispered.

Anne looked at Laura.

Laura shrugged. "I don't know."

Kim grabbed a knife and held it like Laura held hers. "Get behind me, squirt."

Tia stepped behind Kim and wrapped her hands around her waist. She buried her face in the small of her sister's back.

Anne pulled the chair out of the way, and then she stepped back beside Laura. She turned and pulled two knives out of the holder. She held one in each hand. "Am I holding these right?"

"Yeah," Laura said as she glanced at her. "Strike with your elbows, let the blade slide across their skin as you hit them."

"Jesus. Where did you learn this?" Anne asked.

Laura shrugged. "Boyfriend. Knives. Lot of freaky bondage shit. Now is not the time."

"I want a knife too," Tia whispered, her arms still tight around Kim.

"No," they all said to her at once.

"Okay," Tia whined.

"You guys stay back. I'm going to open the door," Laura whispered.

She took a step forward and put her left hand on the knob. "One. Two."

She jerked the door open.

Cold air rushed in along with a chemical odor.

The doorway was empty.

The outside screen door was leaning out, the top hinge ripped free from the door frame.

Laura looked down as Anne joined her.

Smoke wafted up from a hole in the deck a foot across. Foul smelling gray slime lay in puddles by the hole.

A metal bucket lay on its side a few feet away on the deck boards. Anne shook her head. "What the hell?"

Laura leaned out and looked left and right. The backyard was empty.

She stepped back and shut the door. "I had the bucket balanced on top of the screen door. Whoever it was must not have seen it."

"What was in it?" Anne asked.

"Sodium Hydroxide. It's a strong base. Plus I concentrated it."

"Where the hell did you get that?" Anne asked.

Laura smiled. "Household chemicals and a little carbon. It's a three step process. You're out of salt by the way."

Wednesday

The morning dawned with fog.

David checked the straps on the shoulder holster and pulled his hoodie on over top of it.

Gene filled .45 magazines for the boy at the kitchen table. He had five of them lined up. "You reload that magazine in your .45?"

"Yes, sir."

"How many bullets in the gun?"

"Seven."

"Try again."

David frowned. "There's seven in the magazine."

"Yeah, and one more…"

David nodded. "In the chamber."

"Best not to forget that."

"I won't."

Gene slid the magazines to his side of the table. "Here's thirty-five rounds more."

David stuffed them into the pockets of the hoodie. "You think this will be enough?"

"I hope so, kid."

David pulled his backpack onto his back.

Gene looked away. "Once you feel safe, ditch the Colt. Be piss poor luck to walk out of here and get picked up on a weapons charge."

"Mr. Stinson, thank you, for everything."

Gene looked at him with a grim expression. "Don't thank me, son."

David walked to the door.

"I'll be here for another day," Gene said. The words stuck in his mouth, but he spat them out. "You get into trouble, try to make it back here."

Gene watched the boy as he walked into the woods north of the house. Once he thought he was out of Gene's sight, David turned east, which Gene had expected.

"True love," Gene whispered to the empty house.

Miriam stood in the parlor and looked at the mass of bodies. They filled half the room now. The hum from the chaos was deafening inside her head.

The mass parted.

Olc emerged dripping naked and wet. Behind him, he dragged the thing called Chad.

Chad's face was half disintegrated, and his right arm was little more than ragged bone.

Olc's expression was fierce. "Won't heal. Mouth disfigured. Can't feed."

Miriam turned away in disgust. "Put it out of its misery."

"No. For you. Take the blood."

She stole another look at the ruined Draugr. "He went to the girl's house. The boy, David, his girlfriend's house."

Olc snarled. "Is the boy there?"

"No. But, I believe he will come."

Olc stared down at her. "Mae. The boy. He said. Killed *Gwen*..."

Miriam shrugged.

"Who was Gwen?"

"I don't know."

He stopped dragging Chad and walked to her. He placed both hands on the sides of her face and stared into her eyes. "Lie. Protecting someone."

"It doesn't matter," she said slowly, matching his gaze with her own.

"Matters. To me." He pressed into her mind.

Intense pain ran through her eyes. "Darling... if you want to play... let's go upstairs...," she whispered. She smiled at him.

He released her.

Miriam stumbled back. "The boy," she said, catching her breath. "He isn't the one who killed Mae. You know this."

"Your husband."

"Yes. It has to be. He's the only one who could get close enough without Mae sensing him. He used the boy as bait."

"Still. Who was Gwen?"

"A mistake made by one of my own."

"Young man. Your favorite. His mistake?"

"No."

"Perhaps. Take him anyway? Punishment?"

Miriam sighed. "Do what you will. He is not your competition. He's just someone to warm my bed."

"No more mistakes?"

"No. I promise." She took his hand. "We need to find David Connors. If we find him, we find Gene. And, then we can end all this."

The phone was dead when Anne got up at 7:00 AM. They had slept piled on the couch - all but Laura who sat in the overstuffed chair directly across with the butcher knife in her hand.

Anne had dialed the police after the attempted break in during the night.

No one answered.

When she tried to call the state police, the phone never rang. It just gave a busy tone.

The cable was out.

The cell phones worked, but, like the regular phone, it only seemed to work for local numbers. And, the phone internet didn't work at all.

Tia rolled over. "Did the monsters come back?"

Laura jolted awake and dropped the butcher knife on the floor.

Anne reached down and picked it up. She handed it to her sister. "Relax. It's dawn."

"I didn't mean to fall asleep," Laura said.

Anne turned her attention back to Tia. "No, sweetie. There are no monsters."

"Are too. Grandma said. Addie made the one from last night go to the back door instead of the front door. She said, 'That's what he gets for shtupping that Indiana slut.'"

Everyone looked at her.

"What does 'shtupping' mean?"

"It means looking at," Anne said.

"Are we a decade away from having an adult conversation in this house? HBO?" Kim asked. She picked up her phone and dialed.

She rocked forward in her seat. "David?"

"Is it him?" Anne whispered.

Kim nodded. "I can barely hear you. Where are you?" She smiled and nodded. "Stay there. We'll come get you... David? David?"

She looked at her mom and smiled. "He's at the Gas'N'Go. I need to go get him." She jumped to her feet.

Anne grabbed her keys. "I'll drive you."

"No," Laura said. "I'll drive her."

"You stay here," Anne said.

Laura held out her hand. "If she runs into trouble, who's she better off with? Me or you?"

Anne opened her mouth to protest.

"Annie, no offense, but you're about as tough as meat loaf."

Kim laughed. "You've never had Mom's meat loaf."

Laura shook her head and held up the knife. "You know how to slice a guy so it doesn't stop bleeding?"

"No," Anne said.

"I do."

Anne shook her head, but she knew when she was defeated. "You bring her back. The boy too."

"Let's go," Kim said.

Laura looked at Kim. "Then, we're getting the hell out of Dodge. Agreed?"

"Agreed."

The streets were deserted. House after house Laura and Kim passed had their lights off, the front doors hanging wide open. Main Street was a maze of abandoned cars, some idling, others simply stopped.

Many of the car doors were standing open.

"What the hell?" Laura whispered. She touched the hilt of her butcher knife. She had it in the space between the center console and her seat with the handle up.

"Where did they all go?" Kim asked.

Laura shook her head. She had believed something odd was going on, but she thought maybe it was gangs or something.

This was unnerving.

"Kim. I think we should go back and get Anne and Tia..."

"We have to get David."

"We will. But, honey, I think we need to go back and get them before we go to the Gas'N'Go, then we'll just drive straight out of town."

"Please, Aunt Laura, it's not even a mile from here." Kim was looking at her with imploring eyes.

Laura sighed. "Okay."

The Gas'N'Go was lit up, but there were no cars in the lot. Laura pulled up to the entrance.

Kim leaned forward and peered inside through the windshield. "I don't see anybody behind the counter."

Laura looked all around. Nothing moved. "He said he was here, right?"

"Yes."

"No other Gas'N'Go around here?"

"No. The nearest one other than this is the Gas'N'Go truck stop up on the interstate. He specifically said this Gas'N'Go."

Kim took hold of the door handle. "Maybe he's inside."

Laura grabbed her arm. "Sit your ass down. You're not getting out of this car."

"But…"

"No, buts. If I have to lay you out cold, you are not getting out of this car." Laura drew the knife out of its hiding place. "Stay in here with the doors locked. If I'm not out in five minutes, drive home."

"I'm not leaving you."

"Oh, yes, you are. Because if I don't come back, then whatever weird shit is going on in this town got me. It's going to be your responsibility to get your mom and Tia out of here, understand?"

"Don't say that."

"Listen. I know you don't want to be like me, but, sorry princess, you drew the genetic short straw. You're the tough bitch elect." She smiled and rubbed her hair. "Own that shit. Look on the bright side, you're prettier than me."

Laura got out of the car and shut the door behind her. She pointed at Kim and then the car door.

Kim locked it.

Laura looked down at the knife in her hand. *No, I'm not here to rob the place. I'm just armed against terrorists, or zombies, or Mormon Missionaries who've gone cuckoo.*

The doors hissed open as Laura approached the entrance. Warm air blew in her face from the heater above the door. Middle Eastern music played as she stepped inside.

The warm air was laced with something else - something rotted, like bad eggs or spoiled milk. Laura winced at the smell. "Hello?"

She walked up to the counter. "Hello? David? Are you in here?"

She looked at the counter. A plaque under the Plexiglas top read: Gas'N'Go number 08172, Proprietor Ishmar Hamadi, A Division of Osborne Leland Corporation.

She stared at the counter top.

There was a single drop of blood in the middle of the counter.

Nothing ominous there, she thought. *Just somebody with a nosebleed, nothing to worry about.*

There was a door behind the counter standing slightly open. It was dark inside.

"Sure. Let's go look in the creepy room," Laura whispered.

Kim watched Laura walk behind the counter. "What are you doing?" she whispered in the quiet car.

Something moved to her right.

She looked up and smiled. David was standing near the side of the store. He smiled at her.

She opened the car door and ran to him. "Where have you been, you dummy?" She wrapped her arms around his neck.

He kissed her, and she moaned into the kiss.

His lips were so cold, but she didn't care.

His hands slid down to her buttocks.

She opened her eyes as they broke their kiss.

It wasn't him.

A tall brunette woman wearing pearls was smiling down at her.

She tried to scream and pull away, but the woman lifted her into the air, then turned her around and clamped a cold hand over her mouth. "Such a good kisser."

Kim kicked and struggled as the woman carried her away behind the store.

Laura eased the door open. A bank of security camera monitors glowed black and white in the room.

Ishmar Hamadi stared straight up from the office floor, a look of sheer terror in his glazed over eyes.

His throat had been ripped out all the way to his backbone.

"The fuck?" Laura whispered.

A door opened somewhere in the Gas'N'Go.

Laura whirled around. She shifted to the overhand hold on the knife, feeling the reassuring kiss of the steel against her bare forearm. She brought the knife up to chin level as she scanned the room.

There was a cold room in the back of the store with stacks of beer in six and twelve packs. The door was closing slowly on its piston.

Laura brought her empty fist down to waist level, turned it over, drew it back. She was ready to deliver a twisting front punch.

"I'm pretty," a woman's voice said.

It came from her left and Laura pivoted toward the sound.

A girl stood a few feet from the counter. Her skin was dark, her hair long and black. She was wearing a red and white Gas'N'Go golf shirt.

Her name tag said Fatima.

She seemed to be staring past Laura with her black eyes.

Laura stared at her. "Hi. You work here?" Laura asked.

"I'm not ugly."

"No. No, you're very pretty. There's a dead man in here, do you know who did that?"

Fatima looked at her. "I'm so hungry. Can you hear them singing?"

The girl was high on something. "No, I can't. I'm going to come out into the store now. I need you to back away."

"It's a pretty song. So many voices." She was staring through Laura again.

"What are they saying?" Laura asked.

"They're saying: Drink. Drink and be damned. Am I damned?"

"Depends," Laura motioned toward the office with her knife. "Did you kill this guy?"

"Papa? No. The monster killed him."

"Monster?"

She nodded. "I drank. I didn't want to. I drank, and now I'm damned."

Laura felt a pain behind her eyes.

Fatima looked at her sideways. "You're damned too. You killed the man on the bulldozer, even if you didn't make the bomb."

Laura took a step back. She felt the dead man's shoe touching her foot, and she nudged it away. "You couldn't know that…"

"I'm hungry. I'm so hungry," she said as she stepped toward Laura.

Fatima's image flickered. Behind it was a woman with dark gray skin, what was left of her black hair hung in sick tendrils from her bare scalp. She was naked, and her skin looked moist.

"Don't come any closer."

Fatima opened her mouth and hissed through long sharp teeth. She ran toward Laura around the side of the counter.

Laura struck outward with the knife shielded forearm. The blade slashed the girl's throat.

Laura drove her left fist up and out from her waist, turning it as she struck flesh.

The twisting punch caught Fatima in the mouth and teeth shattered.

She staggered back against the counter.

Laura pressed forward, pinning Fatima against the counter. She flipped her grip on the knife and brought it up and under Fatima's ribs. The blade drove high and found the girl's heart.

Laura twisted the knife in place.

Fatima collapsed on the floor as her blood gushed out of both neck and abdomen.

Laura stumbled backward. The blood soaked knife was still in her hand.

The crimson on her hand tingled.

The pathetic thing on the floor stared behind her into the office.

"What are you?" Laura whispered to the empty store.

Laura stumbled out of the Gas'N'Go. *Murder*, she thought. *I just killed someone*. She felt the tingling in her hand and up her arm. Her arm felt strong as if she were pumped from working out.

Kim? What is Kim going to think? She looked up from her hand.

The Prius was idling.

The passenger side door hung wide open.

Kim was gone.

No. "Kim!" she screamed. "Kim, where are you?"

The parking lot was utterly silent.

Laura ran around to the back of the building.

Nothing. The entire area was deserted.

Cameras, she thought. She ran back into the store and almost fell over the dead gray thing on the floor. She went into the back room and pushed the man's body out of the way so she could lean over the security console.

It was a fairly simple setup. She found the rewind button.

She watched herself in reverse: out of the store, around the building, back into the store.

There was a blur of movement on the outside cameras.

She pressed play.

A gray shape like the one she had killed was standing on one side of the building.

The car door opened, and Kim ran straight toward it.

"Why?" Why would she do that?

Kim kissed the gray shape as if it were someone she loved.

And, then Kim was trying to get away.

The gray thing carried her backward, its hand over her mouth.

Laura followed them on each camera leading to the back.

A town cop car pulled up in the alley behind the store. The gray thing opened the rear door and threw Kim inside. It then got in behind her.

The words Rural Retreat Police were stenciled on the side along with a number: 015.

On the video, the car pulled away.

David ran through the woods on the southeast side of town. He flushed out birds and an occasional squirrel as he passed through.

He hadn't seen any of the monsters.

David thought he might be a quarter mile from Kim's house. It was time to leave the woods.

There was a playground a block south of Kim's, and he could see the swing set through the trees.

"You make a lot of noise, bro."

David stopped.

It was Pauly's voice.

He was sitting in a swing staring toward the woods.

David reached for the gun.

"Yeah, we knew where you were. One of them spotted you a half hour ago. Come on out, we'll talk."

David looked around the woods.

"Only, leave the gun. You won't need it. And, if you try to come out of the woods with it, my friends will rip you to pieces," Pauly said. He was looking at his feet and swinging slowly forward and back.

David took out the gun and leveled it at Pauly's head. He thought of a song and sang it in his head: My Sharona. He wasn't even sure who sang it, but it was dull and repetitive.

He hummed it to himself.

Pauly looked off to his left and stopped swinging. "Hey!" Pauly yelled. "Don't do that. My friends aren't music fans. You ain't gonna shoot me anyway, you putz. I'm still your friend."

David hesitated.

"We have her, David. Your redhead? We have her. You shoot me, and, oh man, they will do things to her. Shit, dude. I don't even know the names for some of the shit they can do."

David lowered the pistol.

"That's better. Leave the gun."

Laura looked at her cell phone. The words 'no service' showed under the signal indicator. *They* had turned off the cell phones. She didn't need to pick up the office phone to know *they* had killed the land lines as well.

But, who were *they*? She thought about the gray thing lying on the floor in a pool of blood. Liquid black eyes and long, sharp teeth. The nails on the woman's hands were more like talons.

The stench was coming from her.

Strange, Laura thought. She hadn't noticed the smell the whole time she fought the girl. Only before she saw Fatima and after she died.

What had she been saying? *Hungry, I'm so hungry?*

The woman was insane. Was that what was going on? Some sort of disease that turned people into psychopaths?

Yeah, and caused them to grow vampire teeth and to lose all their hair.

It didn't matter. There was a choice to be made. She could try to get to the interstate and find help; however, she had little doubt that the road would be blocked by men who thought nothing of helping a gray-skinned monster abduct a teenage girl. In comparison, taking Laura down in a hail of gunfire wouldn't cause them any concern.

She could go back home to Anne and Tia, try to get them somewhere safe. But, where was safe? How could you be safe when the town was full of these monsters?

Laura had, at most, a few minutes to find the car that took Kim: police car 015.

She felt around under the counter at the Gas'N'Go. She was hoping for a gun. Instead, she found a nicked and scarred baseball bat.

David walked out of the woods.

Pauly smiled at him. "Unzip the hoodie."

David unzipped it and showed the empty holster.

"Damn, look at you. Holster and everything. That's bad ass," Pauly said. "Lift your shirt and turn around.

David did so. "I left the gun in the woods."

"Man can't be too careful."

David looked around. "Where are your friends?"

"Close by. I told them to keep their distance."

His voice, his mannerisms, his sense of humor - all Pauly.

But the eyes? There was something new behind the eyes, something dark.

Pauly nodded off to his right. "They're all pissed over Mae. If I wasn't here, man, they'd castrate you."

"Mae? Was that the Draugr in the t-shirt I killed?"

"Damn! You even pronounce that Swedish shit right."

"Norwegian."

"Who the fuck cares, David?" Pauly said as he jumped off the swing. "I'm trying to save your pimpled ass, and you're running around here all Johnny Rambo."

"Save me? What are you talking about?"

"This is all a mistake, David. One big SNAFU. You were supposed to be at the damned party. None of this would have happened." Pauly shook his head. "You remember a few months after your Dad killed himself, you fainted in the hall at middle school?"

"Yeah, so?"

"School nurse thought you had a seizure and wrote 'possibly epileptic' on your school records."

"I'm not epileptic."

Pauly laughed. "Yeah, I know that. You know that. Your mom knows that - not that she cares. But, Miriam, she didn't know. You were on the do not invite list. Something about brain abnormalities not being able to accept the virus. You were supposed to become one of the Draugr."

"Lucky me."

"Yeah, man - it would have been. Immortality, powerful as hell. Red, she was supposed to be at the party too. She was meant to be a protector, like me. That date you two went on? Most costly scratch and tickle session of both your lives."

David took a step toward him. "Where is Kim?"

He heard a chorus of hissing all around him. The Draugr were there, somewhere out of sight.

"Step back. I told you, man, they want your nuts." Pauly shook his head. "You went all Van Helsing, so your deal is out the window. Her deal is still on the table."

"She doesn't want it."

"What? You speakin' for her now? She don't seem the type to put up with a guy speaking for her." Pauly laughed. "Yeah, well, anyway, once she gets a taste, she'll want it. Olc will make her want it."

"Is that what he did to you? Didn't know you swung that way, Pauly," David spat.

Pauly laughed. "Naah, I did Miriam. She showed me the light. I just got a little brain surgery from Olc." Pauly grinned as he tapped his head with a fingertip. "I did Regina too, but I got to say, she was nothing compared to your mom. Even Olc went back for seconds on her."

David clenched his fists.

Pauly sneered at him. "Come on over. After what Olc did to my head, I really love turning people inside out with my bare hands. I can do that now if I want to. I mean, it'd break my heart, man, but I'd get over it. That's what Olc does: makes it so you can get over things."

David pushed the anger away. "Why are you telling me all this?"

"Miriam and Olc want to deal. She wants to talk to you."

Laura drove through the empty streets looking for car 015. She didn't see a living soul until she pulled onto a residential street on her way to downtown. In front of a split-level ranch, a woman was buckling a toddler into his car seat.

Laura pulled up to the driveway, and a man came rushing out of the house with a hunting rifle. He pointed it at her.

Laura held up her hands. "Don't shoot. You see any cop cars go through here?"

The man watched her behind the iron sights. "No."

The woman was holding a small revolver pointed at the driveway. Her hand was shaking.

Laura nodded toward them. "Be careful, whatever this is, I think the cops are in on it."

The man nodded, but he didn't lower the rifle. "Thanks."

"I don't think you can get to the interstate."

"We'll risk it."

Laura nodded. "Good luck."

"And you," the man said.

Laura pulled away.

The man and woman drove away in the opposite direction.

She reached Main Street.

She almost drove right up behind a cop car. She cut the wheel left and pulled into an alley.

Facing away from her in the middle of Main Street was car 015.

Laura got out of the Prius and peered around the edge of a brick building.

The patrol car was just idling in front of the stop light.

The light cycled from green to red and back again, but the car didn't move. She could see the driver staring straight ahead.

Laura crouched low and hid behind parked cars as she approached the cop.

She had the baseball bat in her right hand.

She was hiding behind a pickup a few yards from the car.

He had his window up. The backseat looked empty. The cop looked to be about thirty with a buzz cut and a chiseled jaw. He stared straight ahead, motionless.

He took Kim. He took Kim. She repeated it over and over to herself. She needed to justify what was coming next.

She ran out from behind the pickup and swung the bat at the police car.

The driver's side window shattered inward.

Laura didn't hesitate. She swung again, striking the policeman in the mouth. Blood and teeth exploded in a cloud.

He was moving, reaching for his gun.

Laura drove the end of the bat down through the windowless door. She smashed his crotch.

The man grunted, but he forgot about the gun and grabbed for his nuts instead.

She reached in and opened the car door, dragging him out as it opened.

He evidently remembered the gun again, because he scrambled for it as his shoulder landed on the pavement.

Laura swung the bat with her free hand.

His wrist broke under the onslaught.

She dropped the bat and grabbed the pistol out of his holster.

Laura took a step back and pointed it at him. "My niece. Where?"

"Who?" He was smiling through a mouthful of blood and broken teeth.

"The redheaded girl you took from the Gas'N'Go. Where is she?"

"Hell. Same as you. Same as all of us."

The quiet morning air exploded as she put a round into the pavement beside his head.

"Wrong answer."

He started laughing. "The whole town is in hell now. I've met the devil. He's not red, he doesn't have horns. He's a gray man dressed in black." He tapped his temple. "He gets in your head."

Laura shot him in the right knee.

He didn't scream. He just continued to laugh.

"Where is she?" Laura growled.

"Police station. Purgatory. Waiting for the devil."

David sat in the backseat of a Lincoln Town Car and stared at his friend.

Pauly sat in the rear-facing seat directly across from him. "Man, I never would have thought shit would go down like this, David.

Saturday evening, I was going to a senior party, and you were going on your first date. Damn, man."

David just stared at him.

"Hey, listen. That shit about your mom? That was uncalled for." Pauly shook his head. "I mean, it was true and all, but, still... that was cold of me."

David shook his head. "Who are you? I mean who are you really? Because you aren't Pauly Delveccio. You're wearing his skin, but you aren't him. Pauly Delveccio was my friend."

Pauly pointed at him. "Get to use that condom I gave you yet?"

"I don't care if you know what he knew. My friend died Saturday night. You're some sick, demented thing. I don't know you."

"Look at you, all righteous and shit. You don't know anything. That 'monster' you killed? She was a goddess. She would have still been alive and beautiful ten thousand years from now. They're better than people, and you killed her." Pauly shook his head. "Total SNAFU, man. None of this should have happened. You'd be one of them, and you'd understand. We'd still be friends."

Laura sat in the parking lot across from the police station in car 015. The lot was mostly empty. Only one or two patrol cars were parked in front

"Now what, genius?" she whispered to herself.

She had no way of knowing how many cops were inside the station, not to mention how many of the monsters. She had zero chance if she rushed the building.

Laura had dragged the cop she beat up into a coffee shop on Main Street and handcuffed him to an iron pipe behind the counter.

He was still laughing as she left.

Sitting and doing nothing wasn't an option either. They had Kim in there.

There was a twelve gauge pump action locked upright by the center console. She unlocked it and pulled it out of its holder.

With the shotgun and Glock 17, at least she was well armed.

She dropped down in the seat as a Lincoln town car drove by.

It pulled up in front of the station.

Two boys got out of the back - one of them was David.

"Oh, my God," Laura whispered.

The taller kid with black hair shoved David through the doors of the police station.

David almost fell as he was shoved through the door.

He spun and drew back his fist.

Pauly smiled at him. "Go on. I dare you. Take a shot. Maybe you'll get lucky - then again, maybe I'll tie your arm in a knot for you."

David lowered his fist.

"Yeah, that's a good idea."

David looked around. Police officers sat at desks, at least a dozen of them. They were all armed, a few were in riot gear.

Pauly saluted. "Morning, officers. I just want you guys and gals to know how much we admire that thin blue line." He leaned close to David and whispered, "Their brains are totally scrambled. Seriously, man, they can barely zip up after they piss. Old Olc put their gray matter in a blender. But, they can follow orders and put lots and lots of bullets in anything we want."

The cops stared straight ahead, paying no attention.

Pauly opened a door and pointed inside. "Here ya go."

The sign by the door said Interrogation 1.

David stepped inside.

Kim was sitting on the other side of a steel desk. Her right wrist was handcuffed to a steel ring in the middle of the table. She stood up and tried to back away as David walked in.

"I'll just leave you love birds to it," Pauly said as he shut the door behind David.

"Kim, are you okay?" David asked. He took a step toward her.

Kim shook her head and grabbed the small steel chair she had been sitting in. She held it front of her like a cartoon lion tamer. "Don't touch me!"

"Kim? It's okay. It's me. I won't hurt you." He held out his hands to her.

"No. You're not David. You're that... woman or whatever she was." Her eyes were wild with fear.

"No. No. I'm me. I'm David." He walked to her slowly. He reached out and took the chair out of her hands. "It's going to be okay now."

"David?"

He smiled. "Yeah. Yeah, it's me."

"Really?"

He put his arms around her.

She was stiff in his arms and then she wrapped her free arm around him. "Warm. You're warm."

"Did she look like me?"

Kim looked ill. She nodded. "But, cold. She was cold."

He rubbed her hair. "I tried to get to you. Honest, I did."

"David, what are they?"

An old green pickup pulled up beside the town car as Laura slid lower in her seat.

A tall blonde in a skirt got out of the truck.

The black haired boy met her on the street, and then the boy got into the pickup and drove away.

The woman walked into the police station.

Laura needed a plan.

David sat beside Kim at the table.

"Vampires?" Kim asked.

"Yeah, I know. Sounds crazy."

Kim shook her head. "It was so real. She looked just like you. I…"
She sighed.

"It's okay," David said. "Why did you go to the Gas'N'Go in the first place?"

"You called me… only, I guess it wasn't you?"

"No. I lost my phone yesterday. Debbie Kincaid had it."

Kim looked confused. "Cat Lady Debbie? She's one of them?"

"No. Not exactly…"

The door opened, and two women walked in. At the sight of the second woman, a brunette wearing pearls, Kim jumped out of her seat and strained against the handcuffs securing her to the table.

The blonde woman looked at the brunette. "I think she knows you."

The woman wearing pearls smiled. "We kissed earlier."

The blonde sat down and smiled. "My, Miss Lawrence, how progressive of you."

The brunette hovered behind the blonde's chair.

"Who are you?" David asked.

"My name is Miriam. This is my friend Brittney. And, you are the elusive Mr. Connors. We've been looking for you," Miriam pointed at Kim's empty chair. "Sit down, please."

David held Kim's hand as she sat down.

"There now. That's better," Miriam said. "I'll get directly to the point. Where is Gene Stinson?"

"Who?" David asked.

"Please, David. It's not even noon, and it's already been a long day. I need you to tell me where Gene is, or Brittney is going to drain Kim dry while you watch."

Miriam's eyes were like cold shards of ice.

Brittney was smiling.

David shook his head. "I don't know where he is. He dropped me off short of town and drove north." He imagined the scene in his mind. Imagined Gene driving away.

Brittney stared at him.

David felt his mind being sifted through, the same as it had been in the woods by Mae. He showed Brittney the imagined scene.

Miriam glanced up at her.

Brittney shook her head. "He knows about us. Everything. Olc could pry his way inside, but I can't."

Miriam smiled at him. "I believe you're lying, David."

David shrugged.

Brittney stared harder. "She's a beauty. One in a million girls..."

Miriam rolled her eyes. "The Tubes. Points for classic rock. How long do you think you can keep that up?"

"It's a catchy song," David said.

Miriam looked up at Brittney. "Enough."

Brittney nodded.

David felt the onslaught on his thoughts recede.

Miriam leaned back. "There's no need for this to be any more unpleasant than it is. We only want Gene. We know he is the one who killed Mae. Give him to us, and we'll let you and Kim go free."

Kim looked at David.

He stared directly at Miriam. "Free? What? To be eaten or converted."

"We'll let you leave. A police escort to the interstate. You promise to just go away for a few weeks, keeping all this to yourselves of course. You can come home by December. We'll be gone by then, and you can put this whole mess behind you." Miriam smiled.

"My family?" Kim asked.

Miriam smiled. "If you insist."

"What about my mom and Pauly?" David asked.

Miriam laughed. "I'm afraid that wouldn't work out well for any of you. They belong with us. They've made... lifestyle changes."

Brittney smiled.

"What gives you the right to rape people's minds?" David asked. "What gives you the right to turn people into monsters against their will?"

Miriam stared at him. "You mean, like your mother? Oh, she begged me to become a *monster*, David. And Pauly? He was exuberant to have me, no matter the consequences."

David looked up at Brittney. "What about you? Did you beg for this? I've seen you around town. You looked fairly happy whenever I saw you - was this your choice?"

Brittney frowned.

"Do you even know?" David asked.

Miriam leaned across the table. "Normally, I enjoy a good philosophical discussion, but I'm on a schedule, David. We do what we do because of biological imperative. We are going to survive, David. We're older than you, smarter, stronger. We are your superiors in every way. We don't justify ourselves to cattle. We take what we want." She spread her hands on the table. "Now, this conversation is beginning to bore me."

She stood up. "David, I'm going to give you until midnight to deliver Gene Stinson to me. If you do, you and Kim and Kim's family get to leave Rural Retreat. If you don't, I'm going to make Kim into a protector like your mother and Pauly. And, we'll bleed you dry, slowly and painfully."

Miriam looked at Brittney. "Send in one of the officers, please?"

Brittney stepped outside and walked in a moment later with a policeman wearing a brown uniform. His nameplate read Taggert.

Miriam smiled at him. "Uncuff Miss Lawrence, please, Officer Taggert."

Taggert moved like he was sleepwalking. He unlocked the handcuff.

Kim rubbed her wrist.

"Brittney, take Miss Lawrence to the car, please."

Kim jumped out of her chair.

David stood up and got between her and Brittney. "Okay, I'll do it. But, Kim stays with me. I'll get him for you."

Miriam shook her head. "No, David. Kim is coming with us." She looked at Taggert. "Give David your radio, please."

Taggert unclipped his two-way radio from his belt and held it out to David.

"Take the radio. When you find Gene, call us with the position. We'll take care of the rest," Miriam said.

David took the radio.

"Now, stand aside. We're going to take Kim somewhere to prepare her for tonight - in case you fail."

"No!" Kim screamed.

"Don't worry. We won't hurt you," Miriam said. "We might even persuade you to join us."

David and Kim stood ready to fight.

Miriam sighed. "You can't fight your way out of this. Can't you see that? There is no hope. There is no way..." She looked at Taggert. "Officer Taggert, draw your pistol."

He took out his gun and held it pointed toward the floor.

"What are you doing?" David asked.

"Officer Taggert, open your mouth."

He opened his mouth. His eyes were empty.

"Now, put the barrel in your mouth."

"Don't!" Kim whispered.

"I told you, I'll do what you want!" David said.

Taggert put the barrel of the Glock in his mouth.

Miriam nodded. "I know. But, I need you to understand we hold all the cards, David."

"I already know!"

"Pull the trigger, Officer Taggert."

Kim screamed as the gun went off. Blood sprayed against the wall and overhead tiles.

Taggert collapsed on the floor, his legs bent under him.

The barrel of the gun was still in his mouth.

David and Kim clung to each other and shook.

"Brittney."

Brittney smiled and stepped around the table.

She backhanded David and knocked him off his feet. He landed flat of his back on the Interrogation Room floor.

"David!" Kim screamed. She lashed out with her hands Brittney's face.

Brittney caught her hands and twisted them behind her back.

"Ow!"

She gathered Kim's wrists together behind her back and pulled her backward toward the door.

David struggled to his feet. Blood leaked from the right side of his mouth. "Don't hurt her. Please."

Kim was crying and struggling as she was pulled through the door.

"Take her to the car," Miriam said as she followed them.

"Kim! I'll find you," David yelled.

Miriam paused and looked at him. "Twelve hours, David. After that, we're going to enjoy ourselves with her. The results will break your heart."

David glared at her. "One day, someone is going to do this to you. They're going to take everything away from you. And, you're going to know what it's like to be helpless. I only hope I'm there to see it."

Miriam turned her head to the side and studied him. "Perhaps." She turned away. "But, not today."

Laura had decided to storm the police station. There was no other choice. She checked the twelve gauge and put extra shells in her jacket pocket. She had her hand on the car's door handle.

The two women from earlier exited the building.

The brunette was dragging Kim by her wrists.

Kim was kicking and screaming.

Laura started to open the door.

They dragged Kim into the town car.

Laura stopped.

No, she thought. *Let them pull away.* She had a better chance of stopping them away from the police station.

The town car turned and left the lot.

Laura put the car in gear and followed.

In the Interrogation Room, David reached down to take the Glock out of Taggert's mouth. The dead man stared at him with a circular pool of blood spread out under his head.

He heard a clicking noise.

Two more cops stood in the doorway, their weapons drawn and pointed at him.

So much for getting a gun.

He stood up and showed them his hands. He carried nothing but the radio.

The blank-eyed officers stepped to the side and let him pass.

There were Draugr in the police station now. Six. They looked at him with their big black eyes.

They weren't trying to camouflage. They stood, naked and oily looking, baring their teeth at him as he passed.

He walked out the front door into the gloom.

David looked behind him. The Draugr made no move to follow.

He needed a weapon.

Luckily, he knew where to find one.

Miriam sat in the rear-facing seat and watched as Brittney played with Kim's hair. "I think she likes you," Miriam said.

"Please stop," Kim whispered.

"I don't think she returns the sentiment, Brittney."

"Too bad. That was an amazing kiss. He's a lucky boy," Brittney said as she continued to twirl Kim's hair around her finger. "Her hair is so beautiful."

Miriam smiled. "They become obsessed with hair. All of their hair falls out, so it intrigues them."

"Are you going to let us go?" Kim asked.

"No, of course not," Miriam said. She straightened her skirt.

Kim fought back tears.

"Kim, you've only heard one side of all this. I hope tonight to have the opportunity to reason with you. The protectors are my responsibility. I love each and every one of them. I want to love you. I want to show you what unconditional love really means - not this teenage stuff you're experiencing now. Real, true love that lasts for centuries, millennia."

"You're insane."

Miriam smiled. "I suppose. The Draugr are very special. Much more important than…"

Miriam's smile faded. She looked toward the black glass partition concealing the front seats. "What? Are you sure?"

Kim stared at her.

Brittney turned and looked out the back window. "Stop the car. I'll handle this."

"What are you talking about?" Kim asked.

Miriam peered over Kim's shoulder. "Someone is following us."

Miriam looked at Brittney. "No. You stay with us. Contact the house and tell them to send someone in my truck. I've told Edgar to slow down."

Kim turned and looked out the window. "Is it David? Please don't hurt him."

"No. It isn't David. It's someone else. A woman according to Edgar. She's following us because of you. Who might that be, Kim?"

"I… I don't know," Kim said.

Brittney put a hand on each side of Kim's face.

"Ah…" Kim whispered. "What are you doing? Are you in my head?"

"Laura… Aunt Laura. She was with her at the Gas'N'Go." Brittney said. She released Kim's face. "She killed one of the young there. I sensed it just as I took Kim."

Miriam looked astonished. "And, you're just telling me now?" Miriam asked.

"Kim was the priority."

Laura hung back on the road as far as she dared. They were headed back into the country on Kinder Valley Road. Laura tried to remember what was out this way. It was mostly empty pasture land.

The town car kept slowing down. They were barely driving thirty miles per hour. She had to drive slower and slower so as not to catch up to them.

They turned a shallow curve ahead.

Laura entered the curve to find the town car speeding away.

"Oh, shit," she said. She pressed her foot to the floor.

She never saw the green pickup speeding toward her from the left. It had been idling on a small dirt road that intersected Kinder Valley Road.

If she had been an instant slower in pressing the gas, the pickup would have t-boned her. Instead, it struck her rear fender at the tire.

The cruiser spun on the rain slick road.

Suddenly she was facing the opposite direction and airborne as the cruiser spiraled off the road and over an embankment.

Time stood still.

The shotgun floated off the seat as down became up and up became down.

She was looking through the window as the car landed upside down. Her head hit the headliner and pain shot through her neck and back. She passed out.

Debbie Kincaid jumped out of the truck and clapped.

The police cruiser was lying on its top in a six-foot-deep ditch off the road.

"I did it," she said to herself. She skipped back to the truck.

The truck's left headlight was hanging by a cable from the dented front fender, but the chrome bumper had taken the brunt of the impact. She reached into the truck bed for the plastic, five-gallon gas can.

The world was upside down. Laura tried to focus, but she saw two of everything, and the upside down world was spinning. She could see dead grass above her head out the car window.

No.

The car was upside down, and so was she.

She looked toward her lap. She was still belted in the driver's seat.

She looked up the embankment outside the window.

Two cherub-faced women, identical twins, were staring down at her with a look of glee. "I got you good!" one voice yelled. Both of them held up identical red gas cans. "Now, I'm going to watch you burn!"

Laura felt around on the headliner. She found the Glock.

Her head hurt. She aimed it out the window.

Which one to shoot?

The women were walking side by side down the embankment.

She aimed and fired.

The bullet went wild, but the chubby women ducked. They stared at Laura wide-eyed.

They started to laugh. "You're all fucked up! You can't hit me."

Laura fired again and kicked up dirt. "Can one of you bitches stand still?"

They were opening the gas cans. They both fumbled in their pockets for something.

"Screw this," Laura whispered. She dropped the Glock.

Laura picked up the twelve gauge and racked a shell.

The women froze in place.

Laura aimed for both of them and pulled the trigger.

The boom hurt her ears, but both women went down side by side.

"I got to get out of here," Laura whispered as she passed out.

"All with one accord in one place," Tia whispered. She was lying on her mother's lap on the living room couch.

Anne stroked her hair with her left hand.

She held the butcher knife tight in her right.

"What did you say, sweetie?"

"Grandma said we would be okay when we were all with one accord in one place," Tia said.

"Sounds like something out of the Bible."

Tia shrugged. "I want Kim to come home. And, Aunt Laura. They need to come home, Mommy. We need to all be in one place and with one accord. Even David. And, the old man."

"What old man, sweetie?"

"Grandma said he was a knight like Aunt Laura and David."

She hugged Tia tight. "Oh, honey, I wish Grandma would talk to me. I'd really like to hear her voice right now."

Tia nodded. "She says I can hear her because I haven't learned what's impossible yet."

Anne smiled. "Is that right? Well, I hope you never do." She looked at the door and hoped beyond hope they would come home soon.

David ran. He had been a runner since middle school, and he ran through the deserted streets. He thought he saw Draugr at every corner, in every window.

Maybe they were there, shadowing him as he retraced the path he had taken in the town car with Pauly. He was heading for the playground near Kim's house.

It seemed pointless. They wouldn't be so thoughtless as to leave it there in the woods.

He ran onto the playground, past the swings, and into the woods. He slid to a stop in a clearing of dead leaves.

His backpack was lying where he left it.

He dropped down beside it, panting.

David opened the zipper.

The pistol was there, its black silencer gleaming. He checked it. Still loaded.

He unzipped the hoodie. He slid the .45 into the holster and pulled a bottle of water out of the backpack.

He turned slowly as he drank, taking in the woods around him.

There could be a dozen surrounding him, he would never know. He suspected that not only could they look like anyone, they could also look like *nothing* if they wanted.

If so, they didn't consider him a threat with his pistol.

We'll see, he thought as he slung the pack on his back and ran to the west.

Laura blinked. Her head hurt.

She could smell gasoline.

The car. She jolted awake.

She was still hanging upside down.

She unhooked the seatbelt and fell on her shoulders. "Mother..." she hissed.

She tossed the shotgun and Glock out ahead of her as she crawled out the driver's side window.

There was an overturned gas can on the dead grass. The gas fumes were strong.

She got to her feet and picked up the weapons. She slid the Glock into the back waistband of her jeans.

Laura cradled the shotgun in her left arm. She felt in her jacket pockets. The extra shells were still there as were the bullets for the Glock.

There was a dark red stain on the grass. A large pool of blood with a smear leading up the embankment.

She climbed up to the road.

The chubby girl was clawing her way across the asphalt toward the pickup. There was a massive hole in her back, and, from the blood trail, there must have been a matching hole in her front.

Laura hooked her boot under the woman's right shoulder and rolled her onto her back.

There was blood leaking from her mouth, and she was pale as a sheet.

She was smiling. "Got you. I got you good," she rasped.

Laura stared at her. "Looks like I got you better."

The woman laughed and brought up more blood.

She should be dead, Laura thought. Nobody could lose this much blood and still be alive.

"Did what I was supposed to do," the woman whispered. "That's what matters. I did what Miriam told me. I'm a hero."

Laura shook her head. "Bitch, you are batshit insane."

The woman raised her head and looked down at her stomach. "Hurts. First time always hurts." She laughed.

"Where are they taking Kim?"

The woman laughed bringing up a swell of blood. "Won't tell. I'm a hero." She laughed harder. "First time always hurts. It really does."

Laura shook her head. "Second time won't." She pointed the shotgun at her head, racked a shell, and pulled the trigger.

"Hold her down," Miriam said as she retrieved the glass bottle from her dresser.

Kim screamed and fought as Jane Connors knelt behind her and pulled the girl's arms down and back.

Kim was kneeling on the floor, her back arched as Jane bent her almost double.

"Kim, you need to calm down." Miriam stepped in front of her. She unscrewed the dropper from the top of the glass bottle.

Red liquid filled the glass tube.

"No!" Kim screamed.

Miriam put her thumb and index finger against Kim's right eye and forced it open.

The girl thrashed, and Miriam pried harder. "Kim, I want you to stop this. I have medical instruments that will hold your eye open, but I don't want to use them because they hurt. I don't want to hurt you, but I will if I have to."

Kim screamed louder.

Miriam stumbled backward. "Oh, for God's sake. Put her on her back."

Jane picked Kim up by her shoulders and slammed her down on the floor.

Kim was lying flat on her back, the wind knocked out of her.

"Pin her shoulders," Miriam said.

Jane put her knees on the girl's shoulders and put her hands on either side of her head. "Careful, she can still kick."

Miriam straddled Kim's waist.

She reached down and pried Kim's right eye open again.

Kim whined.

"Shh, it'll be okay." She dripped a single red drop in Kim's eye.

Kim arched her back and ground her teeth together.

"There we go. That's better."

She went limp. Kim's lips moved, but no sound came out.

"It's nice, isn't it?" Jane whispered as she stared down at Kim.

The girl's gaze was unfocused.

Miriam gently put a drop in her left eye.

They let her go.

Kim's head slowly turned to the left. Her lips were still moving, speaking without a sound in her delirium.

Miriam picked her up and laid her on the bed.

David ran through the woods. He stopped a few times to get his bearings, but he remembered most of the landmarks. The day grew colder, and his breath fogged in front of his face.

He didn't know what he was going to do.

Were they following him as he suspected? He wanted to think they weren't. He wanted to believe Miriam would live up to her end of the bargain, that she was waiting for him to call on the radio.

He wanted to believe they were leaving Kim alone.

He wanted to believe all that.

And, what was he going to do when he got back to Gene's hiding place? Ask him to help?

Was that his goal?

Or, was he going to make the call on the radio and tell them where to find Gene?

The man had saved his life. Mae would have killed him if Gene hadn't intervened.

Would he give up Gene to save Kim?

Yes, he thought. He would. He wasn't proud of that, but he knew it was true.

Laura rolled the chubby girl down the hill toward the police cruiser.

There was still a mess on the road, but stealth was no longer a concern.

Before today, she hadn't killed anyone. She'd killed a car and made life a nightmare for some logging companies. She had even played a hand in enabling killers.

But, since this morning, she had killed two and disfigured one.

It was starting to sink in.

She wasn't who she thought she was.

She shook her head as she climbed into the chubby girl's pickup. This was about Kim, not her. After Kim was safe, let the chips fall where they may.

If she had to kill half this town to get her niece back, then that was exactly what she was going to do.

The woman had left the truck idling, and Laura drove it west down Kinder Valley Road - the last direction she had seen the town car traveling.

Kim was floating. Her existence was defined in brief snapshots as she regained consciousness and just as quickly slipped back under.

The bed. Warm. The comforter soft under her fingers.

Miriam smiling down as she massaged something red into her skin.

It tingled like peppermint.

She felt strong.

"Not so bad now, is it?" Miriam asked.

"Let me go home," Kim whispered back.

"Shh. Sleep."

Blackness.

Dreams of voices in her head, all speaking at once.

So young.

Hair. Red. Child of Eirinn.

No. Older still. Child of the Lamia.

Wonderful.

Tell her about Die Gute Wolf. Train her to recognize. Protector, better than Miriam.

Die Gute Wolf is our danger.

Nemesis.

Fear Die Gute Wolf.

Only pure metal protects.

Listen, child.

Close, too close.

Olc is a fool.

Miriam's face. "Are you awake?"

"No," Kim whispered.

Miriam stroked her forehead. "You aren't afraid now?"

"No," Kim whispered.

Miriam smiled. "No. You see? I told you." She held up a hand mirror.

Kim stared at her own reflection. Her face was the same color as her auburn hair.

She smiled at herself covered in dried blood.

Pauly stood in the doorway to Miriam's room and watched as Miriam poured Draugr blood down Kim's naked body. She massaged it into Kim's thighs and calves.

Pauly watched as Kim's muscle tone became more defined.

There was a smile on Kim's sleeping face.

He knew the feeling. He'd felt the same during his own baptism.

Pauly stepped inside.

"No," Miriam said without looking up. "You'll have her soon enough. Olc will be first. She belongs to him."

"He's busy downstairs in the group. I don't think…"

"That's right, you don't think," Miriam said. "Not thinking will likely be the end of you."

Pauly sighed and turned away.

He walked into the hallway.

Come to us, boy. The words sounded like trumpets in his mind. He staggered against the wall.

Pauly shook.

They never spoke to him. They spoke to Olc and Miriam.

The ancients never spoke to him.

"I don't know where…"

Outside.

Cellar.

Come now.

Pauly went downstairs and through the kitchen.

He looked at the back yard through the wavy glass of the kitchen door.

Near the middle of the yard was a mound of stones with two old wooden doors on top.

The root cellar dug over a century ago. A cool place to store potatoes and turnips, to protect them from heat and freezing.

Now, it stored something far different.

He opened the kitchen door and walked out into the cold.

The cellar doors were attached to the limestone rocks by rusting metal hinges.

He opened one of the doors.

The smell of earth and decay wafted up to him.

He was used to the stench of the Draugr, but this seemed even more noxious.

The rough-hewn steps descended into darkness.

Down here.

Something laughed. He was unsure if it was in his ears or only in his head.

He descended into darkness.

He reached the bottom step.

The cellar had collapsed in on itself at some point, and plant roots wove through what little space was left inside.

Three gray shapes sat entwined in the roots.

Light.

Cursed light.

A thin gray hand with long, claw-like nails snaked out into the meager sun.

The skin was almost transparent - he could see pale red blood pulsing beneath the skin, pink muscle attached to white bone. The sunlight touched the skin, and the hand began to smoke.

The hand withdrew quickly.

Damned light.

There was laughter again.

The boy's skin. Nice and thick. Maybe we should wear it?

Pauly scrambled backward.

No fear, boy.

Safe.

Need your help.

Pauly stopped crawling backward. "I'm listening."

A place where possessions are traded for gold. Nearby?

Pauly shook his head. "I... I'm not sure what you mean."

They hissed.

Pauly winced at the sound.

A fat spider crawled out of the darkness. It skittered over the limestone.

Pauly squashed it with his foot.

Money. A place where possessions are traded for money.

"A pawnshop? You mean a pawnshop?"

Pawnshop?

Yes.

Lombardy bank.

Damned Medicis.

"What do you need from a pawn shop?" Pauly asked.

Silver.

As much as you can find.

Bring it here from their vault.

Pure metal.

"Why do you need…"

Die Gute Wolf.

Go, now.

The ancients moved within the roots. They crawled toward him, stopping just short of the light.

Pauly scrambled back up the steps.

Laura drove by the old Victorian house on Kinder Valley Road. She had forgotten about it. She had gone there once in high school with a dozen other kids. Not even teenage bravado could coerce them inside that day.

No one dared to enter the dying hulk of a house.

They had stayed on the big front porch and watched the lights of Rural Retreat through a haze of cheap weed and cheaper beer. The only exploring had taken place inside tight jeans.

The house looked just as abandoned as it always had.

She drove past.

Olc walked into Miriam's bedroom.

Miriam smiled at him from where she sat on the edge of the bed.

Kim slept on the bed. She was lying on her back, her bare skin stained red by the blood.

"She's ready for you," Miriam said as she rose to her feet.

Olc touched the sleeping girl's mind.

She stirred.

Miriam leaned against him and stroked his upper thigh. "Make her... suffer. And, make her enjoy that. The way you did with me."

He smiled down at her.

Miriam smiled toward Kim. "Make her cruel. I want the boy to see what we've made of her. I want him to see how we've destroyed his world. And, when he is filled with despair, we'll destroy him."

Miriam stepped past him. "Enjoy her."

He grabbed her arm. "Stay."

She smiled up at him.

David stopped in the woods beside the house Gene was using as a hideout.

The lights were out, but Gene's pickup sat in the yard fifty yards from the brick ranch.

David figured he must have moved it during the day.

The sun had set.

David looked at his watch. Just a few minutes past five. He had less than seven hours to get Kim.

He looked around once more.

There was no sign of the Draugr.

He walked toward the house.

The lights were off, but, as he drew closer, he could hear the familiar sound of Billy Don't be a Hero playing on a stereo.

Nothing moved in the dark windows.

Maybe they had already gotten him. What would that mean for his deal?

He knew what it would mean: no deal.

He reached up to knock on the door.

Before he could touch it, the door opened, and Gene grabbed him by the front of his hoodie, dragging him inside.

He slammed the door behind them.

"Gene…"

The old man was carrying an assault rifle with a long silencer in his hands. He put the silencer under David's nose. "Don't talk…"

Gene pushed him toward the kitchen.

There was an odd smell, like rotten eggs.

"What's going on?"

He slapped the back of David's head and pushed him toward the basement door. "Keep quiet!"

David took the steps down two at a time, and Gene was still pushing him.

Gene slammed the door behind them and braced a two by four under the knob.

Something crashed upstairs.

Gene smiled at him. "You little prick."

"Let me explain."

Gene shoved him toward two Bilco doors at the end of the basement.

There was pounding on the basement door behind them.

Gene was smiling. "Draw your gun." He took a small box out of his pocket and pressed a button. "On three."

251

"What?"

Gene dropped the box and slapped him. "One."

"What are we doing?"

"Two."

Gene took hold of the handle on the underside of the Bilco door.

"Three."

He flung the door open and fired the assault rifle into the darkness beyond.

David ran after him as Gene ran into the yard.

The night was alive with Draugr.

They were inside the house and all around it.

Gene fired calmly.

Gray shapes fell with each bullet fired.

"Six."

He was still counting as he fired at the shapes around the house. He was walking backward toward his truck.

"Seven. Make your choice, kid. You with them or me?"

David turned and fired at the nearest Draugr. The bullet hit the creature in the shoulder, and it spun away.

"Eight. Good choice."

David was walking backward and firing. "There are too many of them."

"Nine. Duck!"

"What?"

The sun rose. At least, that's what it looked like: sunrise on a hot summer day.

The house exploded in a ball of flame.

David was knocked off his feet. He landed beside Gene who was already lying on the ground.

"Told you to duck!" the old man said as the fireball rose into the air.

Draugr were running in every direction. They were burning.

"You... you blew up the house."

"Burn, you mothers!" Gene yelled.

Some of the Draugr were getting to their feet.

Gene started firing again.

David sat up.

"You just going to sit there?" Gene hissed.

David took aim and fired. A Draugr head exploded.

Olc screamed.

An instant later, the Draugr communed together in the parlor screamed as well.

Miriam was forced down to her knees by the pain in her head. "What is it!"

Kim sat bolt upright on the bed.

Olc swung his fist. Part of the door frame exploded from the impact of the blow. "No!"

"Olc? What…"

"They're dead! He killed them."

"What?"

Olc grabbed her by the shoulders and lifted her into the air. "Draugr. You sent. To follow the boy. Dead!"

"How?"

"Your husband. Set a trap," Olc said as he shook her.

He tossed her onto the floor as he stalked out of the room.

Miriam sat up. Her arm was twisted. She took hold of her wrist and pulled the bones back into place.

Kim stared at her uncomprehending.

David and Gene walked around the yard. If any Draugr moved they shot it.

"Well, would you look at this?" Gene said. He was leaning over a gray body.

David stood beside Gene.

One of the Draugr, a male, was crawling through the grass.

"Not a scratch on him. Lucky bastard, just got the wind knocked out of him," Gene said. He pulled a ziplock bag out of his pocket. There was a white rag inside.

Gene put his knee in the small of the Draugr's back and leaned over him.

He pulled the monster's head back and clamped the rag over its mouth and nose.

It struggled weakly for a moment.

"What are you doing?"

The Draugr went limp. He put the cloth back in the ziplock bag. "Chloroform. Works on them same as people." Gene took a pillowcase out of his pocket and put it over the creature's head. He tied it in place with rope.

Then he used two lengths of rope to tie the Draugr's feet and ankles together.

"Grab him by the knees."

"Obviously, you were planning this."

Gene grabbed under the Draugr's arms. "I was hoping," Gene said as they picked him up.

"Where are we going with this?"

"Truck bed."

"Why?"

"'Cause I like torturing the bastards."

They tossed the tied Draugr in the back of the pickup.

David turned and looked at the still burning house. "You rigged the house to explode."

"Yes, I did."

"How did you know we could get out?"

"We? I knew I could get out. You were just a spur of the moment thing, you traitorous little shit."

"I didn't know…"

"Bullshit! You knew exactly. You knew they were following you. And, if they hadn't have followed you, you'd be telling them where I was right now with that radio you're carrying," Gene said. He turned and opened the driver's side door.

"They said…"

"I know what they said. They told you they would let you go if you rolled over on good ol' Gene, right?"

David sighed. "I love her."

"Of course you do. That's why I set a trap. I knew they'd catch you, and I knew they would use you to find me. Been waiting all day to set that shit off," he got in the truck and slammed the door.

The truck started with a rumble.

He backed up and stared at David through the passenger door window. Gene pressed a button, and the window rolled down. "Well?"

"Well, what?"

Gene shook his head. "Get in the damned truck, boy. They'll be on us in a few minutes."

Laura reached the roadblock near the end of Kinder Valley Road. Five town cop cars were blocking both lanes at the bottom of the hill. She had passed at least a dozen side roads along the way.

The town car must have turned on one of them.

She did a U-turn and started searching the back roads.

Gene drove in silence.

David looked at his hands. "Where are we going?"

"I think I'll keep that to myself. Loose lips sink ships."

"Jesus, I'm sorry. What was I supposed to do?"

Gene opened a pill bottle and stuck a tiny pill under his tongue. "Well, if you'd done what I told you, you'd be halfway to Miami by now. You would have lived through this night."

"You knew I wouldn't leave, didn't you?"

"I expected you wouldn't."

"You used me."

The old man laughed. "Damn, kid. You were going to turn me over to Olc in exchange for a piece of tail, and somehow you think you have the moral high ground?"

David glared at him. "Don't you talk about her like that."

"Simmer down."

"Let me out here," David said.

Gene looked around the deserted road. "What the hell are you going to do?"

"I'm going to the house on Kinder Valley Road. I'm going to get Kim out of there or die trying."

"Oh, it'll be the latter, sonny boy. No doubt about that."

"Just let me out."

Gene pulled to a stop and stared at him. "You know what your problem is?"

"No, what?" David growled.

"You go off half-cocked with no plan. You let your nuts do your thinking.."

"If you're such a genius, you tell me what I should do."

"Think like your enemy, you dipshit. What does he expect from you?"

"How the hell should I know?"

"Olc expects you to either run or try to get to the girl. He's betting you'll come back to the house because you're a stupid kid. You do that, and you might as well slit your own throat."

"I'm not running!" David yelled. "I won't leave her. I won't give up."

Gene nodded, his voice became calm. "Okay. Okay." Gene looked at the steering wheel. "Your only move is to try to get to the girl." Gene smiled. "I'm the wildcard. Olc knows I won't go near the house, not tonight anyway. He expects me to go to ground and plot my next move."

"So?"

Gene turned and smiled at him. "Well, let's give the old bastard a surprise."

Pauly returned from his errand to find the house in an uproar. He could feel the Draugr screaming a mile from the house, three minutes before he could actually hear them.

He parked behind the house and went straight back to the root cellar with a cardboard box in his hands.

The sun had set a few hours before.

The ancients stood outside the stone entrance.

They were hard to see. They seemed to stay in motion, and, if you tried to look at them for more than an instant, they darted away.

Their movements reminded him of hummingbirds.

"I brought you silver," Pauly said.

The heavy box was pulled from his hands by a gray blur of motion.

Well done.

A fine boy.

Pleases us.

They huddled together and poured over the contents of the box.

Pauly looked toward the house. The wailing within continued. "What's happened?"

Death.

"Who's dead?" Pauly asked. He took a step toward the house. His first thought was of Miriam.

Draugr.
Many Draugr.
Half.
Yes, half.
"Who killed them?"
The old man.
Nemesis.
Alive too long.
Pauly started toward the house.
No.
You will drive us.
He pointed toward the house. "They need my help."
Find death on their own.
Blinded.
Fool's errand.
You will drive us.
Pauly sighed. "Where do you want me to take you?"
One of the Draugr picked up a handful of silver coins and jewelry.
It let the items sift through its fingers back into the box.
Blacksmith.
"There are no blacksmiths in Rural Retreat."
Find an equivalent.
You will drive us.

Gene drove toward town.

David kept watch in the rear view. He expected to see someone or something behind them any moment.

"Olc is nothing if not cautious. We hurt him. He won't rush out after us, but you can bet we rattled him."

"Everyone is talking about this Olc character, but I haven't seen him," David said, still keeping one eye on the mirror.

"Marcus Velerius Corvus Olc. He's about twenty-four hundred years old if we can believe his history. He was a Roman general in the Republic, three hundred plus years before Julius Caesar and Jesus Christ," Gene said. "He was a stand-up guy from the accounts I've read. Only, somewhere along the way, he started looking for the secret to immortality." Gene looked at David. "He found it."

"All these people dead. How can they hope to get away with it?"

"Somehow it will get blamed on something else. Wildfire, plague, chemical spill - hell, you know there was a town up in Indiana a few years ago, whole damned place was wiped out in a chemical spill. I wonder about that one sometimes." Gene said. He shook his head. "I got to admit though, this is ballsy even by his standards."

"Because you killed so many of them in Minneapolis? That's why he's moving so fast?"

Gene nodded. "Yeah, I think it is."

Gene pulled behind an old gas station off Kinder Valley Road. It was a garage in addition to selling fuel. The pumps were ancient, the aluminum housings dull with age.

"Why are we stopping here?" David asked.

"The beast."

David frowned. "The what?"

Gene pointed to a shed at the far end of the property. The shed itself was an old tin structure that was sagging with age.

Inside it, however, sat the beast. It was a tow truck, fire engine red and bigger than any he had seen before. Flying white letters on the crimson wrecker boom read Jerr-Dan.

White letters were stenciled on the driver's side door: P.F. Decker and Sons.

"Saw it when I drove into town. That's a sixty-ton job, used to haul eighteen wheelers that have gone tits up. The Deckers had a nice setup here. Probably worked all up and down Interstate 81."

"What are you going to do with it?"

Gene smiled. "I aim to do mischief, boy. I aim to do mischief."

Miriam stood beside Olc on the front porch and looked toward Rural Retreat. The lamentations of the young Draugr had subsided to a gentle buzzing in Miriam's ears.

Just south of town, the horizon glowed orange from the still burning house.

She took his hand and looked up at him.

Tears were streaming down his face.

Miriam looked away.

He squeezed her hand. "Not your fault."

"Yes, it is. I underestimated Gene and the boy."

"My fault. Forty years. My fault."

258

"There's no place for them to go. We have them outnumbered, the police will shoot on sight. For the first time in forty years, we have him boxed in with no one to help him other than a sixteen-year-old boy." She leaned up and wiped away a tear. "This will be his end."

"Foolish. Too bold. This place."

Miriam smiled and ran a finger down his bare back. "You are bold. It's why I'm with you. You took me, made me yours. You took me from him."

"Happy?"

Miriam laid her head against his chest. "Of course. Everything you do makes me happy. Even the painful things." She stared up at him. "Those things especially. It's how you made me, remember?"

"I remember."

She pulled him toward the door. "Come upstairs. The girl is ready. She is ripe. Take out your vengeance on her."

"No," Olc whispered. "The boy. I'll make him watch. Vengeance. Sweet."

David looked at the Draugr who now dangled from the end of the tow truck boom. He was wrapped in chains with the pillowcase still over his head. He wasn't moving.

Gene checked the chains.

The creature's feet dangled two feet off the ground.

Suddenly, it moved, swinging its arms wildly.

Gene hit it in the face with a right hook.

The body went limp again.

David turned and looked at Gene's old truck. "I don't know about this plan."

Gene shrugged. "You can still run."

David jingled the keys in his hand. "I've never actually driven before."

"Not even on XBox?"

"Like you said, 'Ain't quite the same.'"

"My truck's an automatic. Lucky for you, I'm lazy. You know which is the gas and which is the brake, right?"

David nodded.

Gene walked up to him. "The road turns off a half mile before you reach the house. Now, it's rough, but the truck can navigate it. Stop short of where you can see the house."

David nodded.

"You loaded?"

"Yeah, full magazines."

"You run into Draugr on the road, you remember you're driving a truck. Mash them flat. Don't hesitate, even if it looks like a person - someone you know. You run them down."

"Yes, sir."

"Go in the back door of the house. If one sees you, it's over. Remember…"

"If one sees, they all see."

"That's right," Gene said. "I'm going to buy you as much time as I can. Lay low outside the house until you see them leave, then you make your move."

David nodded.

Gene sighed. "Boy, if you find her and she ain't… if she ain't her. You owe it to her and yourself to put her down."

David shook his head. "I can't do that."

"Maybe you can't, or maybe you will if it comes to that. You won't know till that instant," Gene said. "You're a good boy, David. She's lucky. No matter what happens, you've made a good accounting of yourself. You ought to be proud."

David laughed. "You do remember I was going to hand you over to them, don't you?"

Gene shook his head. "Priorities. You got your priorities straight. You put the emotion out of the equation and decided what mattered most." He smiled. "I might not have approved of it, but I do respect it."

Gene held out his hand. "I'll take that radio now if you don't mind."

David unclipped the two-way radio from his belt and handed it to him.

Gene grinned. "You know, maybe I ought to see if I can trade you for a free pass out of here?"

David laughed. "Serve me right."

"Vaya con Dios, kid."

Gene watched the boy pull onto Kinder Valley Road. He was driving clumsily, but that was to be expected.

Once the taillights were out of sight, Gene walked to the back of the wrecker and slid the radio into his belt. "Well, now Mr. Draugr. You are in one powerful sticky situation. And, it is about to get a lot worse."

The Draugr's head moved under the pillowcase.

Gene grabbed a five-gallon gas can off the back of the wrecker. He opened the lid and threw it away.

He splashed gas on the Draugr's bare skin and soaked the pillowcase.

The Draugr struggled against the chains around its upper body and under its arms that secured it to the boom.

Gene pulled the two-way radio off his belt and keyed it. "Hello, Miriam."

He waited.

He was just about to key the microphone again when he heard her voice.

"Gene?"

Gene frowned. "How are you, darlin'?"

"This is unexpected. I thought David would be calling."

"The boy? I shot the little bastard."

"Oh, Gene, you're a terrible liar."

"God as my witness. You know, he was going to give me up to you? I couldn't let that go."

"What do you want, Gene?"

"I was thinking prisoner exchange. One of yours for the little redheaded girl."

"Now, why would you want her? A little young for you, isn't she?"

"Well, I promised the kid before I put a bullet in his head that I'd try to save his girlfriend."

"And, you're always a man of your word. As I recall, you also promised to kill me."

"Oh, I'll keep that promise one day," Gene said. "What do you say? Middle of Main Street in twenty minutes? You bring the girl, and I'll give you ol' toothy here."

"Is that all you want?"

Gene gritted his teeth. "I'll settle for that."

"Nothing else I can tell you?"

Gene's hand shook. "We both know you won't tell me that."

"It must be torture for you? The not knowing? I still know you, Gene. I know what makes you tick."

"I'll get the answer to those questions from you personally. When I can take my time and cut the truth out of you."

Miriam laughed. "Torture? You have changed over the years. Tell me, Gene, have you learned to be sadistic over the last forty years, or did you pick those skills up in Viet Nam?"

"Twenty minutes. Tell Olc."

David drove for the first time in his life. It wasn't as hard as he had imagined. He managed to keep the truck between the lines.

He slowed down when the headlights picked out the dirt path Gene had described. Gravel crunched under the tires as David pulled onto it.

It was deeply rutted, a path made by tractors.

The truck tires found their way into the channels and slid in the wet mud.

The path led through fields of dead grass and under a skeletal canopy of dormant trees.

He could see the hill ahead. He stopped just before a clearing at the base of the hill, concealed by a copse of laurel bushes.

He turned off the headlights and the ignition.

He sat in the dark and watched the house on the hill through the bushes.

Olc paced in the foyer.

Miriam sat on the bottom step and watched him. "It's a trap."

"Of course."

"He'll have the boy with him."

"Yes."

"Another fire, most likely."

"Yes."

"I can send a few of mine and maybe two dozen Draugr."

"No."

"Then what?"

"Take your protectors. A few Draugr. Go to the west. Watch the house."

"You're going to Main Street?"

"Yes. Wouldn't want. To disappoint."

"You need to leave some Draugr here, to guard the house. We can't take the girl with us, she isn't ready."

"Yes."

"Also, the ancients are gone. I think Pauly took them somewhere."

Olc hissed. "Games. Senile. I think. Sometimes."

There were no blacksmiths in Rural Retreat. In the end, Pauly had taken them to the high school. The shop classroom was the closest thing to a blacksmith forge he could find.

He had remembered the shop teacher having a crucible. He couldn't remember why, but he remembered it sitting on the workbench.

He watched as the silver began to melt in the crucible as he heated it with a torch.

Skilled.

Well done, boy.

"What do you want me to pour this in? We need a mold," Pauly said as he moved the crucible slightly using long tongs and a thick glove.

Not mold.

Form.

One of the shapes appeared beside him.

He turned off the torch and set it down.

The ancient placed a severed Draugr hand in his.

Pauly stared at the cold thing of gray meat and exposed bone.

The claws.

Dip them.

Need three sets.

Six hands worth.

Pauly dipped the claws in the silver. The meat sizzled.

Once the silver coated claws cooled, he slid them off the nails with a pair of pliers. Then he repeated the process.

When he was done, thirty hollow silver claws lay on the workbench.

"Is that it?"

No.

There was tittering laughter in his head.

One of the ancients appeared by his side and dropped something else in his hand.

It was the upper jaw of a dead Draugr. It had been chipped away from the skull with something rough. The fangs gleamed white in the fluorescent light.

Three sets of teeth.

David got out of the truck when he heard a car start on the hill.

He watched as Miriam came through the back door and climbed into the back of the town car as it pulled around.

His breath caught in his chest when his Mom followed her.

She was lost to him. He knew that. But, he still couldn't bare to look at her.

He expected to see Pauly next, but instead, he only saw Regina who climbed in with them.

The car continued down the driveway.

Draugr began leaving the house. There were dozens of them.

An old blue school bus pulled around, and most of the Draugr got on board.

He couldn't see the figure driving.

Several Draugr followed the town car on foot.

They disappeared on the other side of the hill from where David stood.

The house was quiet.

He counted to one hundred, and then he walked up the hill toward the back door.

Gene reached up and yanked the pillowcase off the Draugr's head. It snarled at him, the face wet with gasoline. "How's it goin', Ace? You hangin' in there?"

It kicked at him rattling its chains as it swung on them.

Gene just stepped to the side. "Hang on, going to be a bumpy ride."

Gene took a road flare out of a tool box attached to the rear bumper.

Main Street was quiet.

The only sound was the throb of the big diesel engine as Gene climbed up in the cab. He turned up the radio. Classic rock. David Gates and Bread singing Guitar Man.

Gene leaned back in the driver's seat and smiled. "Hell, yeah." He rolled down the window and yelled back, "You know, Mr. Draugr. I do like Billy Don't be a Hero, but it gets monotonous. However, Bread? They are the sound of my generation, Amigo."

The school bus appeared two blocks down. It stopped in the middle of the street, the driver facing him.

He was too far away to make out the face, but he knew it was Olc.

"Hello, motherfucker," Gene whispered.

He took the cap off the end of the flare. He held it out the window and struck it.

The red flare lit up the inside of the cab in crimson.

Draugr were pouring off the bus.

With his free hand, Gene popped a heart pill under his tongue. He smiled as it dissolved. "Let's get this party started!"

He flung the flare behind him.

It tumbled end over end in the view from the side mirror.

The chained Draugr screamed as the gas soaking it ignited.

The Draugr from the bus screamed in unison.

Gene put the truck in gear and floored it.

David reached the back door. There was no movement in the yard.

He wished he had remembered to ask Gene for his phone and earbuds. He just tried to think about song lyrics - maybe that would be enough.

He held the .45 in his right hand as he tried the doorknob with his left.

It turned freely.

Of course, he thought. *A house full of vampires doesn't worry about burglars.*

He eased the door open.

The kitchen was empty. The room looked unused. The old farmhouse sink was brown with rust.

He stepped inside and eased the door closed behind him.

He stepped into the hall.

It was also empty and dark. The wallpaper was ripped in places, exposing the lath and plaster beneath.

He suddenly realized another flaw in the plan: he had no idea where Kim was inside this enormous house.

David walked into the foyer. There was a gaping hole in the floorboards near the middle of the floor. A sweeping staircase led up to the second floor.

To the left of the front door, there was a room. The door to the room was shut.

He reached for the knob.

He heard singing in his head. It was droning, like some sort of chant.

His hand touched the knob.

David froze.

A woman was staring at him. She was old and wore a plaid sundress. She stood with her back to the front door. She smiled at him.

David let go of the doorknob.

She walked toward him.

He raised the pistol.

She reached the hole in the floor and kept moving.

The old woman stood in mid air, her feet over the chasm.

David's hand trembled.

And, then he saw her eyes. Emerald green. The whites were tinged with age, but the green was bright.

He had seen those eyes before.

Her smile broadened. A whisper in his ear, "Equal parts horror and wonder. All that live forever are not damned." Her lips didn't move, but he knew the words came from this woman.

This woman who had Kim's eyes.

She held out her hand, and he took it.

The whisper in his ear again. "They are lost, caught between this life and the next. They can be manipulated."

The hand in his own felt like nothing, a breath of air against his skin.

"Do not move."

The door to the room to the left flung open, and the Draugr came out in a screaming wave.

He felt the pressure of the woman's hand in his.

He looked into her eyes.

He stood still.

The Draugr ran past him and flung the front door open.

They passed by him, like water flowing around a rock in a stream. They gave no notice to him or the ghost who held his hand, the ghost who smiled at him and reassured him.

The last Draugr ran out the front door into the night.

The ghost led him across the foyer, around the hole in the floor. She pointed up the stairs.

David looked up the stairs. One of the upstairs bedrooms had light streaming through under the door.

He turned to the ghost.

She was gone. His hand held nothing but cool night air.

David trembled.

He started climbing the steps.

"Damn it," Miriam said. They were sitting in the town car a half mile west of the house.

"What's wrong?" Jane asked from the rear facing seat.

"The Draugr. They're running toward town," Miriam said. "Edgar says something has happened. Gene is creating a disturbance." Miriam rolled her eyes. "The Draugr have abandoned the house as well."

"Should we follow them," Regina asked.

"No. Olc was afraid of an attack from this direction. We'll do as we were told."

Light streamed in through the rear window of the town car.

The pickup pulled in behind them.

Miriam looked through the rear window. "Finally, I was getting worried about Debbie."

Laura pulled onto the shoulder behind the idling town car. Three hours of searching and here it was right back out on the road. She grabbed the shotgun off the seat.

The rear driver's side door of the town car opened.

A leggy blonde teenager hopped out and walked toward the car.

The girl stared at the ruined headlight as she walked up to Laura's side of the truck.

She looked in, and her mouth dropped open. "You aren't Debbie."

Laura leveled the shotgun at the girl's head. "Debbie? Chubby chick?"

"Yes."

"Blew her head off," Laura said. She nodded at the shotgun. "You care for a dose?"

"Olc is going to be pissed."

"Don't know who that is. I'm looking for Kim Lawrence."

The blonde just stared at her.

"Hey, genius Barbie, I asked you a question."

"Never heard of her."

"Yeah, right. Forgive me if I think you're full of shit."

Gene was going sixty by the time he reached the end of Main Street and pulled onto Kinder Valley Road.

The burning, screaming Draugr swayed like a grotesque lantern from the boom.

As fast as he was going, the Draugr from the bus still managed to jump onto the truck.

They crawled over the outside.

A face appeared in the driver's side window. Gene pointed his .357 Magnum at the face and pulled the trigger. The window shattered and a dime sized hole opened in the Draugr's forehead. It fell away from the door.

He saw Olc turning the school bus around in the side mirrors.

The headlights turned toward Gene, and the bus was in pursuit surrounded by Draugr who ran alongside.

He heard a sound on the roof of the cab.

Gene pointed the .357 straight up and pulled the trigger.

A Draugr rolled off the top.

On the radio, David Gates was still singing Guitar Man.

Miriam turned and stared at the pickup.

Regina was standing on the shoulder talking.

She had sent the girl back to tell Debbie to go to the house and protect it.

Instead, she was locked in some animated conversation.

The truck's single headlight was blinding, and Miriam couldn't see Debbie's face.

David opened the bedroom door.

The room was lit with a small candelabra.

Kim was sitting in a small chair in front of the dresser. She was putting on makeup, applying mascara as she stared in the mirror.

She saw his face reflected.

She smiled. "I knew you would come."

David held the pistol in his right hand with the silenced barrel pointed at the floor. "Are you okay?" His hands shook.

She turned and looked at him, her face and eyes beautiful, her long red hair flowing across her shoulders. "Of course."

Kim stood up. She was glowing. She wore a white silk chemise that ended mid thigh. She looked down. "You like it?"

"It's pretty. Are you okay?" His voice choked on the last words.

"I already told you I am," Kim said. "It's a special night."

"Is it?"

Kim nodded. "Miriam told me. I become his tonight." She had a smile on her face.

"Kim? Did they do something to you?" David whispered.

"Miriam talked to me," she said as she walked toward him. "We have it all wrong. They aren't evil, David. Their blood. It's like magic."

David took a step back. "Did Olc do something to you? Inside your head?" He eased his finger onto the trigger.

"I'm sorry, David. I didn't know I would feel this way. You and me, it's just kid stuff. He's a man, not a boy." She bit her lip. "Do you think he's going to care that I'm not a virgin?"

"What are you talking about? They're monsters, Kim."

She smiled and shook her head. "You don't understand."

"What don't I understand?"

"It's not that simple. Now that I've had the blood, I can see that." She was walking toward him. "Don't be upset. They may take you as a Draugr. I'll ask him tonight when we..." She smiled and blushed. "I shouldn't be talking about this with you."

"What about your family, Kim? Your mom, your aunt, your little sister - do you think they will make your sister like you? Or, will they make her a Draugr?"

"No, they don't turn children. It doesn't work," Kim said. She was still smiling.

"Think about that, Kim. What does that mean? What does that mean they will do with her?"

Kim paused. She winced. "I don't... know. I have to ask Miriam. She'll make things clear. That's what she does."

"If they can't turn her into a Draugr or something like you? You know what they'll do to her. They'll drain her."

"You're trying to confuse me," Kim whispered. Her expression changed. She looked furious. "Miriam!" she screamed. "Help me!"

"They're gone. It's just you and me. And, I'm going to take you home," he said as he walked toward her.

"Stay away from me."

"Can't. Sorry. You're going home, or I'll die trying."

Her arm shot out and grabbed his neck.

David felt himself rise in the air. His feet dangled above the floor.

He dropped the pistol and grabbed at the hand clutching his throat.

She smiled up at him. "I'm sorry, David."

He let go of her hand. She was cutting off his blood flow, and he felt his vision going dark.

He fumbled in the pocket of his hoodie and found the zip lock bag there. He tore it open and fished out the rag.

David struggled and pressed the chloroform soaked rag against her mouth and nose.

Kim coughed and stumbled back.

She released the grip on his throat and David fell.

He grabbed at her waist as he fell and pulled her down with him.

David rolled on top of her as she kicked and screamed.

He pressed the rag onto her mouth and nose again.

She wrapped her arms around his chest and squeezed.

David cried out in pain as he felt his ribcage move. He felt the bones snap.

He screamed through the pain and pressed down harder with the rag.

Her eyes bored into his, and then they went unfocused.

She let go of his ribs and went limp under him.

A woman stuck her head out of the town car door. "Regina! What's going on?"

"Miriam!" Regina screamed as she turned toward her. "It's not her!"

Laura pulled the trigger, and the blonde went down as the buckshot hit her.

She leaned out the truck window, racked another shell, and fired toward the woman Regina had called Miriam.

The woman's eyes went wide as she ducked back in the car.

The car started to move forward, but Laura racked another shell and took out the left rear tire.

Something slammed into the truck door.

Regina was pounding on the driver's side door with her fists. The left side of her face was a ragged mess. The eye on that side was gone, and Laura could see the girl's tongue working though the missing cheek. "My face! You bitch!" Regina screamed as she punched. Spit and blood sprayed with each word.

The door was starting to cave in under the force of the blows.

Laura slammed the stock of the shotgun against the girl's nose, and she tumbled backward.

The town car peeled out, leaving the shredded tire behind in a shower of sparks.

Laura put the truck in gear and followed.

Olc sped along behind the wrecker. The Draugr chained to the back had long since burned to death. He hung from the boom, swaying as the truck rounded curves.

Draugr clung to the outside of the wrecker, but they didn't dare go near the cab.

Gene Stinson was an excellent shot.

He was driving toward the house.

Olc thought about this.

He reached out with his mind.

All the Draugr were converging on his position - even the ones he had told to guard the house.

Of course.

Gene was only a diversion.

The boy.

Olc screamed out with his mind.

The Draugr running toward them stopped. They turned and ran back toward the house.

David was in agony. Every breath felt like fire in his lungs.

He ignored it. He put it out of his mind. There were things to do.

He stood up and almost blacked out.

No. He wasn't going to do that.

He leaned down and slid his arms under Kim's shoulders and knees. He slid her along the floor until he felt the gun under his right hand. He closed his fingers around it, letting his right elbow support the back of Kim's knees.

He just had to…

David stood up.

He screamed. Kim's weight put pressure on his mangled chest. He almost fainted again.

No. He stood up straight with Kim in his arms, the .45 in his right hand.

He walked to the bedroom door.

A Draugr was coming through the front door. He fired from the top of the stairs, and it went down. Two more came in, and he fired twice more, two sounds like twigs breaking from the silenced gun. They went down as well.

He reached the bottom of the stairs and walked to the door.

A horde was running up the drive. They were screaming.

The black town car followed behind them.

Five bullets, he thought. He could kill three before saving two: one for Kim, one for himself. "I'm sorry," he whispered.

The Silverado pickup truck whipped around the side of the town car and plowed through Draugr. The gray bodies tumbled through the air.

The pickup spun sideways up against the front steps of the house.

Aunt Laura looked at him, her eyes wide. "Is she alive?" she screamed.

"Yes," David yelled.

Laura turned toward the horde and fired her shotgun. "Get in!"

David laid Kim in the bed of the pickup. He put his hands on the side of the truck bed. He tried to pull himself up, but the pain was too much.

"Get in, I said!"

He opened the passenger side door. "I can't."

Laura groaned. She looked toward the approaching horde. They would be on them in seconds.

The boy was still trying to pull himself inside.

She reached out and grabbed the back of his hoodie and hauled him inside.

She pulled out before the door was shut. "Hang on!"

Laura blasted through the crowd of monsters. Those that didn't get knocked to the side were crushed underneath. She held up her middle finger as they passed the town car.

David sat up. He turned the .45 around in his hand, held it like a hammer. He knocked out the back safety glass window leading to the truck bed.

"What the hell?" Laura said as she fishtailed onto Kinder Valley Road heading east toward town.

"Can't leave her back there. If she wakes up... she'll jump out."

"She'll what?!"

David groaned as he climbed into the truck bed.

The boy was hurt. Laura couldn't tell how bad, but bad enough.

Headlights appeared on the road ahead.

The biggest tow truck Laura had ever seen blew past them in a blur of red. A dead, burned Draugr dangled from the back.

"What now?" Laura asked.

David sat down beside Kim and started waving. "No. It's okay. He's a friend."

Laura watched in the side mirror as the tow truck's brakes locked. It slid sideways and roared after them.

The tow truck was speeding up trying to pass them.

"You sure he's a friend?"

David smiled and nodded. "Yeah."

He tore past them blowing his air horn.

"What is he doing?"

David laughed and held his ribs. "Mischief."

Gene smiled. The boy had made it out alive, and, unless he missed his guess, the girl beside him on the truck bed was Kim.

He had no idea who the dark haired girl was driving Miriam's pickup.

However, their overall chance of survival had just gone up by thirty percent.

Except that Marcus Velerius Corvus Olc was heading right at them.

He pulled ahead of them in the left lane and stayed there.

Olc was somewhere ahead.

The speedometer climbed past sixty to seventy.

The radio station was on a classic roll. Jim Croce was singing Time in a Bottle.

Yeah, Gene thought. *I could die on that one.* Croce was cool.

He topped a small hill at ninety miles per hour. The tow truck's wheels left the road as it went airborne.

Olc was heading straight toward him.

"Surprise, asshole," Gene said.

Gene stared into Olc's black eyes.

The bus swerved to the right, down an embankment, and into a field, tearing out a barbed wire fence as it passed.

"No!" Gene screamed as he slammed on the brakes.

He skidded to a stop sideways.

Gene jumped out of the tow truck with the .357 in his hand.

Olc ran out of the school bus.

"Would you die?" Gene screamed. He fired toward Olc.

The gray man dodged to the left faster than the eye could see.

The Silverado screeched to a halt beside Gene.

Olc hissed from the field.

Gene fired again.

He dodged right. The bullet missed him by a yard.

Olc was smiling.

"Stand still, you mother…" Gene fired again.

Again, Olc dodged.

"Get in the truck, you moron!" the dark haired girl yelled.

"I can…"

"What? Get yourself killed? Look behind you, jackass," the girl said.

Gene turned.

The Draugr horde that had been chasing after Olc was running toward them.

"Damn. Forgot about them," Gene said as he ran around the front of the truck and got in the passenger door.

The girl floored it, and they roared down the road toward the Draugr. "Hang on back there, David."

Gene tipped his Air Cav baseball cap. "Gene Stinson."

"Laura Reynolds. I'm Kim's aunt."

Gene turned and looked into the truck bed.

The Draugr dove out of the way as Laura drove through them at a hundred miles per hour.

"She okay?" Gene yelled.

David shook his head. "I… I don't know."

"Are *you* okay?"

"Yeah," David said. He closed his eyes. "I'll be okay."

"In that case, where's my damned truck?"

Anne heard the truck pull into her driveway and jumped to her feet.

"Are they here?" Tia asked as she sat up on the couch.

She pulled Tia off the couch and got between her and the front door. She held the butcher knife the way Laura had told her.

She heard footsteps on the porch.

"No matter what happens, stay behind me."

"It's okay, Mommy."

Someone pounded on the door. "Anne? Open up, it's Laura."

Anne breathed out and took a step toward the door.

"Wait!" Tia yelled. She grabbed hold of her Mom's belt loop and pulled her back. "Aunt Laura? What's my name?"

"Tia," Laura said from the other side of the door.

"No, my other name."

"Monkey Face?"

"Correct. Why do I pinch you?"

Anne stared down at Tia.

Laura groaned. "Oh, for fuck's sake…"

Tia smiled. "It's okay, Mommy. You can open the door."

Anne opened the door.

Laura had a shotgun in her hand.

"What the…" Anne said.

"There's no time. We have to go."

"Wait. Where's Kim?"

"In the truck," Laura said. "I will explain everything, but we have to move."

Tia ran down the hallway.

Anne leaned out the door.

A beat up Silverado pickup was in the drive.

"Who…"

"We have to go!" Laura yelled.

Tia came down the hall dragging four backpacks behind her.

"What are those?" Laura asked.

"Stuff. Grandma said it was stuff we might need. I packed them earlier."

Anne and Laura looked at each other.

Laura shrugged. "Mom was always prepared."

Laura and Anne grabbed the backpacks.

Laura led them outside.

An old man was standing in the bed of the truck. David was sitting with his back against the tailgate.

Kim was unconscious in his arms.

"Kim!" Anne yelled.

Laura grabbed her. "She's okay. Anne? She's okay, but we have to leave right now."

The old man was watching the street to the north. He had a revolver in his hand.

Tia climbed in the truck, and Anne got in the passenger side, pushing her to the middle.

Laura jumped in the driver seat.

"Where are we going?" David asked.

Anne didn't like how he looked. He looked pale and sweaty.

Laura shrugged. "I don't know."

David nodded at Gene. "Any more hiding places?"

"No," the old man, Gene, said. "Blew up the last one."

"We have to be all together in one accord," Tia said.

"I'm just going to drive until we figure it out," Laura said. "I feel like we're sitting ducks here."

"Sitting ducks?" Anne asked. "What are you talking about?"

Laura opened her mouth. Then she shook her head. "Oh, man. Not a conversation I am ready to have yet." She pulled onto the street.

"What happened?" Anne asked.

"Well, let's see. I found a dead guy and killed a monster. Kim got kidnapped. I beat up a cop with a baseball bat. Got in a car chase. Killed some crazy psycho chubby girl and took this truck from her..."

"Wait, what did you say?" David asked from the truck bed.

Laura looked confused. "Which part?"

"Crazy psycho chubby girl - black hair?"

"Yeah. The bitch whose face I shot off called her Debbie..."

Anne looked at her in horror. "You shot someone's face off?"

"Trust me, she had it coming."

"I know where we can go," David said. "There won't be anybody there, and they won't expect us to go there. Hang a left."

Olc stood on the road by the wrecker. The Draugr huddled around him.

Miriam drove up in Jane's car.

"Edgar?" Olc asked.

Miriam got out. "Pauly is changing the left rear tire on the town car. Some bitch shot it off with a shotgun."

"Allies. Unexpected."

The Draugr pressed in close to him, and he stroked the backs of those nearest.

Miriam was counting in her head. She counted three dozen Draugr. "Where are the others?"

"Bodies. Strewn. Here to town."

"Damn it." Miriam pulled the nearest one close to her and kissed its head. "We lost quite a few at the house as well. Forty-seven left back in the parlor. They took Kim."

Olc hissed. "Loss. Too much. Loss."

Miriam looked into the field. "The bus?"

"Stuck. Luckily…" He pointed to the tow truck.

"Olc, let's pull the bus out of the field and leave tonight. We've lost over a hundred tonight."

Olc shook his head. "No."

Miriam threw her hands in the air. "We can leave here with four protectors and eighty-three Draugr. Let's go someplace far away from here."

"Follow us. Again. Your husband. Kill more," Olc said. "No more. No more. Dead. By his hands."

Laura pulled into the trailer park a little after eleven PM.

Debbie Kincaid's trailer was well kept on the outside with flowers and mulch.

They pulled up in front.

Tia stared out the window at the small trailer. "This is wrong."

Anne rubbed her hair. "What do you mean, sweetie?"

"We can't be all in one accord in one place here. This isn't the right place," Tia said.

Laura smiled down at her. "I know it ain't the Ritz, Monkey Face."

Tia shook her head. "No. You don't understand. The place where we are going to be safe is made out of stone. This place looks like an aluminum can."

"It's just for tonight, baby," Anne said. She glared at Laura. "Just until Aunt Laura tells me what the fuck is going on."

Tia pinched her mother.

Gene stood on the front porch and looked at the trailer door. It was locked. "Might be some tools out in that shed. I can open this with a small pry bar," he said pointing toward the small outbuilding behind the trailer.

The deck railing was lined with potted plants.

"Check under all the plants," Laura said.

Gene shook his head. "That's a one in a million shot."

Laura nodded toward the railing. "Monkey Face."

Tia picked up the first potted plant. She smiled and showed them a brass key.

Laura smiled at Gene.

"Lucky," Gene said.

"Oh, my God," Anne said as they stepped inside.

The trailer reeked of ammonia.

"Whew," Laura said. "Somebody has cats."

"Smells like mountain lions," Tia said.

Anne walked into the kitchen and set one of the backpacks on the island. Her butcher knife was still in her hand.

Gene opened the truck's tailgate. "You ready?"

David nodded. "I had to use the chloroform again a few minutes ago. I was afraid Mrs. Lawrence was going to see."

Gene picked Anne up and carried her toward the house.

David got to his feet. The pain in his chest was excruciating.

Gene carried Kim through the front door. "I'm going to take her back to the main bedroom, Ma'am."

David stumbled through the front door.

Anne nodded. "Now, I want one of you to tell me why my daughter is asleep."

Gene glanced over his shoulder at David. "You're up, kid." He carried her up the hall.

David sat down on the overstuffed green couch. He winced in pain. "Chloroform."

"What?" Anne asked.

"I had to use chloroform."

Anne slammed her hands down on the kitchen island. "One of you had better tell me what the hell is going on…"

Tia tugged on her shirt. "Don't be mad. David, Laura, and Gene saved her. Only, she isn't her right now. But, she'll get better."

"I cannot accept any of this," Anne said. "You come in here and tell me you roofied my daughter…"

"I didn't roofie her. I used chloroform," David said.

Anne pointed the knife at him. "Open that mouth one more time."

David closed his eyes.

"Anne, he's telling the truth," Laura said.

Anne shook her head. "This is something you brought. It all started when you came back here."

Laura gritted her teeth. "Something I brought? Are you kidding me? I spent all day being GI Jane because I was terrified to tell you I lost your kid. This is nothing I brought with me."

"Tell her," Tia said.

"Sweetie, the adults are talking," Anne said.

"Aunt Laura, tell her why you came home."

Laura stared at her. "It was… I just wanted to come home."

"No. Grandma told you to come home," Tia said.

Laura felt a jolt go through her whole body. The dream in Tucson. *Time to go home*, her mother had said. "Time to go home," Laura whispered.

"What?" Anne asked.

"She was standing there in that plaid sundress," Laura said. "You remember it? She wore it all the time. Threadbare and out of style, and every other day, there she was in that damned sundress."

David was staring at her. "Plaid?"

Gene glanced up at the word *plaid*.

"Yeah," Laura said. "Why?"

Tia looked at David and Gene and smiled. She nodded. "Sometimes the dead protect the living. I think they take a vacation from heaven." She looked solemn. "They hate the monsters. Ghosts haunt the monsters, and they'll help us when they can. But you have to listen to them."

David started to say something. Instead, he cried out in pain and hugged his ribs.

Laura ran to him. "Where's the pain?"

"Everywhere," David whispered.

Laura lifted his hoodie and t-shirt. "Christ."

The boy's ribs were black and blue.

"What happened to you?" Anne asked.

David shook his head. "She didn't mean it. It wasn't her fault."

They all looked toward the bedroom at the end of the hall.

David sat on the edge of the bed in the second bedroom. He had his shirt off and his hands in the air.

Laura wrapped bandages around his torso. "Feeling better?"

"Yeah. You're really good at this."

Laura smiled. "When you protest logging in the great Northwest, people end up getting their ribs broke. Either from chaining themselves to trees or from some Paul Bunyan swinging an ax handle their way. I've taped a lot of ribs." She took a step back and admired her work.

"Can I put my arms down?" David asked.

"In a second. I'm admiring the view. No wonder Kim likes you."

David laughed and then winced. "Ow! Don't make me laugh. It hurts."

She handed him two pills and a bottle of water. "Advil. Sorry. Left the hard stuff behind in Arizona." She sighed. "Along with my cigarettes. I'd kill for a cig - you wouldn't happen to have one?"

"I don't smoke."

She rolled her eyes. "Of course, you don't."

He started to stand up.

"Whoa, slugger, back in bed."

"I'm fine."

"No, kiddo, you're a couple of weeks from fine. You need to sleep."

He shook his head. "I need to stay awake. We have to keep watch."

She pushed him gently back onto the bed. "We will. But, not you. You're going to sleep."

"But..."

"Hey. I mean it. I'm playing the adult card." Laura said. She sat down beside him. "What you did back there? Going in there like that?" She shook her head. "You got a pair on you, kid. She's... she's Kim, because of you." She smiled at him. "You're okay in my book, David Connors. Sorry about all that baseball talk on Saturday."

David laughed and winced.

Laura got up.

"Third base," David said. He smiled at her.

"Third?"

"I was late to third. She got there before me."

Laura shook her head. "God, she is so my niece."

Father Tobias knelt in front of the altar and prayed. He was trembling, and his voice shook. No one had come to the church today. He hadn't seen a soul. But, he heard cries in the distance. And he was afraid.

"Lord Jesus, in Your Holy Name, I bind all evil spirits of the air, water, ground, underground, and netherworld. I further bind, in Jesus's Name, any and all emissaries of the satanic headquarters and claim the Precious Blood of Jesus on the air, atmosphere, water, ground and their fruits around us, the underground and the netherworld below…"

Someone clapped slowly behind him.

He turned at the sound.

A brunette woman wearing pearls stood by the font. She stopped clapping and smiled at him. "Such faith. I'm genuinely moved, Father."

Tobias stood. "You are welcome here on this night, my child."

She traced a fingertip through the holy water. She lifted the finger to her lips and licked it. "Oh, I am no child, Tobias." She ran her finger along the side of the font. "Evil is at large tonight, isn't it, Father?"

"Yes," Tobias whispered. "I believe it is. I've been praying for strength."

The woman's eyes grew wide and hopeful. "Oh! And, has your idol answered you?"

"I don't pray to the crucifix, I pray to the One who inspired it."

She nodded. "I'm looking for someone. A boy. Sixteen. Blond hair. Have you seen him?"

Tobias looked at her. "No."

She drew in a surprised breath. "What's this? A lie? Whatever would your friend on the cross think?"

Her eyes narrowed, and her voice changed. She spoke in the boy's voice from the day before, *"Do you believe in evil?"*

Tobias stumbled backward.

Her voice returned to normal. "Does your faith fail you, Tobias?"

"No," he said, steeling himself. "If anything, your presence strengthens it."

She laughed. "I see. You believe in evil when you see it?"

"And, it affirms my faith in its opposite."

She rolled her eyes. "So pious. Tell me, priest, how do you explain my standing here on your holy ground, touching your holy water to my tongue, not cowering at the sight of your idol?"

"In truth, I can't. God gives me faith, but not always understanding. Faith is enough."

She held her hands at her sides. Her clothing faded away, leaving her standing naked in her pearls. The glamour was still there - she projected the nude illusion of Brittney Davis before Olc changed her for all eternity. "I wonder if I can test that faith. Do you like what you see, Father?"

He nodded as he looked at her. "Very much."

She laughed. "Not a very good priest, are you?"

"I'm a man like any other. With weaknesses, like any other. Tell me, were you born a demon?"

She bit her lip. "You think I'm a demon?"

His voice was calm and even. "I think you're the saddest creature I've ever seen."

Her glamour faded away. She stood in front of him in her true form.

Tobias drew in a breath. For the first time, he could smell the stench of her. Her body was glistening and gray, her skin sagging. Her eyes were pools of black ink. Brittney's mouth was filled with sharp teeth.

A tear rolled down his cheek.

She smiled. "I terrify you. Good. Where is the boy, Father?"

He shook his head. "When the boy came to me, I felt... a presence. I felt like he was supposed to come here, and I was meant to give him some counsel. I had only a few words with him, but I pray those words were enough to help him." He smiled. "I don't know where the boy is. And, I'm glad I don't. Because I have no doubt you have come here to torture the truth out of me. I take solace in knowing my suffering cannot betray the child."

"What a shame, priest."

"And, what you mistake as terror in my eyes? It is not. It is pity. I will pray for you. And, I forgive you."

Brittney's eyes flashed with anger. Her lips curled back from her teeth.

The priest died praying for her soul.

Anne and Tia slept together on the living room couch.

Laura sat in the kitchen with the shotgun draped across her lap.

Gene sat in the hallway with his eye on Kim as she slept in the back bedroom. He held the .357 in his right hand.

"So, what's your story, old man?" Laura asked.

He looked at her with tired eyes. "You know that blonde-haired queen bitch in the town car?"

"Yeah, Miriam?"

"I was married to her."

Laura looked him up and down. "Damn, Gramps. You must be the hero at the retirement home."

"She's sixty-seven years old."

"No shit? I want to meet her plastic surgeon."

"No," Gene said. "You don't."

"How many bullets you have?" Laura asked.

"Sixteen, including the six I have in it now. You?"

"Four twelve gauge shells. Twenty-one rounds for the Glock."

"Kid's got about fifteen rounds for the .45. Too bad we couldn't get to my truck. Got a steel case in the back full of ammo and rifles."

"Them's the breaks, old man," Laura whispered. She stared at the front door. "You think they'll find us?"

"Well, I don't know, but if they do, we're spam in a can."

"Yeah," Laura said. "We're totally screwed."

Thursday

Kim slept. In her dreams, the gray man slept curled behind her, his cold hand tracing patterns across her abdomen. He spoke in words she couldn't understand - old words in Latin.

She saw palaces in her mind of white stone and marble, the sounds and smells of a great city from twenty-four centuries in the past.

The gray man was young, his hair black, his skin dark.

"Not the gray man, at all," he said.

She smiled. "No."

"They took you from me," he whispered in her ear.

"I tried to stop them," Kim answered.

"I know. Tell me where you are, and I will move heaven and earth to bring you home." His cold hand found her breast. He massaged the nipple in slow circles.

"I don't know where I am."

"Open your eyes."

The room was dark. She was lying in a bed in almost total darkness.

No. That wasn't quite true. There was light flowing through a doorway, but she couldn't see through to the hallway beyond.

People were standing in front of her.

The bedroom was small, but dozens of people were crowded inside, blocking her view of the doorway.

Her grandmother was there in a faded plaid sundress. She stood closest to Kim's head. She looked down at her with a look of love and fear.

A girl with dark, short hair stood beside her. Addie. She remembered. The girl from TV lost on the Appalachian Trail - but, not lost, not lost at all.

Another girl with long black hair and purple highlights. She was wearing black short shorts and a white halter top.

Mr. Hamadi. He was crying.

"Sometimes, the dead protect the living," her grandmother said in the dark. "We are here. Push him away. Deny him."

"I can't," Kim whispered. "I don't want to."

"He is pain and suffering," Hamadi said. "He is eternal death."

"The darkness of the tomb," Addie whispered.

A priest leaned down beside her grandmother. "He is the Prince of Lies. Everything he tells you is false."

"He's an asshole," the girl in the short shorts said in a stiff east Kentucky drawl.

Her grandmother took Kim's hand. The touch was light but warm. "You will be happy. You will live a long life. All you have to do is push him away."

"Close your eyes!" the gray man commanded.

She obeyed.

She was back in the palace of stone and marble with the gray man holding her tight.

Kim felt something moving in her head.

Tia woke in the dark hours before dawn. Her mother slept on the couch beside her.

Aunt Laura sat in a kitchen chair, her mouth open and her head to the side. She was sleeping soundly.

Tia got off the couch and stretched.

The old man snored in his chair in the hall. The gun had fallen on the floor a few inches from his fingers.

Tia smiled up to her left. She walked through the house as if someone much taller was holding her hand.

"They fell asleep," Tia whispered.

She listened and nodded.

Then, she walked to Gene's chair.

"God, I need a shower," Laura said. She was pissed at herself. Both she and the old cowboy had fallen asleep on watch. They were damned lucky no one had come to the trailer during the night.

Anne fried eggs on the stove. "Go ahead."

Laura stretched. "Where did Gene Autry go?"

Anne snickered. "Front porch. I don't think he's used to people."

"I could eat a horse," Laura said as she leaned over the stove.

"Hey, check the freezer. See if there's microwave sausage patties or something?"

Laura turned to the refrigerator and opened the freezer compartment. She looked inside for a moment.

Then she shut the door.

"No sausage and no bacon. Don't open the freezer," Laura said as she walked toward the bathroom.

"Why not?" Anne said without looking up.

"Found her damned cats."

Anne walked up the hall and peeked into the main bedroom where Kim slept. She opened the door enough for the light to play across her daughter's face.

She was still asleep, breathing gently.

Her face looked far younger when she slept.

She closed the door and opened the door to the second bedroom.

David was asleep. He moaned a little and shifted on the bed.

She smiled. What kind of sixteen-year-old boy walks into a house full of monsters to save a girl he dated once? Gets his ribs crushed and still carries her out? "Oh, Kim, you found a keeper."

He wasn't the kind that spent long hours with a dental hygienist.

She shut the door.

The shower was going in the bathroom.

Tia slept on the couch.

She went back to the kitchen. "Butter," she said. "I need butter." She opened the refrigerator door and found it.

She stood up and shut the door.

Kim was standing beside the refrigerator in the white silk chemise.

Anne smiled. "Morning sunshine."

Kim clamped her hand over her mother's mouth and pushed her backward toward the cooktop.

Anne tried to scream, but Kim's hand was clamped over her mouth.

Her daughter was so strong. Anne felt like she was trying to struggle against a bear.

All the while, Kim's green eyes sparkled with insanity and hatred.

She pushed Anne against the center island.

With her free hand, she grabbed Anne's forearm.

She was pressing her arm to the side.

Anne felt the heat off the frying pan as Kim slowly pushed her right hand toward the burner.

"Kim, stop!" Tia said. She was standing in the living room in her pajamas.

Kim turned her head and smiled.

And, then Tia did what millions of years of evolution have cultivated in small children: she screamed, high pitched and as loud as her lungs could manage.

Gene Stinson burst through the front door. He raised the .357 Magnum. "Let her go!"

"Fuck you, old man," Kim hissed.

Gene grabbed Tia and turned her away from the kitchen. "Sorry, kid."

He pulled the trigger.

Click.

Gene looked at the gun in horror.

Tia looked up at him. "Grandma said I can give the bullets back later."

Laura came out of the bathroom wrapped in a towel. She ran into the kitchen.

Kim released Anne who collapsed, gasping for breath, on the floor.

Kim turned and swung her left arm when Laura was close enough.

Laura flew backward, her feet leaving the ground. She crashed against the trailer wall.

Kim grabbed a butcher knife off the kitchen island. It was the same long knife Anne had brought from the house.

She held it in her right hand and turned back to her mother. "He told me to." She raised the knife above her head.

David charged into the kitchen. He wrapped his arms around her from behind. He raised his arms, locked his hands behind Kim's neck in a full nelson. "Drop the knife!"

He raised her into the air and brought her feet back down hard on the floor.

The knife clattered to the floor.

Kim screamed. "Let go! You fucker! Let go! I have to. He told me to."

Anne watched as David dragged her backward.

Her eyes were flashing with hate.

David stumbled and fell backward on the floor, pulling Kim with him.

She broke the full nelson and her left arm was free.

288

She drove her elbow into his ribs.

David slid out from under her clutching his chest.

Kim laughed.

Anne Lawrence dove on top of her daughter. She caught Kim's wrists and forced them down on the linoleum.

Kim smiled up at her in amusement.

"Kimberly Renee Lawrence!" Anne screamed in her face.

A shocked look went across Kim's face. The fire left her eyes.

"Stop this. Stop it right now! Do you hear me?" Anne yelled.

Kim shook her head and tried to push her mother off.

Anne pressed her back down. "I will not lose you. I have lost my father, my mother, my husband. I have lost my home. But, by God, I will not lose you."

Kim seemed to be losing steam. She still fought, but the inhuman strength she had a moment before was gone.

"Stop it," Anne whispered. "Whatever this is, you fight it. You fight him."

Tears began to stream down Kim's face. "Mommy?"

Anne's tears came then.

David was crying as well.

Laura smiled and nodded, her own face streaked with tears.

Tia took Gene's hand and smiled up at him. She gave him a thumbs up.

Gene ate his eggs in silence.

Tia sat beside him at the small kitchen table and smiled.

He pointed his fork at her. "Next time grandma tells you to mess with my stuff, you check with me first."

"You ain't the boss of me," Tia said.

Gene sighed.

"You were going to shoot my kid," Anne said. She glared at him from the other side of the table.

"Your kid was going to fry you on a cook top."

"I don't care. You don't shoot my child." Anne loaded his plate with another egg.

"Your funeral."

"No," Anne said. "It'll be yours."

Gene nodded. "Noted."

Laura came into the kitchen. "She wanted me to tie her to the bed."

Anne stared at her. "You didn't, did you?"

"No," Laura said as she sat down to her eggs. "I left David in there with her. He won't leave her side. That kid's tough."

"Is he okay?"

"No worse than last night."

Kim lay on her side in the bed.

David sat in a chair a few feet away.

"Don't leave me, okay?" Kim whispered.

He shook his head. "I won't." He winced.

She started to cry. "I hurt you."

"Stop," he whispered. "It wasn't you. It was their blood. It was him. Never you." He leaned over and took her hand.

She smiled up at him. "Hold me?"

He started to get up. He hesitated.

She shook her head. "It's me. I just... if I fall asleep. He's so cold, David."

He climbed over her onto the bed.

He lay down behind her and wrapped his arm around her. "Ow!"

"You okay?" Kim whispered.

"Yeah. I'm okay. Just sore when I move. Or breathe."

He was warm against her, his hand on her stomach. His words in her ear.

They fell asleep surrounded by ghosts who watched over them both.

Olc sighed. He was standing in the parlor. The Draugr clung to each other on the floor in their ever-changing miasma, while he and the protectors stood by the door.

"Lost her," Olc whispered.

"We'll get her back," Miriam said. "They can't hide forever."

"Hold on her. Gone. Broken," Olc said. "Ghosts. Plague us."

"When you had control over her, was there anything you saw? Something to help us find them?"

Olc shook his head. "House. Small. Cramped."

Miriam shook her head.

"Hold still," Jane said. She was picking buckshot and bone shard out of the right side of Regina's face with tweezers.

"It hurts," Regina whined. Her tongue worked in her mouth in plain view through the missing cheek. There was a small orb the size of a grape in her formerly empty right eye socket.

"It will all grow back," Miriam said.

"Tell that to Debbie," Regina lisped. Saliva rolled out of the hole in her face as she spoke.

"Most things grow back, not your brain," Miriam said. "Remember that, all of you. If they destroy your heart, your brain suffocates. You die. If they rip out your throat, your brain suffocates, you die."

"They blow your head off, your brain is mush. You die," Pauly said. "Yeah, we get it."

"Everything else can heal," Miriam said.

Jane looked at the socket. "Move your eye."

The tiny orb rotated in the raw socket. Her left eye was blue, this new one was black.

"I can't see shit with it," Regina complained.

Jane shrugged. "It's only halfway there." She resumed picking buckshot with the tweezers.

"When I get my hands on that skinny bitch who shot me? I'm going to carve her face up good."

Jane grimaced and danced back. Her hand was dripping with saliva. "Shut up, you're drooling all over me."

Laura walked around the trailer to the shed.

Gene was digging through the tools inside.

Laura leaned against the steel door frame. The inside of the shed was a hodge-podge of tools. A big Coca-Cola sign hung on the back wall. One corner of the shed was littered with steel cylinders marked 'Property of Coca-Cola Bottling.' Smaller bottles lay beside them marked 'CO2'.

"What is all this shit?" Laura asked.

"Looks like Debbie's father worked for Coca-Cola," Gene said. He pointed to a hose attached to a backpack mounted tank in the corner. "He was an exterminator on the side."

"Anything in those cylinders?" Laura asked.

Gene shook his head. "CO2 cylinders feel full. The syrup cylinders or whatever they are? They're empties."

Laura shook her head. "Well, the CO2 isn't going to help us. Fire extinguisher would be counter-productive."

Gene held up his hands. "Shed full of useless shit. I was hoping to find some ammo, a hidden gun. All I found was this." He held out a bottle.

Laura took it. "Ames Winery, Bedford, Virginia."

"Not even a decent bottle of whiskey."

"Which is odd, because if Debbie was my kid, I'd drink like a fish." She tore the foil top off the bottle. "Care to partake of the grape, old man?"

Gene stared at her. "It ain't even noon yet."

"Well, I don't know about you, Gene Autry, but I'm parched. It was a long night. And, then my niece tried to kill me." Laura stared at the uncovered end of the bottle. "Son of a bitch. A cork. Not a twist top. You wouldn't happen to have…"

Gene pulled out his pocket knife and opened the corkscrew.

"You know, you're okay, Gramps. If you had a cigarette on you, you'd be perfect."

"Sorry, never picked up that habit."

"Shit." She pulled out the cork and handed the knife back to Gene. She took a swig. She gave the bottle to Gene.

He took the bottle and looked at it.

He wiped the mouth of the bottle off on his shirt sleeve.

"I ain't got herpes, old man."

He shrugged and took a drink.

Laura stared at the empty syrup cylinders and the CO2 cylinders. She looked at the exterminator rig.

She smiled.

Anne walked back to the bedroom.

David was in bed with Kim, his arm wrapped around her.

She frowned. She started to say something.

Then, she saw Kim's hand holding David's in a tight grip as they slept.

She smiled. *Not a little girl anymore,* Anne thought. The boy was there to keep the demons away.

She turned to go back down the hall.

She caught a glimpse of something out of the corner of her eye. A shadow against the wall.

Anne shook her head. She was seeing things. She had seen a shadow on the wall, not her mother looking at her with sad eyes.

Anne left the quiet room as the ghosts screamed.

"It'll work," Laura said.

"Maybe," Gene said.

"You have a degree in Chemistry from the University of Washington, old man?" Laura growled. "'Cause I do. And, I'm telling you it will work."

"Yeah, I'll bet they taught you this in college. Pyromania 101."

Laura had arranged one of the empty syrup cylinders and a CO2 cylinder side by side on the workbench. She had rigged a hose from the CO2 to the syrup cylinder and attached another hose to a valve on the other side of the syrup bottle. This last hose was left open on the end.

"Just watch." Laura clamped her thumb over the end of the loose hose. She pointed the hose at the wall and opened the CO2 valve with her other hand.

A stream of stale Coke syrup sprayed against the wall. "We can get twenty or thirty feet out of this."

Gene screwed his lips up. "Try it again."

Laura smiled and opened the valve.

The hose in her hand popped off the cylinder and sprayed her Grateful Dead t-shirt with Coke. "Shit."

"And, you're dead," Gene said.

"Damn it, cowboy. This is just a prototype. I'm going to tap and connect these cylinders properly - we have all the tools we need." She pointed to the corner of the shed. "I'm going to use the exterminator rig as the actual trigger mechanism."

"Okay, but how are you going to…"

Laura reached down and picked up something from the floor. She set a blue BernzOmatic blowtorch on the worktable. "Few feet of duct tape and we're in business."

"You're going to blow your skinny ass up," Gene said.

"I know my shit, old man."

Gene shook his head. "I don't doubt that. But, hell, one tank? You need at least two."

She frowned. "I know my limitations. I can't carry two full cylinders and the CO2 tank."

"No," Gene said. "But, I can."

Laura laughed. "Seriously? You take a look in the mirror lately? Your lips are blue, Grandpa. And, you're popping those heart pills like they're candy. I don't want to sound cruel, but you have a foot and most of one leg in the grave. Your weightlifting days are over."

"I carried a buddy of mine out of the shit back in Nam. Ten miles to the LZ, and that old boy weighed about two-fifty."

"Yeah? How old were you? Twenty?"

Gene looked away. "I won't have to carry it long. You know that."

Laura shook her head. "Is this a misogyny thing? Those gray-haired little peanuts of yours don't make you the boss."

Gene laughed. "No. It is not a misogyny thing." He turned and looked at her. "I can carry two, and two are what's needed. No slight on you."

Laura sighed and crossed her arms over her chest. She sat down on the edge of the bench. "Okay. It might explode," she whispered. "I mean, in theory, it's safe."

Gene chuckled. "Young lady, I've carried the real thing. Government issue. And, they sure as shit ain't safe."

Rural Retreat slept on that overcast Thursday afternoon with snow falling. The streets were filled with abandoned cars, and the early snow gathered like dust on the windshields.

Ghosts walked the streets in invisible silence.

Most houses were cold. Nothing moved within. What few people who were left huddled in basements or attics and watched the windows and doors.

They watched for the gray shadows to come and asked why their God had forsaken them.

Occasionally, there was a brief sound of screaming, of running feet - it was always brief.

But, mostly there was silence.

At either end of town, police blocked the roads. They had been standing watch for five days. They did not take breaks. They simply sat in cars that had long ago run dry of gas.

They were like mannequins, especially those who froze in the cold night.

When the Draugr left, those who were left would have heart attacks and die, leaving no loose ends.

The phones didn't work.

Sometimes relatives would try to call houses within Rural Retreat. They would get a fast busy signal. Most would try later.

After a few days, a few would drive to Rural Retreat to check on a parent or grandparent. They might get within a mile of the road blocks. A Draugr on watch nearby would convince them to turn around through that odd telepathy. There was nothing to see in the small town. All was well.

Fewer still would call the police and tell them something strange was going on in Rural Retreat.

A car would be dispatched.

The Draugr would convince them to turn around. There was nothing wrong. All was well.

The ancients worked in their burrow, nimble fingers crafting strange jewelry out of silver - bracelets that formed ornate silver exoskeletons on the back of their thin hands ending in sharp silver claws on their fingertips.

They smiled as they worked, each pointed tooth capped with silver fangs.

These were the old ways, and something told them these ways would soon be needed again.

Miriam arched her back as Olc thrust into her. She scraped his cold, gray back with her long nails.

Pauly and Jane sat on the bedroom floor.

Jane watched with a smile.

Pauly frowned.

Jane took his hand. "Jealous?" she whispered.

"Shut up."

She leaned over and whispered in his ear. "Love me. She doesn't love you."

"You don't love me either."

"No," she said. She licked his ear. "But, I love what you do to me."

He pushed her away.

She ran her finger up the fly of his jeans. "What's wrong? Immortality not what you expected?"

Pauly shook his head.

She leaned close again. "You know. He made you pine after her on purpose? He wants you to suffer." She watched as Olc grabbed Miriam's ankles and pounded into her harder. "He's a sadistic fuck, isn't he?"

Olc screamed. He pulled back and rolled Miriam away.

She sat up and wrapped her hands around him as he sat on the edge of the bed. "What's wrong?"

He pointed to his head. "No sign of them."

She laid her head on his shoulder. "Forget about them. You can hurt me if you want."

He shrugged her away.

"Do you want Jane?" Miriam asked.

Jane smiled at Pauly. "My turn. You had your chance."

"No," Olc whispered. "Have to. Find them."

Jane slumped back on the floor.

Miriam stood up and walked across the floor naked. "A small house. Cramped."

Olc nodded. "Two bedrooms. A smell."

Miriam turned. "What smell?"

Olc shook his head. "Ammonia."

"Ammonia?" Miriam asked. A smile crept across her lips. "A small house. A trailer. Ammonia. Cats." She turned to Olc. "Tell me how much you love me."

"I mean, why don't we just stay here till it's over?" Kim said. She was sitting on the couch leaning back against David. Since the morning, they had been inseparable.

All six of them were sitting in the living room as the snow fell outside. The heat was electric thankfully - they didn't have to worry about smoke from a chimney.

Gene shrugged. "I don't know."

"We don't have enough ammunition if they find us," Laura said.

"What about the project you and Gene are working on?" Anne asked. She sat in the rocking recliner with Tia in her lap. She clung to her mother like a toddler.

Laura shook her head. "Offensive weapon. Not defensive."

Gene nodded to the wall. "It would destroy the trailer."

The two of them had been very secretive about their project. Laura had confided that most of the reason for the secrecy was Kim - they had no way of knowing if Olc could use her to spy on them.

Anne had a feeling they were being evasive for a different reason. The contraption they were constructing looked dangerous to the one wielding it.

Tia looked up at her mother. "We have to leave. Right now. We can't be all in one accord in one place here."

Anne smiled and rubbed her hair. "Baby, none of us can figure out what that means. Can't you ask grandma to explain it?"

Tia shook her head. "It doesn't work that way. Sometimes I talk to her yesterday, sometimes it's tomorrow. Time doesn't mean anything to her. If I ask yesterday her what tomorrow her meant, she probably won't know either."

Anne stared at her youngest daughter and tried to wrap her head around what she was saying.

David looked up. "I think we need to get out of here."

Gene laughed. "You led us here."

"Yeah, but I only wanted us to come here for the night. We need to move."

"We have to find the stone house," Tia whispered.

"Tia, honey, there are no stone houses here - at least none that I've ever seen," Anne said.

"Look," Kim said. "No offense, but, she's six."

Tia sat up and pouted. "I know I'm six, but Grandma talks to me. She tells me things." Tia sat back on Anne's lap. "Only. Only she hasn't spoken to me since last night."

"When she told you to take my bullets?" Gene asked.

Tia shook her head. "After."

"What did she say, Monkey Face?" Laura asked.

"She said she loved me."

Anne smiled and hugged her.

The living room window shattered.

A brick-sized rock was laying on the coffee table.

"Hello, in the house!" a girl's voice yelled.

"Everybody down!" Gene yelled. He drew the .357 and stood beside the window casing.

Laura rolled onto the floor and grabbed her shotgun.

"I know that voice," Kim said.

David was pulling her back to the kitchen island.

Anne rolled off the recliner with Tia in her arms. She turned the recliner over and hid behind it.

David pulled his .45 from its shoulder holster.

Laura leaned up and looked out the window. "Damn. I shot that slut's face off."

"That's Regina. She's in my class at school," Kim said as David got her to sit down on the kitchen floor.

Regina was standing in the middle of the yard surrounded by at least fifty Draugr. She was smiling. Part of her face had grown back, but her grin went all the way to her ear on the right side, and her eye looked wonky.

David knelt behind the kitchen island and braced his grip on the .45 on the table top.

"I said, 'Hello!'" Regina screamed. "Okay, so here's the deal. We only want Kim and David, and the old dude, and the old bitch who messed up my face."

"Who are you calling old?" Laura yelled.

"That's all of us, you moron," David yelled.

Regina looked confused. "It is? Well, shit."

Gene nodded. "They don't know about Anne and Tia."

"So, come on out and let's get this over with! " Regina screamed.

"Kid," Gene said. "You got a shot?"

David lined up the sights. "Hell of a long way away."

Gene winked. "Worth a try."

David breathed out and pulled the trigger.

In the yard, Regina's head snapped back, and she fell on her back.

The Draugr began to scream.

"Holy shit," Laura laughed.

"Beautiful shot, kid," Gene said.

"Did you get her?" Kim asked as she raised up and looked over the island.

"Yeah," David said.

"Are all of you psychopaths now?" Anne asked.

David shrugged.

"Hey, assholes," Gene yelled. "Anybody else want to dictate terms?"

The Draugr charged the trailer.

Gene knew the position was indefensible. He knew it when he walked in the night before. He had stood on the porch that morning knowing he had to leave. Staying was suicide.

Forty years of surviving this insanity had taught him that attachments got you killed. It got those around you killed as well, so he blamed himself as he moved them deeper into the trailer.

The shattered window was the weak point, and the Draugr used it. They rushed the trailer as Gene scooped up Tia in his left arm and aimed the .357 with his right.

He walked sideways, the child burying her head in his neck as he backed toward the kitchen. He fired, each bullet finding a Draugr's face. They went down in a pile as he and Laura fired into the mass of gray.

Laura took her sister's arm and shoved her into the kitchen.

David fired between them, picking off those they missed.

The window filled with Draugr dead, and they still came, pushing the dead out of their way.

Kim, Anne, and Tia huddled behind the island.

Gene, Laura, and David stood their ground beside them.

Three knights guarding the castle, but the castle was besieged by an overwhelming force.

Gene looked at Laura. He knew she was almost out.

The roof tore open.

White snow swirled down into the kitchen, and, along with it, a dark shape.

The gray man, Marcus Velerius Corvus Olc, landed on his feet behind them.

Laura turned toward the shape behind them.

He smiled down at her. He seemed ten feet tall.

He grabbed the barrel of the shotgun and bent it. He shoved it toward her and sent her sailing across the floor.

David tried to spin around, but he grabbed David by the belt and tossed him over the island.

Gene had a shot.

Kim stood up and threw a punch toward Olc.

He grabbed her arm and spun her around.

Then he threw her into Gene, knocking them both to the floor.

Tia screamed from the kitchen floor.

Olc reached for her with his long taloned fingers.

Anne grabbed Tia and shoved her on top of Kim.

Olc grabbed Anne by her hands and yanked her to her feet. "Miss Lawrence. I keep. Finding reasons. To hold. Your hands."

The Draugr left silently. They opened the trailer door and filed out. Miriam stepped inside, followed by Pauly and Jane.

Gene and Laura had pulled Kim, David, and Tia back against the far wall of the living room.

Gene and David still held their guns.

Pauly reached down and picked up Laura's nine millimeter with a smile.

It had fallen out of her waistband in the commotion.

Olc stood behind the island. He was holding Anne's wrists behind her back. He had his face close to the right side of her neck.

"Gene, David, drop your guns," Miriam said. "It's over."

Gene had his gun pointed at her. "Ain't happenin'."

Pauly tried to step in front of her, but Miriam pushed him aside. "Not necessary, dear. Gene isn't really going to shoot me. He has other plans for me. Isn't that right, husband?"

Gene ignored her. "David, you think you can hit that limp dicked bastard?"

David held his gun aimed at Olc. "We'll see."

"Don't shoot. My Mom is too close," Kim said.

Miriam shook her head. "Kim, Kim. You are such a disappointment. I wanted so much to see you blossom into something beautiful."

Laura glared at her and flipped her off. "I got your blossom right here, bitch."

300

Miriam laughed. "How vulgar. Obviously, we should have taken the aunt instead of the niece." She looked thoughtful. "Or, maybe the mother?"

Anne whimpered.

"Mom," David said. "If there's anything left of you in that shell. I need you to help us. For once in your life, help me."

"You ungrateful little prick," Jane said. "You see, Miriam. This is why I abandoned him. He's pathetic."

"He's too good a son for you, you piece of shit," Anne said.

Olc jerked Anne back against him.

"Ooo," Miriam said. "Not so limp a dick, is it, Anne?"

"I think. I want her," Olc whispered.

Miriam nodded. "Normally, I get jealous, but in this case, he deserves to have his fun. It was a rough night."

Olc took Anne's wrists in one hand. He smiled as he raised the wrist of his free arm to his lips. He bit down.

Dark blood ran down on the kitchen floor.

He smiled with blood stained teeth.

"This next part is the one I like best," Miriam said.

Anne looked in Kim's eyes as Olc pressed the bloody wrist against her lips.

She held her lips closed.

David fired, but Olc dodged sideways. The bullet passed by his head and buried itself in the cabinets.

Anne's mouth opened.

Her eyes grew wide as she began to nurse at the wound.

"No!" Kim screamed. She turned Tia away and made her hide her face.

Anne drank.

Olc released her hands.

Her left hand came up.

She put her hand on the kitchen island to brace herself.

But, that wasn't what she was doing at all.

She picked up the butcher knife by the handle.

There was a look of realization in Olc's face.

The butcher knife was long.

Anne drove it into her left breast.

"Annie, no!" Laura screamed.

Anne smiled as she drove the knife deep.

The point pushed out of her back.

And, then it buried deep in Olc's chest.

Olc screamed, and everybody dropped to their knees.

They all felt the pain in their own chests.

He shoved Anne away.

David aimed and fired.

The bullet grazed along Olc's temple.

Then Olc jumped straight into the air, up through the hole in the roof.

Miriam was screaming.

Pauly pushed her out of the way as Gene fired two rounds after them.

Pauly grabbed Miriam's hand and dragged her screaming out into the snow.

Jane turned to run after them.

David took aim at the back of her head.

Gene stepped in the way. He raised the magnum and fired.

The back of Jane's head exploded, and she fell face down on the snow-covered porch.

Anne lay on her back staring up as the snow swirled down through the hole in the roof. The pain was gone.

"Mom?" Kim whispered as she dropped down beside her.

Anne smiled. "Hi. It's okay now."

"Mommy," Kim leaned over her and cried.

Laura knelt down beside her. "Oh, Annie. Oh, Jesus."

Anne reached up and touched her sister's face. "Kim. Tia is crying. You have to take care of her."

David led Kim away.

Anne looked up at Laura. "Couldn't be one of them, Laura."

"I know. Oh, God, Annie."

"Shh. You thought you were the tough one? You're bush league, princess."

Laura laughed through her tears. "I'm going to get you to a hospital."

"Liar," Anne whispered. "No. I want to watch the snow. So pretty. I'm lying in a trailer that smells like cat piss, and the sky is so pretty."

Laura held her hand.

"Tell them I love them. Everyday. You tell them I love them?"
Laura nodded. "I will."
"You tried being you, Stringbean. You suck at being you."
"I know."
"Be me. Okay? Can you do that? Just be me?"
"I'm going to suck at that too," Laura whispered.
"I love you, Stringbean."
Laura knelt on the kitchen floor and cried.
Anne stared straight up into the snow storm.

The Draugr were gone. They left their dead in the trailer park.
Gene and David reached the porch as the town car sped away.
They both stepped over Jane Connors' dead body.
David looked down at her. "You didn't have to do that. I could have."
Gene put his hand on the boy's shoulder. "I know. But, you didn't need to live with that. I didn't want you to live with that."
David nodded. "Thank you."

They set the trailer on fire as they left.
There was a semi sitting in front of the trailer beside Debbie's. David supposed it belonged to the dead man who still moldered inside with Gwen.
That night of horror seemed like a century ago. And, it seemed tame in comparison.
Gene filled two five gallon gas cans with the diesel fuel from the semi's tanks.
Then, Laura and Gene loaded a harness in the back of the pickup. It had three large cylinders on the back. Their project from the shed.
David hugged Kim and Tia tight in the front seat.
Laura drove them away.
Gene sat in the truck bed with his back to the cab and watched the trailer burn.
They reached the edge of the trailer park.
Laura sighed and leaned against the steering wheel. "I don't know where I'm going."

David closed his eyes. "There's another place. I'm not sure if it's safe."

"No place is safe," Laura whispered.

They pulled up in front of Saint Mary's Church a little before dark.

Tia sat on David's lap and pressed her face to the glass. "The stone house."

Laura looked at her with red-rimmed eyes. "Are you sure?"

Tia burst into tears. She pointed toward the sign out front:

Saint Mary's Catholic Church
Rural Retreat, Virginia

Below this was a sign that could be changed with plastic letters behind Plexiglas:

...all with one accord in one place.
    Acts 2:1

Laura just stared at the sign and shook her head.

"What do you think?" Laura asked. She was looking at the church from the driver's seat.

Gene stood up and looked over the cab of the truck toward the church. "We should check it out before we go inside."

Laura shook her head. "Let's face it, gramps. You and David have, what, ten bullets between you. Do you really think it matters?"

David opened the passenger door. "We can't split up. We don't have enough ammunition to guard the truck and check out the church. We do one or the other."

He got out of the truck and held out his hand.

Kim smiled and handed Tia out to him.

He took her in his arms. She buried her face in his chest.

Kim got out and took her from him. She balanced her sister on her hip.

Gene climbed down from the truck bed. He walked back and hoisted the pack onto his shoulders. The steel cylinders clinked.

He picked up a diesel can.

Laura got out and picked up the other can.

Gene set his diesel can down. He handed her his .357. "Last six are in it."

They walked toward the front doors of the church.

David held his .45 with the barrel pointed at the walkway. "I met the priest. His name is Tobias. He's nice."

The front door was open.

They walked into the church. Their footsteps echoed on the stone floor.

They passed the font.

Father Tobias hung upside down from the crucifix behind the altar.

The plaster Jesus lay on the floor beneath Tobias's head.

The priest's throat had been ripped out.

Kim turned Tia's face away.

David sighed. "I thought they didn't care about religion."

Gene closed his eyes and shook his head. "They don't. For them, this was a joke."

"I hate them," Kim whispered.

"That's what they are," Gene said. "They're hate."

Laura looked away. "Gene? Can you and David?"

Gene nodded. "Yeah, we'll cut him down."

Tia had been right. The church was safe. They searched the rooms together, one at a time. Tobias was the only body they found.

Afterward, they sat in the chapel.

Tia slept on the pew with her head on Kim's lap.

"Do you think Olc is dead?" Laura asked.

Gene nodded. "God, I hope so."

Laura stared at him. "But, do you believe he is?"

Gene shrugged. "Depends on how much of his heart was destroyed." Gene closed his eyes. "Don't ask me how I know this, but they can survive a lot of damage as long as blood is getting to the brain."

"I can imagine how you know that," Laura whispered.

"What do we do?" David asked.

"The three of you aren't going to do anything," Laura said.

"Four of you," Gene said.

Laura looked at him out of the corner of her eye. "We'll have that conversation in a minute, old man." She reached out and took David's and Kim's hands. "I need you to listen. We have no way of knowing how long they are going to hold this town. They might leave tonight, or they might leave in a week. We have no way of knowing."

"What are you saying?" Kim asked.

"Gene and I have a plan. It's a plan to end this. We're going to the house."

"I am, anyway," Gene said.

Laura rolled her eyes.

"Let's just stay here," Kim whispered.

Laura shook her head. "No. They'll come back for us again." She took a deep breath. "Your mom hurt them bad. If Olc is dead, maybe they'll leave."

"If he ain't, he'll come for us all," Gene said.

"We can't hold them off without more firepower."

"We can search the houses. People around here have plenty of guns," David said.

Laura smiled. "Kiddo, we stick our heads out of here and start trying to rifle through houses? We will definitely die."

Kim wiped tears away from her cheeks. "We'll go with you."

Laura laughed. "Tia too?"

Kim looked down at her sister's sleeping face.

Laura shook her head. She reached out and stroked Tia's face. "She's the top priority. You have to take care of her."

"You can't leave, Aunt Laura," Kim whispered.

"I have to."

"No, you don't," Gene said.

Laura smiled at him. "You can't do this alone, redneck."

Gene sighed and shook his head. He looked at Kim and David. "If we ain't back by morning, you do what I told you that first day."

David nodded. "North to the interstate. Walk to the truck stop. Hitch a ride on a rig going south."

Gene nodded. "Deep south. Warm all year round. South Florida or South Texas will do."

Kim looked at Laura. "Tell me you're coming back."

Laura smiled. "We're both coming back."

"David, you still got my keys?" Gene asked.

David fished in his pocket and handed him the keys.

Gene smiled. "I do miss my truck."

Gene and Laura worked together on the weapon in the parking lot. They filled the syrup tanks with a mixture of the diesel fuel and siphoned gas from the pickup. Then they put the tanks and harness in the back of the truck.

Afterward, Laura sat in the driver's seat.

Gene got in beside her.

She was staring at the church.

"I won't think less of you if you stay. Those kids are your responsibility," Gene said.

Laura closed her eyes. "Yeah, they are. And, if we don't end these bastards, we'll be looking over our shoulders for the rest of our lives. The only way to protect them is to end this."

Gene nodded. "Well, Miss Reynolds, let's go kill the bastards."

Laura smiled. "We have a stop to make first."

Olc bled in the back of the town car.

"Why isn't he healing?" Pauly asked from the rear facing seat.

"He is," Miriam said as she put pressure on the wound. "But, the wound is deep. He keeps losing blood. There are limits to how much he can heal at once."

Olc groaned. "I won't. Die. Today."

He glared at Pauly. "Sorry. To disappoint."

Pauly looked away.

Miriam leaned forward and pounded on the divider between the rear seats and Edgar. "Drive faster!"

Olc took her hand and pulled her back to him. "Calm yourself."

She squeezed his hand. "We should have left."

Olc nodded. "Yes. Tonight. We go."

"Can I ask you a question?" Laura asked as she drove.

"Knock yourself out," Gene said.

"Forty years? I mean I get it, they turned your wife into that... thing. But, shit, forty years? Didn't you want to live a life?"

Gene looked out the window at the gathering snow on the side of the road. "Wasn't that simple."

Laura watched the road. "Don't want to talk about it?"

"No."

"Gene, you are a classic. Bottled up emotions, can't talk. You're a dying breed, old man."

"Literally."

Laura didn't press.

Gene sighed. "We were living west of Fort Worth. That winter, whole damned country was buried in snow and ice - before your time. Anyway, I was working the oil derricks out there. Everything was freezing up."

He looked straight ahead. "I left home about six in the morning. We laid in bed before I left. We were happy." He bit his lip and looked at his hands. "I came home late about seven. I tell people I stopped at a bar before I went home."

"You didn't?"

"No," he said. His hands shook. "Anyway. I walked in the house. She was gone. Sheets on the bed had been stripped off. There was a note on the kitchen table: I'm leaving you. I never loved you. Don't look for me."

Laura turned toward him. "She found out?"

"What?"

"Where you were?"

Gene stared at her for a second. He laughed and shook his head. "She knew where I was."

"I don't understand."

"I was shopping in Dallas," he turned away. His voice broke. "For a bassinet." He clenched his fists together. "Her parents had sold her bassinet, and she had to have one just like it."

"Oh, God. I'm sorry."

"I left my seven months pregnant wife in our bed at six AM. And, I never saw her again for ten years." The old man's face turned hard. "That's what he does. He takes what he wants. Anything he wants."

Gene unclenched his fists. "I didn't know that, of course. My first thought was she had been abducted because nobody falls out of love with you in a half day. You don't go from talking about baby names to telling someone you never loved them that fast. I thought someone had taken her. Cops didn't believe me."

Laura saw his hands shaking.

"It's the not knowing," he said. "That's what eats at you. I tried to live a life, but it's always in the back of your head. And, then, a decade later I was working up north on the Alaska pipeline, and I saw her walking out of a bar. Only, she's like six inches taller and a dozen years younger than she should be. I almost died there, I didn't know shit. I thought she had just left me.

"That's when I met Marcus Velerius Corvus Olc," Gene said. He spat the words out. "Blind luck I survived. There was a crowd there, too big a crowd for Olc. I slipped away.

"I've been tracking them ever since. That is my life. It isn't because of her, it isn't even because of him."

Laura nodded. "The baby."

Gene looked away. "I've cornered her several times over the years. She won't tell me. I don't know if they killed our baby before it was born. I don't know if they turned it. I don't know if they dropped it on somebody's doorstep." Gene squeezed his eyes shut. "Forty years ain't a high price if I could find out what happened." He turned and looked at her. "It was the not knowing."

Laura gave him a weak smile. "Thank you. For telling me."

He nodded.

"Gene?"

"Yeah?"

"Whatever they did to the baby? It was over forty years ago. It's over. Wherever it is? The suffering is over."

He reached out and took her hand. "I know. And, I know she'll never tell me. That's his final cruelty. I could torture her to the brink of death, and she'll never tell me what they did." He squeezed her hand and let it go.

"I wasted my life, Laura." He laughed. "You know, I met a woman in West Virginia on my way here. Ava. She was so beautiful. She wanted me to stay with her. I was sorely tempted. I wish I had."

Miriam and Pauly carried Olc up the steps of the house on the hill. The door was open, welcoming them home.

Olc's head slumped forward on his neck.

The ancients were waiting in the foyer.

The floor.

Lay him there.

Miriam and Pauly lowered Olc to the scarred and dusty floor.

They moved away as the ancients gathered around him.

One of the blurry shapes dragged its talons across the wound. It opened, and dark blood poured out.

Knife went deep.

Heart cannot heal.

As the wound closes, the heart beats.

Tears it anew.

"Can't you do something?" Miriam asked.

Pauly held her hand.

Yes.

Miriam's head filled with laughter.

Kill him.

"What?" Miriam screamed.

Calm yourself.

Stop the heart.

Let it heal.

He dies for a moment.

Bring him back.

"Can you do that?" Miriam asked.

We can do many things.

Let me stop his heart! Never liked him.

Question is: who will bring him back?

More laughter filled Miriam's mind.

"Stop it!" Miriam screamed.

One of the ancients turned and slapped her across the face.

The force of the blow knocked both Miriam and Pauly to the floor.

Whore!

Know your place.

Do not tempt us.

Miriam and Pauly clung to each other as the ancients went to work.

One of them held its long taloned hand over Olc's chest. The fingers slowly closed.

Olc arched his back and screamed.

Heart stops.

Watch the fissure close.

Magic!

There now, done.

"Bring him back," Miriam whispered. "Please bring him back."

Soon he will be like us.

This is why he will live.

The ancient holding his closed fist over Olc's chest unclenched his fingers.

Olc breathed out.

He lives!

The heart is sound.

Should have castrated him. He makes poor choices.

Won't matter to him soon anyway.

They laughed again.

The ancients moved away.

Prepare the cars.

We leave tonight.

Enough play.

Danger here.

Miriam scrambled to Olc's side as the wound in his chest closed. She lay down on the cold floor beside and wrapped her arms around him. "I thought I lost you."

"No." He smiled at her and touched her hair. "We leave. Now."

Laura pulled into a fire station off Main Street. Snow was piling up on the pavement.

The station was a new building with a garage door twenty feet high.

It was open, despite the cold.

A bright red fire engine gleamed under the fluorescent lights inside.

Gene looked at the building. "You want something to put fires *out?*"

Laura smiled. "You'll see, old man."

They stepped out into the cold air. Gene held the .357 in his right hand as they walked into the open garage.

"If there are more than six unfriendlies inside, we're in trouble," Gene said.

The garage was empty.

A hallway led off to the left.

There was a light coming from the first doorway.

Eight men sat inside around a round kitchen table.

They each wore blue fire department t-shirts.

They stared sightlessly at one another.

Laura looked at Gene.

He held the gun ready and nodded at her.

She walked to the nearest fireman. She put two fingers on his throat.

His skin was ice cold. There was no pulse.

"Dead," Laura whispered.

She went to the next. "This one as well. There's not a mark on them. What happened to them?"

Gene blew his breath out in front of him. It formed a cloud. "They froze to death. The heat's off. Or, they died of thirst. Take your pick."

Laura pointed to the wall. "The thermostat is right there. The sink tap is right over there."

"Olc's been in their heads," Gene said. "They weren't programmed to survive."

Laura shook her head. "Why? It doesn't make sense."

"First responders. Cops, firemen, ambulance. He took them first," Olc said. "What are we here for, Laura?"

"Come on, I'll show you. I hope."

They walked down the hall to the equipment room. She opened the door and turned on the lights.

The fluorescents blinked on.

She smiled and pointed to the wall. "That's what I was looking for."

There were lockers on the back wall.

Three suits hung side by side.

"Fire suits," Gene said.

The suits looked like they were made out of tin foil. An overcoat and pants, gloves and boot covers. A large silver hood with a thick glass window over the face completed the ensemble.

Laura walked up and ran her fingers down the closest. "They can take up to a thousand degrees." She leaned down. She held up an air tank and face mask. "These tanks say forty-five minutes."

Gene stood by the door. "If we're in there that long, we're dead."

Gene saw something move out of the corner of his eye.

He turned to see a tall brunette woman wearing a tight skirt and pearls walking toward him down the hall.

"Shit!" Gene turned and fired.

She skipped left and smiled.

"Draugr!" Gene yelled.

She was fast. She covered the distance between them in an instant. She slapped the gun out of his hand and knocked Gene on the floor.

He didn't move.

Laura grabbed a fireman's ax and held it ready. "Gene?"

Pearls looked down at him. "He's having a nap."

Laura squared off with the ax. "Pearls? A little much, isn't it?"

"Always appropriate," the woman said as she walked forward. "You look like fun."

"Not really," Laura said as she took a step sideways.

They were circling each other.

"You're more talkative than your friends," Laura said. She was easing toward the door.

"I'm special," Pearls said with a smile.

"I'll bet you are."

Pearls laughed. "I'll give you a choice. You can be dinner or my new best friend. Your choice."

"Hard pass on both," Laura said as she reached Gene. The old man wasn't moving. She leaned down to get the gun.

Pearls sped forward a few feet, so fast she seemed to disappear in one place and reappear a few feet closer. "No, no. I don't like guns. Let's keep this intimate."

Laura stood up. "Okay. I'll just chop your head off."

Pearls smiled. "I'm Brittney, what's your name?"

"Laura, nice to meet you."

Brittney pointed at her. "Your sister was the one who stabbed Olc, wasn't she?"

Laura narrowed her eyes. "Word of advice - don't talk about my sister."

Laura backed into the hall.

Brittney followed.

"I hear you burned the trailer. You know, she might not have been dead. She took the blood."

Laura backed down the hallway. She was half afraid there were more coming up behind her, but she didn't dare take her eyes off Brittney.

"You know, that was a real shame," Brittney said as she walked into the hallway. "We sleep in a communal group. The sensations of all our bodies pressed together, all our thoughts mingling? It's very erotic. Interested?"

"No thanks, did all my experimentation in college." Laura was at the entrance to the garage.

Brittney threw her head back and laughed. Then she stared directly into Laura's eyes. "Stop moving, Laura. I'm going to take you right here in the hallway."

"What? No dinner? No romance?"

Brittney smiled.

"Oh, thank God," Laura said.

A shot rang out as Gene fired the .357.

Brittney's left ring finger disappeared in a red mist.

"Run!" Gene yelled as Brittney screamed.

Laura ran through the garage as a second shot rang out. She reached the truck and threw the ax on the ground.

"Laura?" Brittney was twenty feet behind her. "Second shot missed. Now, you're going to die just like your sister."

Laura reached into the truck bed and pulled out the exterminator spray gun. She pressed a button and ignited the BernzOmatic blow torch near the tip.

Blue flame licked the end of the exterminator gun.

"I told you, don't talk about my sister, bitch." Laura pulled the trigger. A sixty / forty mixture of gasoline and diesel fuel streamed from the end of the sprayer. It hit the flame and ignited.

A stream of burning fuel jetted out twenty feet and engulfed Brittney in fire.

She screamed.

The illusion was gone.

Laura caught a glimpse of charring gray skin as Brittney ran away down the street trailing fire.

Gene leaned against the garage door with the .357 in his hand.

He watched the burning Draugr disappear into the night.

Laura held up the gun and patted the barrel. "Flamethrower works."

Gene laughed and sat down with his back against the firehouse wall.

The Draugr in the house on the hill screamed.

Olc raised up from the floor.

"Don't," Miriam whispered. "You need to rest."

Olc shook his head. He opened his mouth, but no words came out. His eyes focused on her.

Miriam groaned as his thoughts touched hers.

"What's wrong?" Pauly asked.

"Gene and Laura. They attacked Brittney."

"Where are they?"

"The fire station on Main Street. Take Jane's car. Do you have a gun?"

"Yes. Wait. You want me to go alone?" Pauly asked.

Miriam shook her head. "I can't leave Olc alone. He hasn't recovered."

"Can I take some Draugr, at least?" Pauly asked.

"No. There's fire, Pauly. He won't risk more Draugr," Miriam said. She took his hand. "We're the protectors. This is what we do. Go."

Laura and Gene followed after Brittney in the truck. She had run down a side street.

Pauly drove straight down Main Street. They passed each other with two blocks between them.

Laura gave up after a mile. "I don't know where she went."

"She's dead," Gene said. "They can't take heat, much less fire."

Laura nodded. "I think it's time."

"Me too."

Pauly stopped at the fire station. There was blood in the hallway, and a single Draugr finger - he assumed it was Brittney's.

There were scorch marks on the pavement out front.

He leaned down and touched the burns.

Then he stood up and looked around. They could be anywhere.

He got back in Jane's car and drove east.

Laura pulled onto the dirt track that led to the field behind the house on the hill. The pickup complained and strained in the deep, snow-filled ruts. She turned off the headlights.

The snowy landscape was lit pale blue by the moonlight.

"I'll be damned. It's still there," he said.

Gene's pickup sat behind a laurel bush.

They pulled in behind it and killed the engine.

Gene got out and unlocked the steel case in his truck bed.

He held up an assault rifle with suppressor.

"God bless the second amendment," Laura whispered. She took the gun from him. "Wait, this isn't an AR-15 - this is a fully automatic M4."

Gene stared at her in amazement. "Darlin', if I was forty years younger."

"I don't know, the gray makes you look distinguished." She said as she pulled the fire suit pants on over her jeans.

"No, it doesn't," Gene said as he pulled on his own suit.

Laura shrugged. "You're right, it doesn't."

Gene popped a heart pill under his tongue.

"You okay?" Laura asked.

He nodded. "Now, I want you to listen to me."

She rolled her eyes. "What now?"

"I ain't coming out of there."

"You don't know that."

"Yeah, I do. I need you to promise me something."

"What's that?"

"When the time comes, you go."

"I won't leave you in there."

"Yes, you will." He put his hands on her shoulders. "This is my stop, kid. Not yours. Those children need you. If it comes down to a choice between me or you - you remember those kids and you choose you."

"Shut up, old man."

He smiled at her. "Look at it this way. Odds are both of us are going to die."

"That's what I like about you. Always looking on the bright side," Laura said. "We walking up?"

"Hell no. We're driving."

"Your truck?"

"My truck? Are you kidding? We're taking her piece of shit. I ain't messing up my truck."

Pauly drove slowly past each building east of the fire station.

The door to the Catholic church was closed.

He stopped.

An open door meant the Draugr had emptied a building.

A closed door meant there were people still inside.

The only problem was, the door to the church had been left open yesterday.

He stopped on the street and got out. He walked through the snow to the old stone building.

Pauly put his hand on the doorknob.

The door was locked.

Pauly shook his head.

He turned the knob, feeling the metal within break.

He winced at the sound.

The door was heavy. It opened in slowly.

He held the gun at eye level as he stepped inside.

David stood in the center of the chapel.

Kim stood behind him, shielding the little girl.

David held the .45 pointed directly at him. "Hello, Pauly."

"Hey, man," Pauly said. "Red. Who's the kid?"

Kim leaned down beside her and hugged her.

David's hand was steady.

"Well, here we are," Pauly said.

"Yeah."

Pauly shook his head. "The fuck happened, David? I keep trying to put it together in my head. It just seems like a dream. You think we're going to wake up tomorrow morning and everything is going to be like it was. XBox and high school and you dating Red here and me with the cheerleader?"

"I don't think so, Pauly."

Pauly blinked. "I really want it to, David. I want to wake up, man."

"I'm sorry, Pauly."

Pauly nodded. "Where's the old man and Red's aunt?"

David shook his head.

"Yeah. Okay."

Kim looked at him. "Pauly, put the gun down. You don't have to go back to them. I didn't."

He smiled. "No. He gets in your head. You got out in time. I'm all Jeffrey Dahmer and Charlie Manson up here now. It's like worms in your brain, I ain't fit to be around people. Not now."

He laughed. "Besides, the hell of it all is: I love her. Miriam. She's the love of my life. Ain't that some sick, twisted shit?"

"What are we doing here, Pauly?" David asked.

Pauly shook his head. "You need to leave the door open. Draugr use that as code to say the house is empty. I'll leave it open as I go."

David took a step forward. "I can't let you leave, Pauly."

"Yeah. Yeah, you can."

"You'll tell them where we are."

"I'm going to do one last good thing in my life. Everything after this is going to be a shit show, but I ain't giving up my best friend. Have a good life, David." He started backing away.

"Stop."

Kim put her hand in David's free hand. "David? Let him go."

"I can't."

"Yes. You can."

Pauly smiled at her and nodded. And, he left them alone.

The ancients stood in the front yard as Edgar brought the town car around.

Safer in the car.

Go on to the road ahead of them, I think.

Yes. Too dangerous here.

The town car stopped. It reversed back up the drive as the ancients watched in confusion.

The wheel cut sharp left, and then Edgar drove toward the back of the house.

Too late.

Should we assist?

No. Wait and see.

Laura drove as fast as she dared up the hill in four wheel drive. The rear end spun out a couple of times, but the front tires bit in and pulled them up the hill.

She slid sideways against the back porch.

She was out of the truck before Gene could climb down from the back.

Laura saw herself in the side mirror. She looked like an astronaut in the fire suit.

An astronaut with a rifle.

She had cut a small hole in the right glove for her trigger finger - she hoped her finger wouldn't get burned.

She heard the roar of an engine and saw the town car careen around the back of the house.

Gene was on his feet and stepping off the truck bed. He sent a stream of burning fuel arcing toward the town car.

The driver threw on the brakes and backed away as the flaming mixture landed on the snow in front of it.

The driver laid on the horn.

Laura took aim at the car.

"Leave it!" Gene yelled through his air mask. "Save your ammo." He pushed past her and kicked the door off its hinges.

He sprayed down the kitchen beyond with liquid fire.

Together, they stepped into the growing inferno.

Olc sat up on the foyer floor and screamed.

The town car's horn started to blow, and, a few seconds later, a roar like a freight train came from the kitchen.

Miriam helped him to his feet as a crowd of Draugr erupted from the parlor and ran toward the kitchen.

"No!" Olc screamed.

They stopped, but it didn't matter.

Two people in silver suits came down the hall in a rush of flame and bullets.

Gene directed the fire toward the dazed Draugr. They burst into flames as Olc screamed.

Laura stood beside him and fired.

Gene smiled. He turned the flame spray toward Olc and Miriam.

The town car horn stopped blowing.

The driver's side door opened.

There was a scream from within as something huge and gelatinous began prying itself out of the car.

Pauly drove up the driveway. Flames leaped up the back of the house. He jumped out beside the ancients who simply stood and watched. "What's happening?" He screamed.

The old man.

He has come.

Pauly ran toward the front door with the pistol in his hand. He stopped when he realized they weren't following him. "Do something!"

We are.

Waiting for the car.

Your car is too small.

Screams erupted from inside the house.

Pauly stumbled backward. "Can't you hear them? They're burning."

Heat.

Burning.

Not for us.

Wait here with us, boy.

"Fuck you! She's in there!" Pauly ran to the door.

Love.

Impetuous.

Foolish.

Where is the car?

Two Draugr threw themselves in front of the flamethrower, blocking the stream from hitting Olc and Miriam, incinerating themselves in the process.

Laura worked her way to the left along the wall.

Draugr were still coming through the parlor door, but she shot each one as it emerged.

"Mind that hole in the floor!" Gene yelled.

Laura stepped gingerly around the hole.

Miriam dragged Olc toward the steps. He pulled away from her and screamed at Gene.

Gene took aim with the flame thrower.

The parlor wall crashed outward under a flood of Draugr.

Laura went tumbling against the front door.

She fumbled with the rifle.

"Shit!" Gene screamed behind the air mask.

He turned the flame at the horde of Draugr.

They burst into flame and screamed.

Laura scrambled to her feet.

Pauly opened the front door.

The foyer walls were on fire.

An astronaut with a rifle turned and looked at him.

She slammed the gun stock against his nose, and he tumbled back down the steps.

Olc jumped into the air and flew over the hole in the floor.

He landed on Gene and together they slid across the parlor with its piles of burning Draugr.

The floor to Laura's right gave way and fell into the basement.

Olc was on top of Gene tearing at his fire hood with his long claws.

Gene turned his head right and yelled. "I got this. Take her!"

Laura turned to her left.

Miriam was looking at the hole in the floor. She looked like she was going to try to jump it and reach Olc.

Laura smiled. She raised the rifle and fired.

A fist-sized hunk of lath and plaster vaporized behind Miriam's head.

She looked at Laura in horror as Laura took aim again.

Something hit Laura from behind, and she fell forward just short of the yawning chasm leading to the basement.

After knocking Laura down, Pauly ran to Miriam and took her hand. "We have to go." He dragged her toward the front door.

"No! Olc!"

Laura was getting to her feet.

Pauly yanked Miriam toward the front door.

Laura stitched a line of bullets across the wall in front of them.

Pauly changed direction and pushed Miriam up the stairs.

"Olc!" Miriam screamed.

Gene Stinson stared up into the eyes of the creature he had chased for decades.

He had never been this close. He could see the deep lines beside the man's eyes, the jaundiced age surrounding the black irises.

The long yellow teeth bit at the fire hood faceplate.

He felt a stabbing pain in his left arm - his heart.

Yeah, that's okay, he thought. *It's okay now.*

Olc screamed as they struggled on the floor.

The words were strange. Latin.

He tried to get a grip on Gene's shoulders, but the fabric was slick.

Gene flexed the muscles in his right arm. He felt the flamethrower nozzle push between his body and Olc's.

He gritted his teeth against the pain that racked his left arm and flung it around Olc's waist.

Gene smiled as Olc's face showed the realization that Gene wasn't trying to push him away - he was drawing him closer.

Gene pulled the trigger on the flamethrower.

"Olc!" Miriam screamed from the top of the stairs.

Olc looked up at her as he and Gene were engulfed in flame.

He screamed and thrashed.

Gene's arm stayed locked around his waist.

Laura took a step toward Gene. The room was engulfed, and the gap in the floor was too wide to jump.

Instead, she turned toward Pauly and Miriam and took aim with the rifle.

She fired.

A huge hole opened in Miriam's lower right abdomen.

The boy grabbed Miriam in his arms and ran toward the bedrooms at the top of the stairs.

Oh, no you don't, Laura thought. She stepped toward the stairs.

The steps caught fire.

She shook her head.

Let them burn, she thought.

She looked back in the parlor.

Gene and Olc lay in a burning pile.

The heat coming from the two of them was intense.

Neither moved.

"You got him, Gene." Tears streamed down her face.

Laura stumbled through the front door.

Three Draugr stood staring at her from the yard.

They looked different. They seemed to be in a state of constant motion. They darted from side to side.

She raised the rifle and pulled the trigger.

Nothing happened. Empty.

One of them took a step toward her.

It stopped and hissed at her.

She looked back at the burning house.

She smiled.

It was too hot for them.

She dropped the rifle. She took off the fire hood and mask.

"Just you and me, bitches," she said with a smile.

What a protector you would have made.

The words sounded in Laura's head, and she blinked. "Get out of my head."

No. What a Draugr she would have made.

Still could.

Would you be willing, child?

"No. I wouldn't," Laura called as burning boards tumbled off the roof and landed beside her.

War is coming.

A great war.
An old war.
Nothing like it since Atlantis fell.
Die Gute Wolf.
Rises in the east.
One of them stepped forward, its skin blistering. It held out its long thin hand toward her.
Take the hand child.
We will show you wonders.
We will make you a wonder.
"Fuck you. And, fuck your war."

Smoke filled the upper floor as Pauly carried Miriam to the back bedroom over the kitchen. The floor was smoking.
"Olc," she whispered. She was limp in his arms.
"He's dead."
"No!" she screamed. "No. We were going to live forever."
"You will," Pauly said as he kicked out the old window. It crashed onto the roof of the back porch.
"Leave me. I want to die with him."
He looked down at her. "I know you think that now. But, I can't leave you."
He crouched down and carried her through the window.
Flames were climbing up the back walls.
He reached the edge of the roof with Miriam in his arms. He jumped down onto the bed of the pickup truck and jumped again onto the snow covered ground. He ran to the town car that sat idling a few yards away.
"Edgar! She's hurt." Pauly stopped.
The driver's door was hanging open.
Putrid smelling slime dripped from the inside onto the ground. "Edgar?"
He looked toward the kitchen door.
It was open.
He shook his head.
He slid Miriam across the slick seats.
The inside reeked like a hundred Draugr.

She leaned against the passenger side door and held the hole in her stomach. She was crying. "Why didn't you leave me?"

"I love you," he said as he got in the car and closed the door.

Laura had to step away from the porch as a dozen burning boards fell behind her.

The ancient Draugr laughed in her head and took a step toward her.

She returned the smile. She reached down and picked up a burning board. She pointed it at them.

"Who wants to go first?"

The town car drove around the side of the house.

"Son of a bitch," Laura whispered.

More laughter in her head.

Our ride.

Here at last.

One last chance.

We are for you, and you could be for us.

Immortality.

Pleasure.

"No, thanks. I'm tired. I think I'll skip on the immortality. Ninety or ninety-five years will be just fine with me."

The car stopped.

The driver's side window rolled down.

She could see the boy, and, beyond him, Miriam.

Miriam's face turned to a mask of hate when she saw her. "I'm going to kill you!"

"Sure you are. How're your guts, bitch?"

The boy raised his pistol and aimed it at her.

Laura raised her hands in a welcoming gesture.

The boy rolled up the window as the ancients climbed in the back.

She watched the town car drive away down the snowy driveway.

Laura sat down in the snow and watched the house on the hill burn. "You did good, cowboy. You did good."

Laura took off the fire suit and left it on the ground as the house continued to collapse in on itself.

She walked toward the car sitting in the drive. She leaned in. The keys were gone.

Laura sighed.

She walked around the burning house.

Miriam's pickup was burned down to the tires. "Shit." She shook her head. "And, Gene had his keys in his pocket. Damn."

She turned away from the house.

The old blue school bus sat at the top of the hill. "No way."

She walked up to the bus and pushed the door open.

An overpowering stench poured out of the door.

"Oh, fu... fudge. Fudge cupcakes that stinks like sh... like something really stinky." *Time to make some changes*, she thought.

And, for the first time in months, she didn't want a cigarette.

Laura looked at the front door of the church.

It was open.

"God. No." She ran off the bus.

She shoved the door open.

David, Kim, and Tia stood in the center of the church.

Laura burst into tears.

Kim came running. "What's wrong?"

David watched over their heads and carried Tia toward them. "Are they behind you?"

Laura hugged Kim. She dragged David and Tia close as they got within reach. "The door. It was open. I thought."

Kim shook her head. "It's okay. I'll explain..."

"No. I don't care." Laura kissed them all.

David looked at the door. "Gene?"

Laura bit her lower lip. "No, honey. He didn't make it."

David nodded. He looked out the door toward the parking lot. He was scanning the perimeter. A thousand yard stare they called it.

He would lapse into it for the rest of his life whenever he was out in the open.

"This school bus stinks," Tia said as they climbed on board.

The seats were ripped out, and the floors were stained.

"Nobody touch anything. And, we're getting hand sanitizer the first place we find."

"Hand sanitizer?" Kim asked.

"Yes."

"Who are you and what did you do with my Aunt Laura?" Kim asked as she sat down on the floor and gathered Tia onto her lap.

David sat down on the steps. He glanced back into the bus.

"It's okay. I checked it for monsters," Laura said.

They pulled out of the church parking lot.

Nothing moved in Rural Retreat.

The doors to every house and building they passed stood open.

There was a glow on the horizon to the west where the house on the hill continued to burn.

Laura turned onto Main Street and headed northeast.

The cop cars sat silently at the road block.

"Keep that gun handy," Laura whispered.

David nodded.

The bodies of policemen lay in the snow beside their silent cars. Their sightless eyes stared at the bus as Laura drove past.

They reached the entrance to the interstate.

A steady flow of cars passed by on the overpass.

"We made it," Kim whispered.

"Don't jinx it," Laura said as she pulled onto Interstate 81.

Kim and David were asleep within a minute of pulling onto the highway.

Laura drove in silence.

Tia looked up with a smile on her face from Kim's lap.

She stood up and walked with her hand held up as if she were holding someone's hand.

She walked to the back of the bus.

Two duffel bags were laying on the floor.

She looked up and smiled at the ghost who led her. "Really? Is it okay?"

Tia grinned wide and dragged the bags toward the front.

They pulled into the Greyhound terminal in Wytheville just past midnight.

The old bus creaked and hissed as Laura parked it at the far end of the lot.

"Hey," Laura said. "Wake up. Time to switch transportation."

David jumped.

Laura put her hand on his shoulder. "Gun, please?"

David stared at it. "Are you sure?"

Laura smiled at him. "You're sixteen. Time to be a kid again, okay?"

He nodded and handed it to her.

She put it under the seat.

She turned the bus off and left the key on the dashboard.

Kim stretched and yawned. "What are those?"

Tia was sitting beside her looking inside a duffel bag. She held up a banded stack of one hundred dollar bills. "I can't count this high."

"Holy crap," Kim whispered.

Laura knelt down beside them. "There's ten thousand in each bundle." She opened the other bag. "Holy shit. There must be three million dollars here. Where did it come from?"

Tia pointed behind her. "Back of the bus. It's monster money."

Laura laughed. "Of course. They would have to pay cash, wouldn't they?" She rubbed Tia's face. "How did you know it was back there?"

"Mommy told me."

The Greyhound terminal was empty. The ticket office was closed. A sign said it would re-open at six AM.

The interior of the terminal was lit brightly with fluorescents. Signs on the wall held pictures of every place Greyhound traveled.

It was warm inside with the heat blasting to hold out the cold night air.

The four of them sat huddled together on a wooden bench. David sat on the right, Kim leaned against him with her head cradled on his shoulder.

To her left, Laura sat with Tia in her arms, the little girl's legs laying across Kim's lap.

Tia fell asleep first, and Laura listened to the gentle sound of the girl's breath.

Kim's breathing grew regular and her eyes closed.

David fought against sleep. His head nodded forward, and he would catch himself.

But, eventually, his eyes closed.

Laura sat in the warmth - the air, the child in her lap, the children huddled beside her.

Her eyes closed.

Outside, emergency vehicles rushed by on the highway with their sirens wailing.

She opened her eyes.

Anne sat across from her.

Laura began to cry.

Anne smiled at her.

"Oh, Annie. I failed you."

Anne looked to Laura's right, her gaze falling on David and Kim.

Anne looked at Tia.

She looked at Laura with a wide smile. "You didn't fail me, Stringbean."

The terminal was full of people.

Her mother in the ragged plaid sundress.

Addie, the girl from the Appalachian trail.

A girl in black short shorts with black hair and purple highlights.

A priest smiled at her.

A hundred more, sitting on the benches or standing.

Some stood in front of the door.

Anne smiled at her. "Sleep. You're safe."

With ghosts watching over them, they slept till morning.

The old man who ran the ticket booth raised the metal shutters in front of his desk.

He sat down and did a double take.

Four people stood on the other side of the glass.

A tall woman with dark hair and a dirty Grateful Dead t-shirt stood holding a little girl with the same colored hair.

Beside her stood a tall redheaded teenage girl.

A muscular boy stood beside the redhead and held her hand.

All their eyes looked haunted and tired.

"Where to?"

"What's the warmest place you go to?" the dark haired woman asked.

He stared at her over wire-rimmed glasses. "Well, let's see. There's the Gulf coast. New Orleans?"

"Absolutely not," the woman said.

"There's Florida."

"What's the furthest south you go in Florida?"

"Uh, let me see," he tapped away on his computer. "That'd be Key West."

"Four to Key West, please."

He typed it up. "That'll be eight hundred fifty-seven dollars and thirteen cents."

The woman looked at the boy.

He turned around and unzipped a duffel bag. He turned back to her with a handful of hundreds.

The woman handed the old man the money.

He marked each bill with a counterfeit detection pen. Some of the bills were very old.

His hands hesitated over the keyboard.

There was a printout stuck to the wall behind his computer screen.

Wanted by FBI: Laura Constance Reynolds, domestic terrorism.

The picture was bad, but it looked like the woman standing in front of him.

"Identification, please?"

The woman frowned. "I've never needed ID before…"

"New policy."

The woman looked around.

The old man didn't see a purse.

"It's in your pocket, Mommy," the little girl said. She was smiling.

The woman dug in the pocket of her jeans. She got an odd look on her face and pulled her hand out of her pocket. She stared at the card in her hand.

She looked at the little girl. "Thank you, honey." She handed the license to the old man.

It read: Anne Marie Lawrence.

The picture didn't look a lot like her, but it looked more like her than the printout did.

He handed her the tickets, change, and ID. "Y'all have a pleasant trip."

Laura sat in the aisle bus seat beside Tia.

The little girl was asleep again with her face against Laura's arm.

David and Kim whispered in the seat behind them.

The bus headed south as the sun rose.

Laura held the ID in her hand and stared at it. She hadn't needed to ask Tia why she had taken Anne's driver's license and slipped it into her jeans pocket.

She knew the answer.

"Be me," Laura whispered as she looked at her sister's picture.

And, she did just that.

DENOUEMENT

Gene
Thursday, 10:00 PM

Gene Stinson stared up into Marcus Velerius Corvus Olc's face as it caught fire.

He smiled as the flames consumed the face. The skin flaked away. The eyes exploded in black ichor.

Gene was dying. His heart was thudding in his chest, his left arm alive with pain.

He was content.

He let off on the flamethrower trigger - it was empty anyway.

He pushed Olc's charred remains off him.

The ceiling was on fire, a beautiful plasma of flame that consumed the floor joists above.

Gene stood up. He took off the heavy flamethrower and let it fall on the floor.

His head was spinning.

He walked through the flaming parlor.

He could see Laura through the flames standing just off the porch. She was raising her rifle and pointing it toward the ancients.

Son of a bitch, Gene thought. He took a step toward the door.

The room was suddenly full of people.

The woman in the plaid sundress stood at the front of the group and smiled at him. She shook her head.

The floor in front of the door collapsed.

The ghosts disappeared.

He hugged his left arm against him and limped toward the kitchen. He had to get to Laura.

The room was an inferno.

There was a shape running at him from the kitchen.

It was a Draugr, but misshapen. It was huge and swollen, dragging its balloon-like skin behind it.

It sizzled in the fire as it ran.

The Draugr had one huge eye and a smaller dead eye set beside it in a misshapen skull.

There was a Lincoln symbol imprinted across its swollen, naked chest and, below that, in reversed, backward letters: Air Bag.

The driver of the town car.

He held up his right arm as the massive gelatinous thing collided with him.

He was falling backward through the hole in the floor.

Gene landed on his back, and it jarred his entire body.

The mass of the Draugr lying on top of him forced the breath out of him.

White porcelain rose up on both sides of him.

A bathtub.

He had landed in a bathtub in the basement with the huge Draugr on top of him.

The pain in his left arm became excruciating.

He sucked in air behind the mask.

Gene fumbled with the glove on his right hand. He slipped it off and dug under the fire suit. He found his jeans pocket.

His hand closed on his pocket knife.

He stared up at the distorted face of the Draugr.

For the second time in one day, Draugr teeth snapped at him from the other side of the glass.

He opened the pocket knife one handed and drove the blade into the creature's flesh.

Blood poured onto his hand, and he stabbed harder. He slashed and skewered.

His hand felt warm.

It tingled.

The blood, he thought.

He panicked and dropped the knife.

The Draugr was shaking as its blood poured into the tub.

Gene felt it running into the suit.

"No!" Gene screamed under the air mask.

The Draugr raised up. It looked down at him with drowsy eyes. It's stomach tore open, and it fell back on top of him.

The blood was soaking into him.

His heart stopped pounding.

His left arm no longer hurt.

It felt strong.

He was hyperventilating as the Draugr's eyes went slack.

The tub was filling with blood.

He pushed as hard as he could, but he couldn't lift the Draugr off him.

The blood rose up the side of the mask, but the rubber hugged tight to his face.

He stopped hyperventilating as the blood covered the mask.

Friday
2:00 AM

The firemen directed their hoses at the house on the hill. Embers rose into the cold air, taken aloft on air currents like ghosts rising from the ruin.

Later, each man would wonder why they hadn't done their best. They would wonder why they didn't focus on the largest of the flaming areas, but instead only sprayed the periphery of the fire.

Still, others would wonder at the whispers they heard as the flames grew.

Whispers that seemed to say, "Let it burn."

A fireman walked out of the flames wearing a fire suit. It was charred black and red with blood.

The fire chief looked up from the radio in his hand. "Jesus, somebody spray that man down! Where did all that blood come from?"

The man in the fire suit walked down the driveway.

The fire chief yelled into the radio. "I don't know where Rural Retreat Fire is! I've been trying to call them. I can't get shit on the radio or phone."

The man in the fire suit walked toward the fire engine.

A man ran up and started spraying him with water.

A few minutes later the man tapped on the glass of the fire suit hood. "You okay, buddy?"

The man in the suit gave him a thumbs up.

Gene walked behind the fire engine.

He stripped off the suit.

He looked at his left arm and made a fist. There was no pain.

Gene looked in the fire engine's side mirror.

The face looking back at him was twenty years younger and framed with salt and pepper hair.

Friday
12:20 PM
Huntington, West Virginia

"Trust me, you don't want the meatloaf," Ava said as she took the truck driver's order.

He smiled at her. "Chicken it is."

"You won't be sorry," Ava said.

The front door opened with a jingling bell.

She glanced up. "Just take a seat anywhere." She walked toward the counter.

Ava stopped.

She turned slowly.

Gene Stinson stood just inside the door.

She walked to him and stared. "Gene?"

He nodded.

She touched his face. "You look..." She touched his face and caressed his hair. "Did you dye it?"

His eyes welled up with tears. "I don't know how long this is going to last."

Ava laughed and fluffed his hair. "A few months, I reckon."

He laughed. "When I was here last time, you said you'd like to spend the day with me. Is that still something you'd like?"

She shook her head. "What about your ghosts?"

Gene nodded. "They're put to rest."

"Okay. I get off work at two. Where would you like to go?"

He smiled at her, and she thought she saw tears in his eyes. "Texas?"

"Well, how about we start with Huntington and see where the day takes us?"

"I'd like that."

Bedford, Virginia
Thursday, 2:00 AM
Twenty hours before the house on the hill burned.

Deputy Ward Rickman slept. His wife, Loretta, slept against him in the big bed. The old farmhouse was silent.

Ward Rickman dreamed he was standing on the cliff beside Apple Orchard Falls on the Blue Ridge Parkway. It was late in the day - a summer day, a carpet of green pines spread out from the cliff base, and the setting sun illuminated the valley beyond.

He knew without looking someone stood to his left. This was a place for ghosts, and one stood beside him.

Unlike Ward, the ghost was not looking toward the setting sun. Instead, he peered over the cliff edge at the jagged rocks below.

"My," Clayton Ambrose said in his soft-spoken southern genteel drawl. "That was quite a fall I took."

Ward felt the change ripple through him - the wolf making its appearance. Ward was growing taller in his dream, claws sprouting from his fingertips, fangs growing into his mouth.

"Now, now," Clayton said. "I see no call for such theatrics. As you can see, I have maintained my human, albeit incorporeal, form. I admonish you to do the same."

Ward looked at him. True to his word, Clayton stood in human form, dressed in his khaki shorts and comical safari shirt, his bald head beaded with sweat.

Clayton chuckled. "I find it ironic that I seem doomed to spend the afterlife tied to a man I hated for most of my adult life. Perhaps, we are each other's penance. I forgive you, Ward."

Ward's claws retracted. "I don't want your forgiveness, Clayton. You were a mass murderer."

Clayton shook his head and stared at the sun. "Regardless, my forgiveness is bestowed." He smiled. "Being... passed on has given me a certain, shall we say, clarity. It seems I can now see the past and present from many different points of view. I recognize my failings, and I now understand the tremendous burden put upon you when you were little more than a child." Clayton looked at him. "It's time for you to forgive yourself."

Ward sighed and looked away. He took a deep breath. "Thank you."

"I do enjoy my position as a voyeur in your life. Watching our Missy Nine Fingers grow into a fine young woman. She is the only thing of which I am proud."

Ward smiled. "On that, we can agree."

Clayton laughed. "Oh, Ward, we should have been better. We were supposed to be better. And, now at least our descendants *are* better. *Die Gute Wolf,* the good wolf." He shook his head. "What wonders they are."

"Did you come back just to gab?"

Clayton laughed. "Ever the pragmatist. No, Ward, I came back to warn."

Ward stared at him. "Warn? About what?"

"We are old, Ward. Die Gute Wolf. But, there are things older, and they are coming."

"What kind of things?"

"If I explained, you would not believe. Some things have to be experienced." Clayton squeezed Ward's upper arm. "Ghosts can see the past and present with perfect clarity, and, if we choose, we can see possible futures."

"Another rogue?" Ward asked. "Is there another rogue?"

Clayton shook his head. "Nothing of us. This is something older. This evening, you and Loretta should take the night shift."

Ward stared at him. "You know the future?"

"I know *possible* futures. It is a fluid thing, but it would be best for you and Loretta to face this possible future - two, shall we say lesser beings will not fare well against what might pass this way tonight."

"How do I know you aren't trying to get us killed?"

Clayton laughed. "You don't. But, I promise you I hold you no ill will. Not anymore."

Ward looked at the setting sun.

Clayton shrugged. "Look at it this way: at worst, tonight you will face something I believe only you can face. At best, this future will not transpire, and you will spend the evening alone with a beautiful woman on a deserted road - something I believe a man of your virile nature and proclivities would find enjoyable. But, if you don't take this shift and the thing I fear does come calling? Two innocent deputies will die."

The sun set as Clayton spoke those last words, and the night became pitch black.

Ward awoke in his bed, Loretta curled against him. He put his arm around her and pulled her close.

Friday
3:20 AM

"Not that I'm complaining, mind you, but you do know we have deputies to handle overnight shifts?" Sheriff Loretta Rickman said as she buttoned her tan uniform shirt in the driver's seat of the police cruiser.

Ward leaned back in the passenger seat and smiled. "Well, how else could we christen the hood of this patrol car?"

She leaned over and kissed him. "We already christened this one."

"We did?"

"Yes, dear."

Ward scratched his head. "When?"

"Two years ago. We left a dent in the hood the same shape as my butt because somebody got over excited and changed into wolf form when he was on top of me..."

"Oh! That was this cruiser?" He stared out the windshield. "Body shop did a good job on that dent."

"Stop changing the subject, Ward Rickman! Why are we out here?"

Ward sighed and laughed under his breath. "I had a dream."

She stroked his face. "What kind of dream?"

Ward looked out the window. "A strange one."

"We've been over this," Loretta said. "Whatever this psychic ability is that Karen and Melissa have, you don't have it, honey." She smiled. "Maybe it's only blue-eyed alpha girls that have it? You blue-eyed alpha boy werewolves are just shit out of luck."

"Look, I don't think this has anything to do with psychic ability. It felt like... I don't know, like he was really there in my head, a ghost or something."

"He? Who do you mean?"

"Clayton Ambrose. He told me we needed to be out here tonight. There's some sort of danger, but he wasn't specific."

Loretta went pale, and Ward knew why: almost a decade earlier, the rogue werewolf Clayton Truman Ambrose had almost killed Loretta and her daughter, Melissa. Together, Ward and Loretta's family had banded together and killed Clayton, but in the process, Loretta was infected.

Melissa was infected with the werewolf virus as well, but they didn't know that until three years later with the onset of puberty.

Loretta shook her head. "Why would he come to you? It doesn't make sense, he hated you - honey, it was just a dream."

"I know. But, just on the off chance... I mean, so what if we spend the night in the cruiser?"

She laughed and laid her head on his shoulder. "It's been an enjoyable evening so far."

Ward smiled. "Yes, it has."

"Enjoy me while I'm still bendable. In a few months, I'll be a beached whale."

"Stop it. You'll be glowing and beautiful like you always are."

Loretta sighed. "Four. Four kids. This has got to be the last one, Ward. I'm forty-five. I mean, even werewolves have to stop being able to pump them out at some point, right?"

Ward shrugged. "I don't know."

Loretta counted off on her fingers. "Birth control pills don't work. Tubal ligation doesn't work, everything just grows back. Vasectomy, same thing."

Ward grimaced. "Don't remind me. I don't know what was worse, getting snipped or having it correct itself."

"That leaves us with abstinence."

"Not happening."

"Definitely not," Loretta agreed. "You could wear a condom?"

"Yeah, but, that means we'd always need to be... human when we..."

Loretta frowned. "No. That's half the fun."

"Yep."

Loretta laughed and buried her face in his chest. "We're going to need a bigger house."

The radio crackled to life. "Sheriff, this is dispatch."

Ward reached for the microphone.

Loretta slapped his hand. "Hey! You lost the last election, she's asking for me."

Ward laughed. "Sorry, old habit."

Loretta smiled mischievously and picked up the microphone. "Go ahead, Agnes."

"Staties just called. Been some big disturbance over in Rural Retreat. Multiple fatalities sounds like the whole town is in a shambles. Over."

Loretta sat up. "That's hours from here. What do the state police need? Over."

"We're supposed to be on the lookout for two vehicles heading northeast. Vehicle one: a school bus, light blue, Minnesota tags. Over."

"Blue school bus, Minnesota. Copy."

"Vehicle two: black late model Lincoln Town Car. Minnesota tags. Over."

"Town car. Got it. What's the want? Over."

"Unspecified. But, the state police said to approach with extreme caution. Over."

"Copy," Loretta said as she replaced the microphone.

Loretta closed her eyes. "Can't possibly be that dream, can it?"

Ward looked out the window at the dark, empty road. It was 3:30 AM.

Miriam sat in the front passenger seat and screamed. The bullet was still in her.

The ancient leaned over the back seat, its long claws digging into the oozing wound.

Be still, it is deep.

She wasn't listening to the ancient's thoughts.

Olc was dead, and her world was at an end.

No.

You have saved us.

We can start again.

"Fuck you!" Miriam screamed.

Pauly was driving, and he jumped at her words. He swerved into the left lane and then corrected. "It's going to be all right, Miriam. You'll see."

The ancient's claws twisted inside her and pulled free of the wound. The bullet fell onto her lap.

The ancient raked one of its wrists with the claws of its opposite hand. Blood sprayed onto the bullet wound. It began to close.

Miriam stopped screaming. Exhausted, she laid her head against the window. She sobbed. "None of it matters anymore."

"Don't say that. The ancient is right. Eight hours, we'll be in New York City. It's going to be okay." He smiled at her and took her hand. "My family is in Brooklyn. We'll go there, turn them. Then we'll go deeper into the city. There are places we can disappear, places they won't even notice us."

She pushed his hand away. "He was my life, Pauly."

You will replace him.

You are strong, Miriam.

To make you one of us was always the plan.

Miriam.

You will be stronger still.

One of us.

In time, you will be more powerful even than Olc.

Protect us.

We are eternal.

You are eternal.

Miriam laughed. "Eternal? I don't want to be eternal. It doesn't mean anything without him."

Pauly took her hand and squeezed it. "I won't leave you."

She looked at the boy - as powerful as he was now, he was still just a boy.

She felt the pain of Olc's loss in the pit of her stomach.

Miriam pushed his hand away.

She looked out the window.

A sign by the road said "Blue Ridge Parkway - 3 miles."

The monsters in Bedford are not for us, and we are not for them. "Bedford. *Stay away*," Olc had whispered on that day that seemed like a lifetime ago.

"Where are we?" Miriam asked.

"I'm going to take us on the Blue Ridge Parkway. I think it will be safer. We drive northeast on it for a few hours, and then we'll cut across to Interstate 81."

Miriam looked in the side mirror. Nothing but dark woods stretched behind them. "No, where are we right now?"

"Um, we just passed through some hick town…"

"What hick town?" Miriam screamed.

"Bedford. Calm down."

Miriam started laughing.

The ancients began to scream in Miriam's and Pauly's minds.

No!

We can't be here!

Trap! The ghosts!

"Get us out of here," Miriam said. She swallowed and composed herself. "Olc warned me to stay out of Bedford. He was afraid of it. Get us to this parkway you were talking about." She turned to the ancients.

They were moving in the back seat so fast she could barely see them.

She took a deep breath. "Calm down. We're already driving away from the town."

The black Lincoln passed Loretta and Ward.

"You have got to be kidding me," Loretta whispered. She put the car in gear and pulled off the shoulder.

She reached for the microphone.

"No." Ward took her hand. "I think this should just be you and me."

She looked at her husband and swallowed hard. "Okay."

Red and blue lights began flashing in the mirrors.

Pauly looked up. "Oh, shit."

The ancients hissed in the back seat.

Miriam reached over and pressed a switch on the dashboard. The smoked glass barrier between the front and back seats rose into place. "Stay calm." She opened the glove compartment and pulled out two pistols. She handed one to Pauly. "Put this under your seat. Only use it if you have to."

She put the second pistol under her right hip, pressing it into the seat.

"You want to do the honors?" Ward asked. The town car idled in front of them on the shoulder.

"I'll hang back," Loretta said.

They got out.

Loretta walked up behind the car as Ward approached the driver's side.

There was a smell coming from the car.

Ward looked back and frowned.

Loretta wrinkled her nose and nodded.

He walked up to the driver's door.

The tinted window slid down.

A young boy smiled up at him. "What can I do for you officer?" he asked in a New York accent.

"Drivers license and registration."

The smell coming from inside the car was pungent. Ward's wolf senses were on overload.

"Honey, can you get the registration?" He handed Ward his license.

Pauly Delveccio. Rural Retreat.

The boy was sixteen.

"A little young to be driving after midnight, aren't you?"

The woman smiled. "That's my fault. I got sleepy."

Ward looked at the woman.

There was blood on her blouse.

She was trying to keep it covered with her hand. She handed Delveccio the registration with the other hand.

He passed it to Ward.

"Is that blood?"

"Nosebleed," the woman said

Ward nodded. He read the registration. "This car is registered to Edgar Fuentes of Minneapolis. Who is Mr. Fuentes?"

"My cousin," the woman said.

"And, you are?"

"Miriam Tillford," she said. She reached her hand down beside her. "Would you like to see my license?"

Ward listened closely.

Two heartbeats. Strong.

Something else in the back of the car. Irregular. Very fast.

"That won't be necessary. Who you got in the back?" He stared at the black glass divider behind Pauly's head.

"Officer, is there a problem? Were we speeding?" Miriam asked.

Ward smiled and shook his head. "Just routine. Would you mind lowering the glass, please?"

Pauly Delveccio stared at him. "You really don't want me to do that."

The rear doors flew open.

Gray shapes jumped out.

Ward couldn't see them clearly.

One was running toward him.

The two from the other side ran toward Loretta.

He had another problem.

Pauly Delveccio was pointing a pistol at him.

Ward punched with his left.

Pauly's head snapped to the right.

His neck snapped.

The gray shape dove on Ward.

Once it clamped onto his arm with its teeth. It stopped moving.

He was looking at a nightmare.

The face was old and wrinkled, gray to the point of being blue. It was naked and hairless. The eyes were liquid black

It drove long claws into his chest.

The eyes focused on his.

Something screamed in his head: *Blue eyes? No! It cannot be!*

Ward felt the change roll through him. Thick brown hair erupted from follicles all over his body.

He was growing, dragging the monster into the air with him as he changed.

Ward's clothes tore away, including the gun belt that he had modified with plastic clips.

The creature bit down harder.

Ward's blue eyed wolf face stared down at him.

The creature tried to open its mouth and drop away.

Ward growled and brought a massive right paw down on the monster's head.

It exploded in a spray of gray and red pulp.

Ward tossed the carcass away and jumped over the car.

The other two had Loretta on her knees.

She was staring up at them as if she were in a trance.

They raised glittering claws over her head.

She offered her neck to them.

Ward roared as he landed on all fours on the ground.

Loretta jerked as if she had been jolted with electricity.

The monsters took a step back. The words formed in his head again.

No!

Impossible.

You are all dead.

Loretta changed. Her clothes ripped away, and she dove on the nearest of them.

It screeched like an animal as she ripped into its stomach with her fangs on her way to its heart.

The last backed away toward the woods.

Loretta rose from the dead monster with its blood dripping from her face.

She and Ward stood side by side, nine-foot tall werewolves.

They leaped on the last monster and ripped it in half.

Miriam climbed out of the town car.

She looked at Pauly's face through the open door. He stared at her glassy-eyed, his neck bent sideways.

The monsters rose from the remains of the last ancient.

She held the pistol in her hand.

The monsters, werewolves, walked toward her. They changed as they walked, growing smaller, becoming human.

Ward held up his hand. "That gun won't hurt us."

"We won't harm you," Loretta said. "Just put down the gun."

Miriam shook. "Monsters. You're monsters."

Ward shook his head. "We want to understand what happened here, okay? Nobody is going to hurt you." He walked toward her.

She raised her gun.

"You can't hurt us with that," Ward said.

"You killed them. Oh, God. You killed them," Miriam cried.

"We didn't have a choice," Loretta said.

"Olc is dead. I don't know where to find other Draugr. Don't you understand? They were my family. I'm alone." She raised the gun and pointed it at her temple. "Alone with monsters."

"No!" Ward screamed.

Miriam pulled the trigger.

Ward and Loretta stood and clung to each other surrounded by the dead.

Loretta touched Ward's arm. "You're not healing."

Ward winced and dug in the wound. He pulled out a hollow silver tooth. The puncture closed. "Silver. Their teeth and claws? They were clad in silver."

He dug through the remains of his destroyed clothes. He picked up his cell phone.

Ward dialed and held it to his ear. "Karen? It's Ward. I know it's late. But, you need to hear this. We just killed... Karen, I think we just killed three vampires."

Suburban Seattle
One week later

Sherry Shaunessy, wife of the late Patrick Shaunessy, went to the door just as the postman drove away. There was a plain brown parcel on her front porch.

It was sealed carefully with packing tape.

There was no return address, but it was postmarked Miami, Florida.

She opened the box.

There was a note on top, written in a careful hand:

Mrs. Shaunessy,

Words cannot express my sorrow for your loss. This is no excuse, but please believe me when I say that, had I known what they were planning, I would have stopped them.

I hope this will help with your children's college tuition or allow you to move someplace warm.

Sincerely,
A friend

Below the note was five-hundred thousand dollars in fifty bundles of ten-thousand dollars each.

Brittney
Front Royal, Virginia
Two weeks later

Once upon a time, her name was Brittney Davis. She lived in a big house with her rich lawyer husband. She had everything planned out.

Now, she was alone. She sat in the roadside bar and drank her Long Island Iced Tea which did nothing to quench the true thirst that gnawed into her stomach and made her mouth dry.

There was a big mirror behind the bar, so she sat at the very end of the bar where no one would see her reflection. Anyone who looked at her would see a tall brunette with an upturned nose and perfect white teeth dressed in a white blouse with a short black skirt and tall heels. She wore pearls around her neck.

She was proud of the necklace. It took concentration to hold that illusion and make the light sparkle on the white surface of each pearl.

When she left the bar, later on, she would be wearing an ankle length coat - she had seen it on a magazine cover earlier in the day. Brittney had memorized every crease, every fold in the picture, and she could clothe herself with it at will.

This was the illusion, the glamour.

If they could see her reflection, these men who circled her like sharks, trying to build up the courage to speak to her, would scream.

Her gray skin sagged on her emaciated frame and was scored with scars from when she had burned - the only part of her that didn't hang down were her magnificent silicone breasts, though she assumed even they would decay and abandon her at some point in the distant future.

Anyone standing near her would smell vanilla.

Another illusion. In truth, she carried with her the smell of a shallow grave on a hot summer day.

The bar was hot, stifling. She clung to the icy glass of tea as if it were a life preserver.

A small, chubby man sat down on the bar stool beside her. He took off his hat and laid it on the bar beside him, uncovering his bald head.

"What can I get for you?" the bartender asked.

"Vodka. Do you have Sobieski?" the man asked.

"Yeah."

"Neat, please. I do love Polish vodka. So much smoother than that Russian swill," he said. He finally turned and looked at her with small green eyes. "My God, you are enchanting." He turned back to the bartender. "Another Long Island Iced Tea for the lady. Extra ice."

"Thank you," Brittney said.

"Edward Price," he said. He did not offer his hand.

"Brittney Davis. What do you do, Edward Price?"

"Ahh, I work for the government, Miss Davis. Procurement."

"And, what do you procure?" She leaned toward him.

"Talent. Munitions. A little of both." He smiled at her and looked deep into her eyes. He laughed. "I'm sorry. I don't mean to stare, but you are absolutely gorgeous."

"You're very flattering and very charming." She fought the urge to attack him on the spot. The alley behind the bar would do.

"How do you do it? I mean do you just picture how you want to look in your head? If I were to reach out and try to touch those pearls, would they just vanish? Or, would I actually feel them under my fingers? The mind boggles." His smile never wavered.

Brittney almost dropped her illusion. The pearls faltered for an instant and then flickered back.

He pointed at her. "I saw that. I apologize for rattling you. It's not my intent."

She stood up to leave.

"Please sit down, Miss Davis, may I call you Brittney?"

"No." She focused on his eyes and pressed with her mind trying to induce an aneurysm.

"Sorry, your Jedi mind tricks won't work on me. I know all about you, so..." he tapped his temple with his index finger. "Immune. And, before you decide to just reach over and tear my throat out, I want to alert you to the fact there are three gentlemen arrayed in the crowd behind you, former Navy Seals with submachine guns hidden under their coats." He licked his lips and turned back to the bar as the bartender set his vodka in front of him along with a new tea for Brittney. He pushed the tea toward her. "Please, enjoy the ice. It must be terribly uncomfortable for you in here."

She sat down. "I can move fast enough to disarm them," Brittney said with a smile.

"Perhaps. However, you can't move fast enough to get away from the sniper outside who has his crosshairs on the back of your head at this very moment." He held up his glass and peered through the vodka at her face. "As they say, this isn't my first rodeo. Salut."

Brittney picked up the Long Island Iced Tea and tapped it against his vodka. "Salut." She took a drink and let the cold course through her. "What can I do for you, Mr. Price?"

"We've been following your... family for quite some time. Very promising. It's a pity about Rural Retreat. We were planning on making contact with Mr. Olc and Miss Tillford, alas that is no longer an option. Congratulations, Miss Davis, you are the only 'enhanced' survivor of Rural Retreat, and the world is about to become your oyster."

She stared at him. "I'm afraid I don't follow."

"Our goals are parallel," he said. He took a drink of vodka. "We share a common enemy."

"My only enemies are human," Brittney said. "Like you."

"You haven't met Die Gute Wolf yet, Miss Davis. And, I can assure you they are your true enemy."

"Die Gute Wolf?"

"Beasts, Miss Davis. Ill-tempered and completely uncooperative. Without them, the world would be a... well, not necessarily a better place, but certainly one my associates and I would find more palatable. Hence I would like to negotiate an understanding between us."

She smiled at him and let her long incisor fangs show. "I don't negotiate with snacks."

Price started to laugh. "You are charming." He downed his vodka. "Trust me, Miss Davis, when you finally meet Die Gute Wolf, you're going to want the might of the US government behind you."

She ran her finger down the outside of her glass. "Tell me more."

About the Author

At the time of this publication, Tony Bowman has written five novels. He lives in North Carolina with his gorgeous wife, Laurie, his beautiful daughter, Sara, and a hundred pound Catahoula Leopard dog.

Born in the Appalachian Mountains of southwest Virginia, he will tell you he was born and raised a hillbilly. The hills of his Russell County home are a part of him, as tangible as his fingers or toes. Not a day goes by that he does not miss the steep hills and the dense, fragrant forests of pine and cedar.

He has lived all over the country, from North Carolina, to the Amish Country of Pennsylvania, to the San Francisco Bay, and the bright lights of Las Vegas. But, the lure of travel is lost on him now, and he longs for the view of the mountains of his youth and the cool taste of water from a limestone well.

Mr. Bowman writes stories of Horror, Science Fiction, and Suspense.

Horror seems a strange genre for someone who grew up in such an idyllic setting. But, horror stories are woven into the fabric of Appalachian life, whether they are tales of ghosts, or witches, or things that prowl the hills at night – hungry things that snatch away the unwary or unwise. He is merely carrying on the tradition of telling stories in the dark, albeit with a twenty-first-century outlook.

Mr. Bowman welcomes your comments. Contact him via:

Email: thattonybowman@gmail.com
Blog: http://thattonybowman.blogspot.com
Facebook: https://www.facebook.com/tony.bowman.14289

What the readers are saying about Tony Bowman:

Four members of a mercenary team are marked for death by the CIA. They hideout in the small town of Vales Hollow, Pennsylvania, seeking only to live quiet, peaceful lives. But, can these adrenalin junkies adjust to life in the slow lane? Or, is Vales Hollow really as peaceful as it appears on the surface?

http://www.amazon.com/dp/B00IYZW8DU

"This is one of the best Kindle books I have read to date! If you like military style books that are believable, this is a good one. I had a hard time putting it down, but I read a lot at work and well, I had no choice. If you are into special forces type books without too much gore, this book is a good choice!"

- Alex

"What if a bunch of city thugs and corrupt small town bullies came up against a well-trained quartet of antiterrorists operating to save new friends and a charming town? The heroes may act like brilliant strategists and hold most of the cards, but their characters are well enough developed so that I liked all of them. Except for the killing and mayhem, this is a sweet story, fast moving, simplistic and fun."

- Kathleen L.

Seventeen tales of terror, from a dating site that finds your match in the city morgue, to a sociopath in a beautiful package, to the witch next door. Horror writer Tony Bowman takes you to the edge of horror and suspense. http://www.amazon.com/dp/B00JSLXIYW

"Tony Bowman's Morgue Dreams and Curiouser Things is a fantastic read. The stories are, for the most part, quite short. This makes for excellent quick reads if you need a short break in between work assignments/projects/etc, and there are plenty of them. The stories are all within the Horror genre, but they range the gamut from scary to funny to thought provoking, often within each story. Some of my favorite stories from this collection include Rejected Children, which deals with the nature of acceptance and belonging, Parts Man, which raises some good ethical questions, and Monster, which forces the reader to consider the nature and manifestation of evil. Some great entertainment and interesting stories here."

- Sliphsc

'I just finished Tony Bowman's book, and was intrigued by the combination of horror unleashed by his imagination. His stories remind me of the writings of Richard Matheson and Ray Bradbury."

- Thomas Kleaton

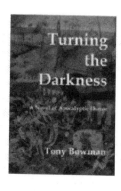

An experiment in teleportation goes horribly wrong, opening a doorway to hell. Eight years after the demon invasion, three heroes journey across what is left of the United States in search of an artifact powerful enough to banish the evil. Can a psychic, a witch, and the last living priest turn back the darkness? Or, will there literally be hell on earth?

http://www.amazon.com/dp/B00KBB5EFY

"I started reading this thinking no way was the author going to pull it off. Ghouls, witches, vampires, werewolves AND demons in the same book ???????......crazy. After a few chapters I was totally drawn in, the 3 main characters are brilliantly described, even the ones with a small part to play you end up feeling like you know them. Very, very good job Mr. Bowman, looking forward to more."

- John Phillips

"Turning the Darkness is an apocalyptic horror mixed with bits of science fiction and fantasy. A group a scientists accidentally open a portal to hell in a groundbreaking experiment gone horribly wrong. Demons escape. Awfulness ensues. I was thoroughly engrossed in this book from the beginning countdown. We get a little taste of everything from witches to werewolves and demons to psychics. Becoming bogged down with such large cast could have been easy, but the author does an amazing job of creating unassuming and interesting characters that kept me turning pages well into the night. I loved watching them evolve as they attempt to save the earth from certain destruction. The writing flows quickly and purposefully, the plot is imaginative, and the characters are some that I'll remember forever."

- J. R. McDonald

An evil has descended upon the small town of Bedford, Virginia. Grisly murders on the nearby Blue Ridge Parkway are being blamed on a rogue bear.

Only one man understands the true nature of the beast that haunts the parkway.

And, Ward Rickman knows the only thing that can stop a werewolf is another werewolf.

http://www.amazon.com/dp/B00OKHDDXU

"Some people prefer vampires, others prefer zombies, but I am certifiably a werewolf fan! Unfortunately, werewolves don't get the same recognition as their supernatural counterparts. But if only some Hollywood exec were to read "Nine Fingers," by Tony Bowman, it could seriously be a game changer in the sub-genre. The book is incredibly entertaining and fast paced. Sure its premise includes monsters that rip apart its victims, yet the violence is surprisingly not gratuitous. There is sexual content but it's not explicit. Bowman doesn't waste time with excessive or unnecessary details, as he keeps the plot tight. There's nothing in this book that would make the reader want to put it down - nothing. This is an absolute page turner..."

- Miss. Thorn

I won't recap the plot and I will keep this short and sweet. This is one of the best books I've read in a while. Really well written - serious character development. This is a complete winner. I couldn't put it down. Thank you Tony Bowman!!

- "Book Diva"

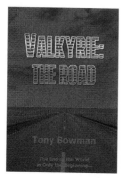

Valkyrie is two-hundred thousand pounds of armor plate, a rolling fortress travelling the road from Chicago to New Orleans in a post-apocalyptic future. Trading goods between vampire controlled Chicago and a New Orleans dominated by Vodou, the human crew of Valkyrie face werewolves, ghouls, and cannibals in the ruins of the Midwest.

http://www.amazon.com/dp/B011J894EE

"Valkyrie: The Road by Tony Bowman is one of the most entertaining post-apocalyptic novels I have read in a long time. The story is unique and does not follow the stereotypical situations of most dystopian and apocalyptic novels. Bowman introduces a story reminiscent of the Mad Max series. The plot is full of thrilling and adventurous journeys and unique characters. You not only get the post-apocalyptic world most fans of this genre love, but you get Werewolves, Cannibals, Ghouls, and Vampires. How could you not love a story that includes every one of your favorite horror story characters?

Bowman introduces his characters and makes the reader love or hate them. The main protagonists are a close knit group and you can not help but feel like you are a part of the family as well. The antagonists have you clenching your teeth at the anticipation of their downfall. Bowman's story is one I would read over and over again!

The novel had the page turning effect you seek when reading a novel about the end of the world. I can not wait to see how this story progresses. I am left sitting on the edge of my seat awaiting the follow up to this story just to see how each character thrives, falls, and/or overcomes whatever this new life throws at them next."

Steph Nizi
NovelIdeaReviews.blogspot.com

Made in United States
Orlando, FL
01 September 2022

21827528R00196